FLEE THE
DARKNESS

FLEE THE DARKNESS

Grant R. Jeffrey

and Angela Hunt

WORD PUBLISHING

NASHVILLE

A Thomas Nelson Company

Published by Word Publishing, Nashville, Tennessee. All rights reserved. No portion of
this book may be reproduced, stored in a retrieval system, or transmitted in any form or
by any other means—electronic, mechanical, photocopy, recording, or any other—except
for brief quotations in printed reviews, without the prior permission of the publisher.

All Scripture quotations in this book are from the HOLY BIBLE: NEW INTERNATIONAL
VERSION. Copyright © 1973, 1978, 1984 by International Bible Society. Used by
permission of Zondervan Publishing House. All rights reserved.

Library of Congress Cataloging-in-Publication Data

Jeffrey, Grant R.
    Flee the darkness / Grant R. Jeffrey with Angela Elwell Hunt.
        p.   cm.
    ISBN 0-8499-4063-X
    1. Hunt, Angela Elwell, 1957–   . II. Title.
PS3560.E436F58   1998
813'.54—dc21   98-8834
                                                                                                              CIP

Printed in the United States of America

8 9 0 1 2 3 4 BVG 9 8 7 6 5 4 3 2 1

Top corporate technology executives polled in February 1998
by *CIO* magazine:

Do you have confidence the Millennium Bug will be fixed by December 31, 1999?

Yes 21%   No 67%   Not sure 12%

Would you fly on a commercial airline on January 1, 2000?

Yes 48%   No 41%   Not sure 11%

Should Americans investigate their banks' plan to ensure the safety of their personal assets?

Yes 60%   No 30%   Not sure 10%

If your company is unable to solve its specific year 2000 problem, will your job be in jeopardy?

Yes 47%   No 33%   Not applicable 20%

—*Newsweek,* March 23, 1998

AUTHORS' NOTE

This is a work of fiction. Daniel Prentice, President and Mrs. Stedman, Brad Hunter, Lauren Mitchell, and Kord Herrick have been created from imagination. Their function, however, is to represent people who will live through situations and circumstances very similar to those described in these pages.

The Y2K Crisis, the first catastrophe in history that cannot be avoided or postponed, is very real, as is the technology we describe. The European Union exists. The character depicted within these pages as Adrian Romulus either does or will exist, and his advent upon the world stage is closer now than when we began writing.

This book is not an attempt to portray how the future *must* occur, but how things may come to pass in the light of biblical prophecy. It is our prayer that you will take this story to heart and walk in purity as the day of Christ's coming approaches.

Maranatha! The Lord returns!

Grant R. Jeffrey
Angela Hunt

Acknowledgments

The authors would like to thank

Rick Blanchette for his excellent editing,

Kaye Jeffrey and Adrienne Tigchelaar, editorial assistant,

for their insightful reading through the rough draft,

and Lee Gessner for his faith in this project.

PROLOGUE

AT PRECISELY 5:59 A.M., KORD HERRICK GLANCED UP AT THE PANEL OF surveillance monitors. Camera three displayed his employer's long form lying as still as death in the mammoth four-poster bed, and through the gray-veiled morning shadows Kord could see the shimmer of black, fathomless eyes.

Romulus was already awake. But still the routine must be observed.

Kord waited silently until the digital clock marked the hour, then pressed the button that sent a soft chime ringing through his master's bedroom. "Mr. Romulus—" Kord leaned toward the microphone—"it is 6:00 A.M." As was his habit, he paused, then added, "I hope you slept well."

Adrian Romulus tossed off the coverlet and swung his long legs over the edge of the bed. He turned to face the window, then sat motionless for a long moment, his face lowered and hidden from the camera.

Kord's gaze roved over the image, mentally approving his master's appearance. At forty-nine, Adrian Romulus exuded a commanding air of self-confidence even in the privacy of his bedchamber. Fluid muscles rippled in his smooth back and shoulders, and even though the passing years had carried him well into middle age, his waistline remained trim, his posture straight and unbowed.

Kord lifted his chin. They were much alike, he and his master. Though

Kord was nearly thirty years older than his employer, either one of them could have passed for men ten years younger.

"General Herrick."

Kord snapped to attention and returned his gaze to the monitor. Romulus had turned toward the camera; one hand pushed at a tendril of dark hair that had fallen onto his forehead.

"Sir?"

"I've just experienced the most remarkable insight. I've lived here for what—five years?—and yet I've just realized why I bought this place." A smile crawled to his lips and curved itself like a snake. "Let's see how well you understand me, General. Look at the view outside my window and tell me what you see."

Kord glanced up at monitor five. The camera mounted within the decorative finial atop a fence post moved in a careful arc, surveying the road and grassy pasture outside the estate. A skeletal tree stood black against the brightening sky; a small flock of sheep huddled beneath its empty branches. Kord could see nothing that he hadn't seen on a hundred other autumn mornings.

Sighing, he turned to the microphone. "I'm sorry, sir, but I see nothing unusual. To what did you owe this remarkable understanding?"

One of Romulus's dark brows arched. "The sheep, General. The little flock. They remind me of my birthplace."

"Sheep?" Kord frowned. "Mr. Romulus, must you speak in riddles at this early hour? Why would sheep remind you of Jerusalem?"

"Forget what you read in my dossier." A trace of laughter lined Romulus's voice as he turned away from the camera and looked out the window again. "I was not born in Jerusalem, but in Bethlehem, a sleepy little town known more for producing trinkets and souvenirs than business-men."

Kord felt a wry smile twist the corner of his mouth. "I should think it is more known for the birth of a well-known Jew."

Romulus cut a look from the window back to the camera. "That was then," he said simply, his black eyes jumping in their quick, electric way. "Things are about to change, General. By the time man's evolution is complete, that fanatical and divisive Jew will be a mere footnote in history."

"I'm certain you are correct, sir." Kord paused as his employer's gaze swung back to the window. "Are you ready for your coffee and morning news?"

"Yes." Romulus's eyes did not move from the pastoral scene. "Send Charles to me at once."

Kord pressed the button that would summon the butler, then stepped out of the control room to personally fetch his master's news reports from the wire services and Internet.

ONE

4:15 P.M., Thursday, November 5, 1998

As a chilly autumn wind blew across the silver surface of Trout Lake, Daniel Prentice jerked on his fishing line and crouched lower inside his heavy jacket. He'd been sitting at the water's edge for nearly an hour, his thoughts centered more on problems at the lab than on the lake, but at least his body was participating in this forced sabbatical.

Rest and relaxation, the doctors called it. A change of pace. And though eight years ago he had resented having white-coated professionals tell him how to order his life, Daniel had to admit that his occasional retreats here at the end of the world brought clarity and freshness to his thinking. Obstacles that seemed insurmountable at the office looked smaller when viewed against the backdrop of the wide Canadian wilderness. In the silence of this lonely place he had found the insight to solve more than one perplexing puzzle.

And, occasionally, he even caught a fish.

Something—probably a frog—splashed into the water from the tall grass at Daniel's right hand, and he shifted his attention to the epicenter of the rings spreading over the glassy surface of the water. That splash was the only sign of life he'd seen all day. His uncle had once told him about a huge northern pike that lived in this lake, longer than a man's arm span and sneakier than a cat. "They call him the monster," his uncle had explained, "and they say he killed the fellow who built the cabin up on the ridge. Seems that old Henry disappeared one day, and rumor has it that he managed to hook that pike, only to get pulled into the lake and drowned for his troubles. While lots of people have seen the monster, no one else has been able to hook him. They say he can't be caught."

Daniel circled his finger, slowly winding the reel in a jerky motion that would set the bait to dancing in the clear water. He liked to imagine the huge fish lurking below, sneaking through shadows and the fading stalks of summer reeds. He wanted to believe that the monster waited for him, that the beast had been destined to snag itself on *his* hook, but the reel clicked in an easy, syncopated rhythm as the unclaimed bait floated through the water.

Daniel hunched inside his coat, ignoring the cold numbness in his hands. Few sportsmen were foolish enough to enjoy sitting on a damp rock; this weather was more suited for hunting than fishing. But the stark, quiet, solitary lake suited Daniel's mood.

A faint wind breathed through the trees as he considered the problem that had sent him scrambling for the serenity of this place. His company, Prentice Technologies, had just been handed a multimillion-dollar challenge. Faced with the realization that their aging mainframe computers would not function properly in the year 2000, First Manhattan Bank of New York had hired Daniel's company to check, adapt, and test over 400 million lines of binary computer code. Such a gargantuan task would ordinarily employ four hundred programmers for ten years and cost at least one dollar per line of code. Confident of his people, however, Daniel had signed a contract guaranteeing that his team of fifty code warriors would complete the job by December 31, 1999, a scant thirteen months away. If they succeeded, Prentice Technologies would earn a bonus of $400 million. If they failed, First Manhattan Bank would owe Prentice Technologies only $30 million, barely enough to cover his costs. Furthermore, Daniel would lose his reputation, and in the highly competitive technology business, reputation was everything.

Daniel turned the handle on his fishing rod, absently counting each distinctive click of the ratchet. Last week's *Newsweek* had splashed his face across its cover beneath the headline "Daniel Prentice—Fool or Phenomenon?". The *Newsweek* coverage had made it clear that every computer expert in the world was betting against Daniel, laughing at him, or both. No one could believe that the board of directors at First Manhattan would trust their entire operation to an unorthodox team headed by a Johnny-come-lately sprung from the wilds of Canada instead of Silicon Valley.

Last week, as the news leaked to the press, the executives at First

Manhattan had come under fire from the bank's stockholders. The resulting turmoil made the front pages of the *Wall Street Journal* and the *New York Times*. The furor grew so heated that the bank's CEO, Ernest Schocken, left for a hastily-arranged European vacation not twenty-four hours after formally announcing that he'd placed the fate of his bank in Daniel's hands. Schocken had flown to Paris; Daniel fled to the lake.

A heavy splash ruffled the waters to the south. The monster? Daniel reeled in his line, then shifted his weight and expertly tossed the lure toward the widening circle. If the pike wasn't lurking in the north sector, he'd fish in the south. A man found success in trying new things, seeking new approaches. Whatever worked.

He knew the answer to First Manhattan's problem would not be found in the painstakingly slow solution favored by every other computer company. People had been talking about the coming Year 2000 Crisis—Y2K, for those in the know—since 1990, though at first few people believed it could truly cripple companies and governments. But as experts considered the implications and likely repercussions, panic set in. Like mountaineers intent on conquering Everest step by upward step, programmers had tackled the challenge using the most elementary approach, attempting to unravel the long strings of computer code digit by digit. Daniel and his team didn't have time for trudging uphill.

There had to be another way—some means of flying *to the summit.*

A sharp beep shattered the stillness, and Daniel frowned in annoyance as he shut off the alarm on his watch. Four-thirty. He had promised himself that he'd return to the Range Rover and check his e-mail before five in case something came up at the lab. He had hoped that he'd be able to send the kernel of an idea to his associates, some brilliant insight that would put Prentice Technologies well on its way to solving First Manhattan's Y2K problems. Unfortunately, inspiration didn't operate on a dependable schedule.

"You got lucky today, Monster." Daniel's voice rang over the silent water and echoed among the barren maples as he reeled in his line. "Catch you next time."

He half-expected to hear an answering splash, but the lake remained smooth and glassy as he worked the slab of bait from his hook and tossed it into a bed of weeds. He wrapped the hook around the end of the pole, then picked up his tackle box and headed up the hill to the Range Rover. It sat beneath a tall pine tree, only a few feet from the ramshackle log cabin that had belonged to the unfortunate Henry.

Daniel opened the car door, tossed his gear into the backseat, then leaned in and picked up his Nokia 9000 personal communicator. He flipped open the lid and punched the power on, then scrolled down the menu and selected the "received e-mail" function.

He grinned as the list flashed across the screen. The first message was from his mother, who'd given herself the screen name Hipgrani despite the fact that Daniel had not yet found the time—or the woman—to provide her with a grandchild.

Sinking back into the vehicle's leather upholstery, Daniel highlighted his mother's note, then pressed the enter key.

Darling Son:

All is sunny and delightful in St. Pete. I wish you were here. Mrs. Davis, from the townhouse next door, has invited her daughter for the week. She's thirty-ish and very charming, from what I hear. Bright, too, and pretty—just your type. She'll be here for a week, so if you can get away, I'd love to have you drop in. Just surprise me if you want to, and we'll think of some good excuse to meet Mrs. Davis's daughter.

I know what you're thinking, and I can almost see you rolling your eyes at me. I know you don't want me to worry about you, but that's what mothers are for. I know you have a great company and a fancy car, but I want more for you, Daniel. Not more things—more love and life. And I know a wife and family would make you very, very happy.

Trust me. Mothers always know best.

Mom

A quick flood of guilt washed over Daniel, and he made a mental note to set aside an hour for a nice long telephone chat with his mother. Her birthday was November 16—less than two weeks away. If the brain cells weren't percolating and he hadn't yet come up with an answer for his Y2K problems, he could even fly down to Florida, stay overnight in his mom's condo, perhaps even meet the neighbors. Daniel was certain nothing would come of his meeting Mrs. Davis's daughter, but at least he'd make his mother happy.

Satisfied with that decision, he tapped the enter key and highlighted the next message.

> *Daniel—*
>
> *Saw your grinning mug on the cover of* Newsweek! *If I had known that I was rescuing a future poster hunk when I pulled your bacon from the fire, I'd have left you in Baghdad. Even my own darling Christine was quite taken with your picture. She kept saying, "This gorgeous fellow is going to be your best man?"*
>
> *I'm warning you, Prentice. If Christine gets a good look at you and calls off the wedding, I'm coming after you with every weapon at my disposal—and maybe a few that aren't.*
>
> *So get into a fight or stop showering, will you, so you're nice and ugly when you come for the rehearsal. And make sure it's on your calendar—December 22, 7:00 P.M., Washington Cathedral.*
>
> *Be there . . . or be very afraid. I will come after you.*
>
> *Later,*
>
> *Brad*

Daniel rubbed his hand across his face and grinned. Brad Hunter had to be getting nervous as his wedding date approached. Like Daniel, he was thirty-eight, and, like Daniel, his career had always held precedence over any romantic relationship. Both men were well past the age when most women thought they should be faithfully and lawfully espoused, but they never would have met had one of them been married. The military didn't send married men on missions like the one that had introduced Daniel to Brad Hunter.

After the Desert Storm mission, Daniel and Brad recuperated together in a Washington hospital. With nothing else to do, they played cards, ogled their pretty nurses, and made a pact—the first to succumb to marriage would pay for the more resistant man's honeymoon. Brad had sworn that he'd be able to remain single for the rest of the century, but then a young elementary schoolteacher named Christine had walked into his life and changed everything.

Now Brad was suggesting that Daniel consider a vow of celibacy.

"Marriage isn't for everyone," he told Daniel the last time they spoke. "Okay, I'll admit it, I'm the weaker man. But you, Daniel, are going to bankrupt me if you get married! You move in lofty and expensive circles, you date rich women, and you'll want to honeymoon in Tahiti or some other exotic place. Remember, I'm just a lowly civil servant—"

"Right," Daniel had interrupted, laughing into the phone. "Lowly like Henry Kissinger. Give it up, Brad, you'll be running Washington in a year or two."

Though he had blustered his way through the compliment, Brad couldn't deny that his heroism in Desert Storm had placed him on the fast track to success. He had transferred from the elite Navy SEALS to the National Security Agency, and now he served as a deputy assistant to the president for national security affairs. Daniel wasn't exactly certain what Brad did in Washington, but he knew his friend was an official mover and shaker.

Daniel touched the save key, consigning Brad's message to a storage folder. He'd respond to it later, when he had time to think of some witty comeback. Perhaps he'd reply that he was dating a European princess and would need extra security if he brought her to the wedding.

He smiled devilishly. Brad would be so distressed by the thought of Daniel's dating a high-maintenance woman that he wouldn't have time to worry about his own wedding.

Daniel pressed the receive button one final time, then frowned as another message flashed across the gray screen. This one, from HKriegel@Prenticetech.com, was heralded by one word in the subject line: "Eureka!"

Daniel pressed the enter key and the message filled the screen.

Daniel:

A breakthrough! Have devised a program to flag category II and III date codes in need of modification—decided to underline them. Color not compatible with monochrome monitors.

Come see.

Howard

Daniel felt a surge of excitement flow through him. The most difficult and time-consuming aspect of repairing COBOL and FORTRAN computer code involved *finding* the hidden category II and III date codes. To the human eye—trained or untrained—binary machine code looked like nothing more than a long string of zeros and ones in random sequences. Computer experts had accurately compared the manual search for hidden date codes to looking for needles in haystacks. If Dr. Kriegel had indeed been able to write a program to find and flag the hidden codes—why, this capability alone would speed their work beyond calculation!

Daniel snapped the Nokia shut, tossed it onto the passenger seat, then slammed the Range Rover's back door. This wilderness retreat hadn't paid off in the way he had hoped, but it had pulled him out of the office and away from Dr. Kriegel. And that gifted eccentric, thank goodness, had used the quiet hours of Daniel's absence to once again prove his genius.

Daniel climbed into the car, closed the door, and smiled in satisfaction as the powerful engine roared. Though the sun had begun to set, the future seemed much brighter than it had an hour before.

-01001111OO-

The jet touched down at 9:00 P.M., and Daniel promptly took a cab to his office in Mount Vernon, New York. He'd chosen to establish his company in Westchester County because the area was close to Manhattan without being in the thick of things. With a population of just under seventy thousand, Mount Vernon offered schools, playgrounds, and community spirit for the few employees of Prentice Technology who had time to care about such things.

Daniel had little time for family or community, but he wanted his employees to be happy. So he bought a dilapidated block of buildings scheduled for demolition, brought in the wrecking ball and explosives crews, then watched a gleaming white stone edifice rise from the rubble. The Mount Vernon Urban Renewal Agency *adored* Prentice Technologies and demonstrated its affection with low taxes and various community perks.

The taxi driver pulled over to the curb, then twisted in the seat and gave Daniel a dubious look. "You sure dis de place, man?" he asked in some indistinguishable accent. "Nobody here dis time of de night."

"This is the place." Daniel ripped three twenties out of his wallet and dropped them over the front seat. "There's always someone here."

He fumbled for a moment with the broken door handle, then stepped out onto the curb. A bitterly cold wind whipped down the deserted street, and as he moved toward the entrance he was grateful for the warmth of his wilderness clothes.

A pair of deceptively simple glass doors and a small black box marked the entrance to the sparkling white building. Daniel lifted the lid on the biometric security system's sensor pad and pressed his thumb to it. The pad immediately glowed with a green light, then a husky female voice poured through the concealed speakers. "Good evening, Mr. Prentice. You are cleared to enter."

"Thank you, Roberta."

"You're welcome."

The locking mechanism inside the glass door clicked, and Daniel opened it and stepped inside the vestibule. He would face three more checkpoints before reaching his office, and each time his unique thumb- and voiceprint would serve as the entry key. The security system at PT was neat, tidy, and precise, shunning external cameras, guards, and guns in favor of cutting-edge technology.

Sophisticated technology guarded the interior of the building as well. Soft recessed lamps lit the windowless offices and computer labs; rubber-lined drapes covered the cafeteria's wide windows to absorb vibration in the event that an industrial spy might try to use a microwave laser to read conversations off the glass panels. Complex combination locks guarded each filing cabinet behind the assistants' desks, and a shredder sat atop every waste container except those in the cafeteria. The state-of-the-art personal computers at each desk lacked floppy and zip drives, so no information could be copied to disk and carried out the door. A secure network of Daniel's own design governed the sharing of information, files, and e-mail. Finally, Daniel banned photocopy machines and required that paperwork be kept to a minimum. Any sensitive reports were printed on flash paper, which burned in an instant and left no ashes.

When at last he passed through the double oak doors that opened into his office, Daniel fished the Nokia from his jacket pocket and tossed it onto his desk. Walking to his computer, he pressed his index finger to the touch-pad and listened to the reassuring sound of the whirring hard drive.

"Good evening, Mr. Prentice. It is 9:47 P.M. What would you like to do?"

"Find Dr. Kriegel, please." Daniel sank into his chair.

The screen flickered, then filled with the professor's black-and-white security photo.

"Dr. Kriegel is in his office. Would you like me to page him for you?"

"Please, Roberta." Daniel leaned forward, ruefully wishing he could create a real feminine presence to match the luscious voice that purred from his computer. He and Dr. Kriegel had decided to name the security system Roberta as a play on the word *robot*, but the Voice Operated Security System, or VOSS for short, had taken on a life of its own within the environs of Prentice Technologies.

On a mischievous whim, Daniel had programmed the operating system so that the words *please* and *thank you* performed the action of an enter key, so Roberta would execute no command unless spoken to politely. Inside the building, anyone—employee or intruder—who gave brusque commands or attempted to override Roberta's protocols would find himself ignored or yelling at a system that had shut down. Outside the building, any intruder who failed to pass either the fingerprint or the voice recognition test would discover that while Roberta stalled with a brief and pleasant monologue on the origin and vision of Prentice Technologies, she had faxed his voice- and fingerprints to Daniel's office, the local police department, and the FBI.

Dr. Kriegel's photo remained on screen while Roberta queried the professor. Daniel could have programmed his computers to eavesdrop on his employees, but he knew how he'd resent the knowledge that someone could spy on him at any moment. More than one hundred digital cameras were mounted throughout the offices and labs of Prentice Technologies, but they served more often as tools for communication than surveillance.

"Daniel?" The photo faded, replaced by a close-up shot of the professor's bulbous nose. "Glad you're back. You got my message?"

"Of course. Is this a good time for me to see a demonstration?"

"Is it what—what time is it, please?" The nose shifted, and Daniel was treated to a tight shot of the professor's graying eyebrow. The cat must have been sitting atop the computer again and upset the camera adjustments.

"The time, Dr. Kriegel, is 9:50 P.M." Roberta's polite voice floated over the speaker.

"Thank you, Roberta," Daniel answered. "Dr. Kriegel, I'm coming down."

"Oh yes." The professor shifted again, and as Daniel stood he saw a large eyeball, dark and wide, peering out from the computer screen. "It's most extraordinary, Daniel. Come whenever you like, come now, come tomorrow. Most extraordinary. Amazing, in fact."

Daniel shrugged out of his coat, tossed it over his chair, then crossed the room in four long strides. After he'd seen the demonstration, he really ought to make the professor get some sleep.

T w o

10:00 P.M., Thursday, November 5, 1998

"WATCH THIS."

Dr. Howard Kriegel slid his finger over the touchpad on his computer keyboard, then lightly tapped it. The monitor's screen filled with what seemed like an infinite pattern of zeros and ones, a marching army of digits moving to its own haphazard beat.

"Binary code," Daniel said, watching the numbers.

"Yes." The professor absently reached out to his cat, Quark, and scratched the animal's head. "This particular machine code is COBOL. Bob Bemer has come up with a rather elegant solution to the Y2K problem, but he still can't find the hidden dates without a painstaking manual search."

Daniel crossed his arms and leaned back upon the professor's cluttered desk. "What's his solution?"

Dr. Kriegel held up a finger. "Mr. Bemer's Vertex solution is based on the fact that date fields in COBOL do not make use of the complete number of eight bits available to them. By using the extra bits, new numbers can be created that represent centuries. On COBOL systems, characters are contained in eight bits of data, but single digit integers never use more than four bits to define a digit. The upper four bits define what the next four bits mean. But out of the sixteen possible combinations, some were never used."

"Well, Bemer should know." Daniel shrugged. "Since he helped write the code years ago."

Dr. Kriegel nodded. "Now he is making use of these unused combinations of bits to identify a number as a decade-specific BIGIT. For example, the top four digits might be 1000 for the century 19xx, and 1001 for the century 20xx. In combination with the next two digits, a century-specific year can be specified in the space of only two characters."

"Well, that's fine for obvious date codes," Daniel said, squinting at the screen. "But searching for hidden date codes will still take thousands of man-hours. How do we find them?"

Like a parent amused by the questions of his child, Dr. Kriegel gave Daniel an indulgent smile. "We call the program X 2000," he said, tapping on the keyboard. "Watch."

The screen flickered and flowed with numbers as the professor typed and talked. "This little program scans the machine code for all arithmetic operations, whether hidden or obvious. X 2000 is linked as a library at compilation with source code. The program replaces the arithmetic operation with a jump instruction, and the replaced instruction is placed in a table, intact. The jump instruction takes the program to the table, where X 2000, not the mainframe hardware, executes the arithmetic operation in virtual memory. The program knows how to add or subtract two BIGIT numbers to get the proper year difference. The resultant values, now in BIGIT format, are returned to the program just as if the original operation had calculated the results. And, voilà! The new codes are underlined, so the programmer can identify and test them in a fraction of the time he would have required. The beauty of our program is that it works on the machine code regardless of the original programming language used. It will work on COBOL, FORTRAN, or even the military's old favorite, Jovial."

Before Daniel's eyes, the numbers of the screen shifted as underlining appeared under various codes. It seemed so simple . . . why hadn't he thought of it?

"That's it?" An anticipatory shiver of excitement rippled through Daniel's limbs. "The underlined digits I'm seeing now—that's replaced code? It's ready for testing?"

Kriegel nodded, then squinted at Daniel through his glasses. "Of course, we could mark the modified code in color if you'd like—I myself am partial to a nice chartreuse—but too many old systems still operate with monochrome monitors. Color just wouldn't be feasible."

"It's perfect!" Daniel slapped the professor on the shoulder, then bent to watch the numbers scrolling by. "How quickly does the program compute?"

"The average programmer can examine and repair a hundred thousand lines of code per year. With our advanced microprocessors, I estimate that X 2000 will find and repair a hundred thousand lines an hour. The procedure could be accelerated, of course, by increasing the speed of the computer, or assigning more computers to the task."

Daniel did quick computations in his head. "So a typical IBM 390 workstation running twenty-four hours a day, for an entire year—"

"Will correct 876 million lines of code," Dr. Kriegel finished. "Multiply that by x number of machines, and you have solved the entire nation's problem."

Daniel stared at the flashing digits, mesmerized by the possibilities. He exhaled in relief. "It'll work. We'll finish the First Manhattan project with time to spare."

"Not much time." The professor held up a restraining hand. "The code must still be tested. And don't forget Murphy's Law: What *can* go wrong *will* go wrong. You've got to allow for the occasional system crash and even minor things like power outages. And we'll have to debug this program as well as the revised code, allowing for the standard one error in every hundred lines—"

"The solar panels will give us backup power," Daniel interrupted. He sank back to the desk and crossed his arms, thinking. "And we'll set up twenty workstation computers running at full tilt to give us an edge. We'll divide our people—one team will supervise the decoding, another will test the revised codes." He looked up at the professor. "You and your team will debug the new program, of course. I know you'll do it at top speed, and I'd trust it to no one else."

"Well, then." Looking faintly pleased, the professor folded his hands at his waist and smiled at his cat. "We are glad to be of service, aren't we, Quark?"

Daniel gazed at the professor in silent amazement. He had studied under Dr. Howard Kriegel at MIT, and after graduation he'd been almost embarrassed to ask such a brilliant teacher to leave education and work in the private sector. That Dr. Kriegel had accepted Daniel's job offer was almost beyond belief. But Daniel would never again regret stealing MIT's best professor. The world would benefit from Dr. Kriegel's work today.

"Howard, you just earned yourself a huge bonus."

The professor dismissed that with a wave. "Daniel, there's really no need. And I had help, you know. The others all contributed."

"Then I'll dish out bonuses all around." Daniel nodded as he stood. "Money is important, and we need to fulfill our dreams. Besides, if I don't treat my people well, some other firm will hire you all away from me."

The professor looked at him with rounded eyes. "Why would I want to leave? Life here is so—" he spread his hands, indicating the cluttered room. "Life here is perfect," he finished, dropping his hands to the keyboard. "Absolutely complete."

"Even so, you'll soon find an expression of my gratitude in your bank account." Daniel walked over to the communications PC, where Quark was batting at the wide, unblinking eye of the camera. "I'll never be able to thank you enough for your hard work." He set the animal in a chair, re-adjusted the focus control, then turned back to the professor. "Now, professor, why don't you get some sleep? Tomorrow you and I will make copies of that program and divide the bank's code into manageable sectors. And when it's all done and First Manhattan is year-2000 compliant, you and I will have a rich laugh at everyone who doubted that we could pull it off."

"A nap." The professor tilted his head. "A very good idea. I am feeling a bit drained. But I think I'll just curl up on my couch. No sense in going home if I'm coming right back tomorrow."

"Fine, Dr. Kriegel." Daniel paused in the doorway, studying the cluttered room, the paper-strewn couch, the chalkboard scrawled with computations. He had seen the professor's one room apartment, and it didn't look much different than this place. At least here the professor had Roberta and Quark to keep him company.

Without further ado, the professor perched on the edge of his couch and removed his glasses. As the older man shoved papers from the couch to the floor, Daniel turned toward the corner computer. "Roberta?"

"Yes, Mr. Prentice?"

"Wake Dr. Kriegel at 7:30 A.M."

Silence.

"Wake Dr. Kriegel at 7:30 A.M., *please*."

"Certainly, Mr. Prentice."

Daniel dimmed the lights, then left the professor sleeping in the soft glow of the monitors.

Daniel left the office just after midnight and nosed his '57 Jag out of the parking garage and onto the road. Traffic was light at this hour, and the red sports car devoured the miles, roaring along the Cross Bronx Expressway as if eager to get home. Daniel switched on the radio and sang along with Three Dog Night on the classic rock station, joyfully ripping the words from his throat.

"Jeremiah was a bullfrog! Was a good friend of mine!"

His left leg thumped heavily on the floorboards, his hand patted the steering wheel in rhythm. He slanted from one lane to the next, dodging slower, stodgier cars.

Let the experts wonder if he'd lost his sanity by accepting the challenge of First Manhattan's code. He'd believed in his team, and his team had delivered. The computer program they had concocted would not only solve First Manhattan's Y2K problem, but could be the definitive answer for every bank, corporation, and government in the world.

"Joy to the fishes in the deep blue sea. Joy to you and me."

He took the exit for the Henry Hudson Parkway and curved into the on-ramp, setting the Jaguar free as soon as he reached the straightaway. The Jag rode the left lane and blew past the tired drivers. Soon Daniel exited the freeway and crept down Park Avenue, where the high and mighty slept in multimillion-dollar high-rise apartments.

He pulled into his reserved space at the garage, saluted the on-duty attendant with a careless wave, and called a cheery greeting to the doorman.

"Good evening, Mr. Prentice." The fellow didn't sound nearly as welcoming as Roberta, but he hadn't been programmed to personify the woman of Daniel's dreams, either.

"Evening, Randall. All quiet tonight?"

"Yes, sir. Very quiet." The doorman flashed a diplomatic smile. "Saw your picture on the cover of *Newsweek*. *People* magazine, too."

"*People?*" Daniel felt a curious, tingling shock. *Newsweek* was one thing, *People* was quite another. Businessmen and politicians read *Newsweek;* businessmen, politicians, and customers in hair salons and auto repair shops read *People*. Furthermore, he couldn't remember giving an interview to *People*, so the article would undoubtedly feature the opinions and recollections of so-called friends and associates he barely knew—

Daniel had a sudden vision of his mother's bridge club snickering behind the magazine's glossy pages as they read what his latest ex-girl-friend had to say about him.

"*People*, huh?" He gave the doorman a forced smile. "I didn't know about that one. I'll have to pick up a copy tomorrow."

"I could go out and get one for you, Mr. Prentice." An always helpful breed, doormen, if the tip promised to be generous.

"No, thanks, it'll wait." Daniel waved the doorman away and moved toward the elevator, his thoughts churning. He really ought to have invested more time in his personal life. Society looked far more favorably on a married man with a wife and a couple of kids than a thirty-something bachelor who dated only when a social occasion required an escort. It wasn't that he didn't care for the company of women; he found intelli-gent, beautiful women as interesting as a well-conceived paradox. But relationships took time, and there were never enough hours in the day as it was.

Daniel stepped into the elevator and pressed the button for his floor, remembering his mother's e-mail message. Even now he didn't have time for family responsibilities, but he couldn't let her birthday slip by without doing something special. He wouldn't be able to go down to Florida, not with all that was happening at the office, but he could send her the biggest bouquet St. Pete had ever seen.

The elevator opened to his front hall. Daniel stepped out onto the marble floors and shifted his briefcase from one hand to the other, won-dering for the hundredth time why he had ever bought such an extrava-gant apartment. After the *Business Week* profile that revealed how he made his first million before the age of thirty, financial planners and real estate agents had besieged him. It seemed only logical that he would move to a nicer place in Manhattan, but this Park Avenue apartment seemed to mock his hard-earned success even as it proved it. This vast, marble space, filled with expensive furnishings and cold statuary, was completely his, but it was not *him*. Sometimes he felt more at home in old Henry's lakeside shack.

An elegant, curving staircase rose from the center of the marble foyer. To the left lay a wing designed for a nonexistent staff of household servants; to the right lay the library and various rooms deemed fit for entertaining.

His real living space lay upstairs. Daniel sprinted up the staircase to his sprawling bedroom, then tossed his briefcase on a chair and tugged at the collar of his shirt. He picked up the television remote and scanned the scores on ESPN, then switched to CNN and studied the stock ticker racing across the bottom of the screen. His personal computer sat on a wooden table in the dressing room, and after a moment he moved toward it and lightly pressed his finger to the touchpad.

The screen brightened instantly. He had not, unfortunately, installed Roberta's program into this system; it operated with Windows 98. Aside from a couple of computer games Daniel was testing for one of the young guys at the office, the hard drive contained only basic communications software and Pretty Good Privacy, or PGP, an encryption program that enabled Daniel to communicate securely with the office over an ordinary modem and telephone line.

Internet Explorer indicated that he had e-mail waiting—two messages from Hipgrani, one marked "urgent."

Sighing, Daniel sank into a leather chair near his wide window, picked up the phone, and punched in his mother's number. She knew he kept late hours, so she wouldn't be surprised that he was calling at midnight.

"Hello?"

"Mom, did I wake you?"

"Daniel? Goodness Son, are you all right?"

"I'm fine. But you sent me an urgent message—what's up?"

"Well, dear, it's about Linda. Do you remember? I wrote you about her."

"Who?"

"Mrs. Davis's daughter. I met her tonight, and honestly, Daniel, I don't think she's your type at all. So don't come down here. Consider yourself uninvited. Forgive me for playing matchmaker, and don't put yourself out on my account."

Daniel blinked in surprised silence. Since his thirtieth birthday, his mother had never met an unmarried woman she didn't think could improve Daniel's life immeasurably. This change of heart was certainly unexpected.

A cloud of suspicion rose in his mind. "Mom?" He propped his elbow on the arm of the chair. "Did this lady—Linda—happen to inquire about my net worth?"

He heard her quick breath of astonishment. "Why, whatever makes you ask such—"

"It's all right, Mom. I know the gold-digging type. And I generally steer clear of them."

"I know, Son, but I've been reading so many things, I can't help but worry about you."

Daniel blew out his breath. "Relax, Mom. I know the *Newsweek* article made me look like a fool, and I can only imagine what *People* had to say. But it's okay. Let people think I'm crazy. I knew I was taking a risk when I signed the contract with First Manhattan."

"But—" He could practically see her, pink-faced and nervous, her chin quivering. "Daniel, you will make it work, won't you? They say you'll be ruined forever in the computer business if you don't find a way to fix those computers."

"We've already found a way." He lowered his voice, suddenly convinced that he'd break the sweet spell of success if he bragged about it. "Don't you worry, Mom, it's all taken care of. We'll have the project done with time to spare. Shoot, we could fix the entire *world's* computers if they'd come to us—"

He broke off, afraid of saying too much. You had to be careful in this business, especially when big bucks and big deals were at stake. "It's okay, Mom," he finally finished. "You have nothing to worry about. In fact," he lightened his tone, "I just may go down in history as the man who saved the twenty-first century."

"Thank the Lord, Daniel." Her voice was like a warm embrace in the chilly apartment. "I have been praying that you'd think of something. And when Mrs. Davis said that you were completely nuts, I told her you'd be all right because the Lord has his hand on you."

Daniel shifted uncomfortably. "Well, somebody had his hand on Dr. Kriegel and his team because *they* came up with the answer. But thanks for sticking up for me."

"Of course, Son." Maternal pride filled her voice and rolled over the telephone lines. "Now it's late, so you get some sleep. And don't worry about coming down here; just keep in touch however you can. And know that I'm praying for you."

"I know that, Mom. Thanks. Good-night."

Daniel waited until he heard the click of the phone line, then he held the receiver to his chest and wondered how his mother could believe prayer had the power to change anything.

-0100111100-

Amelia Prentice hung up her bedside phone, then lifted the covers of her narrow bed and lowered herself to the carpeted floor. On her knees, she pressed her elbows into the mattress and clasped her hands, closing her eyes to the moonlit shadows that danced on the walls.

"Heavenly Father, I gave him to you once," she prayed, her heart brimming with love as powerful as the day she gave birth to the son she adored. "And now I ask you to keep your hand upon him. He has so much, Lord, that he doesn't realize how much he needs. And what he needs most is you."

She paused, listening to the rattle of the palmettos in the wind. A warm sea-scented breeze came in through the open window and blew the fringe of hair upon her neck.

"He's a tough kid, and he won't admit his fears . . . or his needs. It hurts me to see him so successful and yet so lonely. He's rich in worldly goods, but so poor in spiritual treasures. He's so bright, but so unwise about the things that really matter."

Her heart squeezed so tight she could barely draw breath to speak, but she forced the words out. "Heavenly Father, I gave him to you when he was born, but I've always begged you to protect him. You have—you've given him so much, and yet he still resists you. With every success, my Daniel thinks he needs you less."

She clenched her jaw to kill the sob in her throat. "Now I'm asking, Lord, that you would do whatever it takes to open his eyes. Break his strong will . . . break his proud heart, if you must. But protect his life, and bring him to the place where he can choose. I love him so much, Lord."

When she lifted her eyes, the palm tree shadows still flickered on the walls, but the darkness that had shadowed her heart was gone. Amelia slowly climbed back into her bed and pulled the covers to her chin, content to lie in the warm breeze and wait for sleep.

THREE

8:00 A.M., Friday, November 6, 1998

DANIEL DELIBERATELY SLEPT UNTIL EIGHT, THEN ROSE AND ENJOYED A LONG, HOT shower. Driven to come up with a solution for the Year 2000 Crisis, the other employees of Prentice Technologies would have arrived at the office at seven-thirty, if not earlier.

Daniel smiled as the hot water streamed over his back and shoulders. Y2K no longer had the power to intimidate him. He and his people would quietly solve First Manhattan's problems, and when the rest of the world panicked in the spring, he'd market the X 2000 software—with a less alien-sounding name, of course—at some obscene price and make a killing. He'd be able to establish generous pension plans for all fifty of his programmers, and Dr. Kriegel could retire—if he wanted to. Daniel had the sneaking suspicion that Professor Kriegel would happily grow old in his computer lab, with Quark for company and a host of unsolvable problems whirling in his brain.

And everyone who had mocked Daniel's intuition and faith would have to purchase the Prentice Technologies package before the year-2000 deadline in order to save their systems.

Shutting off the water, he glanced into the steamy bathroom mirror and grinned back at his own reflection. Revenge—even one as subtle as this—would taste sweet.

Daniel pulled a towel from the heated rack and made a mental note to call Ernest Schocken's office at First Manhattan. The CEO might still be on his European vacation, but Daniel would pry his phone number out of Schocken's secretary. Despite all the naysaying, the man had placed his trust in Prentice Technologies. He deserved to know that he would not be disappointed.

Daniel dressed in khaki pants, a light blue long-sleeved shirt, and a blazer of navy wool. Glancing in the mirror, he zipped a comb through his brown hair, then picked up his briefcase and strode through the hall. He glanced at his watch as he waited for the elevator. With any luck, he'd be in the office by nine, ready to receive relieved congratulations from the others.

The air was sharp and cold as he pulled out onto the expressway, and Daniel shivered inside his jacket, wishing that his favorite car were more airtight. As the heater blew a torrent of tepid air at his face, Daniel revved the engine, then eased into the snaking traffic.

Throngs of pedestrians clogged the sidewalks by the time he reached Mount Vernon. Daniel parked in the garage, nodded to the parking attendant, then pressed his thumbprint to the sensor pad outside the locked doors.

"Good morning, Mr. Prentice," Roberta purred. "My infrared sensors indicate that you are not alone."

Daniel glanced behind him. Susan McGuire, a young programmer he had hired three months earlier, was hurrying toward him, one pale hand holding her coat closed against the wind.

"You're right, Roberta. Susan McGuire is here, too."

Breathless, Susan stopped a few feet behind Daniel and gave him an embarrassed smile. "I'm sorry I'm late, Mr. Prentice. My little boy was sick, and I had to find a sitter. I couldn't take him to preschool with a fever."

"I understand, Susan." Daniel stepped back and moved toward the door, waiting for Susan to press her thumb to the sensor. Once she had, the pad flashed green, and Roberta's sultry voice called out, "Thank you, Ms. McGuire. You and Mr. Prentice are cleared for entry."

Daniel opened the door for Susan. "A bit cold today, isn't it?"

"Very." Susan hurried past him into the foyer, and Daniel followed, glancing up in surprise as he looked through the second set of glass doors. He couldn't know for sure, but it certainly looked as though every employee of Prentice Technology had crowded into the reception area. As he approached, they burst into applause.

Daniel grinned back as he passed through the second set of doors. Poor Susan, doubly embarrassed by her late arrival and this unexpected greeting, flushed crimson and tried her best to fade into the crowd.

Daniel smiled around the circle, feeling his own face burn at the attention, then held up his hands for silence. Feigning ignorance, he lifted a brow. "I know I'm absent-minded, but did I forget my birthday?"

His employees rocked with laughter, then Bill Royce, director of development, stepped forward. "Your little discovery greeted us this morning. Every computer on the network was running the program." Bill's eyes creased in a flattering expression of admiration. "We knew you could do it, boss. We just didn't expect you to do it so soon."

Daniel stiffened as a flicker of apprehension coursed through him. He hadn't plugged the program into the network. Someone on Kriegel's team might have done it this morning, but the professor wouldn't have approved. This kind of showmanship wasn't like him.

Daniel's eyes swept over the group. "First of all, I didn't do it. Dr. Kriegel's team put the program together, and the professor demonstrated it for me last night. But it is our answer. After the beta version is debugged, we can run multiple computers and have First Manhattan's code tested in a matter of weeks."

The group erupted again in cheers and applause, and after a moment Daniel lifted his hand for silence. "By the way," he said, smiling to mask his uneasiness, "where is the professor? I know he spent the night here."

The group stirred but did not produce Dr. Kriegel. Daniel's sense of unease gelled. "Roberta," he called, lifting his voice to reach the security console near the elevator, "locate Dr. Kriegel, please."

Silence fell upon the group, then Roberta's dusky voice answered. "Dr. Howard Kriegel is in his lab, Mr. Prentice."

Daniel closed his eyes and breathed a sigh of relief. Kriegel hadn't been abducted. He had every confidence in his people and his security system, but the X 2000 program would be worth billions to any thief clever enough to steal it—or its inventor.

"Thanks, people." He turned toward the crowd and gave them a wavering smile. "Dr. Kriegel and I are going to begin testing the program today, and soon we'll assign you to code sections. Some of you will check code, others will test. But *none* of you," he verbally underlined the word, "will breathe a word of this to anyone. This—" he pointed to the program on the monitor—"is top secret. Is that understood?"

Heads bobbed in silence; excited faces immediately grew somber. Daniel glanced around the circle one more time, then moved into the elevator and pressed his thumb to the sensor pad. "My office, Roberta," he said. "Please."

Four

9:23 A.M., Friday, November 6, 1998

IN HIS WASHINGTON OFFICE, BRAD HUNTER TURNED AS HIS COMPUTER CHIMED to signal an incoming message. Words flashed across his screen, then the messaging program automatically fed the e-mail to the printer, which whirred and hummed until a sheet of paper shot out of the tray. The message, from an agent in New York, was short and sweet: "Prentice Technologies perfects Y2K fix."

Brad felt a slow grin spread over his face as he dropped the page to his desk. "So you did it, Danny boy," he breathed, lifting his coffee mug to his lips. He'd never doubted that Daniel would find a fix, but like most of America, he had wondered if Prentice Technologies could solve the problem in time.

Apparently they had.

Brad sipped his coffee, then placed the hot mug on his desk and glanced at his calendar. As a national security counsel in the Office of Records and Access Management, he and his superiors were vitally interested in the Y2K problem. Then again, these days every government agency was crucially concerned with the state of their computers. The old mainframes that had run everything from Social Security to the IRS were in danger of being rendered obsolete as of midnight, January 1, 2000. Their millions of code lines made First Manhattan Bank's problem look puny in comparison.

But Daniel had found an answer.

Brad picked up a pencil and tapped it on his desk. He had felt a stab of guilt when he assigned a pair of agents to Prentice Technologies, but the feeling passed when he considered that he had assigned agents to twenty other innovative software companies as well. Everyone desperately needed an answer to the Y2K dilemma, and, entrepreneurs being what they were, the creative souls who came up with the answer wouldn't be likely to share it without at least a little coercion. These computer whiz kids talked about charity and improving the world through their gifts, but thus far their largesse had been generally limited to free games, redundant productivity software, and programs that hooked the user to some larger and more expensive operating system.

Brad smiled to himself as he thought of his friend. Daniel Prentice was a nice guy, generally altruistic, but he hadn't become a multimillionaire by giving away the store. If he had a Y2K solution, he'd charge handsomely for it, maybe even start a bidding war when the world was desperate and options were limited. Of course, he'd be taking a risk that someone else would hit upon a similar solution, but Daniel wasn't afraid to take a chance. Daniel wasn't afraid of anything in the corporate world.

Well, Uncle Sam would have to take a risk, too. The Washington bureaucrats would have to offer Daniel Prentice more than the private sector ever could, and they'd have to move before Daniel grew comfortable with the idea of upping the ante.

Brad scratched a digit beneath the message, then added an absurd number of zeroes and a dollar sign. The figure was more than the operating budget of the NSA and the Treasury Department combined; but if Daniel could save the government's computers from disaster, he would, in effect, be saving the nation from disaster. Not everyone would see it that way, of course. The sharks would come out in full force when this figure began to be bandied about in committee meetings, since such an amount would take a slice from every budget in Washington. But if Washington wanted to keep the nation together, it would have to pay the price . . . whatever Daniel Prentice demanded.

Brad stared at the message a moment more, then fed it into his shredder. "Danny, my boy, I hope you're open to negotiation. You'd be cheaper to kill than to employ."

He waited until the shredder stopped churning, then stood and tugged out the wrinkles of his jacket. Straightening his shoulders, he moved out into the hall, dreading what he had to do next.

FIVE

10:04 A.M., Monday, November 9, 1998

"GOOD MORNING, MR. PRESIDENT."

The greeting came in near-perfect unison from more than a dozen throats as Lauren Mitchell walked in the wake of the looks of awe and respect directed at President Samuel Stedman. As the president moved around the oval table, giving each member of his cabinet a smile and a handshake, Lauren found an empty chair against the wall. As the president's executive assistant, her position was almost as significant as any cabinet member's, and she felt no need to wrangle for a seat near her boss. After all, she had known the president and first lady since Sam Stedman was a freshman senator from the great state of North Carolina. Her genuine friendship with the first couple involved far more than mere politics.

"Good to see you, Hank." The president moved easily through the group, enchanting his cabinet members as easily as he had charmed the voters when he defeated Bill Clinton in the '96 election. Standing as tall as any man in the room, his thick, dark hair gleamed in the artificial light. At sixty-three, Samuel Stedman possessed a younger man's energy and an older man's wisdom. Tired of the hip attitudes and faltering moral leadership of the previous administration, the voters had flocked to cast their votes for Stedman—a staunch Republican, loyal American, and traditional southern gentleman. On the campaign trail, not one reporter had dared ask what kind of underwear the candidate preferred.

Lauren's gaze moved around the oval table, mentally checking the list of attendees. The secretaries of the Departments of Defense, Agriculture, Education, Transportation, the Treasury, Energy, and Housing and Urban Development flanked the right side of the table, mirrored on the left by the heads of the Departments of State, the Interior, Justice, Labor, Health and Human Services, Commerce, and Veterans' Affairs. Like a referee in a volleyball game, John Miller, the vice president, stood at the far end of the table, his hands clasped at his waist, his head bowed in a posture of polite and patient waiting.

Lauren sank into a chair by the door, opposite Tom Ormond, the White House press secretary. As soon as the preliminaries were observed, Tom would slip out and get back to writing press releases about everything from foreign policy to the president's new litter of puppies. Lauren knew he'd buzz by her desk later to pick up a copy of her notes from this meeting.

John Harper, the official White House photographer, knelt at the edge of the table and got a few shots of the president pressing the flesh. After a few bright flashes, John grabbed his gear and scooted out of the room, much to the dismay, Lauren noticed, of the officials who hadn't been in the right place at the right time.

She tilted her head and studied the line of suits and uniforms. The lucky recipient of today's photo op was General Adam Archer, secretary of the Department of Defense and special assistant to the president for national security affairs. He'd probably call tomorrow and complain that having his picture sent over the AP wire violated his privacy and national security, but that hadn't stopped him from barreling his chest for the camera.

Once the photographer left, the president sank into his chair, and the other bureaucrats sat, too. The formal atmosphere softened slightly as the president leaned forward and rested his arms upon the gleaming conference table.

"I appreciate you all for taking the time to come out on a Monday morning," he said, his voice reverberating with southern charm. "But you know that I signed an executive order back in February directing each department to move on this Year 2000 Crisis." His brows knitted in a frown. "I want to hear what we're doing to solve this computer problem. I've received some troubling reports, and it's time we made this a top priority before we run out of time."

The secretaries looked at one another, and Lauren felt a rush of sympathy for the poor soul who would have to report first.

"I recently read in *Newsweek*," the president went on, a suggestion of annoyance hovering in his eyes, "that the American people might be wise to celebrate the millennium by candlelight next to a mattress stuffed with greenbacks—and we can't have people hoarding money. One of the reasons we have not talked publicly about Y2K is the fear that we might trigger a panic that could result in a stock market crash or even a run on the banks. But time is working against us. Representative Stephen Horn recently evaluated the problem and handed our administration a report card on our year-2000 efforts. Our overall grade, I'm sorry to say, was D minus. The departments of Defense and Transportation received an F."

A flurry of nervous coughing seized the cabinet members as the president peered around the table, then nodded at Dr. Anna Hall, Secretary of the Department of Energy. "Why don't we start with you, Dr. Hall. Surely your people have known about this problem for a while."

"Of course we have." Dr. Hall, a brilliant woman who rather looked like she'd been middle-aged since birth, opened her leather portfolio and drew out a sheaf of papers. "And we are most concerned about the repercussions. The so-called Millennium Bug could, for instance, paralyze the offshore oil industry in the North Sea. In a worst case scenario, oil platforms would be forced to shut down simply because their automated systems fail to recognize the year 2000. Companies such as Royal Dutch/Shell and British Petroleum are racing to check millions of microprocessors— computer chips with the programs embedded, or burned into them—but we fear smaller firms have not yet taken the necessary precautions to ensure the oil supply."

"Why on earth haven't they?" the president demanded.

"Well, sir," Dr. Hall went on, her face clouding, "a single offshore oil platform may contain over ten thousand microprocessors, and some are deep below sea level. And, to put it into perspective, there are over one hundred oil platforms in the North Sea alone."

"Are you saying," the vice president asked, "that somebody's got to check one million little computer chips—some of them *underwater*— before next year so we can ensure our oil supply?"

Dr. Hall opened her mouth as if she would say something else, then snapped it shut and simply nodded.

The Secretary of Housing and Urban Development, Dr. Jeff Stock, lifted a finger. "Excuse me, Mr. President, but that's not the worst of it." Stock cast an apologetic look toward Dr. Hall, then continued. "We should be more immediately concerned with the power grids. Within the United States there are six thousand electrical generating units, half a million miles of bulk transmission lines, and twelve thousand major substations. They are all linked together on a complex grid by computer mainframes, and few of those mainframes are year-2000 compliant. Each of those six thousand generating units has its own computer system to regulate the amount of electricity generated by hydroelectric dams or an oil-burning or nuclear generator; but if one of those computers, *just one*, is not compliant, the entire network could go down."

"Those power plants have embedded computer chips, too," Dr. Hall added, her voice low. "Just like the oil platforms. There might be up to ten thousand embedded chips in a single power plant, and most of them are so buried in mechanical hardware that we won't even be able to find them. And if we do find them, some of them are so old the original programming information has been lost."

President Stedman leaned sideways in his chair and laced his fingers together. "I am beginning to understand the depth of the problem," he said simply, his eyes drifting from one secretary to another. "Go on. Let me have it all. Lay it out, ladies and gentlemen, and let's figure out what has to be done to escape the darkness that will descend on this nation if we don't lick this problem."

Emboldened by the president's openness, the others began to speak freely. Lauren gripped the arm of her chair as the facts and figures began to blur together. The news was far worse than she had anticipated—the secretaries spoke of an approaching stock market crash, widespread catastrophic bank failures, telecommunications blackouts, and crucial miscalculations in Social Security, Medicare, and the Internal Revenue Service.

"I don't even know how we will get food to grocery stores," the secretary of the Department of Commerce said, his face brightening to the shade of a cherry tomato. "Food travels by rail and truck, and the railways are controlled and monitored by computer. The old manual switches are gone, entirely replaced by computerized switching systems."

"Air traffic is another nightmare." Steve Aldridge, secretary of transportation, cleared his throat. "Earlier this year, IBM announced that they will not certify a single FAA air traffic control system after January 1, 2000. Planes, trains, buses, trucks, autos, boats, red lights, radar systems—

everything will be affected, sir. Almost overnight, the friendly skies over America are going to become the *empty* skies."

Dr. Carolyn Wilt, secretary of the Department of Health and Human Services, spoke up. "Mr. President, I will confess that I did not realize the extent of this danger until I began to investigate." The blue in her eyes went as cold as ice, though her lips stayed curved in a professional smile. "Every individual in this country may be affected, some in drastic ways. A recent report by the Nuclear Regulatory Commission stated that computer software used to calculate the dose of radiation treatment—for cancer, for instance—may not recognize the turn of the century, which could lead to incorrectly calculated doses or exposure times for treatment."

Dr. Wilt's blue eyes darkened as she looked around at her colleagues. "Would you like to be the doctor who's responsible for poisoning a sick child with radiation? Or perhaps you'd like to live in the neighborhood where in 2005 all the children are developing cancer as a result of a year-2000 nuclear accident. Our nuclear power plants are extremely vulnerable. If the computer problems are not fixed, we will either have to shut them down or risk another Chernobyl."

"But even if a system is Y2K-compliant, it could be shorted out by an overload in an improperly programmed power grid," Dr. Hall added. "The entire system must be repaired or all systems are vulnerable."

"That's the worst aspect of this entire dilemma." David Whitlow, secretary of the State Department, waved a finger at the president. "Even if by some miracle we manage to get all our computers and embedded chips repaired or replaced, we are still connected to the world in a thousand different ways. And one single bug in the system might bring us all crashing down."

"I think I can offer a good analogy for the situation." Every eye turned toward Dr. Hall, who tented her hands upon the table. "Let's suppose that a train—without brakes—is thundering down a mountain toward a bridge with four spans missing. You know the train can't be stopped or slowed. And you only have time enough to fix three of the four spans." A look of intense, clear understanding poured through her eyes. "Mr. President, even if we fix three spans, that train will still crash. Unless every computer is fixed, every noncompliant chip replaced, we will experience devastation. How much, we can only guess."

"The true tragedy," Dr. Gerald Wilkerson, secretary of the Department of Labor, added, "is that this situation could have been avoided. If we had begun to implement solutions as late as October 1997, we could have corrected the problem and kept our allegorical train on track. But we didn't. We procrastinated, and now we will have to face the inevitable."

"Well." The corners of the president's mouth tightened. "It appears that we may have to pay for our presumption that the experts would find a way to fix this thing in time. Everything seems to indicate that we are moving toward the first economic disaster in human history to arrive on a fixed schedule." His eyes, alive with calculation, moved around the table. "So what do we do about it? How do we keep the Millennium Bug from inflicting a fatal bite?"

Dr. Wilkerson cleared his throat. "I guess that's my cue." He tried to smile at the president, but his features only flinched uncomfortably. "We've studied the situation thoroughly and estimate that finding, fixing, and testing all Y2K-affected software would require over seven hundred thousand person-years. The good news is that already the demand for fixes has created three hundred thousand jobs since 1996. The downside is that programmers' wages are soaring with the demand for skilled workers, so Y2K has the potential to increase inflation."

"Great," the vice president muttered, twisting in his chair. "Greedy little twits are demanding too much."

Ignoring the vice president, Dr. Wilkerson continued. "We estimate that the Y2K Bug will have a profoundly negative impact on the U.S. economy as companies shift their work forces from production to dealing with the problem. Y2K could shave half a percentage point off economic growth in 2000 and early 2001. All told, the bug could cost the U.S. as much as $119 billion in lost economic output between now and 2001. In addition, the respected Gartner consulting company estimates that Y2K will cost over $600 billion to fix the worldwide computer systems. To put that in perspective, in today's dollars, that is more than the total cost of the Vietnam War."

"Growth will decrease as inflation rises," the Treasury secretary added. "That's a perfect recipe for a major recession."

The president winced slightly, then shifted his weight in the chair. "So what do we do about it?" he asked, lifting his brows. "We are the leaders of the free world, ladies and gentlemen; we are the most powerful nation on earth. We must set our own house in order, and then we'll reach out to the rest of the world. But how do we begin?"

General Archer lifted his chin. "I believe we may have an answer," he said, his voice cutting through the silence like a steel blade.

Every person in the room leaned forward, and Lauren wondered why he had not spoken until this moment.

"It has recently come to our attention," the general continued, spacing his words evenly, "that Daniel Prentice, of Prentice Technologies, has designed a program to solve the Y2K problem."

"Daniel Prentice?" Anna Hall frowned. "I know that name."

"*People* magazine." The vice president snapped his fingers. "I read the article just yesterday. He's some kind of entrepreneurial computer nerd. A multimillionaire by age thirty, the next Bill Gates."

"He's far more than Bill Gates, I assure you." The general reached into his leather briefcase and pulled out a folder, then slid it across the polished table toward the president. "I've assembled a complete dossier. Our people believe he will cooperate, given the appropriate incentives. He has cooperated with us before."

"When?" President Stedman's dark eyes bored into General Archer. "Don't be coy with me, General. I haven't the time for games. You may speak freely, as this concerns all of us."

The thin line of the general's mouth clamped tight for a moment, and his Adam's apple bobbed once as he swallowed.

"In Desert Storm," he began, drumming the tabletop with his fingers, "we needed a stealth device the Iraqis would never suspect. One of the NSA chiefs had read about Prentice and brought him on board. While he worked for us, Prentice designed the first hardware virus, a deceptively simple-looking black box that slipped into a printer, yet had the power to scramble the Iraqis' computers every time they powered up their air defense systems."

The president caught his breath in an audible gasp. "It worked?"

Archer's broad face cracked in a sarcastic smile. "Of course. We flew sortie after sortie while the Iraqis scrambled below us, trying to figure out what sort of voodoo we had conjured up for them. By the time they discovered the device, the war was already won." He looked across the table to the vice president. "It was a highly classified operation, of course. We paired Prentice with Brad Hunter, one of our SEALS commanders, and sent them in alone, though we nearly lost them both outside Baghdad. A sniper caught them just inside the border. Hunter threw himself in front of Prentice, but one bullet got both men. We lifted them out and let them quietly recuperate at Walter Reed. Afterward, Prentice went back to his millions, and Hunter joined the NSA."

Archer gestured toward the folder on the table. "It's all there, plus Prentice's history for the last eight years. He's still single, still brilliant, still in touch with Hunter. I think we can approach him."

The president reached out and drew the folder closer, then nodded around the circle. "If no one has a better suggestion, I think we're just about done here."

"Mr. President, I have collected some other data," the vice president called from his end of the table. "For instance, I've polled the various government agencies. Social Security says its computers will be compliant on time, while FEMA will finish by June of the year 2000. The Department of Justice projects it will be compliant by 2001, the Department of the Treasury by 2004, and the Department of Transportation by 2010—"

"Thank you, John," President Stedman said, pushing back his chair as he stood. "But we don't have any more time to debate how bad the situation is. The time has come to act."

He flashed a grim smile around the circle, then moved out through the doorway. Taking her cue from her boss, Lauren rose and followed.

Six

11:39 A.M., Monday, November 9, 1998

DANIEL PRENTICE'S DOSSIER ENDED UP ON LAUREN'S DESK, AS SHE KNEW IT
would. As she'd hurried into the Oval Office after the cabinet meeting, the
president had tossed the folder to her with a brusque request. "If the guy is
solid—and heaven knows he ought to be, if he's earned Archer's recommendation—then call him, write him, do whatever you must to get him on
the team. The sooner, the better."

Now Lauren sat in her small West Wing office, the folder spread on her
desk and a black-and-white photo in her hand. From the physical description cited in the report she knew that Daniel Prentice, age thirty-eight,
stood six feet three inches tall, had brown hair and brown eyes, and
weighed 185 pounds. But that rudimentary description did not do justice
to the striking young man in the photograph.

Some camera had caught Daniel Prentice outdoors, for he was squinting slightly in the sunlight and a breeze ruffled his short hair. He wore a
flight suit, so apparently the photo dated from Desert Storm and his short
stint with the navy. The clean, straight look of him impressed her; even as
a civilian he had a certain no-nonsense look she associated with the military. His handsome square face framed his dark eyes, and the set of his chin
suggested a stubborn streak. But even in this candid black-and-white he
held his head high, and Lauren had always admired men who knew who
they were.

By all reports, Daniel Prentice was someone special . . . and apparently
he knew it. The guy probably had a different woman for every night of the
week.

She slid the photo onto her desk and read the background report Archer
had prepared. Daniel Prentice, born on October 2, 1960, was the only child of

John and Amelia Prentice. Amelia Prentice lived now in a St. Petersburg town-house, where Daniel Prentice paid the annual property taxes of $2,560. John Prentice, former navy pilot, was deceased, killed on a routine mission over North Vietnam in 1967.

"Poor kid." Lauren mentally subtracted one date from another. "Seven years old is a tough time to lose your father."

She read on. After John Prentice's death, Amelia and her son moved to her childhood home in Canada, where Daniel grew up outside North Bay, Ontario. After a rather uneventful childhood and teenage employ-ment at a North Bay marina, he graduated *summa cum laude* from MIT and established Prentice Technologies at the tender age of twenty-three. In the fifteen years of the company's existence, Prentice Technologies had developed and marketed antivirus software as well as advanced technolo-gies to aid the blind and deaf. The company was a leading manufacturer of personal identification computer chips, used in the identification of livestock and lost pets.

Lauren flipped the page, and her eyes widened when she realized she was staring at Daniel Prentice's personal financial records.

His assets included an apartment on New York's glitzy Park Avenue, purchased in 1990 for $3.2 million. He owned a 1957 Jaguar, license num-ber IMAPID, a 1999 Range Rover registered and licensed in Ontario, and a $700,000 yacht docked at a Montauk Point marina.

Her eyes skimmed over the rest of the report. Daniel Prentice paid taxes in the top bracket, yet still was able to deposit thousands of discre-tionary dollars in various stocks, bonds, and mutual funds, and he donated a healthy percentage of his income to his mother's community church in Florida. In the fifteen years he'd been filing income tax returns, he had never taken a deduction for gambling losses, alimony, or child support.

Lauren's mouth twitched with wry amusement as her image of Daniel Prentice, playboy, vanished like a morning mist. The guy was a Boy Scout. A rich scout, to be sure, but definitely an all-American do-gooder. He probably stopped outside his office complex in Mount Vernon to help little gray-haired ladies cross the street. The fact that he had never married most likely meant that he was shy. Despite his striking good looks, Daniel Prentice had to be a quiet, retiring computer nerd.

"Finding anything interesting?"

Startled by the sound of a gentle voice, Lauren looked up. Victoria Stedman, the president's wife, stood in the doorway with a teasing smile on her face. "Sam tells me that he just dropped a nice and eligible young man in your lap. I had to come and see this for myself."

Lauren's smile deepened into laughter. "Is he still trying to marry me off? I thought he put that idea aside when we came to Washington."

"Just because Sam couldn't fix you up with anyone in North Carolina doesn't mean he's going to stop trying." Victoria's clear blue eyes softened. "You know he only wants what's best for you. We both do. Our time in the White House, whether it's two more years or six, is going to fly by, Lauren, then Sam will retire. We just want to make sure you're settled."

Lauren took a deep breath and adjusted her smile. "You don't have to worry about me. I can take care of myself, and besides, I promised to stick to the job until the president retires."

"No one questions your loyalty." Victoria came into the room and leaned over Lauren's desk, the light scent of flowers preceding her. "But there's a lot more to life than taking care of yourself and working at a career. I've always found that joy comes when I'm taking care of someone else."

Lauren felt a warm glow flow through her. Victoria Stedman, the pundits proclaimed, could charm the stripes off a tiger, and Lauren knew she'd just fallen under the woman's spell. But could a little fantasy hurt?

She turned the photo so that it faced Mrs. Stedman. "Here's his picture, but it's eight years old. His name is Daniel Prentice, he's a computer genius, and he saved our necks in Desert Storm—but you'll never hear anything about that. It was a classified mission."

Mrs. Stedman lifted her brows as she picked up the photo. "A nice-looking young man! How old is he?"

"Thirty-eight."

"And not married?"

"No." Lauren glanced down at the file in her lap. "He seems to spend all his time making money—much of which he gives, by the way, to his mother's church."

"Well!" Mrs. Stedman placed the photo back on Lauren's desk and tapped it with a manicured fingernail. "Honey, what are you waiting for? Call the man and invite him to dinner."

Lauren laughed. "I can't. We need him to sort out this Y2K computer crisis. I can't ask him to take me out when we need him to save the country."

Mrs. Stedman laughed softly, her fascinating smile crinkling the corner of her eyes. "Lauren, honey, even superheroes have to eat." She tilted her head. "I think I'm going to start praying for you and this Daniel Prentice."

"Now, Mrs. Stedman—"

"Surely you wouldn't mind a few prayers?"

"No." Lauren felt an unwelcome blush creep onto her cheeks. "I wouldn't mind prayers. A few. But I'm not going to hold my breath."

"Whatever suits you, honey." Mrs. Stedman turned to leave but paused in the doorway again. "What are you waiting for? Samuel says we need that man, so pick up the phone. I think now would be a good time."

Lauren pressed her lips together, then lifted the telephone receiver. She'd just received a direct order from the first lady, so how could she refuse?

-0100111100-

Daniel sat at his desk, watching Dr. Kriegel's X 2000 program run through its paces. The program was a marvel, complex and yet utterly simple in its function. Of course they'd have to rename it before they introduced it to the market—X 2000 would mean nothing to the average consumer. He'd have to put the marketing team to work on it.

But the program worked. He'd had a team of programmers work through the weekend to test and debug the program thoroughly, and the beta version had required only a few minor tweaks and patches. Best of all, the professor had even come up with a version for systems with color monitors.

"Mr. Prentice, you have a phone call." Roberta's voice floated out from the speakers.

"Route it to voice mail, please."

"Yes, Mr. Prentice."

Daniel typed in another string of test code, then clicked the enter key and sat back, his hands behind his head, as the program whizzed through and swiftly made its repairs in living color. A slow grin spread across Daniel's face. Maybe he'd commission a statue to honor Dr. Kriegel. In bronze. The man deserved *something* extraordinary.

"Daniel!" A muffled voice came from behind his office door. Daniel looked up, annoyed.

Roberta explained the intrusion. "Mr. Prentice, Taylor Briner requests admission."

"Let him in, Roberta. Please." Daniel frowned in exasperation. Taylor served as Daniel's personal secretary, and he knew better than to barge into the office while Daniel was working.

"Daniel!" Taylor's flushed face appeared in the doorway. "The White House is calling! You've routed them to voice mail—twice!"

"The White House?" Daniel shifted uneasily in his chair, searching for a plausible explanation. "What do they want?"

Radiating offended dignity, Taylor stepped into the office. "I couldn't come right out and ask! Lauren Mitchell is on the phone."

Daniel closed his eyes, summoning an image to fit the name. He'd seen the president's executive assistant on television, usually in the president's entourage. From all appearances she was polished, competent, and more attractive than any politician had a right to be. So what in the world did she want with him?

Daniel swiveled his chair back toward the keyboard and tapped his fingers on the desk. "I've sent her to voice mail twice?"

"Yes." Taylor's voice was heavy with exasperation. "She finally spoke to someone in development, who put her through to me. She says it's urgent. The *president* wants to speak to you."

"Take a message."

Taylor's brows shot up to his hairline. "You can't be serious."

"I am. Tell Miss Mitchell to call back in five—make that ten—minutes. I'll speak to her then."

Taylor gave Daniel a sidelong glance of utter disbelief, then he nodded. "All right. I'll tell her."

The door clicked, and he was gone.

Daniel leaned back in his chair and rubbed his hand over his face. The White House was calling. The White House had called him once before, eight years ago, and Daniel had been pleased and flattered enough to nearly get himself killed. Now the man behind the call would be Samuel Stedman, not George Bush, but the request would likely be in the same vein: *Daniel, we need a man of your expertise to risk his life. Surely you'd be honored to volunteer.*

Honored? Not any more. He'd been honored the first time, but then his eyes were opened.

With nothing else to do in the hospital, he and Brad Hunter had begun to discuss Vietnam. Brad's father was a Vietnam vet, too, and Brad had promised that as soon as Walter Reed released him, he'd pull some strings at the NSA and the Department of Defense and unearth what he could about that fatal bombing mission over Hanoi.

Three months after Daniel's return to civilian work, a plain brown envelope had arrived in the mail with no postmark or return address. Taylor had been about to scan the package for explosive devices when Daniel pulled it away and carried it into his office. Somehow he had known that the envelope had come from Brad, and when he opened it and began to read, he saw that his friend had kept his promise. It was all there— exhaustive details about his father's ill-fated bombing raid, including the names, ranks, and serial numbers of the fallen pilots.

On the last page, Daniel had read the orders, then saw that someone had scrawled a note at the bottom of the page: *Bombing raid ordered to demonstrate destructive capabilities to visiting congressman Orson Tobias.*

Even now those words echoed in the black stillness of his mind, and Daniel's face burned as he remembered his first reaction to them. His emotions had ricocheted from horror to disgust, from anguish to rage. There had been no compelling reason for those pilots to risk their lives on that autumn morning. His father had died just to impress some hotshot congressman, some idiot who wanted to go back to Washington and report that we were bombing the blazes out of the VC in Hanoi.

What a joke. Vietnam was a disaster, and it had imprinted Daniel's life with sorrow. His mother had to leave their home and return to Canada, where they lived off a government pension and the charity of relatives until Daniel was old enough for a part-time job. He'd gone to MIT on scholarship, working after hours in a grocery just to pay his rent, buy books, and send a little something to his mother.

And now Washington was calling again! Lauren Mitchell should be grateful he hadn't picked up the phone the first time she called. He would probably have hung up on her.

He swiveled his chair to face the door, then spun around and stood up, feeling a powerful need to pace.

He couldn't hang up on the president's representative. No matter what his personal feelings, as a loyal American he owed a certain amount of respect to the country's leader. And he admired Stedman—the man seemed to have worthwhile principles. He had already demonstrated his commitment to several moral and spiritual issues that had largely been ignored by previous administrations.

So why was Stedman calling?

The country was not at war, so they couldn't want him to devise another hardware virus or other stealth device. The economy was as robust as it had been in years, so they didn't need his knowledge about financial planning, which, truth be told, wasn't all that remarkable. Crime was a problem, of course, but most law enforcement was handled on a local level, so the president wouldn't be calling him about a new stun gun or weapons system. Except for its aging computers, the country seemed to be in fairly decent shape—

The Y2K Bug.

The thought brought another in its wake, with a chill that struck deep in the pit of Daniel's stomach. *Do they know about X 2000?*

With a shiver of recollection, he remembered his entrance into the company vestibule Friday. The professor's program had been playing on the network monitors, and Daniel had just assumed someone on the professor's team had demonstrated the program in a burst of enthusiasm.

But what if that scenario was false?

The sound of Roberta's voice made him jump. "Mr. Prentice, you have a phone call."

Daniel's voice emerged as a rusty croak. "Identify, please."

A soft electronic hiss came over the computer speakers as Roberta queried the caller, then Daniel heard a tight, controlled voice: "This is Lauren Mitchell with the president's office. I need to speak to Daniel Prentice at once."

Forcing himself to calm down, Daniel moved to his chair and sat, then picked up the phone. "Daniel Prentice."

"At last." Lauren Mitchell's voice was soft with disbelief. "That's quite a screening system you have, Mr. Prentice. I've been trying to reach you all morning."

"I was . . . involved." Daniel smiled, pleased with how nonchalant he sounded. "How can I help you?"

"Well—" she paused—"the president wanted to talk to you himself, but he's in a meeting now and can't be disturbed. If you like, I could have him call you later, or I can try to explain his proposal."

"Please, go ahead and explain." Daniel leaned back and propped his shoes on the edge of his desk. "I have the feeling none of us has time to waste."

"You're exactly right." She paused again, and Daniel imagined her sitting at her desk, shuffling through papers in a mild panic. She hadn't really expected to get through this time, either, and he had caught her unprepared.

"We would like to invite you—" her voice was clear and confident now—"to serve on the Presidential Year 2000 Crisis Committee. You are aware, no doubt, of the current situation involving our national computer systems, and you have been recommended—"

"No thank you," Daniel interrupted. "I'm flattered by the recognition, but I'm going to have to decline the honor. Thank the president for me, but give him my regrets."

He heard her quick intake of breath. "You won't—well, perhaps you'd like a few days to think about this opportunity."

Daniel forced a smile into his voice. "That won't be necessary. We are very busy with our own work, and I simply cannot take the time to leave my company. The year 2000 is bearing down on all of us, you know. But thank you for the call, Ms. Mitchell."

"Miss."

"I beg your pardon?"

"It's Miss Mitchell. The president is a traditionalist; he doesn't care for the Ms. designation."

"Fine. Thanks again for the call."

"Wait—we are prepared—I'm sure the president could authorize— some form of compensation." Her voice strengthened. "I know we could make it worth your time, Mr. Prentice."

Despite his best intentions, Daniel found himself grinning at the phone. The woman was persistent, he'd give her that. "Miss Mitchell, let me reiterate my position. I have served my country. Now I'd like to step aside and let someone else receive the honors."

"We know about Desert Storm. You did a very brave thing and we're grateful—"

"Sure you are."

"—but this opportunity is not at all dangerous." She cleared her throat. "We're not asking you to risk your life this time, Mr. Prentice. We're only asking for your intellect, which, I understand, is formidable."

Daniel looked up at the ceiling and shook his head. No wonder the ultratraditional Senator Stedman had won the election. He'd probably hired this little bulldog to collar voters and shake them until they agreed to vote Republican.

"Miss Mitchell," he spoke slowly and distinctly, "thank you very much for this high honor, but I must decline. I have already given my country more than enough."

"May I tell the president you'll be in touch later?"

"No."

"May I tell him that you'll at least consider the offer?"

"Good-bye, Miss Mitchell."

Daniel held the receiver over the phone base for a moment, then very deliberately dropped it into its cradle.

-0100111100-

Three hours later, Lauren picked up Daniel Prentice's file and walked slowly toward the Oval Office. She'd spent all afternoon racking her brain, trying to come up with another angle that might snare Daniel Prentice, but she'd come up with nothing—nothing respectable, anyway. She figured she could always beg or threaten, but those tactics were beneath her principles. There remained intimidation, but Daniel Prentice didn't seem the type to be easily intimidated.

She gave Francine Johnson a distracted smile as she moved past the secretary's desk, then rose on tiptoe to peer through the peephole into the Oval Office. "I think he's in the dining room," Francine called over her shoulder. "The first lady and General Archer are in there with him. You can go on in."

"Thanks."

Lauren pulled open the door, then padded across the plush blue carpeting. Another doorway off the Oval Office led into a private hallway, flanked by a private bathroom on one side and the president's study on the other. Beyond that lay a cozy dining room, and Lauren could hear the clink of china as she approached.

"Lauren, honey." Victoria Stedman saw her first. "Come sit down and have a cup of tea. Sam and the general are jabbering in computer lingo; see if you can interpret it for me."

"I'm afraid I have bad news." Lauren dropped Prentice's dossier on the table and sank into the chair the president pulled out for her. "I spoke with Daniel Prentice on the phone earlier today. He's not interested in helping us."

"Not interested?" Victoria lifted a brow.

"Not even for money." Lauren propped her elbow on the table and rested her head on her hand. "He said he'd already served his country and it was someone else's turn. His exact words were, 'I have already given my country more than enough.'"

"Arrogant fellow." A cold flash lit General Archer's eyes as he scowled at Lauren.

"Would it help if I called him?" the president asked, folding his hands. "No offense, Lauren, but sometimes a call from the Oval Office can work wonders." He gave her a bemused smile. "Even with Democrats."

"That's the funny thing—Prentice is a registered Republican." Lauren pushed the dossier toward him. "You can certainly try to convince him, but he sounded very definite. We know his own company is working on the Y2K, and he may be too busy to spare the time to be part of our committee."

Archer slammed his hand on the table. "He has the answer—he's just an arrogant, greedy little—"

"That's enough, General." Victoria Stedman's delicate mouth thinned in disapproval. The empty air between them vibrated, and a steward, his arms laden with a silver tea service, paused in the doorway as if afraid to disturb the absolute quiet.

"There's always a way to bring people around." Changing his tactics,

General Archer glanced at the president, his eyes bright with speculation. "We'll just have to dig a little deeper on this Prentice fellow. Every man has his price and his motivation. We'll just have to find out what sort of man Daniel Prentice really is."

"Please, whatever you do, take the moral high road." Victoria Stedman's hand flew to the string of pearls at her neck. "We made a promise to the American people when we took office—no more shenanigans from the White House. We promised to be trustworthy."

"Don't worry, ma'am." The general's mouth twisted in something not quite a smile. "We'll be careful."

"You've got to be more than careful." The president accepted a cup from the steward, then held it aloft while the man poured tea. "You've got to be downright circumspect, General, do you hear? No dirty tricks— nothing that's going to jump up and bite us on the rear end when we least expect it."

The general lifted his own teacup to his broad mouth. "Mr. President, you can trust me. Depend upon it."

SEVEN

10:45 A.M., Tuesday, November 10, 1998

BRAD HUNTER SHOOK OPEN THE NEWSPAPER SOME CONSIDERATE SOUL HAD LEFT on the end table, but the newsprint blurred before his eyes. After a moment, he dropped the charade and folded the paper again, then tossed it back to the table. The secretary at the oak desk seemed not to notice him; she had scarcely lifted her eyes even when he announced his name and the fact that he had an appointment with General Archer.

"Be seated," she had said, her eyes glued to the computer screen at her desk.

Brad blew out his cheeks, then leaned forward, his hands on his knees. He had a vague idea of why he'd been summoned to this office, but you could never tell with these Department of Defense guys.

The door to the inner sanctum opened, and General Archer himself stood in the opening, as broad and impressive in person as in the framed photographs that decorated every office in the Pentagon and the NSA. The overhead light struck the stubble of gray hair on his shaved head, creating an impression of an almost saintly halo.

"Colonel Hunter?" Archer turned with nonchalant grace and gestured toward his office. "Please, come in."

Brad walked toward the general, extending his hand even as he reminded himself that he was now a civilian and didn't have to salute. "Thank you, sir. I'm pleased to see you again."

General Archer motioned toward a pair of chairs before his desk, then sank into one as Brad took the other. Brad found himself smiling—he admired a man who came out from behind his desk for an underling.

The man wasted no time in coming to the point. "Colonel Hunter, I'm sure you have been kept abreast of the Y2K problem. I'm told by your superiors in the NSA that you have conducted a good deal of industrial surveillance in the field." .

Brad felt heat begin to steal into his face. This had to be about Daniel.

General Archer smiled in a way that only emphasized that he hadn't been smiling before. "I understand that you have established a friendship with Daniel Prentice."

"Yes, sir." Brad nodded perfunctorily and lowered his gaze. "Next month Daniel will be the best man at my wedding."

"That's very nice." The general cocked his head to one side and kept smiling. "Friendship among comrades in war is a unique and wonderful thing. Given what you two went through together in Baghdad, I would imagine that you will remain close for years."

"Yes, sir, I'd imagine so."

The general pressed his lips together, then tilted his head to the other side. Crossing his legs, he shifted his weight to one arm of the chair and looked directly at Brad. "I've read the reports, of course." His smile vanished. "But I'd like you to tell me, moment by moment, what happened in Baghdad. Just tell the story, Colonel, and let me decide which details are important."

Unable to make sense of the request, Brad looked down at his hands. This was old news, ancient history, and there could be no harm in repeating the story. Perhaps it would even do Brad good, for still there were nights when he woke in a cold sweat, fearing that another bullet had caught him and spun him around.

The busy distant chorus of telephones and muffled voices faded as Brad submerged himself into memory. "We'd been anchored off the shores of Saudi for three months when I first met Daniel Prentice," he began, keeping his eyes upon the dark blue carpet of the general's office. "He was a civilian, and I couldn't figure out why in the world they'd brought a rich computer wizard over to train with a group of SEALS. But then I got to know him, and I realized Daniel was brilliant. And when they chose me to go in as his partner and briefed us on the mission, I realized that our mission could guarantee the success or failure of the entire war."

His hands tightened on the armrests of the chair. "I had to admire Daniel Prentice for leaving his company, his entire life behind. He was a patriot back then, a soldier's kid, raring to go in and defend those who were being tortured and trampled by Saddam Hussein."

"And the mission?" The general's eyes were flat and dark in the fluorescent lights, unreadable.

Brad shrugged. "We were dropped by helicopter in the desert. Dressed like Bedouins, we made it into Baghdad with the help of a couple of Mossad agents. The scariest part was breaking into the air defense headquarters, but Daniel had put together some gadget that scrambled their electronic locks, so we waltzed in like we belonged there." He grinned. "By this time we were wearing Iraqi uniforms, and each of us wore heavy mustaches and beards. Our own mothers wouldn't have been able to tell us from the Iraqis."

The general smiled faintly.

Brad went on. "It's late at night, of course, when we go inside, and there are still a handful of soldiers on the premises. But Daniel walks over to a printer, cool as a cucumber, and lifts the lid. I'm just standing behind him, looking bored, and suddenly this Iraqi captain starts jabbering at us. I'm thinking we're toast, but then Daniel opens his mouth and starts to speak Arabic like a native. I hide my face, sure that the captain is going to see the sweat dripping from my brow, but Daniel places the device, lowers the printer lid, and dusts his hands like he's some kind of Epson repairman. Next thing I know, he's waving to the captain who accosted us, and I'm wondering if he's nuts enough to invite the guy to join us for dinner or something."

"Prentice is a linguist?" A gleam of interest flickered in the general's eyes.

"Not really. I asked him about that, and he said that he'd learned the language from his roommate at MIT—he helped the guy with English, and in turn, Prentice learned Arabic. I suppose that's another reason he was tapped for the mission. Anyway, we leave the headquarters, slip out into the desert where we're supposed to meet with the Mossad agents, but there's an Iraqi security detail there instead. They found the Bedouin garments we'd stashed there, and they're all excited. So Daniel and I just turn to walk away, and when we think we're at a safe distance, we begin to run." Brad paused, his heart beating heavily in the memory. "We couldn't help it; I guess the old fight or flight mechanism just kicked in. But our running caught someone's attention, and a sniper fired his weapon. I tried to protect Prentice—after all, he was a civilian—and one bullet got us both."

He could feel each separate heartbeat now, like blows to the chest. Brad took a deep breath to slow his pounding heart.

"How did you get away?"

"The Mossad agents." Brad looked up, suddenly grateful that he sat in a plush Pentagon office and not in the desert sands. "They were hiding out of sight, waiting for the Iraqis to leave. Fortunately for us, they were close enough to grab us before the Iraqi sharpshooter called in reinforcements. We made it to our rendezvous point and were picked up by a marine helicopter."

Brad transferred his gaze from the walls to the general. "That's it. We were shipped to Walter Reed, and we spent a couple of months relaxing at Uncle Sam's expense. After that, I retired from the SEALS and joined the NSA. Daniel went back to New York."

The general drew his lips in thoughtfully. "Your mission was a great success. Statistically we should have lost three thousand bombers and their pilots, and we lost only a dozen planes, largely due to you and your friend."

Not knowing how he should reply, Brad only nodded.

"But if your mission was a success," the general's eyes narrowed in speculation, "why does Mr. Prentice seem so bitter about it now? The president approached him to help with the Y2K Crisis, and Daniel Prentice refused to offer his assistance."

Brad blinked in surprise. "Daniel refused?"

The general nodded with a taut jerk of his head. "Lauren Mitchell spoke to him. She seemed to think that his reasons for refusing had something to do with Desert Storm. He implied that he had already done his duty. I believe his words were, 'I have already given more than enough.'"

A spasm of panic shot across Brad's body like the trilling of an alarm bell. Even coming from the general's lips, Daniel's words had the power to wound.

"What did he mean by that, Colonel?" The general's voice was low, conversational. "As you put it, two months of relaxation at the taxpayers' expense is not so much to give for one's country, particularly when the effort was so successful. So why would Daniel Prentice be reluctant to help us now? Is he intimidated by the enormity of the problem?"

"No." Struggling to mask his anxiety, Brad shifted his eyes to the broad desk at his right hand. "Daniel Prentice would never be intimidated by a computer."

"Afraid of failure, perhaps?"

"I don't recall that he has ever failed at anything he chose to do."

"Then why won't he help us?"

With an effort, Brad met the general's gaze. "I can give you part of the truth," he said, resigned to face the inevitable. "But if you want the entire story, I'll have to plead the Fifth Amendment."

"Ah." The general leaned back in his chair, his eyes like shrewd little chips of quartz. "All right, then. Tell me what you can."

Brad took a deep breath, then plunged into the story. "Daniel Prentice probably—no, definitely—feels that he has given enough to his country because when he was seven he lost his father. John Prentice was a navy pilot, and his jet was shot down in Vietnam."

"MIA?"

"No." Brad swallowed. "They found the body and sent it home. Daniel knows his father died."

The general's eyes closed as he considered this new information. "That is certainly understandable," he said, absently fingering one of the gold buttons of his uniform, "but it begs the question of why his father's death would trouble him now when it didn't bother him in Desert Storm." Archer's eyes opened and focused directly on Brad. "What happened between 1991 and yesterday?"

Brad wiped his damp palms on his trousers. "I'm afraid I must refuse to reply on the grounds that my answer might incriminate me."

"Come now, Brad." The general's eyes softened. "Desert Storm is over, Vietnam is ancient history. No one cares about the past, but I care immensely about the fact that the entire nation might crumble around our ears if we don't solve this computer crisis."

Archer leaned forward. "You and I both know that Prentice has come up with the answer that we need, and we're going to get it. So tell me what you know. I give you my word of honor that any part you might have played in Daniel Prentice's life will not leave this room."

Shifting in his chair, Brad found himself wishing that he'd stayed in bed that morning. He had never dreamed he'd be sitting before the most powerful general in the country, forced to reveal a secret he had buried years ago, but he had no choice. Better to tell the truth than to leave the powers that be in the dark and force them to come up with alternative means to harass Daniel. They wouldn't give up because they knew Daniel had their answer . . . and Brad himself had given them that information.

"As I said," Brad began, "Daniel and I became good friends. Naturally, we talked about our parents, and he told me about his father. He had so many unanswered questions—and I promised to help him discover the answers."

"I see." The general leaned back in his chair and steepled his hands. "What did you do?"

Brad shrugged. "I went through the files. Once I came to the NSA and the Department of Defense, I had clearance to many of the old records. I found a record of the bombing mission in which Daniel's father died, and I sent a copy of the file to him. That was in the summer of '91."

The general lifted his head like a dog scenting the breeze. "What was in the file?"

"A notation stating that the bombing raid was staged to impress a visiting congressman." Brad shot the general a cold look. "So if Daniel Prentice has lost his taste for serving his country, that might be the reason why. I can't say that I blame him."

"I can't, either." The general straightened in his chair, tapped his fingers on his broad knees for a moment, then nodded at Brad. "Thank you for your honesty. You have shed a great deal of light on this situation."

Brad felt his shoulders slump in relief. "Thank you, General . . . for keeping this to yourself. I don't know if there's a statute of limitations on snooping through old files, but I wouldn't want to broadcast my activities in that regard."

"Oh, we can prosecute spies and thieves anytime we wish," the general said, standing. He moved behind his desk, then stood directly in front of the picture of President Stedman and gave Brad a steely smile. "And if you do not wish to be prosecuted, you will convince Daniel Prentice to cooperate with us."

Brad's mood veered sharply to anger. "You said my confession would remain in this room!"

"And it will, as long as you cooperate." General Archer pressed his hands to the back of his chair and squeezed the leather cushion. "You will fly to New York and meet with your good friend, and you will convince him to join the president's committee."

The muscles in Brad's face tightened into a mask of rage, and General Archer laughed. "Don't waste your energy, Hunter," he said, pulling out his chair and falling into it. "This is not a dangerous mission like Desert Storm. The man is a computer genius; we just want to pick his brain for a few days. That's all. Surely you can convince him that your friendship is worth a few hours of his time."

Biting back an oath, Brad stood and faced the general. He had stumbled into one of the most blatant traps one soldier could set for another, and he hadn't even seen it coming. Eight years in a Washington office had dulled his wits.

"Am I dismissed?" he asked, throwing his shoulders back.

"You are. But I will expect to see Mr. Prentice in Washington within a week. Good day, Colonel."

EIGHT

4:00 P.M., Tuesday, November 10, 1998

"SO WE'LL HAVE THE PROGRAM OPERATIONAL BY NEXT WEEK?" DANIEL GLANCED up at the four men who sat in the casual conference area of his office—Dr. Kriegel, Taylor Briner, Ron Johnson, head of production, and Bill Royce, director of development.

"No problem, boss," Ron said, his brows rising in obvious confidence. "My people are already in touch with plants in Singapore. When you say the program is ready, we'll start production."

"We're running a series of tests through a demographic survey," Royce added. "By next week I'll be able to show you how we plan to develop different versions of the product. We're thinking governmental, corporate, and individual, with versions for DOS systems as well as Windows-based workstations that will examine and correct the machine code for mainframes."

"Dr. Kriegel—" Daniel pointed to the professor—"don't let us forget that First Manhattan is still our top priority. When your team is finished with the debugging, I want you to oversee the First Manhattan project. Could we have their systems ready by Christmas?"

"Think spring, Daniel." The professor smiled. "Definitely by Passover."

Daniel mentally translated the professor's Jewish holiday to his own calendar. "An Easter present," he mused, nodding. "Why not? We'll still be months ahead of schedule."

"The press will love that," Taylor said, spilling a sheaf of papers in his enthusiasm. "I'll write up a press release when we make the presentation, and Daniel can go on national television—"

"That reminds me." Daniel cut Taylor off with an uplifted hand. "The name. We need something elegant, something that addresses the problem, and it came to me this morning."

The professor painted on a look of disappointment. "You don't like X 2000?"

The others laughed.

"No offense, Professor, but that name just doesn't do it for me." Daniel paused until the last man had stopped laughing, then spread his hands in a dramatic gesture. "How about the Millennium Code." He shot a look to Royce. "What do you think?"

Royce screwed up his mouth, then nodded. "I like it. You're right—it's elegant, and it's laymen's language. By now everyone has heard of the Y2K problem, and they'll know almost instinctively that this is the answer."

"Yeah, it's good." Johnson added his vote of approval. "We can market that name internationally. It's got real panache." He nodded again. "I like it. It'll sell a zillion copies."

"However many that is." Daniel swiveled his gaze to the professor, who sat silently on the couch, his hand absently stroking his cat. "Dr. Kriegel? I should have spoken to you first. After all, it was your team that came up with the code."

"But it is you, Daniel, who will carry it to the world." The professor's eyes glowed with enjoyment. "It is a good name. And it will bring the world safely into the next millennium."

Daniel sat back, momentarily basking in the approval of his associates. The professor was right, of course—without this program, untold computers would crash and burn in the first weeks of the new century; but Prentice Technology's Millennium Code would provide an answer. Corporations, governments, and individuals would rush to buy it, and *TIME* magazine might choose Daniel Prentice as its Man of the Year.

Aware that the others were watching, Daniel looked down at his notes and abruptly slammed the door on his imaginings. "Well—" he scanned his notepad— "if there's no more new business . . . wait." He glanced up at Taylor. "Don't forget to send flowers for my mom's birthday on the sixteenth. And remind me to call her."

Taylor shrugged. "Done. I set the reminder on my computer calendar this morning. And I told Roberta to remind you to call. On the sixteenth, she'll remind you every hour or so until you take care of it."

Daniel groaned. "I've created an electronic nag."

"Mr. Prentice?"

All five men grinned as the aforementioned nag broke into the conversation.

"Yes, Roberta?"

"You have an urgent e-mail message."

Daniel looked up at his employees. "Are we finished here?"

"All done," Johnson said, standing with Taylor, Royce, and the professor. "We'll get busy and let you know if there's a problem."

"There won't be any problems," Dr. Kriegel muttered, pushing his glasses up on his nose as he followed the other men out of the office. "It's as simple as A-B-C. Why should there be a problem?"

Daniel waited until his office door closed, then tapped his touchpad. The monitor blazed with color, then he clicked his e-mail program. A dozen messages waited in the incoming mailbox, but one was marked with a red flag. Daniel felt the corner of his mouth twist when he recognized Brad Hunter's screen name. It certainly hadn't taken the White House long to discover *that* connection.

He highlighted the message, then tapped the touchpad.

Daniel:

What's this I hear about you snubbing the commander-in-chief? Not very smart, my friend. Now they're sending me out to rough you up. I figure we can start by hitting that steak place around the corner from your shop, then venture out for a drive in the speedster.

Whaddaya say? Care to put me up for a few days? They won't be happy until you crack, you know. So make it easy on me.

Brad

With his finger on the touchpad, Daniel moved the cursor to the reply button, then tapped the key. He was just about to peck out an answer when Roberta interrupted.

"Mr. Prentice, a visitor on the street has requested to see you."

"Identify, please."

"He is not entered in our company database. But his thumbprint matches FBI file number 268350474002. His name is Brad Milton Hunter."

Milton? Daniel pressed his finger over his lips, stifling the urge to laugh. Brad was up to his old tricks; he must have sent this e-mail from his cell phone. "Allow Mr. Hunter to enter, please."

He pushed back from the keyboard, resigning himself to the fact that he'd have to either fortify himself against his best friend or agree to participate in the president's brain trust or whatever it was. Perhaps—if he was very lucky—his capital visit would coincide with Brad's wedding, and he could kill two birds with one stone.

He heard a rap on the door. "Mr. Prentice?" Taylor called, remembering to display a little dignity before a visitor.

"Send Mr. Hunter in," Daniel called, leaning back in his chair.

A moment later the door blew open with the force of a whirlwind. Nattily dressed in an expensive black suit, white shirt, and black tie, Brad stood in the open doorway and stared at Daniel in a pose designed to be boldly intimidating.

"Great heavens," Daniel drawled. "You've joined the Men in Black."

"Get real, computer nerd," Brad called, striding across the room.

In an instant Daniel was out of his chair, then the two men embraced and slapped each other on the back.

"How long are you here?" Daniel asked, pulling away. He gestured toward one of the empty chairs near the sofa.

"Didn't you get my message?" Brad dropped into the chair and grinned up at Daniel. "I'm here to annoy you until you agree to come to Washington and let the Feds pick your brain. This is a no-win situation, buddy. They've got you where they want you."

"They don't have me at all."

"No." Brad's broad smile faded. "Actually, they've got me. They know I showed you the file about your father. And General Archer, brilliant strategist that he is, is willing to do his utmost to twist my arm. If he doesn't try to send me to jail, he'll have me fired."

"You're kidding, right?" Daniel sank into the chair opposite Brad, then gestured toward the hallway. "You thirsty? Want me to send for some coffee?"

"Whatever." Brad shrugged. "Sure, I could use something with caffeine."

Daniel turned his head toward the computer microphone. "Roberta?"

"Yes, Mr. Prentice?"

"Would you have Taylor bring in the coffee service, please?"

"Right away, Mr. Prentice."

Brad let out a long, low whistle. "Daniel, you've been keeping something from me! Who is that woman?"

"Roberta?" Daniel lifted a brow. "She runs things around here."

"I didn't see her when I came in." Brad shifted toward the door as if Roberta might magically appear there at any moment. "The only person I saw was that shaggy guy you've posted to keep the thugs out."

"Actually, Roberta keeps the thugs out." Daniel leaned his elbow on the armrest of his chair and rested his chin on his hand. "So tell me how I can get out of this Washington gig. What if I came down with a communicable disease? I could break my leg in a freak accident—"

"Won't work. You'd have to be in a coma to be brain-disabled." Brad flicked an imaginary speck of lint from his dark suit, then looked back at Daniel. "I'm telling you, buddy, you're it. You're the only guy they believe in."

"What about Robert Bemer?"

"The man's a hundred years old. Sure, he's a genius, but it was his original COBOL language that got us into a large part of this mess, remember?"

The door clicked, and Taylor came in, wheeling a cart loaded with coffee mugs, a coffee pot, sugar, and cream. Brad craned his neck to catch a glimpse of the hallway, and Taylor gave Daniel a questioning look.

"He's looking for Roberta," Daniel explained.

"Oh." Taylor laughed as he poured the coffee. "Mr. Hunter, do you take cream or sugar?"

"Neither." Brad put out his hand and accepted the mug. "Where do you keep that sultry little vixen? Man, what a voice!"

"Roberta is very nearly omnipresent," Taylor said, handing a mug to Daniel. "Just when you least expect her, she's there."

"Man." Brad shook his head, then sipped his coffee.

Taylor pushed the cart aside, then slipped out of the room. For a moment the two men drank their coffee in silence, then Brad lifted his brows and met Daniel's gaze straight on.

"I'm not kidding, Daniel. We need you to do this. Right now, my bosses are asking politely. For your sake—and mine—don't make them ask forcibly."

Daniel swirled the liquid in his coffee cup. "It's just a committee?

Meetings and briefings and the like? No midnight jaunts through the desert with mad Iraqis at our heels?"

"Nothing like that, I promise you." Brad cupped his mug in one hand while he thumped his chest with the other. "Look at me, a prospective bridegroom! I'm days away from becoming a family man! Would I lead you into something I thought was dangerous?"

"You'll be along for the ride?"

"Of course—and I'll probably be bored to tears the entire time."

Daniel sighed and placed his mug on the desk. "We've an awful lot of work to do here, Brad. Did you see last week's *Newsweek?* The entire world is betting I won't get the First Manhattan project done on time."

Brad stared into his coffee cup. "Tell me the truth—will you succeed?"

"Oh, yes. No doubt about it."

"Then you aren't needed here." Brad looked up, his eyes shining. "Let your staff handle First Manhattan."

Daniel leaned forward. "There's more to it, Brad. I can't forget how I feel. I went to Iraq because I believed in the American way. But then I discovered that the idiots who run this country stole my father, my childhood, even the life my mother should have enjoyed. Politicians have already taken too much from me. Why should I give them my time and energy?"

"Because it's your *country!*" With an intensity that matched Daniel's own, Brad hunched forward and met Daniel's gaze. "Because you're an American citizen, and you know there are millions of hard-working, optimistic, loyal Americans who still believe in the good things, in right and truth." He lowered his voice. "You're right, of course—there are some politicians who've let power go to their heads, but there are plenty of others who still believe that every American deserves a chance to find his own way, to fulfill his destiny. And I happen to believe that this Y2K Crisis may be *your* destiny, Daniel. Think of it! You will have an opportunity to save the country, maybe even influence the world. Can you honestly tell me that the idea doesn't intrigue you?"

Daniel sat back and grappled with his thoughts. As much as he hated to admit it, Brad had touched a nerve. Even as a child, he had felt that he was special, unique in some way, and his mother had constantly reinforced the feeling with her praise, support, and unceasing reminders that God himself had created Daniel with a purpose in mind. When Daniel grew older, he realized that nearly every mother loved her child with that sort of single-minded and blind devotion, but still the feeling had persisted. Even now it prodded him forward. Though part of him wanted to remain in New York and nurse his righteous anger, another part wanted to prove his abilities to the world.

Besides, an honorable man, a courageous man, always rose to a challenge.

His father would have.

"All right." A reluctant grin tugged at Daniel's mouth. "I'll go. Just tell me where, when, and how long it will take."

"*Where* is Washington, *when* is as soon as possible, and it will take as long as you need to come up with an idea to save the world." Brad slapped his hands on his thighs in satisfaction, then leaned forward as if to stand up. "Now that we've got that out of the way, how about giving me directions?"

"To what?"

Brad winked. "To Roberta's desk. I want to see if this female is as gorgeous as her voice."

Daniel laughed. "Roberta lives on an entirely different plane," he said, standing. "Besides, you're getting married soon."

As Brad frowned in bewilderment, Daniel pulled his coat from the antique clothes tree behind his desk. "Come on, I know a great place for dinner."

–01001110–

By seven o'clock, Daniel and Brad were boarding the chartered Learjet that had brought Brad to New York.

"You were pretty sure I'd come, weren't you?" Daniel said, tossing his briefcase into the empty seat beside him. "Keeping the jet at the airport— isn't that like telling a taxi to keep the meter running?"

"I was *hoping* you'd come," Brad answered. He sank into the pair of seats across the aisle. "But I wanted to get back to Washington. Christine's waiting for me."

"The joys of an almost-married man." Daniel reclined his seat and folded his hands across his waist, ready for a catnap. He sat quietly, his mind whirling with thoughts and the trivial conversation he and Brad had shared over dinner, until the jet lifted and began to climb through the clouds.

Brad tapped his shoulder. "Awake?"

"Am now."

"So how'd you do it?" Hanging over the empty aisle like a vulture, Brad managed a small, tentative smile. "You said you had come up with a way to fix First Manhattan's mainframes. So how'd you do it?"

"It's a program." Daniel yawned and closed his eyes, hoping Brad would take the hint and back off. He had agreed to help the government, but he certainly hadn't agreed to give away his corporate secret.

"Will the program work for us—for the government?"

Daniel turned his head until he stared directly at Brad. "I don't see why not. But fixing the vital mainframe computers is only a first step. Millions of desktop computers will need replacement BIOS chips to operate properly after 2000. You'll still have to replace embedded chips and take a few precautionary measures. There's no simple fix when you're talking about millions of computers and their parts."

Brad backed off and settled into his seat, but from the preoccupied look on his face Daniel knew the conversation wasn't over.

He turned and looked out the window, wanting to laugh at the absurdity of the situation. Just five days ago he'd been about to pull his hair out because he couldn't determine how to repair 400 million lines of code, and now the United States government wanted him to repair a *zillion* lines in just over thirteen months. He could, of course, sell them copies of the Millennium Code, but the program would only fix obvious problems. Even if they fixed the code in every governmental computer, and corporate America followed suit, it would only take one tiny bank in Kalamazoo, or one lazy hospital administrator with a noncompliant system to bring the fragile house of cards crashing down. And when it fell, every accusing finger would point to Daniel.

Daniel looked down through the clouds and allowed his thoughts to drift. At the lake, hadn't he been thinking that he should approach the problem from a different perspective? He was in the air now, looking through a heaping pile of cumulus clouds, and the earth below had vanished. Yet he knew it was there, just as he had known an answer to his problem existed—somewhere.

Different perspectives . . . his mother had a favorite story about perspectives. It was a riddle, really, a cute little word trick he had used to stump his fellow students at MIT—especially the rich guys in designer sweaters. How he had enjoyed outsmarting them! They couldn't believe that a kid from the Canadian wilderness could ascend to their lofty heights and teach them a thing or two.

Different perspectives. Trading places. The prince and the pauper.

Suddenly, he sat bolt upright, as wide awake as if he'd just been given an intravenous dose of pure caffeine. He felt a tremor run down his throat and heard the gulp as he swallowed his excitement. "I've got it."

Brad leaned forward and examined Daniel's face with considerable absorption. "What did you say?"

"I know how to do it." Daniel felt a sudden wetness behind his eyes. Only twice before in his life had a brilliant insight struck him with such force; the power of it was breathtaking.

"Tell me."

Daniel shook his head. "No. You've got to discover it."

"Okay." Brad pulled himself up and assumed his vulture pose over the aisle again. "Help me."

Daniel lifted a finger. "Once there lived an eccentric old king with two sons. He could only give his throne to one of them, so he arranged that they would have a horse race. The winner would get the laurels and win the race, but the *loser* would win the kingdom."

Brad looked at him in patient amusement but didn't interrupt.

"The two brothers, of course, were both afraid that the other would cheat by not pushing his horse to run as fast as the animal could. So they went to the court jester, who gave them a two-word answer that satisfied them." He grinned at Brad. "What answer did he give?"

Lines of concentration deepened along Brad's brows and under his eyes. "I . . . don't know."

"Think, man!"

Brad lowered his head, ran his hand through his hair, then at last looked up. "Don't cheat?"

"No."

"Kill the king?"

"Spoken like a true SEALS commando. But no, and that's three words."

Brad clenched his fist in frustration. "I don't know."

Daniel grinned and crossed his arms. "When you find the answer," he said, sinking back into the cushions of his seat, "you have found *your* answer. You'll see."

NINE

10:00 P.M., Tuesday, November 10, 1998

TUCKED DEEP INSIDE AN OPULENT CHAMBER WITHIN ADRIAN ROMULUS'S PARIS chateau, Kord Herrick paced over Oriental rugs and tried to keep his expression under control. The European Union's Council of Ministers would convene in less than eight weeks, and Kord was no closer to solving their perplexing problem than he had been two years before.

"Relax," Romulus had told him over dinner last night. "The Americans will solve the crisis. Like cats, they always manage to land on their feet. We will follow their example."

Still, Kord was not assured. According to the American papers, the overconfident, arrogant Yankee lords of creation had found no shortcuts to solve the Y2K problem. Yet time, like death itself, was bearing down on them with a slow and stately deliberation.

The council ministers had laughed last year when Kord voiced his concerns. "Why should we worry about dates on a computer?" they cried. Even though a few had heard horror stories about possible difficulties, their banks, treasury departments, and markets were scrambling to convert their computer systems to handle the euro, the common currency that would officially link the European Union on January 1, 1999. Few people had taken the time and energy to think about Y2K, but the clock was ticking, the computers were faulty, and Kord Herrick did *not* want to rely on the Americans for a solution to the problem.

Kord spun around as the wide white doors, accented with gold leaf, opened to the soft sounds of Mozart's *The Magic Flute*. Romulus had a gentleman's tastes.

"General Herrick, thank you for joining me." Romulus stood in the doorway now, wearing a fine suit and an attitude of self-command. His powerful body moved toward Kord with an easy grace, and his hand, long-fingered and smooth, gestured toward a decanter on the mantle.

"Can I get you something to drink, General?"

"*Nein*, but thank you."

Romulus stopped and smiled, his smooth olive skin stretching over high, angular cheekbones. "Then let us not waste another moment. It is time for you to go to Washington. They are ready for you now."

How do you know? Kord thrust his hands behind his back and gripped them, hesitating to voice his thoughts. For all he knew Romulus had a spy in the White House or the CIA; the man always seemed to know things before anyone else did. But it did not seem proper that Romulus's own head of security would not know if a spy operated among the Americans.

"Can you tell me anything?" Kord's words came out hoarse, forced through a tight throat. "Have you heard from one of our operatives?"

A twinkle of candlelight caught Romulus's eyes as he glanced at Kord. "General, surely you don't think I would keep such information from you? I have no operatives in Washington, . . . but I do have a friend."

"And he has talked to you?"

Romulus's smile softened his angular features. "You worked for Hitler, General. You know he was fascinated by the occult."

Kord nodded, even as he felt fear blow down the back of his neck. The Führer had dabbled in everything from seances to collecting occult relics, but the dark forces had, in the end, overtaken him.

"But I am not a madman like Hitler. Supernatural forces do not control me; I have learned to control them." Romulus moved toward the window, and with one hand pulled back one of the lace curtains. "They have brought in a civilian," he said softly. "A man who will give us our answer . . . and much more."

"Do I know of this man?"

Romulus smiled, a quick curve of thin, dry lips. "All you need to know is that he yearns to make a mark on the world. Ambition is his guiding principle; success his personal mantra. We will offer him what he wants, and he will be ours."

Romulus let the curtain fall and folded his hands. "Go to Washington immediately, and contact General Archer. He will see that you are properly introduced to Daniel Prentice."

"Archer?" Kord lifted a brow. This, then, had to be the friend to whom Romulus had referred. "The American general who contacted us in Paris?"

"The same." Romulus's voice was dry. "Apparently he has grown tired of waving the red, white, and blue. Archer is willing to do his utmost to bring Samuel Stedman around to our way of thinking."

"Very well." Kord picked up the briefcase he had brought into the room, then lifted his head to say farewell to his employer. But Romulus was staring out the window again, apparently lost in his own thoughts.

Kord slipped out though the gilded doorway and left his master alone.

TEN

1:00 P.M., Wednesday, November 11, 1998

LAUREN'S FIRST THOUGHT AFTER MEETING DANIEL PRENTICE WAS THAT EIGHT years had only improved the man's appearance. He wore a navy blue blazer over tan slacks, a vast improvement over the flight suit, and his brown hair now curled over the edge of his collar. His features seemed as clean and transparent as they had in the dossier photo, but his brown eyes were far more powerful in the flesh than in a black-and-white glossy.

Upon learning that Daniel Prentice was en route to Washington, the president had asked Lauren to call an emergency meeting of his cabinet and the National Security Council. The various secretaries who had been present at the regular cabinet meeting were joined on Wednesday afternoon by the chairman of the Joint Chiefs of Staff, the director of the Central Intelligence Agency, the U.S. representative to the United Nations, the assistant to the president for national security affairs, and the assistant to the president for economic policy. Lauren again took a seat by the door, flanked by the press secretary and Brad Hunter, who attended the meeting more as Daniel Prentice's friend than in any official capacity as a representative of the NSA.

Lauren frowned as she caught sight of an unfamiliar face in the room. A short, balding man sat behind General Archer. He wore some sort of uniform, though Lauren couldn't place it. A visiting dignitary, perhaps?

Like all White House gatherings, the meeting began with a round of hand-shaking, insincere fawning, and a flurry of photographs. General Archer had escorted Daniel Prentice and Brad Hunter into the room and directed them to prime seats near the president, upsetting several self-important Washington insiders. When the president called the meeting to order, several of the secretaries offered excruciatingly boring descriptions of the Y2K Crisis—information Lauren could now recite in her sleep.

Finally the president took control of the meeting and turned to the expert they'd worked so hard to enlist. "I assume, Mr. Prentice, that you are completely familiar with the scope of this problem."

Lauren wanted to snap, "Of course he is!" but she bit her lip as Daniel Prentice smiled and looked around the table.

"Certainly, sir. The Year 2000 Crisis, or Millennium Bug, concerns anyone with more than a working knowledge of our computer systems." A short silence followed, and his words seem to hang over the long table as if for inspection.

General Archer broke the stillness. "Well, sir, have you given much thought to how our government can solve the problem before January 1, 2000? We hear that you have undertaken a colossal challenge with First Manhattan—and yet I believe you will rise to the occasion."

"Thank you for the vote of confidence." Daniel gave the general a humorless smile. "But what will work for First Manhattan will not work for the United States government. You should have listened to the experts who began to speak out in the early years of this decade. You didn't, and now you will pay the price."

"The price?" The vice president's brows lifted. "Are you, sir, intending to hold this nation hostage?"

"Now, John." The president put out a soothing hand. "We certainly intend to pay Mr. Prentice for his time and expertise."

"Frankly, I don't think the government can afford what I would charge for the kind of overhaul you need." Daniel Prentice glanced around the table, and Lauren felt herself flush when his gaze caught and held hers. He smiled, acknowledging her, then directed his attention toward the president. "When I say you will pay the price, I mean you will pay in terms of energy and thought. This country will have to learn how to conduct business in an entirely different manner."

"What are you talking about?" The secretary of the treasury leaned forward and spread his hands on the table. "Please, Mr. Prentice, be specific."

Daniel Prentice smiled and leaned back in his chair. "Your challenge, Mr. Secretary, has three distinct faces. First, you have the problem posed by Y2K and noncompliant computers. Fortunately, my company can repair the mainframe computer systems. We have developed a new program, the Millennium Code, which will find even hidden date codes and replace them."

"I'd like to hear more," Dr. Hall interrupted. "Beginning with an explanation of how the program works." Leaning back, she draped one arm over her chair in an almost masculine pose. "In laymen's terms, of course."

Prentice rested his elbow on the conference table and lifted one shoulder in a self-assured shrug. "I'd be happy to explain. Our program looks for short dates within executable, data, and library files. It recognizes forty thousand different date structures and replaces all of them with long date formats. It will work at the binary or machine level, so it is platform-independent and works on all systems from the family PC to mainframes. As long as a file is not encrypted or compressed, the Millennium Code can repair the date bugs. We'll be marketing the program in a matter of weeks, so you no longer have any reason to worry about your computers."

The warm, deep sound of the president's laughter filled the room with relief. As the others murmured in surprise, Daniel Prentice held up his hand. "Don't rejoice too quickly. We can solve the first problem. Two others remain."

The president's face froze in an expression of incredulity. "I thought the problem was all those blasted dates."

Prentice shook his head, then rested his elbows on the table and folded his hands. "We can't just run a utility program on a single computer and pronounce it *cured*. The problem, sir, is consistency. Vast networks link computers. The mainframes at the IRS receive information from thousands of banks; the banks are tied to mainframes at the Treasury Department; the Treasury Department computers are linked to hundreds of brokerage firms. Virtually any computer in the world can be connected to any other computer via modem."

"It's the crashing train scenario, isn't it?" Anna Hall said, her eyes shifting from Daniel to the president. "If one computer is not year-2000 compliant, it can crash any other computer with which it attempts to interact."

Daniel shrugged. "That's essentially correct. So you're not only dealing with faulty codes on your own computers, but you must make certain that every computer in the country—even the world—is compliant as well. Now, we have no authority over the world, but we can implement roadblocks that will keep foreign users off our systems unless their computers meet our Y2K-compliant specifications. As for our own country—" he shifted slightly in his chair and flashed a smile around the table—"I'm well aware that what I'm about to suggest may violate all sorts of antitrust legislation, but the only way to be certain that all computers are repaired to the same exact standard is to use my company's Millennium Code program. You'll have to pass a law, no doubt, to make the fix required. Of course," he deepened his smile, "Prentice Technologies will keep its profits at a respectable minimum. We are not out to fleece the American people."

"We can't require people to use your product!" The vice president's eyes narrowed with fury. "We've just finished going after Bill Gates and Microsoft with antitrust legislation."

"But we have established other precedents," David Whitlow, secretary of the Department of State, interrupted. "There is presently a law on the books requiring all taxpayers to file electronically in the year 2000. How can we expect them to file on computers that won't work?"

"Good grief, think of the headache." Hank Leber, secretary of commerce, held his head. "All those computers transmitting into our mainframes—" He glanced up at the president. "Mr. Prentice is right. If you have to sign an emergency executive order, Mr. President, I suggest you do it. If Prentice Technologies was the first to devise the Y2K fix, let them reap the benefits. Just tell the public what they'll have to do, and make it easy for them to comply with the legislation."

Lauren glanced around at the sea of somber faces. Several were nodding in support of Leber's suggestion, but the vice president and a handful of others seemed reluctant to agree.

"If we make this a national . . . *order*," the president stumbled over the word, "and we require every American computer to run this program, how can we enforce it?"

Prentice leaned forward, an expression of satisfaction glowing in his eyes. "It's very simple, sir. We can combine it with something more useful—a virus checker, for instance—and design the program to be memory-resident. If some sweet lady in Idaho never takes her computer online and doesn't run the Millennium Code, well, she won't upset anyone else's system. But we can patch the program into a computer's modem-dialer so that it activates a handshaking protocol as soon as a computer goes online. Any computer—national or international—not running the Millennium Code in resident memory will be bumped off the system." Settling back in his chair, Prentice grinned. "Beautiful, isn't it?"

Lauren smothered a smile as the president lifted his brows and glanced at the vice president. "Did you get all that?"

John Miller nodded silently.

"You said there were other problems, and I can think of at least one." Dr. Hall, of the Department of Energy, rested her hand beneath her chin as she stared at Prentice. "What about the embedded chips at the bottom of the sea? And those that were launched in satellites? We can't replace them, Mr. Prentice. What's done is done."

"You're right." A frown flitted across Prentice's features. "I said we could fix the mainframes, and we can. But only time and the second law of thermodynamics will solve our problem with the embedded chips."

"The second law of what?" The vice president gave Prentice a cold, hard-eyed smile. "Mr. Prentice, we're not all scientists. I'm afraid you'll have to explain yourself."

"Essentially, Mr. Prentice is saying that you will have to wait until the embedded chips wear out." The unfamiliar voice caught Lauren by surprise, and it took her a moment to realize that the stranger sitting by General Archer had spoken. The older gentleman stood, then bowed stiffly to the room.

General Archer, his face brightening, straightened in his chair and gestured toward his guest. "With the president's permission, of course, let me present General Kord Herrick, special assistant to Adrian Romulus, commission president of the European Union's Council of Ministers. General Herrick has expressed interest in the Y2K situation, and the president has graciously allowed him to join our meeting."

The old man's hawk-like eyes had fastened to Daniel Prentice. "As I was saying," he said, his deep-timbred voice rumbling through the room, "Mr. Prentice believes that no matter what we try to do, some misfortunes cannot be avoided."

Prentice met the old man's gaze without flinching, then nodded soberly. "That's right. It's Murphy's Law—what can go wrong will go wrong. Unfortunately, we have no way of knowing what will go wrong. Some of the things we fear—a total failure of the oil pumps in the North Sea, for instance—will not happen. But others will."

A flurry of panic rippled around the room. "What about our weapons systems?" Dr. Carolyn Wilt pinned General Archer with an icy stare. "Can you promise that your satellite-controlled weapons won't suddenly fire on our cities?"

Mild confusion reigned as the secretaries tossed questions and accusations back and forth, then the president held up his hand. "Perhaps," he said, turning again to Daniel Prentice, "we've just discovered the third problem you mentioned."

"Yes," Prentice answered, his eyes narrowing. "Panic. No matter what we do, we can never be 100 percent sure of the chips we cannot replace. And if you think the media has enjoyed whipping up disaster scenarios thus far, wait until this time next year. Not only will you have people building bomb shelters in their back yards and stocking up on dehydrated survival foods, but you'll have bank runs like nothing this country has ever seen." He looked across the table toward the secretary of commerce. "You're going to have quite a problem, Mr. Leber."

Silence reigned in the room, and Lauren looked toward the window, suddenly realizing that the gray day outside had turned to rain. The whispering water on the window seemed to mock the baffled silence.

After a long moment, the president spoke. "Panic," he said, his gaze swinging to meet General Archer's. "Short of martial law, what can we do to prevent it?"

"If you'll allow me, sir." Prentice lifted his hand like a wiseacre in school. The president nodded, and Prentice continued. "While we were flying to Washington, I offered my friend Brad this riddle: A king had two sons, and could only leave his kingdom to one." Prentice swept his audience with a piercing glance. "You, ladies and gentlemen, have many systems on many mainframes. The Treasury Department has its own system; the IRS has another. Europe has its own system; so do the Asian banks. We only need one."

Prentice's dark eyes darkened as he studied the assembled group. "The king in my riddle arranged a horse race between his sons but decreed that the kingdom would go to the *slower* rider. That left his two sons in a quandary—how could they race and yet be certain that the other brother was not restraining his horse?"

He paused, and Lauren noticed that the room had gone as silent as the grave. Not a person stirred; not a page fluttered.

Brad Hunter lifted his head. "I've been pondering the question since last night," he told the group, "and I still don't get it."

Daniel laughed softly. "There was one sure way to guarantee that neither brother would cheat—they would have to *switch horses*."

Lauren tilted her head, considering his answer, then nearly laughed aloud. It was a clever puzzle, but none of the dignitaries around the table seemed to appreciate it. They were all staring at Daniel Prentice as if he'd suddenly begun to speak Chinese.

"Your answer, ladies and gentlemen," Daniel said, returning his gaze to the president, "is just as simple. Switch systems. Merge all your computer systems into one."

"Combine systems?" The president voiced the thought uppermost in every mind.

"Impossible!" General Archer slammed his hand on the table. "Why, it's taken years for us to compile the information in our databases! We're not giving up our classified files!"

Confusion erupted as several others echoed the general's opinion, but Daniel Prentice merely smiled. Finally the president called for order.

"You've heard the arguments," the president said simply, looking at Prentice with an inscrutable expression. "Convince me that these folks are wrong."

"It's only natural that they'd feel possessive of their own networks," Prentice said. "But just as these *United* States came together to share resources, it only makes sense that we share information as well. I am proposing that we create a national network to control the exchange of currency, monitor health, and regulate the economy."

"A national network?" Dr. Wilt clicked her long nails on the polished tabletop. "Why do we need one?"

"To streamline information." Prentice shifted his weight in his chair. "Do you realize that our law enforcement agencies have begun to fully share resources only in the last two decades? Ted Bundy wreaked a path of murder across the United States because law enforcement officials in one state did not have access to records of his crimes in other states. Think of deadbeat fathers—how often do divorced dads skip out and move to another state, evading responsibilities even as they manage to hide from their ex-wives?"

"We're working on that." Dr. Wilt's voice had a sharp edge. "The federal government is involved now, and we're making progress—"

"I'm not judging your intention, Dr. Wilt. But, if your computers were connected to Dr. Wilkerson's computers—" Prentice pointed toward the secretary of labor—"you would know the instant John Doe, deadbeat dad, applied for a job. If you programmed his Social Security number or I.D. code into a scanner, you'd know if he so much as walked into the local grocery store. And if your computers, Dr. Leber," he shifted his gaze to the secretary of commerce, "were connected to the other two, you'd know what brand of soap John Doe used, what kind of produce he buys, and how much he spends every month on groceries. You, Dr. Hall," he said, smiling at the secretary of energy, "would know if he signed on for electricity or natural gas at his new condo. And you, Mr. Whitlow—" he nodded at the secretary of state—"would know if he took an unexplained side trip into Mexico before settling in Los Angeles."

The vice president rapped on the table with his knuckles. "How would we know these things? We don't keep track of groceries and soap."

"Yes, we do." Dr. Wilkerson's voice was hoarse. "Somebody keeps track of all those things. But there's no central repository of information."

"There could be." A secretive smile softened Daniel Prentice's mouth. "And I know just how to do it."

In a dramatic, almost theatrical gesture, he rested his elbow on the table, then lifted his hand, slowly rotating it back and forth. "Raw data," his voice filled with quiet emphasis, "will be stored here, on the back of each individual's hand. Several years ago my company began to manufacture identification chips for pets—the Personal Identification Device, or PID, is implanted beneath the animal's fur. If the animal becomes lost or injured, with the simple swipe of a scanner we are able to read a number that will lead us to a pet owner's name, address, and phone number."

He lowered his hand and looked toward Dr. Dana Barnett, the secretary of agriculture. "After we perfected the pet PID, we began to work on bovine PIDs. Now we manufacture chips that tell a dairy farmer when a cow is lactating, when she is in heat, when she is pregnant. And he knows it in the instant that a dairy cow walks past a scanner in the barn."

Dr. Barnett nodded, her eyes wide.

Daniel looked next at General Archer. "The military has been talking about ID chips for years. DNA identification was first implemented in Desert Storm, and part of President Clinton's proposed health care legislation involved a 'safe, ingenious, inexpensive, foolproof, and permanent method of identification using radio waves.' Since 1992 health care professionals have been talking about a compact microchip, the size of a grain of rice, which would be placed under the skin in a procedure as simple as a vaccination."

Daniel looked around the circle. "Your complete medical history, employment history, a record of your DNA, even your voice- and thumbprints can be recorded upon a PID and embedded beneath the flesh on the back of your hand." With a smooth, polished gesture, he pulled a mechanical pencil from inside his coat pocket, then clicked the tip several times. "This pencil lead is so thin most of you would not even feel it if I dropped it into your palm," he said, concentrating on the pencil. With a deft motion, he broke off the lead, then pressed it to the tip of his index finger. From where she sat across the room, Lauren could barely see it.

"A PID no bigger than this could contain all your personal records," Daniel went on. "The PIDs could be updated as needed—after marriage, for instance, or an employment change, or every decade. Theoretically, by scanning the PID, a bank could credit an individual with a certain amount of spendable credits, enabling a consumer to shop without cash, credit, or debit cards. Best of all, every time an individual's PID is scanned, every iota of information about his transaction or movement is relayed to the central network."

A general hubbub broke out in the room.

"It's an invasion of privacy," Hank Leber protested.

"Why? We're not recording any information that isn't already being recorded," Dr. Wilkerson answered. "We're just improving the collection and dissemination of that information."

"It's just too bizarre." The vice president threw up his hands. "And bound to cost more than it's worth! The taxpayers would never stand for it."

Tom Ormond, the White House press secretary, leaned over and whispered to Lauren. "Why not? They tolerated $640 airplane toilet seats, didn't they?"

"Wait, think about it." Steve Aldridge, secretary of transportation, spoke up. "We could put scanners at all airports, train stations, and ports of entry. We could monitor who goes where—we'd find wanted criminals and illegal aliens in a flash. That capability alone would save us millions every year."

The secretary of commerce looked at the president with excitement shining in his eyes. "Why not do this now? We've talked about it for years, but we've never had a sufficiently powerful reason. But this will be simple— we tell the American people the truth about the Year 2000 Crisis and ask them to come forward for their PIDs. We could even offer some sort of tax deduction or incentive for those who are willing to be microchipped in the first six months or so."

"Negative consequences would drive the laggards." The secretary of the treasury picked up the thought. "If we do nothing, the media frenzy over possible Y2K crises could conceivably ignite a run on the banks—people would rush to withdraw their funds before all records of those funds disappear into cyberspace. But there simply isn't enough money to distribute. Only three percent of our national currency is actually available in paper bills and coins. The rest is represented on paper, in stocks, bonds, and investments, but mostly as electronic digits in our computer systems. If even a small minority of our citizens become nervous and withdraw their cash, our entire Federal Reserve banking system will collapse."

The president pressed his finger to his lips, a sure sign that he was about to begin a story. Lauren knew the sign and apparently the others did, too, for they all quieted and settled back in their chairs.

"Reminds me of a marvelous scene in *It's a Wonderful Life*, that Christmas movie with Jimmy Stewart." The president glanced up at Lauren. "You remember it, don't you, Miss Mitchell? The scene where the entire town comes storming into the old Bailey Building Savings and Loan, determined to take their money out."

"I remember it," Lauren answered, feeling more than a little uncomfortable. Every eye in the room, including Daniel Prentice's, had turned to her.

"Anyway," the president went on, "poor George Bailey is trying to explain that he doesn't have their money in the vault, that it's all loaned out. It's in the taxi driver's house, and the policeman's, and in that little housing development he started."

President Stedman looked around in the pregnant pause, then nodded at the secretary of the treasury. "George Bailey solved the problem by talking the people out of running the bank. I may not be as charming as Jimmy Stewart, but I think I could give a televised address and convince people that we need to move to a cashless economic system. Probably 90 percent of the country already uses credit or debit cards. We'll just tell the American people that it's time to take a giant leap forward . . . and that everyone has a duty to become involved in the Millennium Project."

"Exactly." The treasury secretary thumped the table with his fist. "That's a great title, sir."

"Wonderful idea, Mr. President."

As others called out their support, Daniel Prentice leaned on the arm of his chair and smiled at President Stedman. "The technology is already in place, Mr. President. Just as you can buy a prepaid telephone card and spend the allotted minutes, you can buy a cash-stored value card, swipe it at registered merchants, and spend money without ever touching a paper dollar. The benefit of having the card used in tandem with a PID is obvious: Persons who try to use the card registered to one individual won't be able to validate the transaction if the number on the PID doesn't match the card."

"The danger of technology," General Archer pushed his way into the conversation, "is that criminals will always try to subvert it. Suppose we implement this PID—how do we prevent criminals from duplicating it and creating false identities?"

"Biometrics," Daniel said, shifting to face the general. "Your thumbprint is unlike any other in the world. And, just in case some terrorist manages to slice off your thumb in order to steal your identity, your unique voiceprint will serve as a failsafe. Together, voice- and fingerprints provide a remarkable degree of security."

"I have a rather obvious question." The vice president, noticeably annoyed that Daniel Prentice had stolen the show, waved his hand.

"Yes, John?" The president asked.

John Miller's mouth twisted into a cynical smile. "What do we do with a man who has no right hand? Or even a left hand? We might have people purposely chopping off limbs in order to get around this thing."

"Alternatively, we could implant the PID under the skin of the forehead." Daniel Prentice set his chin in a stubborn line. "If a man is walking around, he certainly has a head. And unlike an arm or leg, the forehead is visible, and could easily be scanned with remote sensing technology, even at a distance."

"How do we keep people from cutting them out?" The vice president folded his arms. "That little chip isn't going to stop someone who doesn't want us to track his movements."

Prentice did not flinch before Miller's steely gaze. "I suppose we'd have to bury it between the tendons in the wrist. Yes, people could cut them out, but it's not the sort of thing they'd want to do. If they accidentally cut a nerve, they *could* lose the use of their hand."

The secretary of commerce met Prentice's gaze. "I suppose, Mr. Prentice, that you will want your company to manufacture these PIDs."

Daniel smiled. "We would be happy to serve as the senior contractor in charge of design, setting specifications, and ensuring quality. But there's no way my company can produce the number of chips we'll need for the president's Millennium Project. We'll certainly enlist Intel, Motorola, and other companies with the capability to work with us as sub-contractors."

General Archer narrowed his eyes as he looked at Prentice. "Sounds like a very profitable venture for you."

"A very *challenging* venture, General." Prentice grinned. "It will certainly keep us busy. And though I like to provide for my associates, I'm not especially interested in money. I end up sending most of it to you guys in Washington, anyway."

Lauren lifted a brow as the room broke into laughter. Not especially interested in money? Every successful businessman she'd met was more interested in money than anything else. If Daniel Prentice was telling the truth, he certainly didn't fit the typical millionaire mold.

The president cleared his throat and brought the room to order. "Well, ladies and gentlemen," he said, glancing at his watch, "I appreciate your time, and I'm certain we all have much to think about. Let's go back to our offices and consider the implications, then reconvene on Friday morning." His blue eyes flashed a gentle but firm warning. "Of course, this is all strictly classified. Do your research, discuss this in confidence with your highest-ranking officials, but say nothing to the press or anyone outside your departments." His gaze moved toward the foreign visitor. "General Herrick, I'm certain you understand the need for sensitivity in these matters."

As the general nodded, President Stedman shifted in his chair and extended his hand to Daniel Prentice. "Thank you, young man, for coming. You've given us much to consider."

Prentice took President Stedman's hand and gripped it tightly. "My pleasure, sir." He smiled at the president, then his gaze shifted to the corner where Lauren sat. She saw the snap of his eyes as he added, "I trust I shall enjoy my time in Washington."

The president stood, officially ending the meeting. Along with the others, Lauren rose from her chair and respectfully waited for President Stedman to exit the room, then she hurried after him, afraid that the blush that burned her cheek said far more than she wanted Daniel Prentice to know . . . just yet.

ELEVEN

5:45 P.M., Wednesday, November 11, 1998

"PINCH ME." DANIEL STOOD IN FRONT OF THE MASSIVE EAGLE EMBLAZONED ON the deep blue carpeting of the Oval Office. He turned to Brad and grinned. "Tell me I'm not dreaming."

"You're not dreaming, pal." Brad thrust his hands in his pockets, then walked over to the fireplace. "Nice looking couple, aren't they?" he said, studying the series of family photographs along the mantel. "He's the most photogenic president since Ronald Reagan."

Daniel came to stand beside Brad. "The first lady's not bad looking, either." He nodded toward one picture of the Stedmans waving from a bunting-draped platform. "Isn't that Lauren Mitchell with them? Good grief, how long has she worked for this guy?"

"Lower your voice." Brad grinned, but by the look in his eye Daniel knew he was only half-joking. "We're probably being recorded on the surveillance system right now."

Daniel lowered his voice as ordered. "What's the big deal?" He glanced up at the photographs again. "I wasn't accusing her of anything improper."

"It's just—well, you know what the political climate is like these days." Brad turned away and smiled toward the center of the room, mugging for whomever might be watching. "This president is so wary of scandal that he's taken pains to be certain his relationships with female associates are perceived as strictly professional. He's *especially* careful around Lauren Mitchell. You'd never catch him hugging her."

"Why?" Daniel frowned, a little surprised to realize how disappointed he'd be if Lauren Mitchell had some kind of a fling going with her boss. The president had seemed rather casual with her in the cabinet meeting today. That sort of casualness could come from working together, or it might mean something more. . . .

"Lauren Mitchell is like a daughter to the Stedmans." Brad glanced over his shoulder at a photograph of the three of them together on a deserted beach. "I don't know if you'll remember it, but the Stedmans had a daughter about Lauren's age, and the two girls were friends. But Jessica Stedman died nearly thirteen years ago in a boating accident off the Outer Banks."

Daniel closed his eyes, remembering the story. Samuel Stedman had been a senator then, and the news had made the front pages. For a few days there was talk of foul play, but the inquest had eventually ruled that Jessica Stedman had been riding with a group of college students too drunk to handle their power boats.

"Oh man, I remember now." Daniel turned and moved closer to the beach picture. From a distance he had assumed the girl was Lauren, but on closer observation he could see that this was a different young woman, with slightly darker hair and a narrower face. This had to be Jessica Stedman. And though it must give the Stedmans pleasure to work with Lauren, the sight of her must pain them, too. How could they look at Lauren and not think of their deceased daughter?

"So whatever you do," Brad dropped his voice even lower, "don't talk about the beach, boats, or booze. The Stedmans are teetotalers."

"No problem."

The door opened. As the president and his wife came in, trailed by Lauren and General Archer, Daniel thrust his hands in his pockets and tried to mimic Brad's nonchalant attitude.

"Gentlemen, I'm so glad you joined us." The president flashed a genuine smile, and Daniel felt himself relax. "I think the steward has dinner ready in the dining room, so let's eat, shall we? Mr. Prentice, I do hope you like southern fried chicken. I can't seem to get enough of it, but the chef has orders to serve fried foods only on special occasions."

"I love it."

The president and first lady led the way into the small hallway off the Oval Office, and Daniel fell into step beside Lauren Mitchell, leaving Brad to walk with General Archer.

"I'm glad you made it," Lauren said as they moved through the hallway and into the elegantly-appointed but comfortable dining room. "But I'll have to ask Mr. Hunter what he said to convince you to come. I might need to know his secret."

"Mr. Hunter has no secrets," Daniel whispered, pulling out a chair for Lauren at the table. "At least, none that I wouldn't share with you, too. All you have to do is ask."

"Well." The dusky rose of Lauren's cheeks deepened as she sat down. "I'm flattered."

"Don't be," Brad Hunter answered with a smile, taking a seat beside Daniel. "Daniel charms every woman he meets, but no one has managed to snag him yet."

"I can't imagine that no one is interested."

Daniel looked up, slightly embarrassed as Mrs. Stedman offered her opinion. He was sitting directly across from her, and for a moment he was reminded of his mother—Mrs. Stedman had his mother's bright, bold blue eyes.

He sighed in quiet relief when the president returned the conversation to more important matters. "Mr. Prentice, General Archer will want to meet with you tomorrow. And, of course, I'd like you to meet with several of the cabinet secretaries who might have reservations about implementing the sort of national network you suggested today."

"It is nothing to be afraid of," Daniel said, leaning back as the steward placed a salad plate on the table before him. "Most Americans have no idea how often the details of their lives are tracked even now. Every time John Doe makes a phone call, buys something with a credit card, subscribes to a magazine, or pays his taxes, that information is recorded in a database somewhere. If John goes to buy a car, the moment he gives his Social Security number to a salesman, the business office can get a detailed credit history. In a few minutes, they will have more accurate information about who and what John owes than John does himself."

"That doesn't mitigate the fact that people don't like the government knowing those kinds of details," the president pointed out. "We're very privacy-oriented in this country. No one likes a snoop, and we've been conditioned to resist anything that smacks of Big Brother."

"That is actually an advantage the identification chip offers." Daniel waited until the president picked up his fork, then he did the same. "No one can read the PID with the naked eye. Personal information is only visible to scanners, and different institutions will only be able to decipher certain codes. The encoded information can be segmented by category. Stores and merchants, for example, only need to know whether a person is authorized to use a debit card and the level of available credit. Medical centers have no business knowing of an individual's criminal record. The porter at the train station doesn't need to know that his passenger carries the gene for sickle cell anemia."

"So the government controls the dissemination of information." General Archer had not yet begun to eat; he simply stared at Daniel, his eyes narrow and his back ramrod straight.

Daniel paused and stabbed at his salad. "I suppose. Someone has to be in charge, but that authority must be trustworthy. You're quite right, Mr. President, about privacy issues. We cannot allow technology to take away the basic rights guaranteed by our Constitution."

"I don't understand." Lauren's eyes widened with concern. "It all sounds so convenient and controllable. What's the downside?"

Daniel threw a glance at Brad, then looked back at Lauren. "Brad and I were talking about this earlier. The downside is that in a technological age, he who holds information holds great power. I believe that information is like water—it must be checked in some situations and allowed to flow freely in others. But there are those who would dam information for their own purposes."

Lauren smiled and shook her head. "You've lost me, Professor."

Daniel lowered his fork. "Information is money. Marketers routinely shell out big bucks to companies who collect information about who buys what." He bent his head slightly to look into her eyes. "Tell me, Miss Mitchell—have you a hobby? Some outside interest that has nothing to do with your work here?"

"Just one." She dimpled. "I have a champion Samoyed. When my schedule allows, I handle her in dog shows."

"Have you ever ordered pet supplies from a catalog?"

She nodded slowly. "Yes. Once or twice."

"And how many pet supply catalogs do you now find in your mail?"

Her smile vanished, wiped away by understanding. "More than a dozen. Most of them are from companies I've never heard of."

Daniel spread his hands. "There you have it. Information about your buying habits has been spread throughout the catalog kingdom."

"That's not so bad." Lauren gave Mrs. Stedman an uncertain smile. "I mean, there's no harm in getting a lot of junk mail. Everyone does."

"But suppose you couldn't buy groceries because the powers that be decided that you had registered with the wrong political party?" Daniel met the president's eyes. "No offense, sir, but you won't remain in this office forever. What if your successor dreams of an authoritarian society? What if he decides to crush rebels by denying them the right to travel freely? To buy medicine? To attend school?"

Mrs. Stedman's fork dropped to her salad plate with a resounding clatter. Her face seemed to open for a brief moment as Daniel's words took hold in her imagination. He saw bewilderment in her eyes, a quick flicker of fear, then certainty.

"'He also forced everyone,'" Mrs. Stedman breathed the words in a hoarse whisper, as if they were too terrible to utter in a normal voice, "'small and great, rich and poor, free and slave, to receive a mark on his right hand or on his forehead, so that no one could buy or sell unless he had the mark, which is the name of the beast or the number of his name.'"

An awkward silence followed, then the president reached out and patted his wife's hand. "Honey, this isn't the Bible we're talking about here. It's just business."

The Bible? Daniel lowered his gaze, wishing he'd paid better attention all those Sundays his mother had dragged him to church. He didn't remember hearing anything like Mrs. Stedman's dire pronouncement, but her reference to a mark on the right hand or forehead, coming so soon after the cabinet meeting, was enough to send prickles of cold dread crawling up his spine.

"The Antichrist," she said, looking at Daniel. A warning cloud settled on her elegant features. "It's a prediction found in the book of Revelation, chapter thirteen. According to the ancient biblical prophecy, a future world dictator will lead the world into great tribulation, and he will require every living soul to take a mark on his right hand or his forehead."

"Victoria, darling, if we want a sermon, we'll call in a preacher." Annoyance struggled with affection on the president's face as he looked around the table. "You may not know, gentlemen, that Victoria has become quite involved in religion. She finds that it comforts her—and since she's needed quite a bit of comfort in the past few years, I support her entirely."

Quiet sounds of agreement came from everyone at the table. Daniel looked at Lauren—she bent over her salad, methodically eating, but the color in her cheeks was brighter than it had been a moment before.

No matter what her husband's wishes, Victoria Stedman was not one to be ignored. "Thank you, Sam." Her voice was soft but filled with a quiet determination all the more impressive for its control. "But this is a private meeting, off the record. If any of the men at this table are offended by my belief in the Bible and Jesus Christ—" her eyes moved from General Archer to Daniel—"then I apologize for giving offense. But I do not apologize for my convictions."

Brad was quick to regain his composure. "No apology is necessary, Mrs. Stedman."

"I agree," Daniel echoed. "My mother is a Christian, too. I have a feeling she would be very interested in your views, Mrs. Stedman."

The first lady's left eyebrow rose a fraction. "Really? Well, it is reassuring to know that you have some sort of spiritual background. Are you a believer, Mr. Prentice?"

Daniel's face grew hot. He was conscious that everyone at the table was staring at him, but what could he do? If he claimed to be a believer like Mrs. Stedman, the president might lose all faith in Daniel's ideas. Worse yet, General Archer might imagine that Daniel was trying to implement some sort of fulfillment to the prophecy Mrs. Stedman had just mentioned.

But if he said he didn't believe, Mrs. Stedman would be disappointed. And if the story leaked somehow, the news of Daniel Prentice's supposed atheism would break his mother's heart.

Daniel closed his eyes. When in doubt, he reminded himself, the easiest way out was always to tell the truth.

He looked up. General Archer was watching with what looked like wry amusement, Brad had lowered his gaze, and the president appeared to be studying the crown molding at the ceiling. Lauren, though, had put down her fork and stared at Daniel with wide eyes.

"I find religion very interesting." Daniel met the first lady's bold gaze. "I can't say that I'm as devoted to Christian dogma as my mother, but I'm not at all ready to discount the fact that God could exist. Until we know all there is to know, how can anyone deny God with any certainty?"

A smile played at the corners of Victoria Stedman's mouth. "You are an honest man, Daniel Prentice," she said, running her finger around the rim of her crystal water goblet. "I appreciate honesty wherever I find it. There is too little truthfulness in this world."

The pantry door swung open, and the president clapped his hands in open relief. "The fried chicken." He gave Daniel an apologetic smile, then lifted his salad plate toward the steward. "No more talk of business, gentlemen, let's discuss more pleasant things. Who do you think will play in the Super Bowl this year?"

And with that deft command, all conversation about computer chips, religion, and world dictators vanished. Daniel, Brad, Sam Stedman, and General Archer spent the rest of the evening munching on fried chicken and talking football.

-0100111100-

Shortly after ten that evening, General Adam Archer climbed into his limo and told the driver to take him directly home. As the long, black car pulled away from the curb and passed through the iron gates bordering the White House, Archer pulled his secure cell phone from his pocket and punched in a number.

His aide answered on the second ring. "General?"

"I need a wiretap, full team surveillance, and anything else you can get me on Daniel Prentice." To be certain there were no misunderstandings, Archer spelled the name.

"Isn't this the computer guy in the news?"

"Yes."

"All right. I'll get right on it."

"I want to know everything—where he goes, who he knows, and everyone who sent him a Christmas card last year. Use every means at your disposal."

"You've got a green light from Brown?" Alexander Brown was the director of the FBI, and Archer was supposed to clear any sort of domestic wiretapping and surveillance through his office.

"I'll be responsible for this one. Just get on it."

Archer snapped his phone shut, then dropped it back into his pocket. Outside the limo, the streetlights cast an orange, shadowless glow over the row houses that lined the aging streets. The lights were an anticrime device, neither inexpensive nor pretty, but very necessary in this crime-wasted capital.

Archer stared out the window, gazing at the deteriorating buildings on the outskirts of the District. A different law ruled here, a system made up of paroles and second chances, of time off for good behavior and early prison releases. Murderers lurked in those shadowed doorways; rapists, thugs, and thieves lingered at the corner markets and sized up new prospects.

For some time Archer had known that the proud America of his youth was dying. The harder he tried to ignore the truth, the more it persisted. Decadence, sloth, and moral weakness had infected the lower classes and risen steadily upward, corrupting even the White House and Congress.

Most Americans had not considered how a weak, faltering America would function in a world where the United States was no longer the de facto leader. While Americans cocooned in their homes in an effort to avoid the rampant crime on the streets, the rest of the world had begun to flex its muscles. China was an awakening giant, and dedicated, oftentimes suicidal Islamic oil barons controlled the vital distribution of oil. Europe had been energized with a new sense of purpose found in unity, and only Adrian Romulus seemed to fully appreciate the forces at work in the world outside the boundaries of the United States.

The future belonged to men like Romulus. That charming and charismatic leader had impressed Archer with his ideas, his commitment to a united world community ruled by strength and power, and his "iron hand in a velvet glove" approach. In a strict society, each individual knew his place. In a society with regulated laws and absolute justice, those who broke the rules knew they'd pay the consequences. Black was black, white was white, and truth was truth.

While Samuel Stedman didn't exhibit the obvious symptoms of depravity many of his predecessors had manifested, he was a conservative, bound in his thinking and habits to the old ways that had destroyed the nation. Though Archer personally liked Sam Stedman, the man couldn't even prevent school children from shooting each other on the playground. Romulus, on the other hand, had already instituted street curfews in Europe and strict gun controls.

Archer lowered his eyes, resigned to the inevitable. The old ways—and those who clung to them—had to be eliminated. Whether America realized it or not, the country was at war for its survival, and every war had casualties. . . .

Romulus would bring about a new world order, and he had promised Adam Archer a key place in it.

Closing his eyes to the depressing street scene, the general crossed his arms over his thick chest and wondered what the next few days would bring.

-01001111000-

Daniel pulled the comforter up over the rumpled bed, then sat on the edge of the mattress and slipped on his socks. He'd just spent a night in the Lincoln Bedroom, and found the experience strangely deflating. The bed wasn't comfortable, the antique furnishings weren't to his taste, and the tiny desk wasn't big enough for his laptop, his notebooks, and the stacks of papers he wanted to organize. Still, it was the Lincoln Bedroom, and he figured the news was worth sharing with a friend or two.

He picked up the phone on the night stand and gave the operator the number for Prentice Technologies. As he waited for the call to go through, he noticed that gray winter light poured through the sheer lace panels at the windows, so the office was bound to be humming with activity.

Roberta answered after the first ring.

"Prentice Technologies."

"Roberta, may I have Dr. Kriegel, please?"

The VOSS program recognized his voiceprint immediately, and Daniel thought he could almost hear a smile in Roberta's voice. "Certainly, Mr. Prentice. You have been away for thirty-seven hours. Are you enjoying your trip?"

"Yes, Roberta. Thanks for asking."

Daniel shifted on the bed and moved the telephone receiver from one ear to the other. The last few hours had been distracting, but he couldn't allow himself to forget that business continued as usual back in Mount Vernon.

"Daniel?"

He felt a sudden surge of relief at hearing Dr. Kriegel's voice. "Professor! How are you? How are things progressing?"

"Fine, Daniel, fine." A soft beep sounded over the phone line, and Daniel tensed as the professor cleared his throat. "One minute, Daniel, Roberta is signaling."

A sense of unease crept into Daniel's mood like a wisp of smoke. Roberta monitored the phone lines as well as the physical building, and that soft beep could only mean that a security breach had occurred. In order to avoid tipping off an intruder, Roberta had been programmed to interrupt quietly and display a warning message on the computer monitor.

Thirty seconds passed, then the professor came back on the line. "Daniel," he said, his voice thick and unsteady, "Roberta says we're not alone."

Daniel sat in silence, digesting this information. Someone was monitoring the phone line? If the bug originated at the office, other lines would be tapped, too. But if it was coming from his end—

He pressed his hand to his forehead. Of course! He was calling from the White House, after all. There were probably fewer than two or three clear lines in the entire building.

"I'm calling from the White House, Professor." Daniel frowned, perturbed by the lack of privacy. Even though he understood the need for security, the invasion was unsettling.

"Ah. Well, that must explain it."

"All the same," Daniel shifted his weight and glanced around the tidy bedroom, "I think I'll move to a hotel room ASAP. I wanted to see how things were going, but let's discuss it later."

"Good idea, Daniel. Take care."

Daniel hung up, then tossed the rest of his clothes into a suitcase. For Brad's sake he was willing to volunteer his time and energy to help the government, but he was not willing for some government spook to access and catalog his every word.

He slipped into his coat, closed his suitcase, then tossed a few remaining papers into his briefcase. He'd move out this morning, and he wouldn't leave a forwarding address with anyone but Brad. He'd take a taxi to any other meetings and save the taxpayers whatever bucks it would have cost to send a limo to fetch him.

Whistling, Daniel picked up his bags, gave the infamous Lincoln Bedroom a final rueful smile, then sauntered out and down the hall, ready to move into more hospitable quarters.

Before leaving the White House, Daniel flashed his ID badge at a couple of security guards and visited the West Wing. One of the guards directed him through the maze to Lauren's office. Once he found the tiny room, he paused for a moment in the hallway. She was sitting at a cluttered desk, her golden head bent low over a notebook, her hand curled around a still-steaming cup of coffee.

Except for the desk, the rest of the office was as neat as a museum. Daniel glanced at a bookcase lined with leather volumes, then noticed that only two personal pictures were framed for display with the books. One was a casual snapshot of Lauren and Jessica Stedman; the other appeared to be a formal portrait of a fluffy white dog with gleaming black eyes.

"Miss Mitchell?"

She jumped at the sound of his voice but recovered quickly and gave him a warm smile. "Mr. Prentice. I trust you slept well?"

"Probably better than Abe Lincoln ever did in that bed." Daniel pushed aside his complaints in order to concentrate on the young woman before him. Her gleaming blonde hair clustered in short curls around a perfectly oval face, and he knew that in addition to beauty she possessed wit, directness, and intelligence. Yes, Lauren Mitchell was a very interesting woman. The trouble was, Daniel had no time to pursue other interests.

She had to be keenly aware of his scrutiny, yet she kept her features composed. "Can I help you with something, Mr. Prentice?"

"Call me Daniel. After all, we ate fried chicken together last night. If we were in North Carolina, wouldn't that mean we were courting?"

Lauren tilted her head. "All right—Daniel. Now, is there anything I can get for you? Your meeting with General Archer isn't until one o'clock. He'll probably want to meet in his office at the Pentagon."

Daniel cocked a finger at her. "I'll be there. But I just dropped by to let you know that I'm checking out of the First Hotel today and taking another room."

Her face clouded with what Daniel hoped was disappointment. "Oh, dear. Was the Lincoln Bedroom that bad?"

"No." He waved her concerns away. "It's just that I have a lot of work to do, and there are too many distractions here."

"Shall I have a car take you someplace? I could arrange another room—"

"No, thanks. I'll take care of it myself."

Her velvet blue eyes went wide with curiosity. "How will we reach you?"

Daniel grinned. "Don't worry. I'll call you once I'm settled to see if the president wants to take me to lunch." Her eyes widened further, and Daniel laughed. "Don't be alarmed, Miss Mitchell. That was a joke. But I will call you to see if I'm needed."

He turned to go, but the sound of her voice caught him in mid-step. "Call me Lauren," she whispered, her accent soft and sweetly seductive. "After all, we did eat fried chicken together. In North Carolina, that's practically a proposal."

He tossed a smile over his shoulder, then picked up his bags and moved away.

Once Daniel passed the security checkpoint at the Southwest Appointment Gate, he walked past the Old Executive Office Building and stepped out to the intersection of Seventeenth Street and New York Avenue. From a concrete island in the fork of the road, he spied the Ambassador Hotel, an aging building that remained aloof to the grandeur and self-importance of its marble-faced neighbors.

Daniel nodded in satisfaction. He'd bet his bottom dollar that the Ambassador was not on Lauren's list of alternate housing for overflow White House guests.

After crossing the street, he stepped through a brass-framed revolving door into a threadbare but comfortable lobby scented with cigarette smoke and disinfectant. He signed in at the desk, paid with his company credit card, and carried his own luggage up to his room. The oak door swung open to reveal a clean little apartment with sun-bombarded curtains, rather drab furniture, and carpet the shade of gray specifically designed to hide dirt. A shaft of sun angled down from the only window, highlighting slow spirals of dust that shifted in the moving air.

Daniel dropped his luggage and walked to the window. The ancient panes of thick glass blurred his view slightly, but on the busy street below he could see nothing unusual, only throngs of suited pedestrians and taxis moving through the marble purlieu surrounding the White House.

He reached for the bedside phone and punched in his company's number. A moment later Roberta answered and transferred him into Dr. Kreigel's lab.

"Daniel?"

"How are you, Professor? I've moved to a hotel, so the phone line should be clear now."

The professor laughed softly. "If it isn't, we'll know soon enough. How are things in Washington?"

"A little interesting, a little boring, and very predictable. Have you begun to run the Millennium Code on the First Manhattan project?"

"Yes, Daniel, and the technicians have not reported any problems. Apparently it's working like a dream."

"Good. I may have even more astounding news soon. Of course, I'll expect we'll have to bid on certain aspects of the job, but—"

A soft beep sounded in his ear, and Daniel caught his breath.

"One moment, please." Daniel heard sounds of someone fumbling with the phone, then dead silence. A moment later the professor came back on the line. "How odd. Roberta says we have another guest."

Daniel blew out his breath in exasperation. No one knew where he was, so how could his phone be tapped? The problem had to lie with the company's phone lines.

"Has anyone else been *visited* today?"

"No." Urgency underlined the professor's voice. "We've been calling out all morning, and Roberta's said nothing."

"I have just walked into this place." Daniel's thoughts raced. "There's no way anyone could have time to follow me."

Picking up the telephone, he moved toward the window, stretching the cord as far as it would go.

"Any sign of a remote?" the professor asked.

Daniel looked up and down the street. The eavesdropper could be stationed in a van, but Daniel couldn't see one in this particular cross section of the street. But a parking garage stood across the road, and he couldn't see around the corner.

"Impossible to tell," he finally said, frowning into the phone. "And I left in such a hurry, I didn't think to pack my Nokia. Listen, Professor, I'll e-mail you later with a PGP-protected file. This thing has me bugged—" he managed a choking laugh—"in more ways than one."

"Take care, Daniel."

Daniel hung up, then sat on the bed and hunched forward, thinking. Given the speed with which the intruder had followed him and latched onto his phone call, the intruder almost had to be using a laser—not exactly a nickel-and-dime security toy. The technology was state-of-the-art, real bleeding edge stuff. That could only mean government—or one of Daniel's competitors.

Daniel turned and propped up his back with pillows, then stretched his legs out on the bed. The very real threat of industrial espionage had motivated him to design and install Roberta, a virtually unbeatable security system; but aside from the customary encryption devices for telephones and e-mail, he hadn't given much thought to the risk of industrial espionage *outside* the office. Thus far most of his competitors had been content to ignore the Y2K problem and concentrate on software for the broader market of personal computers. Nearly half of American homes would have a PC by the end of the millennium, and the easy money lay in peddling software for household machines. Microsoft and CompuWare had been content to stick their heads in the sand and pray the Y2K Crisis would go away.

But now someone was very interested in Daniel's work. He had no trouble understanding why, for billions of dollars were at stake. But *who* had access to the kind of technology that could follow him and clamp onto his phone call in a matter of minutes?

The question hung in the air, shimmering like the spiraling dust motes lit by the window's slanting light.

TWELVE

10:30 P.M., Thursday, November 12, 1998

KORD HERRICK CHECKED HIS WATCH, THEN MOVED EASILY THROUGH THE smoke-filled bar until he spied Archer's close-cropped head and unnaturally bright cheeks above a corner table. The general was prompt, and Kord appreciated a man who understood the value of time. A man had only so many hours allotted to his life span, and a wise man knew that when time was wasted, life itself frittered away.

The soulful sounds of some sentimental song from the eighties blared from the speakers, and Kord steeled his nerves as he moved across what passed for a dance floor. He dodged an Asian couple locked in an embrace, skirted a table where a businessman and a woman sat only inches apart, then slid into a chair at Archer's table.

Archer grunted a greeting, then pushed a manila envelope toward Kord.

"This is complete?" Herrick asked.

Archer caught the waitress's eye, pointed to his empty glass, then crossed his arms. "It's complete. I filled in the details after my meeting with him today."

"The meeting went well?"

Archer fell silent as the waitress approached with another drink, and spoke only after she had exchanged glasses and moved away. "Yes. The man is safe, I assure you. I don't think you'll find anyone more trustworthy."

Kord fingered the clasp of the envelope and wondered if his American host would think it rude if he opened it. Probably. Archer would want him to accept his word; the report could wait.

"What is, then, your overall impression of the man?"

Archer smiled at a pretty brunette who sidled close to the table, then paused to sip his drink. "He's not a raving patriot, if that's worrying you. He spent most of his youth in Canada."

Kord lifted a brow, impressed. Prentice would naturally see himself as a man of the world.

"He's not religious, not politically partisan, not affiliated with any social causes," Archer went on. "He gives money to his mother's church, but that's probably an act of familial duty, nothing more. His employees have publicly stated that his company runs on the team concept, so he's no authoritarian."

"Will he be sympathetic to the coming movement?"

Archer shrugged. "He's a bit of a loner; I think he would like nothing better than to be left alone to tinker with his technological toys. But he is adaptable, yes. Best of all, the man has no apparent agenda. From what I can tell, he will be content to exercise his gifts to benefit the world—as long as he gets the recognition, of course."

His mind burned with the memory of Romulus's words: *All you need to know is that he yearns to make a mark on the world. Ambition is his guiding principle; success his personal mantra.* As always, Romulus was right.

Kord picked up the envelope and ran his finger over the creased edge. "In the last few days, has he called anyone of note?"

Archer drew his lips into a tight smile. "He called his company a couple of times. Got off the phone quickly, though, because he detected our tap. He's implemented some kind of advanced security system, and it caught us each time."

"He's as clever as they say."

"Yes."

Kord turned the envelope in his hands. Romulus would be pleased, and so would the council. Daniel Prentice seemed tailor-made for the task they had in mind. But, of course, Romulus had known he would be.

Kord tucked the envelope under his arm, then slid out of his chair. "My compliments, General." He extended his hand toward Archer. "Your people have done excellent work. After I let my employer know, I'm certain he'll want to demonstrate his gratitude."

"There's no need," Archer replied in a gruff voice, but Kord knew that automatic response was totally meaningless. A man in Archer's position couldn't accept lavish gifts without getting snagged in a mountain of bureaucratic red tape, but if a Swiss chalet or a house in the Azores just happened to be available for a month-long, expense-paid vacation, the general would be happy to accept.

Just as he had hinted he'd be happy to accept a position in the coming world community.

"Good night, Archer." Kord shook the general's hand, nodded in farewell, and left the bar.

-0100111100-

On Friday morning Lauren Mitchell informed Daniel that his third day in Washington would be spent in a series of meetings with cabinet members who had asked for further clarification. The prospect of long hours in the White House conference room brought Daniel little joy, but as the day passed he sensed a growing enthusiasm for the Millennium Project. Despite the initial reluctance voiced by several of the president's advisors, by Friday afternoon the cabinet members' questions had shifted from "if we do this" to "when we begin to move." By the time night had spread her wings over the White House lawn, Daniel realized the Millennium Project was well on its way to becoming reality.

As he exited the conference room Friday night, Daniel impulsively asked Lauren Mitchell to spend Saturday with him. "Sorry," she said, pushing a limp curl off her forehead, "but there's a dog show in Vienna tomorrow, and I'm handling Tasha. It'll pretty much take all day." Daniel felt his face stiffen but kept gallantly smiling when she tilted her head and looked at him intently. "Of course I'd hate for you to be bored in some hotel room. You're welcome to join us if you're looking for something to do."

"No, thanks." He lifted his hands and took a half-step back. "I'm really not much of a dog person."

"Are you sure?" Her eyes softened with concern.

"Quite sure." Her quick refusal had stung his pride, and he wasn't about to accept a counteroffer motivated by pity. She would probably have felt sorry for any stranger in town, but Daniel didn't need either a babysitter or a tour guide. "I've actually got a lot of work to do, so I ought to hibernate and log some hours on the laptop. Good luck, though, in the dog show."

Before she could utter another word, Daniel spun on his heel and moved down the hall.

-0100111100-

As Daniel Prentice moved away, Lauren retreated to her office, then shut the door and slouched against it. "That was not very diplomatic," she muttered, chiding herself. "Why didn't you just tell him to take a flying leap off the Washington Monument? He probably thinks that's what you want him to do. You should have been slower to say no; you could have at least *acted* like you were disappointed that you couldn't spend the day with him."

She opened her eyes and caught sight of the photo of Jessica Stedman on her bookcase. Jessica had never had a problem with men; even in college she'd had a real knack for knowing how to keep a guy interested without revealing too much. Lauren's problem was that she spoke too quickly, too often, and too openly. The tact and diplomacy she'd learned to use when dealing with bureaucrats and politicians seemed to fly out the window when she faced an attractive man . . . particularly one she was personally attracted to.

"Stop it, Mitchell." She straightened and moved quickly to her desk, then dropped her notebooks on a pile of correspondence she'd spent the day ignoring. Daniel Prentice had occupied entirely too much of her mind and imagination in the last three days. She was a competent woman with an important job to do; she had no time for romance, intrigue, or even innocent flirtation. The president would need extra help in the next few weeks as his administration launched this Millennium Project, and Lauren would need to be on her toes.

She moved to her telephone and pressed the button that rang the extension in the White House private family quarters. A moment later, Mrs. Stedman's soft voice answered, "Hello?"

"Mrs. S? I just wanted to remind you of your brunch tomorrow with the congressional wives. I'll be in Vienna most of the day, but call my cell phone if either you or the president needs me—"

"We'll be fine, Lauren. You and Tasha have a great time." Mrs. Stedman's voice brimmed with warmth and concern. "Bring home a blue ribbon, or whatever it is you win in those things."

"The ribbon we want is purple." Lauren grinned, then smacked her hand against her forehead. "That reminds me, Mrs. S, did the physician bring up a refill of the nitroglycerin prescription? I had a note to call him on my to-do list, but with all the goings-on around here—"

"Don't worry, Lauren, my secretary took care of it. But it's sweet of you to worry about us."

"It's the least I can do." Lauren felt a sharp sob rise in her throat and wiped a sudden wetness from her eyes. The Stedmans had brought her out of poverty, arranged for her education, and trusted her with responsibility and position far beyond her dreams or expectations. And yet, for all their loyalty and kindness, they routinely behaved as if *she* were actually useful to *them*.

"Well, if there's nothing else—I guess I'll go home."

"Good-night, dear."

Lauren dropped the phone back into its cradle, then shook off the wave of sentimentality and surveyed her desk again. She'd bundle the pile of correspondence and tackle it on Sunday afternoon, so at least she'd be halfway up to speed on Monday morning. Maybe the combination of routine work and two days without a glimpse of Daniel Prentice would be enough to remind her of who and what she was—Lauren Mitchell, executive assistant to President Sam Stedman for as long as he remained in the White House.

Until he left public office, nothing else mattered.

-0100111100-

Daniel spent Saturday munching on room service snacks while he painstakingly typed out detailed memos to his associates in New York. He warned Dr. Kriegel that a new code would have to be devised for human PIDs. He alerted Ron Johnson that the company would probably be retained as senior contractor to oversee the manufacture of over 266 million individual chips. For Taylor, Daniel typed out a long task list that included investigating new security devices for PT employees located outside the physical plant. Bill Royce would receive a long memo detailing several spin-off ideas Daniel had conceived while listening to the cabinet members drone on about how the Millennium Project would change the American way of life.

Before plugging his laptop modem into the wall, Daniel selected the PGP program and encrypted all four messages. Satisfied that his data was safe, he plugged the modem in, dialed into the company's network, and uploaded the files.

On Sunday afternoon Daniel relaxed at Brad's apartment and finally met the charming Christine. Brad tried to make Daniel comfortable, but with just over a month until the wedding, he and Christine had eyes only for each other. Watching their obvious bliss with a rueful smile, Daniel sipped his iced tea and thanked his lucky stars that Lauren Mitchell had turned him down. In the past few days he had discovered that behind her air of professional competence lay a bright and inquisitive mind. She didn't know much about technology or computers, but she was a quick study and kept pace with him every time he explained a new concept. Moreover, she was extremely knowledgeable about world affairs, having spent most of her career trying to ensure her boss's success in politics.

Yes, Lauren Mitchell was the kind of woman Daniel could fall for, but if he fell, he'd be mooning about like Brad Hunter while there was serious work to be done over the next year.

Thankfully, Brad seemed to be in a more businesslike frame of mind when he met Daniel at the White House on Monday morning. As he escorted Daniel to the semicircular drive on the north side of the building, he explained that they would ride together to an important meeting. Brad gave few details, but as he slammed the car door he assured Daniel that the meeting concerned national security.

They rode through the District streets in silence, then the long black limo steered toward the curb. Daniel lifted a brow in surprise when he saw that the vehicle had pulled up outside the entrance to a Ramada Inn. He turned to Brad with an incredulous grin. "We're holding a national security meeting at the neighborhood Ramada?"

"This isn't just any Ramada." Brad reached for the door. "The Ramada Renaissance has one of the few electronically secure safe rooms in the District. We could have met at the Pentagon, of course, but the president is trying to distance the Millennium Project from the military."

Brad opened his door and slid out, then walked around the car and stood stiffly on the sidewalk and waited for Daniel. With his dark suit, sunglasses, and stern demeanor, Brad looked so much like the stereotypical Secret Service agent that Daniel wanted to laugh.

"Lighten up, Brad," he said, joining his friend on the curb. "No one followed us. And I don't see a single suspicious character."

The corner of Brad's mouth drooped as he buttoned his jacket. "If they're watching, we won't see them," he said simply, leading Daniel away from the hotel's front entrance. "And believe me, lots of people are interested in what you're doing."

Daniel did not answer but slipped his hands into his pockets and followed Brad down the sidewalk toward a short wall that jutted onto the street. When Brad disappeared behind the wall, Daniel followed and discovered a back entrance to the hotel. A uniformed marine at the door snapped to attention and moved aside when Brad flashed his ID card. Feeling a little chagrined by the melodrama, Daniel pulled his ID from his coat pocket and held it before the guard's eyes. As the guard studied the photo, Daniel jerked his thumb in Brad's direction. "I'm with him."

The marine's resolute expression did not soften, but he nodded and pulled the door open so both men could enter.

"Why do you call it a safe room?" Daniel asked, looking around the foyer as Brad pressed the elevator call button. "Is it guarded by marines, or—" he cracked a smile—"have you shielded it against Superman's x-ray vision?"

Brad rolled his eyes. "Joke all you want, but we thought we'd need a secure meeting space. The Ramada's safe room has specially insulated wiring, soundproof walls, state-of-the-art locks. Special audio sweeps have been installed on all exterior doors to prevent passersby from eavesdropping. Even with all that, we still sent a team in to sweep the room for bugs. We were lucky this time—we didn't find any." He gave Daniel a cocky grin. "Don't tell me you don't have something similar at that fortress where you work."

"We have taken precautions with the building's designs. And we have Roberta." The elevator dinged, and the double doors opened. Daniel waited until he and Brad entered before continuing. "Roberta represents the latest in biometric technology. She tracks every individual inside the building by voiceprint. I could ask where you were, for instance, and she would instantly eavesdrop on a selection of voiceprints, then report your whereabouts."

"What if I was silent?"

"She'd examine the thumbprint keys for the room where your voice was last heard. If you had exited, she'd simply look for the room you had accessed next." He crossed his arms and leaned against the elevator's wall. "She'd find you in less than five seconds. She's a good system, and we haven't had any trouble."

"Haven't you?" Without explanation, Brad reached out and pressed the emergency stop button.

Daniel felt his stomach drop—and it wasn't from the elevator's braking.

"Daniel," the stern aspect of Brad's countenance softened, and for a brief moment the familiar spark of friendliness lit his eyes. "If we were on government property, I wouldn't dare speak to you about this. I probably should keep my mouth shut, but it doesn't matter anymore."

Daniel spoke calmly but felt that eerie sense of detachment that always preceded impending disaster. "What are you talking about?"

"We knew about your Y2K fix before you ever arrived in Washington. Right now there are probably a hundred copies of your Millennium Code circulating through our CIA and NSA mainframes."

Daniel glared at Brad, his uneasiness spiced with irritation. "You're not making any sense."

Brad sighed heavily, then turned and braced himself against the opposite wall. "You're a genius, Daniel, but you don't have a criminal mind. We know everything you did last week. You went to Canada; you got an e-mail from the professor; you came back to see a demonstration of his program. The CIA spooks had copies of the program the next day. I knew what you'd done before you had your first cup of coffee the next morning."

Daniel fought back a sudden surge of fury. Had they placed a spy in his company? He would never have imagined that one of his loyal associates would sell secrets to the government, but apparently he had made a serious error in judgment.

He clenched his fists and glared at Brad. "You knew they stole our program?"

"You would have never known." Brad thrust his hands into his pockets, apparently not caring that he'd left himself unprotected while Daniel wanted to smash his face in. "You have to understand. We're talking about *national security* here, and the Y2K problem is our first priority right now. We're dealing with the survival of the USA, and we had no choice but to appropriate your program. We wouldn't have sold it, and you will still make a fortune." He looked at Daniel with the faint beginnings of a smile. "If it makes you feel any better, yours wasn't the only company under surveillance, but you were the only one that rose to the challenge. We knew before you came to Washington that your Millennium Code wouldn't solve every Y2K problem. But we saw enough to know you were the man to head up this Millennium Project."

Daniel gasped through impotent anger. "So why are you telling me this now?"

"Because I want you to know what you're getting into." Brad stepped away from the wall and stood right in front of Daniel. "Now—do you want to hit me? If you do, here's your chance. Get it all out of your system before we go into the meeting."

"No." Daniel turned away, his voice taut with anger. "But tell me the truth—have you been tapping my phones since I arrived in Washington?"

He thought he saw a faint flicker of unease in the depths of Brad's brown eyes. "My department didn't order it. But I wouldn't be surprised if someone else did."

"Who? The president?"

A flash of humor crossed Brad's face. "Definitely not. Maybe the CIA, the Secret Service, the Defense Intelligence Agency, or the FBI. But not the president. He has to remain above the law."

Daniel hesitated, reluctant to voice his next thought. "What about Lauren Mitchell? The other day one of my calls was breached not twenty minutes after I left the White House. Lauren was the only person who knew I was leaving."

Brad gave him a look of faint amusement. "Really? How many people did you pass on the way out? Two guards at the door? Four marines at the gate? And don't forget to count the people you *didn't* see. Probably a dozen people knew when you left, and if you're marked for surveillance, probably a half-dozen followed you. If they want to bug you, they will. You can't outrun them, and I don't think even *you* can outsmart them."

Alarmed and more than a little perturbed, Daniel ran his hand through his hair in a distracted motion. "Brad, what have you gotten me into?"

"You'll be all right, just don't talk about company secrets over any telephone." Brad gave him an exaggerated wink as he leaned forward to release the emergency stop. "When this is all over, you'll be a hero and a billionaire, too. But stay on your toes, Danny boy. Don't let them lull you into a sense of complacency. And remember—just because you're paranoid doesn't mean they're *not* out to get you."

Disconcerted, Daniel crossed his arms and pointedly looked away. He would have sworn that Brad Hunter was a loyal friend, and maybe this was an example of what passed for loyalty in Washington. If he weren't a friend, would he have told Daniel about the government's theft of his Millennium Code program? Or was this all some elaborate deception?

No—Brad had to be telling the truth. He had too much accurate information to be bluffing. Brad's people, whoever they were, had definitely been spying on Prentice Technologies.

As the elevator creaked and hummed, Daniel closed his eyes and replayed the events of the morning he'd returned to the office. He'd come to work late, pausing outside the building for Susan McGuire, who'd been eager to assure him that her son was sick—

Did she even have a child? Susan McGuire was one of Daniel's newest employees; she'd been with Prentice Technologies for less than six months. Daniel couldn't remember her mentioning a child before, but he didn't have too much contact with the lower-level programmers. Was it possible that she had come into the office early that morning, set the program to run on the monitors, and managed somehow to arrange a feed to someone else? She could have gone outside to set it up and returned just as Daniel himself was entering the building.

He glanced over at Brad, half-tempted to ask if the name Susan McGuire would mean anything to the CIA, NSA, or FBI. But if she were working for the government, she'd be working under an alias.

The elevator chimed; the doors slid open. Daniel shoved his troubling thoughts into a far corner of his mind, determined to sort through them later.

"What's happening in this meeting?" Daniel asked, leading the way out. "If I have to answer another question about the feasibility of a cashless society—"

"Relax, Danny boy," Brad answered, following. "We're just going to sing your praises. That's the agenda."

-01001111OO-

Daniel's first thought was that the Ramada Renaissance's safe room looked more like a plush three-hundred-seat auditorium than a safe haven from spies. Daniel sank into one of the theater-style chairs and rested his chin on his hand as he scanned the room. Apparently several congressional committees had been invited to this impromptu gathering. An air of excited expectancy hung over the moiling crowd.

The vice president, John Miller, opened the meeting with the sharp rap of a gavel. After thanking the various honored congresspersons for taking time from their busy schedules, he proceeded to describe the threefold aspect of the Millennium Project in a manner so dry and dull that Daniel wondered if anyone in the audience would still be awake when he had finished.

In an effort to fight off his own weariness, Daniel looked away and tried to imagine why a dynamic man like Samuel Stedman had chosen John Miller as a running mate. Miller was a classic beta male, subservient to the core, and Stedman seemed to value free-thinking team members who offered divergent opinions. This yes-man, Daniel decided, had probably been tapped to fill the veep spot for geographical political reasons rather than intellectual ones. Miller had been a senator from California before the election, and whoever won that state earned a wealth of electoral votes.

Finally, Miller sat down. Daniel pretended to be enraptured as several cabinet members, General Adam Archer, and the director of the CIA stood and enthusiastically endorsed the Millennium Project, including the new national information network and the national identification system. Finally, at the end of a long list of speakers, Kathleen O'Connor, the United States ambassador to the United Nations, walked to the lectern.

"It gives me great pleasure to personally thank Mr. Daniel Prentice for convincing us that this system should be implemented as a solution to the Y2K Crisis," she said, her eyes crinkling as she acknowledged Daniel with a smile. "And we would like to take this opportunity to offer his insights to the world. As you know, the United States is not the only country threatened by a coming computer collapse, and, as Mr. Prentice has so ably demonstrated, the world is now interconnected as one global computer network. We are all linked to one another through the United Nations, international banking and trade, and interdependent relationships."

She looked into the audience, found Daniel again, and lowered her head until she peered over the rims of her glasses and met his gaze. "We would like you, Mr. Prentice, to represent the United States at a summit meeting of the European Union, to be held in January. I have already spoken to a representative of the Council of Ministers, and he has urged me to extend you this invitation."

A light pattering of applause began from somewhere in the back of the room, and soon a great wave of sound engulfed Daniel. He smiled reflexively, nodding to the ambassador, while his brain whirled in tumult. Europe? He'd just signed on for the biggest project of his life, he'd learned that his high-tech security system wasn't as infallible as he thought, and he had to host a bachelor party for his best friend.

Europe was the last place in the world he wanted to go.

The ambassador to the UN backed away from the lectern, still applauding, and an elderly, dignified man in an elegant black dress uniform moved to take her place. Daniel's smile flattened. The fellow had been present at the first cabinet meeting—Archer had introduced him as General Kord Herrick, special assistant to some hotshot on the EU's Council of Ministers. That introduction had done little to explain why a foreign official had been invited to an American president's cabinet meeting.

The applause died down as the older man gripped the edges of the lectern. "My name," he proclaimed in a heavily-accented voice, "is General Kord Herrick. I am the personal ambassador of Adrian Romulus, commission president of the European Council of Ministers, and I am a citizen of the new European community!" He lifted his hand at this last comment, as if he expected additional applause, but the assembled representatives only gazed at him with polite interest.

Unruffled, Herrick lowered his arm and continued, appearing to concentrate his attention on the area of the auditorium where Daniel and Brad were sitting. "We of the European Union," he said, his voice deep and

creaky with age, "would welcome Mr. Daniel Prentice to join our committee, just as we welcome the chance to work with the United States to
solve our mutual problems as the new millennium approaches. For the
past several years, we of the European community have concentrated on
tearing down the walls that divided us for centuries. Today we embrace
each other, and tomorrow we would like to embrace our fellow citizens
across the sea."

Twisting his narrow frame, he nodded toward the seats where the vice
president sat with his wife. "Mr. Vice President, Mrs. Miller, honored senators, honored representatives, ladies and gentlemen, we now stand on the
threshold of a new age. I have been a guest in your capital for the last several days, and my imagination has been stirred by the imaginative propos-
als I've heard your leaders expressing. We are all citizens of the world; we
all belong to a global community. The Millennium Project is but a tool that
will break down the last barriers and unite us. I foresee a strengthened
World Commission with the authority to enforce international environ-
mental laws to guarantee a safe world for our children. I foresee an international court of law with the capability to enforce international
covenants, eradicate terrorism, and ensure basic human rights to all. I foresee a world where each individual is separate and distinct, yet joined with
his fellows in an orchestration/of universal harmony and peace."

"He's quite the optimist, isn't he?" Daniel whispered to Brad. "Who *is*
this guy?"

Brad lifted his shoulder in a slight shrug, then turned his head slightly.
"I don't know how he got clearance, but Romulus must have powerful
friends. Herrick's been in Archer's shadow virtually all week."

"If I may paraphrase your brilliant American scientist Robert Oppen-
heimer, creator of the first successful atomic bomb," Herrick went on, "it is
the open society, the unrestricted access to knowledge, the uninhibited association of men—these are what may make a vast, complex, ever growing,
ever changing, ever more specialized and expert technological world, never-
theless a world of human community." Herrick paused, looking out at his
audience with the soul-searching gaze of a soul-burdened preacher. "And it
is men like Mr. Daniel Prentice who will help us create a true global community. Thank you, Mr. Prentice, for your willingness to share your ideas to

protect us from the Year 2000 Crisis as well as to create innovative solutions. We of the world community thank you for your largesse."

Herrick stepped back and lifted his arms in a flourish, and this time the audience responded to his cue. Applause rang from the insulated walls, and as Daniel raised his hands to join in, he saw that General Herrick was applauding and nodding at *him*.

"I think this one's for you," Brad muttered out the side of his mouth. "Acknowledge the guy, will you, so we can get out of here."

Daniel smiled and nodded slightly, then rose halfway out of his chair and lifted his hand in a half-hearted wave. Clenching his teeth in a smile, he glanced down at Brad. "What does he mean, exactly?"

"I'm not sure," Brad answered, clapping with the others. "But I think he just thanked you for agreeing to work with the European Millennium Project. So act pleased, Daniel, and get it over with."

Biting back an oath, Daniel dropped back into his seat. As the applause died down, he covered his hand with his mouth and leaned toward Brad. "What if I don't *want* to go to Europe?"

"They need you, Daniel. You've said it yourself—if their computers aren't up to speed, our Y2K fixes won't amount to anything." Brad's broad mouth curved in a one-sided smile. "Think of it as an all-expense-paid vacation, Danny, and have a good time. They'll pick your brain, put you up in a fine hotel, and let you talk about computers until your jaw aches. You'll be home in a couple of months, at the latest."

Daniel rested his chin in his hand as the vice president advanced to the lectern and finished with a droning treatise on American technological advancement. The guy was painfully sincere, but his material was about as interesting as an obsolete almanac.

Daniel leaned toward Brad again. "You know, if I go to Europe, I'll need some help. Maybe an assistant."

The corner of Brad's mouth twisted. "Don't you have an assistant?"

"Taylor will be busy in New York. I was thinking more of a political assistant—someone who knows the ins and outs of world politics and pro-tocol. I'm a complete klutz with etiquette, you know that."

Brad lifted one eyebrow, suggesting in shorthand that Daniel get to the point.

"I was wondering—do you think the president could be convinced to let Miss Mitchell come to Europe with me?"

Brad's mouth curved in a wry, knowing smile. "Right now you could ask for just about anything and get it."

Daniel pressed a fingertip over his lips as he considered his options. He had set himself up for a gargantuan task within the United States, but his PT executive team could oversee it. And this General Herrick, no matter what his politics, was right about one thing—Europe would need a Y2K fix like everyone else; and if the American Millennium Project was to be truly successful, the rest of the world would have to come aboard. Any country that did not repair its computer systems with the Millennium Code would be a broken span in the bridge, with the out-of-control train inexorably advancing.

This was his chance to make his mark on human history.

"All right." Daniel kept his voice low and his temper under control. "I want two things: Lauren Mitchell by my side in Europe, and a guarantee that there are no more spooks tapping my phones or spying on my company. Find out who's shadowing me and call them off, Brad. Then I'll go to Europe—and your own people can breathe easier."

Brad's jaw moved sideways, then he nodded in an almost imperceptible movement. "Sounds reasonable to me," he said, standing to applaud the conclusion of the vice president's speech. He glanced down at Daniel. "I'll have to talk to my superiors, but I think you may have yourself a deal."

Satisfied, Daniel stood and joined in the applause.

Thirteen

12:01 A.M., Tuesday, November 17, 1998

THE SHRILL RINGING OF THE BEDSIDE PHONE WOKE AMELIA PRENTICE FROM A sound sleep. A pulse of anxiety spurted through her—middle-of-the-night calls never brought good news—unless it was Daniel calling. That boy kept the strangest hours. . . .

She fumbled in the dark, grasped the receiver, then lifted it to her ear. "Hello?"

"Happy Birthday, Mom!"

Amelia felt her heart race as she held the phone. God bless the boy, and never mind that it was the middle of the night and he'd just scared her half to death. He hadn't forgotten her birthday.

"Daniel, it's good to hear from you! Where are you?" she said, propping up her pillows, then nestling back against them.

"Right now, Mom, I'm on a pay phone in a Washington hotel lobby, so I'm sorry for the noise. But I wanted to catch you before I was officially a day late." He hesitated. "It is still the sixteenth, isn't it?"

Amelia smiled as she glanced at the clock. It just changed to 12:02 A.M., but she'd give him credit for making the effort. "You're so thoughtful, Son. So tell me, what are you doing in Washington? I saw the First Manhattan Bank executive on the news; he certainly was thrilled with what you'd done for him."

"Yeah, he's going to be just fine. Now they want me to do something similar for the government. I was a little reluctant at first, but Brad Hunter talked me into it. You remember Brad?"

"Of course." How could she forget the young man who had saved Daniel's life? After their mission in Desert Storm, she had flown up to Washington and spent a week praying by the bedsides of both young men.

But Daniel wouldn't want to be reminded of how close he'd come to eternity.

"Well," she said, smoothing a wrinkle in the blanket over her lap, "can you tell me what this government project is about? Will I be seeing your picture on a dollar bill anytime soon?"

Daniel laughed, and Amelia's spirits lifted at the sound. "I wouldn't think so, Mom. But you may hear about our project soon enough. We're implementing a national computer network to streamline operations. Everyone in the country will have a personal identification chip, and we figure the United States will be a completely cash-free society by the year 2000. Did you know that Finland has been cashless for months? And the Canadians have taken to debit cards like ducks to water. It really is time for us to put technology to work like the rest of the world."

"An identification chip?" Amelia felt a tremor, a disturbing quake in her serenity. "How would that work, Daniel?"

"It'll be simple, Mom." His tone was carefree and breezy. "You'll just get a tiny little PID in your right hand. It will contain your personal identification number, medical history, financial records, and digital renderings of your DNA sequence, and voice- and thumbprints. It's just one aspect of what we're calling the Millennium Project."

The darkness around Amelia seemed to grow cold. "The Millennium Project?" To her dismay, her voice broke slightly.

Daniel seemed not to notice her uneasiness. "Yes. Believe it or not, the government is sending me to Europe for a few weeks. I don't really want to take time away from my own work, but leaders over there have been keen on this idea of a computerized society ever since they began discussions about a unified Europe. So it's only natural that they'd be interested in how we solve our year-2000 problems."

Amelia felt a cold, thin blade of foreboding slice into her heart as Daniel rambled on. Europe—the old Roman Empire. A worldwide system. And her son in the thick of it.

She took a deep breath and felt bands of tightness in her chest. "Honey, I wish you wouldn't go."

"Why?" Genuine surprise laced his voice. "I thought you'd be proud. Your son helping to save the world, and all that."

"You can do lots of things, Daniel, but I'm afraid you can't save the world. Something bad—something *evil*—is going to come of this, and I don't want you to be in the middle of it."

"Now, Mother." She heard the determination in his soft voice. This was the voice he'd used when she had protested against moving to Florida, when he had insisted that she have household help, and when he'd told her he was going to start his own company instead of working for someone else. When Daniel spoke in that tone, she knew she couldn't win.

"Why are you doing this, Son?"

She could almost see him shrug. "I got involved because I owed Brad a big favor. And I'm still involved because—well, this should please you. I've met a most interesting woman on the president's staff. I think you'd like her."

Oh no, she wasn't going to rise to *that* particular bait. Daniel thought he could distract her by insinuating that he might be thinking about settling down, but he'd waltzed down that particular aisle too many times. And if he was involved in what Amelia feared, marriage was the last thing he should be considering.

She decided to switch tactics. "Daniel, do you still have that box of your father's books?"

He hesitated. "Um, yeah. I think it's in the back of my closet."

"Promise me something."

"Now, Mom—"

"Just this one little thing. When you get back to New York, promise me that you'll look through your father's books. He was a great student, your father, and I know he filled those books with all sorts of personal notes. I think he'd want you to read them now."

He answered with a marked lack of enthusiasm. "Okay."

"Promise me, Daniel!"

"I promise." He paused a moment, then asked, "Did you get the flowers?"

"Yes. And they were very nice. But they won't mean a thing unless you keep your promise to me."

She heard him sigh heavily. "I promise I'll look through the books. As soon as I find some free time."

"And when will that be?"

"Maybe next week. I have to spend some time at the company and get ready for the European trip, but I think everything's under control."

"That's good, Son." There was less darkness in the darkness now, and Amelia relaxed against her pillow. "Be careful. There are spiritual battles raging all around you, wars you aren't even aware of. The Bible warns us that 'our struggle is not against flesh and blood, but against the rulers, against the authorities, against the powers of this dark world and spiritual forces of evil in the heavenly realms.'"

Daniel did not answer, and Amelia knew he was staring off into the distance, probably searching for a polite way to tell her to get a grip on her imagination and go back to sleep.

She'd make it easy for him. "Good night, Son. I love you—please be careful."

-0100111100-

"Who's waiting, Lauren?" The president looked up from his desk, where he was busily signing letters of appreciation to the cabinet members who had put in extra long hours last week.

Lauren checked the peephole in the curved door. Adam Archer and Kord Herrick, the European Union representative, waited outside the Oval Office with stony expressions, probably miffed at the delay.

"Generals Archer and Herrick are outside," she said, glancing over at the president. "And after this meeting you have a lunch appointment with the vice president. He wants to discuss details of the new antismoking campaign."

"Who'd have ever thought that a North Carolinian would be talking about the dangers of tobacco?" The president grinned up at her, then stood and stretched. "I'm going to excuse myself for a moment, Lauren, so why don't you show the generals in. And see if Eddie can rustle up some tea and coffee—if they start talking about computer codes again, I'm liable to need some caffeine."

As the president sauntered off down the hallway that led to his private study, Lauren opened the door into the secretary's office, then nodded to Archer and Herrick. "Gentlemen, please come in." Both men rose and followed her with stiff, military dignity, then paused in the empty space between the chairs before the president's desk and the more relaxed seating arrangement in front of the fireplace.

"I'm going to see about bringing in some coffee," she said, smiling as she gestured toward the comfortable sofas. "If you two would sit and relax, the president will be with you shortly."

Leaving the men to make their own conversation, she hurried down the hallway that led into the private dining room. Eddie Kasper, the steward, was clearing away the remains of the president's breakfast. She asked him for tea and coffee, then nodded when he promised to deliver it immediately.

Lauren paused in the hallway outside the larger space of the Oval Office. The two generals were whispering, and she felt a jolt when she heard one of them mention Daniel Prentice.

A smile ruffled her mouth. If Daniel Prentice wasn't motivated by money, perhaps he craved fame or influence. He would probably be very happy to know that his name was being bandied about in the Oval Office. Maybe she ought to invite him for dinner, just to sound him out and examine his motivations. She could express her appreciation for all he had done to help with the president's Millennium Project and possibly make up for the abrupt way in which she'd brushed him off last weekend. All in the name of business, of course.

Lifting her chin, Lauren walked through the room, inquired after the generals' comfort, then moved out through the secretary's office toward the warren that housed her own private domain.

-0100111100-

"Oh, bother!" Lauren rushed to the stove as the pot of spaghetti noodles filled with white frothy bubbles and threatened to spill over. She turned down the heat and held her breath as the bubbles gradually receded, then she checked her watch. Daniel Prentice was officially late. He'd promised to come for dinner at seven o'clock, and her watch told her it was one minute past. So, Superman had a flaw after all.

She grimaced as the doorbell rang. Okay, maybe her watch was fast. She moved toward the door, checked her reflection in the foyer mirror, then looked through the peephole. Daniel Prentice stood on her front porch, his arms brimming with flowers.

She was still gaping when she opened the door.

"Too much?" Daniel held the bouquet of roses and daisies at arms' length and gazed at it skeptically. "I wasn't sure what kind of statement I wanted to make."

With an effort, Lauren smoothed her expression and offered him a smile. "It's perfect." She gathered the flowers into her arms and breathed deeply of the scent of roses. "My two favorite flowers—how did you know?"

"I read it in your Millennium Code."

She looked up, startled, and saw Daniel smiling at her. "That's a joke. Actually, I just guessed. You seemed like the kind of girl who might like daisies in the morning and roses at night."

Lauren stepped back to let him in, a little unsettled by the feelings he evoked. She met all sorts of men in her work—most of them powerful, many of them rich, more than a few hungry for feminine attention. But she had never yearned to see any of them outside the office, and she had never invited any of them to her Georgetown townhouse. But though Daniel Prentice interested her, this was still business. His work in Washington would be finished soon, and he would be going back to New York.

"I just want you to know," she stammered, feeling like a star-struck schoolgirl, "that you're the first man I've invited to dinner in . . . well, years. First of all, I don't cook. And second, I don't like to mix business with pleasure."

Daniel gave her a lopsided smile. "Sounds like the story of my life. I don't cook, either. And I rarely do anything outside of the business. So I guess we were cut from the same bolt of cloth."

"Apparently." Lauren closed the door, then led the way into the kitchen. "Let me put these in some water. How nice that they're fresh-cut! Most guys would have picked up an arrangement already in a vase."

She gestured for Daniel to take a seat on a stool at the kitchen bar, then opened a cupboard and rummaged for a vase.

"I thought you'd prefer them this way," he said. "You seem to have a gift for arranging things."

Lauren laughed in appreciation of his wit. "In my job, you have to." Giving up on the vase, she pulled the empty spaghetti sauce jar from the trash and rinsed it under the sink.

"I'll find a vase later." She looked away, hoping to hide the flush that burned her cheeks. "This may not be very elegant, but it'll keep the flowers from dying of thirst."

"Very creative."

Daniel grinned as she haphazardly arranged the flowers in the jar. "I must say, Miss Mitchell, your invitation really caught me by surprise. I had planned to spend the night working and sampling the wonders of room service, but since you asked—well, a home-cooked meal beats hotel food any day."

She shrugged and thrust another long-stemmed rose into the arrangement. "I hope you don't mind plain old spaghetti. It's not very fancy, but I've made a salad and used my mom's recipe for salad dressing. It's a lot better than anything I've ever bought in a jar."

"I'm sure it will be delicious. By the way, how'd you do at the dog show?"

"We did great." Lauren put the last of the flowers into the jar, then flashed him a triumphant smile. "Tasha took best of breed, and reserve in the best of show. She's beautiful. I finished her before she was a year old, and next year I'm hoping to breed her."

"If she's finished," confusion filled Daniel's dark eyes, "then why are you still showing her?"

"*Finished* means that she's already earned her championship," Lauren said, moving toward the stove. "But she can still compete. I'm thinking about taking her to Westminster next February, and all the dogs entered there are champions. But I also want to breed her, and that means I have to find the right male dog—"

"Um," Daniel interrupted, a rich blush staining his throat as he looked around, "where is the little whippersnapper? I'd love to meet her."

Lauren choked back a laugh. She'd forgotten that not everyone found the breeding and training of dogs as fascinating as she did. "Tasha's at the trainer's house," she explained, pulling two potholders from a drawer near the stove. "I keep such crazy hours, it's not fair for me to keep her crated in the house while I'm at work. So she spends the week with the girl who helps me train her. I get her every weekend, though, and we spend every moment together."

"So—she's used to being away from you? And if you had to, say, take an extended trip, you'd have someone to take care of the dog?"

His lids came swiftly down over his eyes, and Lauren hesitated at the stove, a little perturbed by the personal question and the sudden change in his manner. Moving slowly, she dumped the pasta into a colander in the sink, then set the empty pot back on the stove.

Crossing her arms, she leaned against the counter and fixed him in an unrelenting stare. "What's up, Daniel?"

His brown eyes lifted. "What? Who said anything was up?"

"Part of my job is reading people, and I'm pretty good at it. You're hiding something, so you may as well get it out now. Because if you've some kind of bombshell to explode for me, I'd rather you didn't drop it in the middle of dinner."

He gave her a bright-eyed glance, filled with shrewdness. "You *are* good. Does Stedman pay you enough? Maybe you'd like to come to work for Prentice Technologies."

"I work for love, not money. And don't try to change the subject. I really *hate* that."

"Okay." He sighed in pretended exasperation, then looked up and met her gaze. "How attached are you to the Stedmans?"

"Very, but why do you ask?"

"Because I think you're going to be, um, transferred for a couple of months. You'd still be working for the president, but you'd be working in Europe as my advisor and the president's unofficial ambassador to the European Union for the duration of this trip."

Totally baffled, Lauren stared at him. Since when did Daniel Prentice tell her what her job would be? What kind of authority did he think he had, and who had given him the idea that he had any control over her life or job?

Her lower lip trembled as she returned his stare. "What are you talking about?"

A faint line appeared between his brows as he felt his way through the conversation. "As you probably know, I've been asked to go to Europe for a few weeks; they want me to introduce the Millennium Project to the European Union. I was honored by the invitation, of course, but the thought of two months in Europe with only a team of security guys for company is not my idea of fun. And you've seen my presentations—I'm not exactly the most diplomatic person in the world. I need help."

His brown eyes softened, as did his voice. "I said I'd go, but only if you could go with me."

Lauren snapped her mouth shut, stunned by his bluntness. He wanted her with him? As *what?*

A surge of white-hot anger caught her by surprise. She felt half-choked with it but clamped it down, steeling herself to maintain her dignity and her composure. "I don't know what you think I am, Mr. Prentice," she said, her words as cool and clear as ice water, "but I am not at your command. If you think the White House will send me to Europe with you like some kind of glorified escort, you're more misinformed than I would have believed possible."

Daniel lifted his hands. "It's not like that at all."

"Isn't it?" She pulled herself off the kitchen counter and swallowed a hysterical surge of angry laughter. "Good grief! Just when I thought America was finally beginning to recognize the achievements of women! I meet you, I like you, and I think you appreciate and respect me. Then you come up with this idiotic plan! No, Daniel Prentice, I will not go to Europe as your bimbo!"

"Lauren." He leaned over the bar and reached for her hand, which she angrily snatched away.

"Don't you dare touch me!"

"Have I ever?"

Her heart was hammering, her breathing came in ragged gasps, but something in his words stemmed the anger and alarm rippling along her spine.

"Lauren, listen to me. I want you to go to Europe with me because I *do* respect you. You've seen me—sometimes I come across like a cocky smart aleck, and I need someone with political experience and enough charm to keep the critics at bay. I've spoken to Brad Hunter, who thinks this is a great opportunity for you to act as a representative for the president and first lady. The media knows about your close relationship with the Stedmans— why not take advantage of it? You can accept some of those European invitations the first lady hasn't the time to accept. You can play Lady Bountiful, cut ribbons, collect bouquets, and visit hospitals, all in the name of Victoria Stedman. The American Heart Association is one of her pet projects, isn't it?"

Lauren ran her hand through her hair in frustration, amazed that she was still listening to the man. "Yes."

"Then take advantage of the opportunity. Contact similar organizations in Europe and arrange to speak to them on the first lady's behalf. Brad Hunter and General Archer are going to present this idea to the president and first lady tomorrow, and we think they'll approve. But I wanted to talk to you first—" he sent her an irresistibly devastating grin—"to prevent this little scene from happening in public."

Lauren moved away and leaned against the far end of the counter, purposely lowering her eyes. He was right about the opportunity. Mrs. Stedman received close to two hundred invitations a month from around the world; she simply couldn't accept all of them. And cardiac research was particularly important to her. If there were any cardiac hospitals in Europe that might benefit by her endorsement, Victoria would see this as a heaven-sent opportunity.

"Where are you going in Europe?"

"Brussels."

Lauren bit her lip and crossed her arms. She should have known. Brussels was considered the capital of the European Union, and any speech she gave there on behalf of the first lady would reach millions of people. And though she hated to admit it, the thought of leaving her tiny office *was* appealing.

She looked up and met Daniel's eyes. "Excuse me for asking," she kept her voice dry, "but are we agreed that this trip is completely platonic? We will travel as two professionals, sleep in separate hotel rooms, and maintain two separate itineraries?"

Daniel held up his hands again. "Except for the occasions when I'll need you to charm some of those feisty council ministers, you'll be completely on your own. You arrange your trip, I'll arrange mine—or I expect someone at the White House or State Department will arrange it for me." His tight expression relaxed into a smile. "Though I hope you won't object to having dinner with me at least once or twice."

Lauren tilted her head and considered him in the light of this new information. A woman could do much worse than traveling to Europe with Daniel Prentice, handsome genius millionaire.

Slowly uncrossing her arms, she nodded. "I'll consider it." She turned to lift the colander out of the sink. "But only if the president approves and my schedule allows."

She had the feeling he would respond with some wry—and truthful—comment about her schedule being completely subject to the president's whim, but he only smiled and slipped off his stool. "What can I do to help you?" he asked, moving to the sink. "Can I chop lettuce, butter bread, or set the table? My mother trained me well, you know."

"You can stir the sauce." She poured the steaming spaghetti noodles into a large ceramic bowl, then handed him a wooden spoon and pointed toward the saucepan on the stove. "And try to be careful. I hate a spattered stovetop."

"Yes, ma'am." Humming contentedly, he lifted the lid and began to stir. Lauren watched him, mystified, then slid a plate over the hot noodles to keep them warm while she finished the salad.

She wasn't certain what Daniel Prentice wanted of her, but he had given her no reason to suspect any ulterior motives . . . yet.

-0100111100-

Daniel sank into the overstuffed sofa by the fireplace and watched as fire shadows danced around the walls of the comfortable room. Lauren had lingered in the kitchen to put away leftovers and stack dishes in the dishwasher. Daniel had offered to help, but she'd chased him away, saying he would only disrupt her system if he interfered.

Had he disrupted her life? She had certainly blown a fuse when he mentioned the European trip. Given the fact that this administration worked overtime to avoid even a hint of sexual impropriety, he could understand why she reacted as she did, but he hadn't intended to imply they would be anything more than business associates. He didn't need to enlist a woman just to have an attractive companion on his arm as he strolled the streets of Brussels—money attracted beautiful women by the dozens. But hard experience had taught Daniel that beautiful, brainless women were like sugar—sweet when a man was hungry, sickening when he'd had enough.

Lauren, however, was certainly not brainless. Nor was she as hardened as the female cabinet members who'd spent hours grilling Daniel on everything from the political to the psychological ramifications of the

Millennium Project. Lauren seemed genuinely compassionate when she talked to people in her office and on the phone—and he'd overheard her talking to heads of state as well as welfare widows.

The soft sound of her slippers on the carpet made him look up as she joined him on the sofa and carefully pressed a mug of hot chocolate against his palm. "I took a chance," she said, clasping her own mug with both hands. "My mother used to say there's nothing better than hot chocolate on a cold night."

Daniel took a sip of the cocoa and resisted the sudden urge to slip his arm around her shoulders. In light of their earlier conversation, touching her might not be a good idea.

He sighed in appreciation of the sweet cocoa, then gave her a smile. "It's delicious." He studied her face. "Does your mother live nearby?"

Dewy moisture filled her expressive blue eyes. "No. She used to live in Raleigh, but she died just before I began working for Sam Stedman. Heart attack."

"Your father?"

Her lips parted in an expression that was not a smile. "Who knows? He left us when I was nine, and I've never once heard from him. We went from middle class to welfare, from a nice house in the suburbs to a housing project. But I don't regret it, not really. I learned how to be tough, how to survive. And when I tell people that I know how frustrated they are with governmental red tape, they believe me."

Caught up in a wave of sympathy, Daniel looked toward the fire. She wouldn't want his pity any more than he wanted hers. But it was comforting to know they had something besides politics in common.

"I lost my dad, too." His voice sounded flat to his own ears. "In Vietnam. He was a navy pilot. He died because some pompous general wanted to impress a visiting congressman."

When he looked over at her, surprise had siphoned the blood from her face. "I would think that you would hate the military."

He grunted in response. "Part of me does."

"So why are you here . . . helping the government?"

Her gaze was as soft as a caress, and Daniel steeled himself against her irresistible aura of femininity. Thinking of the impending trip, he figured he had better retreat than make an ill-advised advance. "I'm here," he said, "because you invited me for a spaghetti dinner. And unless you have another round of pasta waiting in the kitchen," his eyes wandered to her lips, then darted away, "I think I'd better go."

Was that disappointment in her eyes? Whatever the emotion, it faded as she looked away and reached out to place her mug on the coffee table. "Of course. You probably have work to do tonight."

"Sure." He didn't really, but he'd think of something to do. Maybe he'd jog up and down New York Avenue. The way his pulse was pounding, he could certainly take any mugger foolish enough to accost him.

She stood and held out her hand. "Let me take your mug. Do you remember where we left your coat?"

He handed her the mug and stood as she walked quickly to the kitchen. His coat was on the hall tree in the foyer, and he went to get it, regretting this clumsy departure. The good thing about mindless beauties was that they didn't care if you made a less-than-graceful exit from their lives. But this woman, Daniel suspected, cared very much.

He was shrugging his way into his coat when she met him in the foyer. "Thank you very much for dinner," he said stiffly, feeling like a sixteen-year-old on his first date. "It was delicious."

"It was nothing."

She lowered her head, and Daniel reached out to catch her chin with his fingertips. Cupping her chin, he searched her upturned face. "It was wonderful, and I thank you. I'd kiss you on the cheek, but I would hate to do anything to jeopardize your coming to Europe with me." She smiled, and he took that as a good sign. "And I do want you to come, Lauren. I think it would be good for both of us . . . and who knows? It might be fun."

"Fun?" Feather-like laugh lines crinkled around her eyes. "Heavens, we can't have that. What would the taxpayers think?"

"I don't care." He tapped the side of her cheek, then released her. "I told you, I'm not into politics." He turned and opened the door, then paused on the threshold when he heard her response.

"All right."

"What?" Amazed, he turned to face her. "You'll go?"

"Yes." She crossed her arms and gave him a jaunty smile. "It'll be good for the Stedmans. And I've actually never been out of the country."

Daniel felt his smile broaden in approval. "All right, then." He moved across the porch, then turned again on the steps. "Are you sure? You're not just saying this to make me feel better?"

"No." She leaned against the doorframe, her blonde hair glinting in the porch light. "Now good-night, Daniel. I've got work of my own to do."

Smiling, Daniel turned and walked to his rented car. The holidays in New York wouldn't seem so lonely if he was busy thinking about Europe and the work ahead . . . and Lauren. Of course, he'd have to get through Brad's wedding, Christmas, and New Year's Eve without her.

He unlocked the car and slipped inside, then sat in the driver's seat, paralyzed by a sudden thought—he was behaving as if he had fallen in love with the woman. But it had been so long since he'd had a serious relationship that he wasn't certain if this slightly queasy feeling was infatuation or the aftereffects of an amateur's home-cooked meal.

"Get a grip, Prentice," he murmured, turning the key. "You're just in unfamiliar water, that's all."

The car roared to life, and Daniel backed out of the parking space and thundered away into the night.

FOURTEEN

1:05 P.M., Wednesday, November 18, 1998

ENERGIZED BY A NEW SENSE OF PURPOSE, DANIEL HAD SCRIBBLED NOTES throughout the short jaunt from Washington to New York, then drove directly to his office. Now that the First Manhattan project was practically a done deal, three new challenges faced his company: producing and mass-marketing the Millennium Code so that all mainframes would be year-2000-compliant within thirteen months; designing computer codes for human personal identification devices and a corresponding array of PID scanners; and overseeing the physical production of the Millennium Chips and scanners. Ordinarily he'd have to worry about marketing any new devices, but if Congress passed legislation requiring PIDs by January 1, 2000, marketing was a moot point. Scanners would fly off the shelves as businesses, hospitals, law enforcement agencies, and transportation centers rushed to meet the government's regulations.

Daniel knew his people would rise to the occasion; they had never let him down. But before he called in the other executives, he wanted a few moments with his most trusted associates. He asked Roberta to call his administrative assistant and the professor, then pressed his thumb to his computer keypad and listened to the whir of the hard drive.

"Dr. Kriegel and Mr. Briner are here to see you." Roberta's throaty voice warmed the area around his desk.

"Thank you, Roberta. Allow them to enter, please."

Daniel looked up from his keyboard and flashed a smile as the two men entered the office. "Gentlemen—I trust all is going well?"

"Things are great, Daniel." Taylor dropped into one of the empty chairs before Daniel's desk and pulled a mechanical pencil from behind his ear.

"Things are moving along at a prodigious rate," the professor added, perching on the edge of his chair. He looked around, distracted, then slid slowly back, apparently ill at ease.

"Is something wrong, Professor?" Daniel asked.

Kriegel pushed at his glasses. "No, not really. It's just that this office smells different than mine." He looked over at Taylor. "Do you notice it?"

"Um, Dr. Kriegel—" color rose in Taylor's cheeks—"maybe it's the cat box. Mr. Prentice's office doesn't have one."

"Oh." The professor's eyes widened. "Yes, that could account for it. Very good. Yes, I see." He nodded, then folded his hands in his lap and looked at Daniel. "We're glad you're back. Rather dull around here without you."

"How was Washington?" Taylor's eyes glowed with envy. "How was the White House? You'll have to write up a little something about your trip; everyone wants to know all about it."

"Soon enough." Daniel grinned at his eager assistant. "You'll get full details, I promise, but right now I'd like to talk about something else." Shifting in his chair, he approached the matter that had been bothering him for several days. "Gentlemen, we have a security leak. I don't know how, but not only did the Feds manage to obtain a copy of the Millennium Code, but they tapped my calls the entire time I was in Washington. Roberta caught them whenever I called the office, but I want to know how they did it." He bent his head slightly forward and caught the professor's eye. "I especially want to know who sold them the Millennium Code."

"Oh, dear." The professor went pale. "Surely none of our people—"

"The Feds had a copy of the Millennium Code the morning after you demonstrated it for me, Dr. Kriegel." Daniel leaned back in his chair and dropped his hands to the armrests. "It was running on the network monitors when I arrived. Who ran it through the network? And how did the Feds get a copy?"

Taylor furrowed his brow and tapped his pencil on his thigh. The professor frowned and scratched behind his ear. Daniel felt their frustration; he'd been wrestling with the problem for two days.

Taylor spoke first. "A diskette?" He lifted one brow. "I know we don't have floppies on our computers, but maybe someone brought in a portable zip drive and hooked it in."

"There's an alarm; Roberta would have noticed the new device and reported it," the professor said, shaking his head. "No way could anyone hook into the system. But perhaps someone managed to override the network or the e-mail system. They could have sent the file over a modem. . . ."

Daniel turned to his computer. "Roberta?"

"Yes, Mr. Prentice?"

"Check your records for the twelve hours between 9:00 P.M. on November sixth to 9:00 A.M. November seventh, please."

"Checking, Mr. Prentice. Data is loaded."

"Report any unusual activity, please."

"There are no unusual entries, sir."

"Look for modem transmissions, please."

"No modem transmissions."

"Look for e-mail, please."

"No messages until 6:48 A.M. Forty-four messages between that time and 9:00 A.M."

"Report outbound messages only, please."

"One message, sent 8:05 to Jokeaday at Joke.com."

Daniel shook his head. This was ordinary stuff, nothing unusual. "Report employees present in the building after midnight, November seventh, please."

"One employee present: Dr. Howard Kriegel."

The professor leaned forward. "I slept here that night, I remember. And I left my computer powered on, of course, but I don't remember setting it to run on the network. There were still a few adjustments to be made, and we hadn't even begun to debug the beta version."

"Roberta—" Daniel swiped his hand through his hair in frustration— "report Susan McGuire's arrival time, please."

"You suspect Mrs. McGuire?" Taylor asked, his brow lifting.

"I don't know what to think, but she's new, and she came in late that morning—with me." Daniel pressed his fingertips together. "She could have loaded the program onto the network, gone out to alert a waiting accomplice with some kind of eavesdropping laser, then returned as I was coming in."

Roberta interrupted his thoughts. "On Friday, November seventh, Mrs. Susan McGuire entered at 9:56 A.M."

"Report any earlier entries for Susan McGuire, please."

"No data available in the specified twelve-hour field."

Daniel rubbed the bridge of his nose, simultaneously troubled and relieved. He had hoped that Susan McGuire would prove to be the leak. Though he'd be disappointed to lose one of his people, it'd be a relief to know how his system had been infiltrated. He was beginning to suspect that Roberta was no longer impenetrable. What had Brad said? *You're a genius, Daniel, but you don't have a criminal mind.*

Obviously, a good defense was no match for a cutting-edge offense.

Unless—had Brad lied to him? Perhaps he had learned about the Millennium Code through another source. After all, by the time he told Daniel about the supposed leak several people knew about the program and its success, including Ernest Schocken of First Manhattan. Maybe *his* phones were tapped, and maybe Brad was bluffing about Prentice Technology's vulnerability.

But Schocken hadn't known about Daniel's trip to Canada . . . or exactly when Daniel had first seen the program. And Brad knew both details. And someone had definitely been eavesdropping on his calls from Washington.

"Taylor," he turned to his assistant, "find out everything you can about the latest surveillance systems and wireless interception. I want to know everything going on in this field—legal and illegal."

Taylor clicked his mechanical pencil. "Got it."

"What would you like me to do?" The professor crinkled his nose. "The Millennium Code is running like a dream."

"Professor, I need you to begin a much bigger project. And if you'll permit me to change the subject for a moment, I'll explain it." Daniel pulled a folder of notes from his briefcase, then slid them across the desk toward the professor. "We need to devise a code that will convey the most useful specifics of an individual's life history—medical and financial records, DNA markers, voice- and fingerprints. I need you to sift through all the available data and let me know which will be most feasible to include in a human personal identification chip. I believe we're about to begin the mass production of human PIDs."

"A government contract?" Taylor's eyes widened. "We got a government contract?"

Daniel returned Taylor's smile in full measure. "It's bigger than that, Taylor. If Congress approves the president's legislation—and it's a certain bet they will, with the year 2000 breathing down their necks—we'll be the senior contractors for the entire nation. And, if all goes well when I travel to Brussels in January, we may very well find ourselves in charge of PIDs for the entire world."

Daniel smiled when both men gaped at him in astonishment.

"But before you breathe a word of this, Taylor, write up a memo guaranteeing triple time for any hourly employees willing to work through weekends, on Thanksgiving, and Christmas Eve. We'll let the hourlies have Christmas Day off, but I'd like to have the Millennium Chip specs ready for production teams by December thirty-first."

"Triple time for those willing to work that night?" Taylor asked, his pencil driving furiously across his notepad.

"No." Daniel looked at the professor and grinned. "Book a band and call a caterer for New Year's Eve. If all goes according to plan, we'll spend that night celebrating with the biggest party Mount Vernon has ever seen."

Fifteen

10:00 P.M., Thursday, December 31, 1998

LAUREN MITCHELL HISSED IN EXASPERATION AS SHE BENT AND YANKED ON THE hem that kept catching on her narrow heel. If she couldn't manage to make it from the taxi to the entrance of Prentice Technologies without snagging her heel on this ridiculously expensive designer dress, how could she expect to get through a gala New Year's Eve party?

"You okay there, Miss Mitchell?" The gray-haired limo driver shifted in the front seat and gave her a look of worried concern.

Lauren slipped her hem free and opened her sequined evening bag. "Yes, fine. I'd like to give you a little something for your trouble—"

The driver waved his hand. "No thank you, ma'am, that's not necessary. Mr. Prentice takes good care of me."

Lauren snapped her bag shut, her embarrassment turning quickly to annoyance. She was behaving more like a country bumpkin than a polished Washington insider. She would feel more together if she'd had more time to prepare for this evening, but Daniel's invitation had come only yesterday . . . and, like a fool, she had accepted.

"One moment, ma'am, and I'll get your door."

As the driver stepped out of the car and circled around to the curbside, Lauren took a deep breath and tried to steady her pounding heart. Some part of her wanted to run back to the Washington sharks and barracudas, where she felt safe. Her boss, her *friend*, was the president of the United States; and though the Washington waters might boil with trouble and turmoil, she lived in the safe shadow of an upright man. But here—this techno-world was Daniel's turf, and Lauren had no idea where she stood with him. Tonight she would be surrounded by his friends and his brilliant employees, few of whom would appreciate or even care about her

Washington connections. Surrounded by bona fide geniuses, she'd probably be babbling like an intimidated ingenue long before midnight.

The chauffeur opened the door, and Lauren took another deep breath and stepped out onto the sidewalk. The headquarters of Prentice Technology rose like a white monument before her, a clean, spare building of gleaming white stone. Double glass doors and a brass marker adorned the entrance. She glanced around, looking for a doorman or security guard, but the driver motioned toward a small box just to the right of the marker.

"Just go there, Miss Mitchell, and lift the lid. Place your thumb into the tiny oval, and—well, it might be easier if I just show you."

"I can manage, thank you." Lauren clutched her purse, then walked forward on legs that suddenly felt as insubstantial as air. Why had she come? She'd been flattered by Daniel's invitation, surprised at the e-mail that flashed across her screen. It was a clever bit of work, animated and enhanced by sound. Maybe it was the old song "Close to You" that did it, or the simple fact that Daniel had written, "Got Brad married off and on his way. Would love to spend New Year's Eve with you in Mount Vernon . . . because *I miss you.*"

Those three little words had been her undoing. Because she had missed him, too.

She lifted the lid of the little box, then hesitantly pressed her thumb to the red oval. She had seen fingerprint scanners before, but how in the world had Daniel managed to snag her thumbprint?

She tucked the question away as the touchpad glowed beneath her thumb. Nothing Daniel did should surprise her. He could have lifted her fingerprints off any object she'd given him, or perhaps he had some sort of arrangement with the FBI. The monstrous bureau computers held more than 100 million sets of fingerprints of anyone who had ever been arrested, applied to adopt a child, enlisted in the military, or applied for a security clearance or a weapons permit. Cab drivers, bus drivers, civil service employees, criminals, and cops. In Washington, it would have been harder to find someone not in the bureau computer than in it.

The gray box beneath her thumb hummed for a moment, then the touchpad flashed green. A pleasant, well-modulated female voice drifted out across the sidewalk. "Good evening, Miss Lauren Mitchell. My sensors indicate that you are not alone."

"No." Lauren absently waved her hand over her shoulder. "The limo driver is here, too."

"Please advance through the front doors, but be advised that the second door will not open unless the individual with you is cleared for admittance." The voice paused, then added, "Mr. Prentice is waiting for you in the auditorium."

The limo driver caught her eye as she turned. "I know the drill," he said, smiling as he moved back to the driver's side of the car. "And I'll take off, seeing as how you won't get in unless I leave."

Lauren forced a smile to her lips. "It appears you are right. But thank you very much for your help."

The man paused outside his door. "You'll be fine, Miss Mitchell," he said, his eyes twinkling with elderly gallantry. "Don't be nervous. Mr. Prentice is a very nice man."

Lauren lifted her chin, mortified by the thought that this man could see how anxious she was. "I'm not the least bit worried." To prove her lie, she pulled on the first door and stepped inside the narrow vestibule between the two glass entrances. A sensor above the inner door glowed red, then flickered green as the limo pulled away. When Lauren pulled on the second silver handle, it opened easily.

She stepped into a carpeted vestibule, as elegant and understated as the building's exterior. A clean-cut white sculpture stood on a black marble dais in a sea of emptiness. There was no reception desk, no sofa or coffee table, no magazines scattered about for waiting clients. Presumably everyone who entered through those double doors knew exactly where to go.

Lauren sighed in relief when a young man in a tuxedo appeared from behind a pillar. "May I take your coat, Miss Mitchell?" he asked, extending his hand.

How did he know her name? As she walked toward him, Lauren was half-tempted to reach out and pinch his arm to make certain Daniel hadn't installed an android to man his coatroom, but the blue eyes that twinkled at her seemed human enough.

"Roberta told me you were coming in." The young man answered her unspoken question as he helped her out of her coat. "And Mr. Prentice asked me to watch for you. He asked me to be certain you were properly greeted and sent upstairs."

Lauren listened with a vague sense of unreality. If Daniel cared so much, why wasn't he down here waiting for her?

"Allow me to show you the way." The young man tossed her coat over his arm, then stepped across the gleaming marble floor to the elevator. He motioned toward the call button. "You'll have to press the button yourself," he said, his tone slightly apologetic. "And just tell Roberta that you'd like the fourth floor. That's where the auditorium is located."

"I feel like Alice in Wonderland," Lauren whispered, half-laughing as she reached out and pressed the call button. "Everything in this place ought to be labeled 'press me.'"

The pleasant female voice Lauren had heard earlier floated from a brass-plated speaker. "Good evening, Miss Mitchell. Welcome to Prentice Technologies."

Winging a smile toward the helpful young man who had taken her coat, Lauren stepped into the elevator and bit her lip as the doors glided closed. Again, the robot—or whatever it was—spoke. "Where would you like to go?"

"The fourth floor." Lauren tilted her head, waiting for the familiar hum and whir of an elevator, but heard nothing. She marveled, wondering how Daniel had managed to invent a silent elevator. Then she realized the car had not moved.

"That is an inappropriate response." The voice sounded slightly chiding. "Miss Mitchell, where would you like to go?"

"The fourth floor," Lauren repeated. "The auditorium. Wherever Mr. Prentice is."

"That is an inappropriate response." No doubt about it, irritation definitely laced the intrusive voice. "Miss Mitchell, where would you like to go?"

Lauren moved to the doors and slid her hands over the brass walls, hoping for some hidden control panel, for some button to bypass the voice-controlled system. But there were no controls on the inside of the car, no phone, nothing whatever of use.

"That is an inappropriate response," the computer repeated. "You will be returned to the main foyer unless you respond correctly within thirty seconds. Where would you like to go?"

Sighing, Lauren sank to the back wall and felt the cold brass through the sheer fabric of her dress. "The auditorium," she murmured, no longer caring if she reached Daniel or not. "Anywhere. Just get me out of here. Please."

At once the elevator began a swift ascent, and the doors slid open a moment later. Puzzled, Lauren stepped out into a carpeted hall and spied a pair of wide doors across the hallway. Under the word *Auditorium* was another touchpad.

"Touch me," she murmured wearily, moving forward to press her thumb to the pad.

To her surprise, the doors swung open instantly. She caught her breath, gripped her purse, and then glided inside. Several knots of people, many of them dressed quite casually for New Year's Eve in New York, milled around with fluted glasses in their hands. One man, an elderly fellow in a white lab coat, squinted up at a much taller lady who seemed intent upon lecturing him in a technical language Lauren didn't understand. She moved to the wall and slowly surveyed the room from right to left. She saw no sign of Daniel.

Lauren turned toward the door, her heart sinking. She had been wrong to come, and she'd only make a fool of herself if she remained. Daniel Prentice was brilliant and delightful, but this techno-wonderland left Lauren feeling as helpless as a kitten up a tree. Her work involved people and politics, not machines and mathematics. These people probably solved technical equations in their sleep, while Lauren wondered if she and her computer had confused the master/servant relationship every time her desktop flashed an error message.

She lifted her chin, determined to make a quick and inconspicuous exit, but then a long-haired young man in a tweed coat hurried toward her, managing to spill his coffee down the front of his white shirt as he approached.

"Wait, Miss Mitchell! Good grief—I mean, good evening." Holding a Styrofoam cup with one hand, the young man swiped at his stained shirt with the other, then fumbled in his trousers pocket—for a handkerchief, Lauren hoped. "I'm Taylor Briner," he said, looking at her with a chagrined expression. "Mr. Prentice's administrative assistant. And I've been dying to meet you. I'm a real fan."

Since a handshake seemed out of the question, Lauren smiled. "Thank you, I think. I was supposed to meet Mr. Prentice here."

"Yes, he's expecting you." A handkerchief appeared from Taylor's pocket, and the young man absently wiped his shirt as he explained. "He was called away for a moment, though—some problem with one of the mainframes running a sample Millennium Chip code—but he told me to keep an eye out for you."

"Well, I must thank you." Lauren gave him a pleasant smile, then looked away. She shouldn't have come. She was overdressed, overanxious, and over-wrought. She would have had a much more festive holiday if she'd stayed in her townhouse and curled up with a nice novel and Tasha by her side.

"Come on." The young man tossed his coffee cup into a nearby waste-basket, then gallantly took her arm. Too surprised to object, Lauren let him pull her out of the auditorium and down another corridor. In a moment they stood outside an impressive looking pair of carved oak doors. Her skittish abductor pressed the security button and announced, "Taylor Briner and Miss Mitchell to see Mr. Prentice, please."

"Thank you, Mr. Briner."

The domineering biddy who controlled the doors didn't give *him* any lip. The lock clicked, and Taylor pulled the door open, then ushered Lauren into a wide, spacious office. A huge semicircular desk, the obvious center of power, dominated the office, but the overall effect was airy and pleasant. Amber-colored lamps softly lit the space, and warm shadows filled the cor-ners where graceful ficus trees added a splash of color. A matching pair of leather sofas faced each other in a corner, and a series of computer monitors ran along the opposite wall, bathing that part of the room in a soft gray glow.

"Please have a seat." Taylor motioned toward the sofas. "May I get you something to drink?"

Could he manage it without spilling? Lauren cast a pointed look at his stained shirt, then smiled and shook her head. "No, thank you," she said, sinking onto one of the leather sofas. "I'll just wait here."

"He won't be long, I promise." Taylor stood in the center of the room, nervously rocking back and forth on his heels, then snapped his fingers as if he'd had a sudden flash of inspiration. "Let me check on him now. He's probably in the lab, but he won't want to miss you."

Lauren crossed her legs and smothered a smile as he flew from the room. Leaning back on the sofa, she propped her elbow on the supple leather and rested the back of her head on her hand.

What a sucker she was. The man said he missed her, and like a moth to a flame she'd flown to be with him, leaving her dignity and self-respect behind. She could have gone to any of a dozen Washington New Year's Eve parties, any one of which would have done more to advance her career than this last-minute dash to New York. Worse yet, she wouldn't be surprised if Daniel Prentice kept her sitting on this sofa all night. After all, the man had money, success, power, and a room full of eggheads to entertain. Why did he need her?

But he'd said he missed her. And something in Lauren was very, very glad to know she was missed.

-0100111100-

"Lauren!" Daniel felt his spirits lift at the sight of her.

"Mr. Prentice, I presume?" Her lips smiled at him, but a definite trace of annoyance hovered in her eyes. She made no move to rise from the sofa but lifted her hand toward her mouth, deliberately masking a rather obvious yawn.

"I apologize." He reached out and caught her hand, then sank to her side on the couch. "I would have been downstairs to greet you, but something came up in the development lab. I thought it would only take a moment, but time got away from me."

He leaned back to better observe her. Heavens, he'd forgotten how beautiful she was. She had arranged her hair differently tonight—she wore it upswept, away from her face, and it gleamed like gold in the lamplight. She wore a simple black dress that accented her slim figure, and a tantalizing slit ran from the hem to just above her knee. How could any of those stuffed suits in Washington resist her?

Daniel closed his eyes for a moment, feeling slightly drugged by the light, feminine scent that surrounded her. "Dare I say that you've grown more lovely since we've been apart?"

One elegant brow lifted as he opened his eyes. "Have you been taking etiquette lessons, Mr. Prentice? Or do you think flattery will get you off the hook for abandoning me?"

"I said I was sorry." He squeezed her hand. "And I want everyone to meet you. More than that, I want you with me when we make our big announcement at midnight."

"A big announcement?" Despite her cool mien, interest flickered in her blue eyes.

"Yes. Something you'll appreciate."

Standing, he took both her hands and lifted her from the sofa, then paused as they stood close together. He studied the gentle curve of her mouth, the intelligence in her eyes, the graceful strength of her hands. She met his gaze and made no attempt to hide the attraction that leapt like an electric spark between them.

Women were such a wonder. He'd always been aware of Lauren's beauty, but he'd been struck speechless at the wedding when he stood at Brad's side and saw Christine look up at him as if she'd found her fulfillment in Brad's eyes. Brad had been no less moved, promising to love, protect, and cherish the young woman who stood trembling beside him. And in that moment, as he watched two become one, Daniel had realized that something very important had been missing from his own life for far too long.

Now he looked down at Lauren, who trembled slightly, too. Over the past few weeks as he thought about her, he'd come up with a dozen good reasons why they'd make a perfect team, but the feelings that swept through him now had nothing to do with reason.

"Thank you for coming." His voice sounded husky in his own ears. "It means a lot to me."

For once, she did not look away. "Thank you for asking . . . and for showing up. I was beginning to wonder if I should have come."

"Mr. Prentice?"

Roberta's voice jarred him from his thoughts. Daniel turned toward the microphone, irritated by his own creation. "Yes, Roberta?"

"You asked me to remind you of the time. It is eleven o'clock."

"Thank you, Roberta." With a giddy sense of pleasure, Daniel slipped Lauren's hand through his arm. "Shall we go?"

She nodded, and a feeling of pride swept through Daniel as he led her from his office and into the auditorium. As they mingled among employees and spouses and sampled various hors d'oeuvres, Daniel fancied that he knew how a crown prince must feel when introducing his ladylove to the realm. Though everyone received Lauren with graceful smiles, a host of curious eyes followed her as they moved throughout the room. He knew gossiping tongues would wag in the cafeteria tomorrow. His employees' approval, however, was a moot point—by bringing Lauren to this exclusive company gathering, he had indicated to one and all that she was more than a passing fancy. If all went well in the next two months—and if she'd have him—Daniel fully expected to ask Lauren Mitchell to become a permanent part of his life.

When all the introductions had been made, Daniel took Lauren on an abbreviated tour of the complex, then returned her to the auditorium just as the oversized television screens filled with images of Times Square. "Five minutes and counting," a fresh-faced entertainment reporter told the television audience. "The crowd here is jubilant, simply ecstatic, eager to begin this next-to-the-last year of the twentieth century. And just in case you think the year two thousand is the first year of the twenty-first century, here's Adrian Romulus, commission president of the Europoean Union, to explain why it's not."

Daniel crossed his arms as the camera shifted to a man who looked vaguely familiar. The fellow was in his forties, tall, with dark hair and arresting good looks that completely captured the camera's attention. "Well, it's not difficult to understand, Cyndi," he said, brushing his gloved hands together as if he were cold. "After all, if we were counting from one to ten, we'd understand that *ten* was the last item in the first group of ten, not the first item in the next group. So the year 2000 actually ends one millennium, while the year 2001 begins a new one. But we're excited to see a new year arrive, regardless of what number it's wearing."

"That's a wonderful way to explain it," the reporter gushed, her cheeks glowing red on the color monitors. "But I understand that you have a special announcement for us. Would you like to tell us about it?"

"Greetings from your friends across the Atlantic," the man said, giving the camera a professional smile. "My name is Adrian Romulus, and on behalf of the citizens of Europe I'd like to extend a personal wish for a successful new year to each and every soul in the United States. We have wonderful news to share with you—a much-anticipated final peace and unity has come to the troubled Korean peninsula. After long negotiations and five decades of conflict, I'm pleased to announce that peace now permanently reigns over that divided land, and two halves of one people are now permanently united. To the millions of Americans who served in that area, may I offer my heartfelt gratitude!"

Beaming at Romulus, the reporter lifted her hands to applaud his announcement. As the dull thump of her pounding mittens echoed across the airwaves, the lighted ball began to drop and the Times Square crowd roared.

"What a wonderful way to begin 1999!" the reporter crowed. Romulus disappeared from the screen, and the reporter stopped clapping and spoke to the television audience. "Adrian Romulus, for those of you who don't know, is one of Europe's foremost negotiators. We are certain to be hearing more from him in the coming months."

"Ten! Nine! Eight!" The crowd in the Prentice Technologies auditorium took up the chant. "Seven! Six! Five!"

Daniel turned to Lauren and shouted over the noise. "I've heard that name."

"What?"

"Didn't General Herrick tell us he worked for Adrian Romulus?"

"Two! One! Happy New Year!"

Inside the Prentice Technologies auditorium, whistles blew, the nets over the ceiling dropped their cargo of bright balloons, and the band began to play "Auld Lang Syne." Prentice employees who would never think of embracing one another during the year hugged and slapped each other on the back. Taking advantage of the moment, Daniel pulled Lauren to him and kissed her.

It was a quick gesture, a kiss as light and tender as a summer breeze, but it had the desired effect. When they pulled apart, Lauren's eyes were wide with wonder and surprise, her cheeks blazing with color.

Daniel smiled as he shifted his attention back to the television screens. If the kiss had meant nothing to her, she would not have reacted at all.

His employees turned to him as someone lowered the sound on the television monitor. "Speech, boss!" someone shouted, and Daniel squeezed Lauren's arm briefly before ascending to the platform where the band played. He stood there, grinning broadly while his enthusiastic team applauded, then he held up his hand for silence.

"When I was asked to go to Washington a few weeks ago, I'll confess that I was more than a little reluctant." He put one hand in his coat pocket and looked out over the crowd. "After all, we were busy with our own Y2K fix and the First Manhattan project. But as some of you know, the windows of opportunity opened while I was in Washington."

"Tell us!"

"Come on, boss!"

Daniel grinned. "It's no secret anymore, so I might as well tell you. Two days ago, just before breaking from their special Year 2000 emergency session, Congress passed a series of laws guaranteed to keep this country on track into the twenty-first century. First, all computers must be certified before they will be able to connect to any modem, network, or the Internet." Unable to help himself, he grinned. "And the program they'll require to be certified is our own Millennium Code."

Silence hovered over the room for a moment as the full significance of his words took hold.

"Are you saying," Taylor Briner called out, "that you're finally going to make millionaires of us all?"

"What I'm saying," Daniel threw the answer back, "is that if we were a football team, we've just won the Super Bowl. But that's not all. Included in this legislation are two other provisions. One, the United States will become a completely cash-free society by January 1, 2000. Transactions after that will be handled only by debit cards or other forms of electronic transfer. And two, Prentice Technologies has been named senior contractor for the design and production of over 250 million personal identification devices and scanners."

He pressed his hand to his shirt and tried his best to look humble. "Yes, Taylor, you just might be a millionaire before this century ends. Beginning Monday, we will be interviewing to staff new divisions. As we reshuffle our present employees, probably half of you will find yourselves in management positions with new salaries and new responsibilities." As excited whispers vibrated through the room, Daniel lifted his hand and snapped a jaunty salute to his people. "Congratulations, team. This coming year will be the most profitable, most exciting year any of us has ever known."

He stepped down amid a wave of applause, then caught Lauren's arm and escorted her back to his office.

"That was some announcement," she said, gracefully sinking into the sofa. "I didn't know you knew about the special congressional session. The president wanted to keep everything under wraps until he was sure he had the votes."

"I've been spending a lot of time on the phone with General Archer," Daniel answered, sitting next to her. "The Department of Defense helped orchestrate the vote, and he thought it wise to keep me in the loop. Each department represented in the president's cabinet will devote 10 percent of its 1999 budget to Millennium Project development. And by the end of the year, when every person in the United States has been chipped, each department will recover savings amounting to far more than the amount they budgeted. Health and Human Services, for instance, will virtually eliminate fraud in Social Security, Medicare, and Welfare. Illegal aliens will become a part of the past. The black market, illegal drug trade, and money laundering will vanish overnight. Who knows? The tax rate might even fall when everyone begins paying their fair share. Right now officials in the Treasury Department estimate that up to 25 percent of the economy operates underground and is not taxed."

"Amazing." Lauren twisted to face him. "I suppose the Department of the Treasury will begin to phase out paper money almost immediately."

"They're very eager to do so." Daniel leaned forward and slipped his tight shoes off, wiggling his toes to stimulate circulation again. "Do you realize how many crimes are facilitated with cash? Drug runners, smuggling, even those tens and twenties you slip the babysitter and your cleaning lady—all that is unreported income that Uncle Sam can't tax. If you do away with paper money, every transaction will go on the record."

"So how do I pay my cleaning lady?"

"You write a check, of course. Or you sit at your home computer, call up your account, and have the amount transferred from your account to hers via electronic banking. Very simple, economical, and efficient."

"Anything to make life easier."

She murmured the words in a sleepy tone, but Daniel wasn't feeling at all tired. He turned slightly and laced his fingers together as a thought resurfaced in his memory. "I meant to ask you, have you ever met Adrian Romulus? What have you heard about negotiations between North and South Korea?"

Lauren absently raked a stray strand of hair from her forehead. "No, and nothing. I've never met Romulus, and I've only heard bits and pieces about Korea. There was talk last spring about the beginnings of negotiations, but I had no idea they'd advanced so quickly." She dropped her hand to his and tapped it lightly with a manicured fingernail. "That's not really my field. You probably ought to talk to the president's advisor for foreign affairs."

"I might." Daniel hesitated, still wanting to put all the pieces together. "Did Romulus's speech strike you as a little odd?"

"Odd?" She frowned. "What's odd about wishing the world peace in the coming year?"

"Not that." Daniel narrowed his eyes, recalling the memory. "He said he wanted to extend a personal wish for a successful new year to each and every *soul* in the United States." He focused on her eyes. "Doesn't his use of the word *soul* strike you as a bit antiquated? Some scientists will argue that man doesn't even have a soul, while there are theologians today who will swear that even animals and trees do."

"He just sounds like a politician to me." Lauren curled her knees up on the sofa and rested her head on the back cushion. "He didn't want to offend the tree and animal lovers, so, like a wise and considerate diplomat, he included everything. Most people, Daniel, wouldn't give another thought to his choice of words. Sometimes I think you think too much."

Seeing the glint of humor in her eyes, Daniel leaned toward her. "You might be right. Maybe I need someone to distract me."

Her cheeks colored under the heat of his gaze, and for an instant he thought he saw a flicker of desire light her own eyes, but when he reached out to caress her shoulder, she stiffened beneath his touch.

"Daniel." She pulled away. "This has been nice, but I really have to go. I need to be back in Washington tomorrow."

"It already is tomorrow. And it's a holiday."

"I mean Saturday, January second. Mrs. Stedman is hosting a luncheon for heart transplant patients, and I've got to see to the details."

"So why do *you* have to go? Mrs. Stedman has her own staff."

"Yes, but this is special to her. And she's special to me."

His eyes reached into hers, inviting her to stay, but she smiled and shook her head. "Daniel, I told you I'm going with you to Europe as an associate. I'm here tonight as a friend. Let's not confuse the issue with . . . well, you know."

Daniel sighed, torn between pursuing a battle he was fairly sure he could win and waiting for long-term success. If he pushed her now, she might back out of the European trip, and he was counting on the beauty and ambiance of Brussels to tip the scales in his favor.

As usual, his reason bested his passion. "All right. I'll call the pilot and ask him to ready the jet. He'll have you home in a couple of hours." He reached out and pressed his hand to her shoulder. "Sure I can't convince you to stay? We could just sit here and talk—"

"And I'd be a zombie on Saturday. I also have a thousand details to work out for my European trip."

He squeezed her shoulder lightly. "I'm looking forward to it."

Her mouth curved in a wry half-smile. "I hate to admit it, but so am I."

Daniel laughed, then stood, and slipped into his shoes. "Come on, Miss Mitchell," he said, turning to help her up. "Let me get you to the airport so you can go home and get some rest."

"By the way," she said, obediently following, "you haven't said much about Brad Hunter's wedding."

"It was beautiful." Daniel opened the door and let her precede him into the hall. "Christine made a lovely bride, and Brad wasn't as nervous as I thought he'd be. But he did break out in a cold sweat when he thought I'd lost the wedding ring."

"I'll bet his bride won't appreciate him leaving her at home so soon after the wedding."

Daniel closed the door and stopped in mid-step, looking at Lauren with surprise. "Is he going somewhere?"

Lauren nodded. "Didn't he tell you? He's going with us to Brussels as part of the security detail. General Archer arranged everything."

"That's funny, Brad didn't mention it." Daniel patted his pocket for the reassuring jingle of his car keys, then took Lauren's hand and led her toward the elevator. "Then again, I suspect he had other things on his mind. The wedding, you know."

"Of course." Lauren smiled. "Weddings do tend to take your mind off work. That's why I've always avoided planning one of my own."

"Really?" Daniel released her hand and smiled as he summoned the elevator. "That's odd. Until recently, I felt the same way."

Sixteen

4:34 P.M., Friday, January 22, 1999

THREE WEEKS LATER, ON A FRIDAY AFTERNOON, DANIEL STOOD IN A LINE OF passengers at Ronald Reagan Airport and mentally reviewed his task list. Lauren stood in front of him, her briefcase in one hand and a satchel-sized shoulder bag in the other, and he'd already found himself distracted by the mere sight and sound of her. He hadn't seen her since New Year's Eve, and though she was never far from his thoughts, he'd been grateful that she had remained in Washington to make her own arrangements for Brussels. They had exchanged a few e-mails and a couple of friendly phone calls, but each had made a determined effort to concentrate on business and the upcoming trip.

Daniel had spent far more time talking to General Archer and other Washington advisers. The campaign to educate the public about the value of Millennium Chips would begin on Valentine's Day. Officials from the National Endowment for the Arts had already begun to shoot a commercial. Daniel read a copy of the script—the whimsical sixty-second ad featured a leading TV star who takes an attractive woman to a post office where they are both to receive their microchips. The man's chip is inserted by the injector, but as the postal employee searches for the woman's registration card, the man takes her hand, looks deeply into her eyes, and says, "Would you mind changing her name before you do that?" The woman squeals and kisses him, the postal employee grins, and the happy scene fades to black.

Other commercials would air in the months from February through July, reminding people to stop in at their post offices and banks to leave thumb- and voiceprints, sign releases to permit the encoding of their financial records, and exchange any cash for credits. Microchipping would officially begin on the Fourth of July, General Archer told Daniel, giving the government six months to assimilate each individual's records from various computer files and transfer them into binary code. While the government labored to gather information, Daniel and his people would work to assemble the code into a useable format and oversee chip production through several subcontractors throughout the nation.

The final public service announcement, which would begin airing on July 4 and would run until the end of the year, featured a couple at an Independence Day fireworks display. As rockets sputter and trail streamers of light in the velvet sky, the husband dreamily looks at the wife and says, "You know what this Fourth of July will mean to me? True freedom. Freedom from the hassles of cash, of long lines at the grocery store, of all that paperwork every time we go to the doctor's office. Now, because of the president's Millennium Project, we are truly free."

They move closer, as if for a kiss, then the woman's mouth quirks in a smile. "Do you think we'll still have to stand in long lines at amusement parks?"

"One world crisis at a time, darling," the man answers, slipping his arm around her. "Just give us a little more time."

The underlying message, of course, was that the Millennium Chip would turn major frustrations into simple conveniences. Daniel had to admit that the president's cabinet members had done an admirable job of keeping their promises to help him implement the program.

The employees of Prentice Technologies had risen to the challenge, too, and Daniel's dreams were well on their way to becoming reality. New staff had been hired for the purpose of forming a Millennium Chip oversight committee that would sublicense other contractors for PID production and distribution. Dr. Kriegel and his team had managed to condense several critical areas of information to minuscule sections of code. The unchangeable data—an individual's birth date, Social Security number, blood type, voice- and thumbprints, DNA sequence, and birth certificate information had been condensed into a single line that would serve as the basis of the Millennium Chip code. Other information, such as bank account numbers, name, and health records, could be added to the chip at implementation time and updated as often as necessary.

Daniel's purpose for going to Brussels, he reminded his staff before he left New York, was to educate European leaders about the necessity of the Millennium Code fix for noncompliant mainframes, to urge them to consider the advantages of microchipping their populations, and to promote the services of Prentice Technologies—though not necessarily in that order. General Archer had assured Daniel that General Herrick had already prepared the European Union Council of Ministers for the changes that would have to be made in order to prepare for the Y2K Crisis, but Daniel would have to convince them to use the Millennium Code and the same Millennium Chip the Americans were using. If he could win them over, more than half of the world's economy would operate on Daniel's system. And other nations, if they wanted to trade or communicate at all, would have to join what would ultimately become a Millennium Network.

"Move over Robert Bemer," Daniel muttered to himself as they clumped down the passenger ramp toward the Boeing 767. "Make way, Bill Gates. I have seen the future and it belongs to—"

"What are you mumbling about?" Lauren turned and flashed a smile over her shoulder. Though Daniel had practically pulled her out of her office, apparently she had left all her misgivings behind. She had fretted about leaving the president and first lady all through the cab ride to the airport, but she seemed relaxed and happy now.

Once she decided to go to Europe, she attacked her empty itinerary like Teddy Roosevelt at Sam Juan Hill. Now meetings and functions and duties jammed her schedule, and she had guiltily confessed that her suitcase bulged with a new wardrobe, too. "I couldn't represent the first family looking like a frump," she told Daniel in the taxi on their way to the airport. "So Mrs. Stedman called in the designers, who donated several suits and gowns, all in the glorious name of free publicity. The new clothes are so pretty I'm almost afraid to wear them."

"Just make sure they're all *American* designers," Daniel warned, grinning. "Or be prepared to suffer the slings and arrows of those who would discredit your bosses."

"Mrs. Stedman thought of that," she had answered, lifting her chin in a flash of defensive spirit. "These clothes are as American as hot dogs and baseball."

Daniel had tried to reach Brad before he left New York, but Brad was either on assignment or purposely ignoring Daniel's phone calls and e-mails.

Brad had seemed like his old self at the wedding, full of jokes, hope for the future, and love for Christine, but Daniel had already seen how that friendliness could disappear behind the dark suit and sunglasses that were *de rigueur* for a government security officer. Though he had sent at least four e-mails and left half a dozen greetings in Brad's voice mail, he'd only received one cryptic e-mailed answer: "Yes, I'll see you in Brussels."

Which meant, Daniel realized, that the two of them might never actually meet. If Daniel and Lauren were under protective surveillance, Brad might spend the entire time squirreled away inside a van on some crowded Belgian street.

Daniel handed his boarding card to a tall, blonde flight attendant, then followed Lauren to their wide first-class seats. She took the window seat and was carefully placing her briefcase in the space in front of her when Daniel put his leather bag on the floor and casually kicked it out of the way.

"Good grief, aren't you worried about your laptop?" Her brow wrinkled, and Daniel had to restrain himself from reaching out to smooth the anxiety from her face.

"Don't worry, I could drop it off the side of a mountain and it would still run." As Lauren fumbled with her seat belt, Daniel settled back into his seat and folded his hands at his waist. The flight attendant paused in the aisle and smiled at him. "Excuse me, *monsieur*. Aren't you—" she snapped her fingers—"it has something to do with computers."

"That's right."

Her smile deepened. She leaned her arm on the seat in front of Daniel, then slid toward the side of the aisle, clearing the way for other boarding passengers. "Daniel Prentice." One hand gently fluffed her soft, platinum-blonde hair. "I read about you in the Brussels newspapers. They say you are coming to help unite the European Union and the United States. They say you are a genius."

From the next seat, Lauren snorted softly.

"Thanks for noticing." Daniel answered her smile with a tentative one of his own. "I wonder, miss—I don't want to be any trouble, but I'm really tired. Do you think you could find me a pillow?"

"Certainly, Mr. Prentice."

Daniel experienced a haunting moment of déjà vu. Except for the slight trace of a French accent, the woman sounded amazingly like Roberta.

The attendant nearly knocked a small child from his mother's arms as she yanked a pillow from an overhead bin, but she was all consideration as she offered it to Daniel. "The lights will dim once we take off," she said, fingering the lace collar of her blouse. "And if you need anything—a blanket, headphones, anything at all—you will ring for me, no? My name is Chantel."

"Thank you, Chantel." Daniel tucked the pillow behind his head, then smiled up at her. "I'll ring if I need anything."

Lauren snorted again once the attendant had moved away. "Honestly, don't you get tired of that?"

"Tired of what?" Daniel gave her a look of wide-eyed innocence. "Helpfulness?"

Lauren screwed her lips into a tight knot. "If that was mere helpfulness, I'm a European princess. That woman is already planning to follow you off the plane and ask you to buy her a drink in Brussels."

"That's not likely." Daniel shifted in his seat, trying to find a comfortable position. "And I'm tired, remember? So you just go ahead with whatever you brought to keep you busy, but let me catch a few winks. It will be morning when we land in Brussels, and I don't intend to wander around all day in a jet-lagged fog."

From behind his closed eyes, Daniel heard her sigh of exasperation, followed by the sounds of papers rustling in her attaché case. She'd undoubtedly spend most of the flight working, and Daniel wanted some quiet time to mentally sort through everything he had left behind. He had taken pains to be sure that things were progressing as planned at the company, and he had even attempted to set his family life in order.

His mother hadn't been happy to hear about his trip. Oh, she had tried to act bright and breezy when he called to say goodbye. She was excited about his opportunities in Brussels and thrilled that his relationship with Lauren Mitchell seemed to be advancing at a slow and steady pace. But then she had asked about that box of his father's books, and Daniel had to truthfully tell her that he'd forgotten to look for it.

In the silence that followed his confession, Daniel felt the heavy weight of guilt drop onto his shoulders. Though it was totally irrational, he felt like an irresponsible boy who couldn't manage to do the one little thing his mother had asked him to do.

She didn't berate him. She didn't accuse or weep or storm in anger, but disappointment dripped from her one-word response: "Oh."

"I'm sorry, Mom." Daniel tried to explain. "When I got back from Washington we were busy negotiating the details of the Millennium Project. Do you realize what an incredible opportunity this is? The president is putting his complete faith in me. This is my opportunity to improve the world."

Hear what I'm saying, Mother. Be proud of me! I finally did it! But he couldn't say what he was thinking. And his mother had no idea how far Daniel's influence had extended in the last two months.

"Honey, there's some important information in those books," she said, reverting to her previous train of thought. "Things you should know. And since you didn't read them, I'll just tell you about the most important thing—the Resurrection. It's coming, Daniel, and it could come at any moment. And right after the Resurrection, when all the Christians are taken up into heaven, the Antichrist will seize power."

"Mom," he whispered with returning impatience, "can't this wait until I get back from Brussels?"

"No, Daniel, it can't." Her clipped, terse tone forbade any other interruptions. "Honey, I've been reading the papers, and I know about this European Union. And the Bible tells us that a world leader is going to come from the revived Roman Empire. He'll be a persuasive, charismatic individual who will charm the world by talking about peace and safety."

Something clicked in Daniel's mind—a New Year's Eve address about peace in Korea. "Are you talking about Adrian Romulus?"

"I wouldn't know. People have been trying to identify the Antichrist since the Lord's ascension into heaven, and I'm not going to hazard a guess. But he is coming, and he will deceive many. He is *evil*, Daniel, and he will come from Europe—and possibly from the organization you're traveling to Brussels to help."

"Well. . . ." Daniel hesitated, casting about for some way out of the uncomfortable conversation. "If all the Christians are going to heaven before this guy hits the scene, then you and I will be gone. So there's nothing to worry about."

"I know I'll be gone." Her voice broke with huskiness. "But will you, Daniel? Following Jesus is more than simply acknowledging him with your intellect. It's personal faith. Trust. The surrender of your life to Jesus Christ."

Daniel drew in a deep breath and swiveled in his office chair. Some part of him wanted to hang up, then to e-mail his mother and apologize for the bad telephone connection, but she wouldn't be fooled.

"Mom, thanks for sharing this with me." He propped the phone on his shoulder, clapped it into place with his chin, and began typing on the computer keyboard. "But I've got a thousand things to finish before I leave. So you take care of yourself, okay, and if you have any problems, either e-mail me directly or call Taylor at the office. One of us will get right back to you."

"Good-bye then, Son," she had said, her voice stifled and unnatural. "I'll be praying that the Lord will guide your footsteps."

Her words came back to Daniel now, and he gripped the armrests of his seat, determined not to let the memory trouble him. The idea of a babysitting, life-directing God was for weak-minded simpletons and wide-eyed dreamers. Jesus Christ had lived and died, the historical record proved that much, and somehow his followers had managed to change the fabric of human existence.

But that was the full extent of it. Through a series of happy genetic happenstances, the divine Creator who designed human engineering and DNA had provided Daniel with an exceptional brain whose resident intellect had managed to find the answers to most of life's perplexing questions. If God wanted Daniel to depend on him, why'd he do such a good job ensuring that Daniel wouldn't need him?

"Ladies and gentlemen, welcome to PanAir flight 3099 to Brussels, Belgium. My name is Chantel, and I'll be the chief flight attendant tonight as we make our way over the Atlantic."

Daniel turned his head toward the window and felt the sun through his closed eyelids. He knew without looking that if he opened his eyes, Chantel would meet his gaze, promising with her smile that if it were up to her, his flight would be nothing but comfortable and pleasant.

Daniel slipped down in his seat and willed himself to sleep.

-0100111100-

"Does your boss want to sleep through the dinner service?"

The flight attendant's stage whisper broke Lauren's concentration. Irritated, she looked up from the folder on her tray table. "Excuse me?"

"Does your boss want—"

"I heard that part—and he's not my boss."

The seductive Chantel pursed her lips. "Sorry. But we'll be serving dinner soon, and I need to know—"

"Dinner?" Daniel's eyes flew open. "Bring it on." He gave the attendant a bleary smile. "Thanks for asking."

"My pleasure, Mr. Prentice." The woman turned and made her way up the aisle with a great deal more hip-swing than was strictly necessary. Lauren pressed her lips together and turned her attention back to her work.

Daniel sighed, then shifted slightly in his seat, bending and unbending his long legs in an attempt to get comfortable. Despite her annoyance with the melodrama being played out at her side, Lauren felt a little sorry for him. If he found first class uncomfortable, how had he ever managed to fly tourist?

Her mouth twisted in a dry, one-sided smile. Maybe he hadn't. Even before he was rich and successful, Daniel Prentice had probably insisted on the best.

"What are you reading?" He had lowered his head closer to her ear, and his voice came over her shoulder.

"Brussels information." She arched her brow and gave him a coy look. "Have you been briefed yet, Mr. Prentice? Or are you planning to swagger into that council meeting and bowl the Europeans over with your New York charm?"

"New York charm? That's an oxymoron, isn't it?" Daniel grinned. "So brief me, advisor. You've got a captive audience."

Struggling to hide her exasperation, Lauren flipped through several pages of her file. "Okay. Let's just start from our arrival, shall we? We'll be landing at Brussels National Airport, located in the suburb of Zaventem."

Daniel began to snore in her ear. She elbowed him sharply.

"Hey!" He laughed and opened his eyes. "All right, I'm sorry. But the airport is a *fait accompli;* don't waste time on it. Tell me something I *need* to know."

Lauren bit her lip. One would think he'd need to know where he was when he got off the plane, but apparently Daniel Prentice knew the world like his own backyard.

"We're staying at the Eurovillage Brussels Hotel," she offered, eyeing him to make certain he wouldn't start snoring again. "It's very near the European Union Council of Ministers Building, where we'll both have several meetings. There's a pool and a health club if you're interested."

"Fine." He leaned on the armrest of her seat and smiled. "Please, continue."

"Driving in the city is not easy. Cars are driven on the right—"

"Thank goodness."

"—and seat belts are required at all times."

"Of course."

"Taxis will not pick up fares on the street, so if you don't use the limo service, you'll have to call ahead and order a cab by phone."

She paused, waiting for some sort of smart remark, but he only smiled when she looked back at him. Nonplused, she kept going. "French, Dutch, and German are the official languages of Belgium, but French is the dominant language in most of Brussels. English is fairly popular, though, and street signs are written in English and French."

"Good. I don't like using an interpreter, though I have a nice one on my computer."

"Let me guess—Roberta?"

His eyes widened. "How'd you know?"

"A lucky guess." She skimmed down her list. "Though the euro became the official currency on January first, many people still use the Belgian franc—it won't be withdrawn until July 2002. Business hours are nine to five, and many offices and shops close for lunch. European Union offices operate with reduced staff during all major holiday periods."

"Typical government." Daniel parked his chin in his palm. "And I'll bet they have more than a dozen major holidays."

"That's not all. If a holiday falls on a Thursday or Tuesday, Belgians take off a Friday or Monday. The practice is called *faire le pont*, that's French for—"

"To build a bridge," Daniel finished. He shrugged at her surprised expression. "I had to take four years of high school French. I grew up in Canada, remember?"

"Then why would you need an interpreter?"

"I can understand it, but I never claimed to be *conversant* in the language."

Lauren ignored him. "Generally, suit and tie are the norm for business meetings, a small umbrella is often useful, and the average January temperature ranges from thirty to forty degrees Fahrenheit. The time there is six hours ahead of Eastern Standard Time."

"I know."

"Pickpockets operate enthusiastically in Brussels, especially on public transport and in department stores. We're warned to stay away from the vicinity of the Gare du Midi-South Station and the areas of Sainte-Josse, Place Sainte-Catherine, and Fontainas."

"It's a shame, isn't it, that so many places named after saints are riddled by crime?"

"Indeed." Lauren skimmed the protocol section of her notes. "Oh—this is important. People are quite formal in Belgium. You must always shake hands when you arrive and when you leave. Even if you are late to a meeting where fifteen people are gathered around a conference table, you should shake hands with all fifteen."

"Sounds like the presidential drill."

Lauren smiled, realizing that he was right. President Stedman did have to shake hands with every person around every table he ever visited. No one could be allowed to feel excluded.

"Belgians do not use first names immediately—you must wait until a Belgian addresses you by yours before using his or her first name. And don't take off your jacket unless your Belgian host has already removed his."

"Anything else?" His voice was slow and drowsy.

"Just one more thing." She shifted in her seat in order to look him in the eye. "The entire country practices the *quart d'heure academique*—the practice of waiting fifteen minutes for a latecomer. So if your friend Chantel is late for her rendezvous with you, you have to wait at least fifteen minutes before you can find another flight attendant."

"There will not be any rendezvous with Chantel or any other Belgian beauty." Daniel let his head fall back to his headrest. "I'm too tired for a romantic liaison."

Lauren closed her file and thrust it back into her briefcase, wondering why she cared what he did. She herself had set the ground rules for this trip—they were two professionals, each intent upon doing a job. And no matter how attracted she might be to Daniel Prentice, she could not consider him as anything more than a friend and occasional escort. President Stedman had another two years remaining in this term and the possibility of yet another term to come. Until he and Victoria were ready to retire, she would not leave Washington.

She turned her head and caught Daniel's eye. "Don't let me stop you. If you see someone you like, by all means, follow your heart—"

His hand abruptly caught hers; his touch sent a shiver of awareness rippling through her. His voice dropped in volume as he leaned closer. "Why would I be interested in Belgian girls when a fascinating American woman is sitting right next to me?"

Lauren tried to throttle the dizzying current racing through her. This was not good. This was a working diplomatic trip, not a lovers' vacation. She was aboard this jet to represent the president and first lady of the United States, not to get all warm and cozy with one of the world's most eligible bachelors.

If she had to act the part of Isabelle Iceberg until they landed on American shores again, so be it.

"I'll thank you to keep your fascinations to yourself." She pointedly removed his left hand from her right. "Remember what you told me back in my apartment. We are professionals, and we will act like professionals . . . at all times."

Daniel sighed heavily, then leaned back into his own seat. "Yes, ma'am."

Seventeen

10:30 A.M., Sunday, January 24, 1999

DANIEL TUGGED AT HIS JACKET ONE FINAL TIME, THEN LIFTED HIS CHIN AND walked into the chamber where the ten major leaders of the European Union's inner circle waited . . . for him. This Sunday meeting was unusual, the aide who greeted him explained, but the Council of Ministers was most anxious to hear how the United States proposed to solve the Y2K computer crisis.

Daniel had a sneaking suspicion that the council members already knew quite a bit about various aspects of the Millennium Project, but he played along and smiled as if spies did not exist and electronic eavesdropping were not an everyday occurrence.

Suffering from jetlag, he had spent his first day in Brussels in his hotel room, and he suspected that Lauren had done the same. This morning she had gone out to address a gathering of European Women Against Heart Disease, and Daniel knew that she had risen early to rehearse her speech. Though she was quite competent in the White House with Sam Stedman's influence firmly behind her, she had confessed on the plane that the thought of making speeches on the president's behalf made her more than a little nervous.

"Look at the audience and remind yourself that they are just people," Daniel had reassured her. "Under their clothes, they have a bellybutton just like you."

The idea had made her laugh, but Daniel found no comfort in the ridiculous thought as the door to the Council of Ministers' chamber opened for him. He stepped inside the cavernous space, glancing up for a moment at a shallow balcony that ran around the curving walls of the chamber—just room enough, he realized, for a TV camera, not for spectators.

Walking with long steps and a bold confidence he didn't feel, he dropped his briefcase into an empty chair, then made his way to the lectern. The representatives of the European Union rose as a collective body as he approached. Remembering Lauren's briefing on the plane, Daniel placed his leather folio on the lectern, then began at one end of the semicircular table and shook hands with each minister. He recognized a few faces and more than a few names but was startled to find himself face-to-face with the man he'd last seen on television during the New Year's Eve party. Adrian Romulus occupied a place of honor at the center of the table, and his dark eyes gleamed with intensity as he clasped Daniel's hand between both of his own.

"A very great pleasure to meet you, Mr. Prentice. I have read a great deal about your accomplishments and look forward to having you on our team." He spoke in perfect, cultured English, his voice a silken whisper in the chamber. "Together, we shall create a one-world community."

His presumption left Daniel fumbling for words. *On our team?* Daniel had agreed to give a presentation in hopes of expanding his corporate empire; he had never promised to join any sort of political crusade.

Daniel pasted on a nonchalant smile. "The honor is mine, Mr. Romulus."

He moved on down the table, saying the right things, smiling politely, though his mind still buzzed with Romulus's words. Daniel had the uneasy feeling that he had stumbled into a sea of shifting tides and treacherous currents. He realized that his knowledge of European politics and agendas was not all it should be—and he might be in over his head.

He'd ask Lauren for a background briefing . . . later. Right now he had to present the Millennium Project and hope that the Council of Ministers would agree to invest a significant part of its huge computer budget to acquire Prentice Technologies' breakthrough Y2K solution.

With protocol duly observed, Daniel moved back to the lectern and opened his folio. From the corner of his eye, he noticed that a handful of observers had slipped into the room and taken seats in a row of empty chairs behind the council table. He recognized Generals Kord Herrick and Adam Archer; both men wore full uniform and fairly gleamed in ornamental splendor. Another man sat with them, a thin fellow with a narrow face and a dark beard.

"Esteemed councilors, ladies and gentlemen," Daniel flashed his smile across the group, "let me begin by telling you a very simple, very true story. In March of last year, Marilyn Baxter, a housewife in Warren, Michigan, walked into her local grocery, a small operation called the Produce Palace. There she gathered her purchases, then paid at the register with her new VISA card—one with an expiration date of March 2000."

He looked at Lady Bowes-Lyon, the councilor representing Great Britain. Her arms were casually folded on the table, but her eyes burned with interest.

"When the clerk tried to run Mrs. Baxter's VISA through the verification system, the computer rejected the card. The grocer's expensive computer could not process the year 2000 date, and his computer system froze. The manager of the Produce Palace suddenly found himself unable to use any of his cash registers, even for customers with cash and check purchases. In the end, in order to sell any fruits and vegetables that day, he and his clerks had to pull out an old-fashioned adding machine and systematically total all produce sold. By closing time, the manager estimated that the Millennium Bug had cost him almost two hundred employee hours—time he would have to pay employees to repair the system, reenter the day's charges into the computer, and adjust his inventory. He could not, of course, even estimate the financial loss due to frustrated customers who left and vowed to shop elsewhere."

Daniel regarded the impassive ministers with a level gaze. "Imagine that little scenario on a worldwide scale. Imagine computers that freeze and remain inoperable for a month or more. Imagine every shop, bank, hospital, government agency, and airport without computers for just one day—and now you have a clearer picture of what Saturday, January 1, *next year*, will bring."

The plastic, polite smiles vanished. Lady Bowes-Lyon wore a cold, congested expression, and Adrian Romulus's mouth went tight and grim.

"You, my friends, have a much bigger problem than my associates in the United States. I understand, of course, that your conversion to the euro has required thousands of hours of preparation. Unfortunately, you no longer have thousands of hours in which to prepare for the unavoidable calamity bearing down upon you. The year 2000 will arrive in just 341 days, and you are not prepared."

Daniel thrust his hands behind his back, and when he spoke again, his voice was firm and final. "Fortunately, my company has developed a program that will convert your mainframe software in a matter of hours. It is known as the Millennium Code, and its implications are quite staggering."

Nodding with confident satisfaction, Daniel walked to the chair where he had dropped his briefcase and pulled out a small, handheld scanner, a prototype Dr. Kriegel had developed over what should have been his Christmas vacation. Daniel punched on the power, then handed the device to the British representative.

"Would you be kind enough to hold this for a moment, ma'am?" he asked, sliding the gun-like scanner into her hands.

"Ladies and gentlemen." He strolled before the conference table, his confidence spiraling upward. "I know you have concentrated on converting your computer systems from various European currencies to the euro. I applaud you for your willingness to lay aside petty differences in order to come together as one unified force." He broke into a leisurely smile as he glanced back at General Archer. "After all, my own country consists of fifty states. Two hundred and twenty-three years ago we established a common system of law, of currency, of trade, of government, and subsequently we grew to be a world power. And now we are evolving yet again, ready to take our place in the community of nations . . . in the new millennium."

Dramatically, he raised his right hand and turned toward the British councilor. He stood at the far side of the half-circle now, at least fifteen feet from the woman. "Lady Bowes-Lyon," he called in his most authoritative voice, "would you please point the scanner toward my hand and press the green button?"

Playing her part with aplomb, Lady Bowes-Lyon lifted the device and emphatically pressed the button. In less time than it took Daniel to blink, the monitor behind him filled with an astounding array of shifting images—his digitized photo, his Social Security number, his address, phone numbers, next-of-kin information, even twenty-year-old medical records from Daniel's pediatrician.

Daniel walked to the other side of the table and smiled his thanks at Lady Bowes-Lyon. "This particular information is on a loop purely for the purpose of demonstration," he told his astounded audience as he picked up the scanner. "But I want you to see that the information is not in the monitor, nor is it contained in the scanner. Every bit of this information—up to 5 million bits—is contained within a tiny personal identification device implanted on the back of my right hand."

A flutter of amazement moved through the group, and Daniel held up a finger, predicting their first concern. "The chip will be programmed with all pertinent and necessary information," he said, lifting a brow. "But the scanner will only be able to download specific sectors of that information. For instance—a merchant will want to confirm my identity and that I have sufficient funds in my personal bank account. He does not need to know how much I have tucked away in mutual funds, nor does he need access to my medical records. The scanner he will be issued, then, will only access the information he needs. Everything else will be encrypted so that personal data remains secure."

Lady Bowes-Lyon waved her hand in the air. "This is fascinating, Mr. Prentice, but why should our citizens want to be injected with a foreign object?" She shuddered slightly. "Implantation seems so . . . invasive. Rather like George Orwell's novel *1984*."

Daniel thrust his hands into his pockets and smiled at her. "Vaccinations once seemed invasive—after all, what thinking person would *want* his body injected with a virus? But when we learned that the cowpox virus would naturally protect against smallpox, the walls of resistance fell quickly."

He looked up and let his gaze play over the assembled panel. "My mother, who lives in Florida, told me about an extremely vocal group who protested the state law requiring seat belts." He smiled, recalling that Lauren had told him that Brussels law mandated the use of seat belts, too. "The opponents of the seat belt requirements claimed that government had no right to intrude upon an individual's right to choose whether or not to be belted into a car. But they were wrong, of course. Seat belts save lives. We will never know how many lives have been saved because government dared to act, but thousands undoubtedly owe their lives to the government's foresight."

"Saving a man's life is one thing; tapping into his private financial records is quite another." Adrian Romulus's words carried a unique force; every head turned in his direction. He tapped his fingertips together, then looked at Daniel with a fixed stare. "But I have a feeling, Mr. Prentice, that you will be able to demonstrate how we might convince our citizens that this type of government action is in their best interests. Can we count on you to address us next week with the details?"

"Certainly." Daniel stepped back, pleased that he'd won round one. In round two he'd give them demonstrable specifics that would astound them.

"Very good." Romulus leaned forward and pressed his hands to the armrests of his chair. "Shall we adjourn for lunch?" He cut a quick look toward Daniel. "Mr. Prentice, I'd be honored, of course, if you could dine with me."

"Thank you, I'd enjoy the opportunity."

The ministers stood and huddled in small groups, speaking to each other in hushed whispers and the melodious tones of romance languages. Daniel dropped the scanner and his folio back into his briefcase, then snapped it shut. As he stood apart from the others, waiting for Mr. Romulus, a soft and familiar voice came from behind him.

"Did it go well?"

Daniel turned in surprise. Lauren stood there, elegant and cool in a navy suit, her face aglow with some secret success.

"It went very well. I'm to come back again to explain the next logical steps, of course. And Mr. Romulus has invited me to lunch."

"I know." The corner of Lauren's mouth dipped in a slight frown. "I received an invitation from him at the hotel. I wondered how he knew I'd have the afternoon free."

Daniel glanced back at the man under discussion. Romulus was talking to Lady Bowes-Lyon, his hand cupping her elbow. It was almost certainly an innocent encounter, but if Romulus had looked at and touched Lauren in that way, Daniel would be tempted to take a swing at the man.

"Well," Daniel took Lauren's elbow himself, "let's hope the lunch conversation is more interesting than I was this morning. I scanned the Millennium Chip in my hand for them, and all Lady Bowes-Lyon could say was that the device seemed invasive."

Lauren pulled back, and her blue eyes widened in astonishment. "You've already implanted a Millennium Chip? In your own hand?"

Daniel tugged her forward. "Of course. It's no big deal. The professor had my base code ready last week, and I injected the Millennium Chip this morning. It felt like a mere pin prick."

"Amazing." Lauren shook her head and let Daniel lead her. "You never cease to surprise me."

-0100111100-

They dined in the restaurant of the Stanhope Hotel, a thoroughly charming English establishment situated in an old, patrician house in the heart of Brussels' business district. After thanking Adrian Romulus for the opportunity to join him at lunch, Lauren took a seat at the round table and noticed with some dismay that she was the only woman present. Daniel sat at her right side, which was some comfort, but Romulus seemed intent upon monopolizing his attention.

General Archer, who had always ignored Lauren or treated her as a necessary evil, sat at her left hand. To the general's left was Kord Herrick, who sat next to a stranger introduced as Elijah Reis. Reis sat at Romulus's right hand, and though his eyes flitted uneasily around the table, his attention centered on Romulus's conversation.

There had to be a connection between them, Lauren mused, toying with her salad. In politics and bureaucracy, silent men with roving eyes were usually responsible for security or held some sort of advisory position. Elijah Reis seemed an obvious part of Adrian Romulus's entourage. Judging from the deferential way General Herrick scraped and nodded and twittered at Romulus's pleasantries, he was on the payroll, too.

What about General Archer? Lauren leaned back and studied the general as the waiter came to take her salad plate. Ostensibly Archer was along to provide security for her and Daniel. Security was Brad Hunter's job, too, but she'd seen more of the hotel chambermaid than she had the general or Hunter. If those two didn't take a more obvious approach in their security measures, Lauren thought she might place a call to Washington. Security people who hid themselves usually practiced more spying than guarding, and spying was not supposed to be on the agenda for this trip. From where she sat, Lauren thought Archer seemed far more concerned about Romulus's safety than hers or Daniel's.

Romulus turned to whisper something to Reis, and Daniel took advantage of the silence to toss Lauren a smile. "How was your salad?"

What an inane question—or was it? She looked into his direct and piercing eyes. "Fine," she asked, playing along. "Yours?"

"The dressing was a bit different."

"Everything is different here." She lowered her voice. "And I'm not sure I really like it."

"Perhaps," he answered, covering his mouth with his hand as he leaned toward her, "you don't like being the only woman at the table. I'm sorry, but this has to be somewhat uncomfortable for you."

She swallowed hard, trying not to reveal her irritation. "I'll have you know my gender has nothing to do with it. If I'm uncomfortable, it's not because of the situation . . . only the company."

"Ouch." Daniel straightened and turned to Romulus, who was asking another question about Y2K. Lauren exhaled slowly, allowing her sudden rush of indignation to drain away. Why did she always have to react like a belligerent feminist? Daniel understood her position, and he had always demonstrated respect for her work. She felt her mouth curve in a rueful smile. Worst of all, he was right. She would have felt ten times more comfortable if another woman had been present, even if that woman never even looked Lauren's way.

She bit her lip, closed her eyes, and wished she were more like the first lady. Victoria Stedman would know how to handle this situation. With one smile, that lady would charm the dark-eyed Romulus and his sinister-looking companion and put Lauren completely at ease. On the campaign trail Lauren had watched Mrs. Stedman quiet a rabid throng of pro-abortion demonstrators with a few quiet words, and once a mob of avowed Satanists had disbanded and quietly disappeared from a crowd while Victoria waited to give a speech. The powers of darkness—real or imagined—seemed to dissolve and retreat whenever Victoria Stedman walked into a room.

What would the first lady say to Adrian Romulus?

Lauren opened her eyes, and felt an icy finger touch the base of her spine when she realized Romulus was staring at her. His dark eyes, large and luminous, seemed to shine with understanding, almost as if he knew what she had been thinking . . . and found her uneasiness amusing.

She shuddered faintly and fought down the momentary doubt that twisted her stomach. Why was she torturing herself? She had no reason to be at this luncheon. Romulus must have invited her as a courtesy to Daniel, but she wasn't Daniel's lover or his possession.

She tugged on the sleeve of Daniel's jacket. "Daniel, please make my excuses," she whispered, reaching under her chair for her purse. "I'm feeling a little queasy, and I'd like to go back to the hotel."

She felt the weight of his gaze, concerned and tender. "Should I go with you? Or would you like me to ask General Archer for an escort?"

"No, I'll ask the concierge to call a taxi. Don't worry, I'll be fine."

She was up and away before he could respond, and she was a little surprised when he caught her in the hotel lobby a moment later. "Are you sure you're all right?" he asked, his eyes searching her face. "If you're feeling sick, perhaps I should call for a doctor."

"No." She pressed her hand over his. "Maybe it's just—oh, I don't know, jetlag or something. I'll be fine, Daniel, but you should be careful." She leaned toward him so her words reached his ear alone. "Maybe it's feminine intuition, maybe it's something else. But I don't have a good feeling about any of the men at that table."

His look of concern twisted into an uncertain smile. "Present company excluded, I hope."

Lauren smiled. "You're all right, Daniel." The concierge caught her eye and pointed out the glass doors, where a taxi had just pulled up to the curb. "At least, I think you are. Just be careful to stay that way."

Leaving him alone to consider her words, Lauren hurried through the lobby toward the safety of the cab.

-0100111100-

Daniel returned to the lunch table with Lauren's warning ringing in his ears. The other men accepted his explanation of her hasty departure without comment, and the rest of the luncheon conversation centered on the potential uses and abuses of the Millennium Code and Millennium Chips.

Despite Lauren's warning, Daniel felt complete and confident support from his companions at the table. As the lunch meeting broke up, Adrian Romulus praised Daniel's foresight and ingenuity. "The dawning of a new age will surely reward men with the courage to dream of the unconventional," he said, his voice booming through the restaurant so forcefully that other diners stopped eating to stare. "The unsurpassed explosion of knowledge in the last century will pale in comparison to the coming information boom. Mankind stands on the threshold of a major evolutionary change. Aided by technology, man will soon rise above the barriers of physical, moral, and spiritual limitations. All the old taboos and restrictions will be left behind, just as we abandoned our medieval superstitions and primitive ideas about medicine." With theatrical grace, Romulus extended his hand to Daniel. "I am looking forward to the future, and I congratulate you for having the courage to face it with us."

Now as he walked down the busy Rue du Commerce, Daniel's head whirled with dreams and ideas. He had never let anything but practicality and ethics suppress his imagination, but now even practicality and ethics seemed like foolish barriers. Why not let his mind roam free to discover and explore any and all possibilities? Romulus had a point—if truth was ever changing and government continually shifted the standards of morality, anything was possible! The future was theirs to create.

Holding his briefcase behind his back, he slowed his pace and stared past the crowds on the sidewalk. Why not test a child's DNA at birth and assign him to a place in society? Why not implant violent criminals with special "alarm" chips and exile them to some Arctic island where they could live without endangering law-abiding citizens?

He smiled, knowing that those ideas would seem ludicrous to most of the world. But sometimes a seed of ingenuity resided in a crazy idea, and if he just let it rattle around in his head for a few weeks, the idea would bear fruit—something real, useful, and highly profitable. Money he had, fame was too confining, but perhaps, if all went well, he could find a way to change mankind itself. Why should nation rise against nation? Why should the poor always be among us?

Caught up in a wave of imagination, Daniel looked up and grinned at the first person he saw—a very pretty brunette who held his gaze and cast him a smile like bait for a hungry fish. Daniel turned and hesitated for a moment, half-wishing he could follow her and not feel guilty later, but his smile faded when a dark figure on the sidewalk suddenly ducked behind a newsstand, avoiding Daniel's glance.

Daniel turned slowly and resumed his walk, his thoughts sharp and uneasy. He'd caught a glimpse of a dark coat and trousers, a wide-brimmed hat, and a black beard. That was the chosen garb of an orthodox Jew, a disguise Brad and his cronies would be unlikely to adopt under any circumstances. From his short time in the military, Daniel knew that a professional agent would not run and hide if a subject abruptly turned around; he would hold his ground and appear uninterested.

So who was the mysterious man in black?

Daniel frowned as he considered Adrian Romulus and his cohorts. Romulus had explained at lunch that General Herrick served as his security chief, Elijah Reis as his chief advisor. Elijah Reis—the name had a Jewish flavor, and the man's physical features certainly had a Middle Eastern look. But if Reis was Jewish, he was not devout; at lunch he had devoured a plate of steamed shrimp with great gusto.

Calm down, Prentice. You've been spending too much time with Brad. You're paranoid, delusional. No one is tailing you. There's no mysterious rabbi dogging your footsteps.

To put his mind at ease, Daniel stopped at the corner intersection, then spun around. Street vendors, flower sellers, and scurrying men and women choked the sidewalk, but Daniel could see no sign of an orthodox Jew.

Sighing in relief, Daniel waited for the light to change, then continued on his way.

EIGHTEEN

11:38 A.M., Monday, February 8, 1999

AFTER TWO WEEKS OF PRESENTATIONS, QUESTION-AND-ANSWER SESSIONS, AND planning meetings, Daniel sank into a seat in the Council of Ministers' assembly chamber and heard good news: By unanimous vote, the council had approved the recommendation to implement the Millennium Code and pattern its Millennium Project after the American plan.

"In the sincere hope that we will be joined by the people of other nations," Lady Bowes-Lyons, acting secretary, read the declaration, "we have selected Thursday, July 22, 1999, as Community Identification Day. Every government agency in each European Union country will transfer each citizen's data to a personal identification device approved by the Millennium Committee. We will urge each citizen to visit his local postal office for the painless insertion of his Millennium Chip."

As one, the members of the council looked to Daniel for his reaction. "I don't know that I'd call the insertion procedure painless," he said, wincing. "It does smart a bit, and children are particularly adverse to anything that even *looks* like a needle."

"Oh, it will be quite painless." Romulus smiled and leaned back in his chair. "We'll use an anesthetic spray. One spritz and the skin is numbed for ten minutes or so. The insertion is accomplished, and the patient feels nothing."

"Great idea, but why July 22?" Daniel looked to Romulus.

"Will there be a manufacturing problem?" A disturbing light smoldered in Romulus's gold-flecked eyes. "You said we could have the required number of devices by June."

"It's no problem." Daniel lifted his hands in a defensive gesture. "I was just curious about the date."

Alexandre Futetre, the French councilor, leaned forward. "We chose July because it is a mid-year month; we wanted to give ample time for both the manufacture of the chips and the implementation procedures. We asked the computer to pick a date that would be significant in several European countries, and July 22 proved to be our answer. On that date Poland celebrates National Liberation Day and Germany recognizes the anniversary of the Pied Piper of Hamelin. It is also the anniversary of John White's expedition to the first British colony at Roanoke Island and the birthday of Austria's Gregor Mendel, the founder of modern genetics."

Daniel smiled. "An auspicious day, indeed."

"We're glad you approve." Romulus leaned forward and clasped his hands on the table. "Daniel, we've been discussing several things in private, and we have decided to set another proposal before you today. In the past few days we have all been impressed with your knowledge and your commitment to the new-world community. We foresee a great future for you, and we'd like you to join us."

Caught off guard by the sudden vibrancy of Romulus's voice, Daniel took a quick, sharp breath. Spend his future with the European Union?

"Of course, I expect we'll continue to work together." Daniel smiled, not certain what Romulus meant. "After all, you have contracted with my company to repair your mainframes and oversee the manufacture of over 300 million Millennium Chips. It's my hope that more nations will join the Millennium Project, and I'd really like to continue in my role as senior contractor—"

Romulus's firm mouth curled as if on the edge of laughter. "That will take some time, Daniel, and, quite frankly, I don't think you're equipped to handle the political challenges involved in forging a worldwide community. But we are." He leaned across the table, a glittering challenge in his dark eyes. "We will create a community out of chaos, Daniel. We will unite the world. And I want your creative genius at my disposal. I want you to be a permanent part of my team."

With an apologetic glance at the others on the panel, Romulus rose from his chair and pressed his hands to the table. "If the others will forgive me for taking a moment to tend to business not directly affiliated with the EU, let me state my position frankly. The day is soon coming, Daniel, when the creative power of the world will be located here, in the European

Union, not in the United States. Your president is a traditionalist, not a visionary. Your American economy is stagnant, dependent upon massive loans by foreign investors and an overindulged, overextended population. Your people are lazy and complacent. But a renaissance is underway, and it is centered here, in Europe."

Daniel stared into Romulus's eyes, trying to divine what had motivated this unprecedented offer. Romulus, however, had a diplomat's face; almost anything could have been concealed behind that handsome and appealing facade.

"I'd like some time to think about it." Daniel shifted in his chair and gave the council a noncommittal smile. "I'd like to speak to my associates in New York. And I have an agreement with the United States government, so there are certain political considerations—"

"Don't confuse politics and business," Romulus interrupted, his lips parting in a dazzling display of straight, white teeth. "Your work with the American government is business. Your politics—well, you don't really have any, do you, Daniel?"

A sense of foreboding descended over Daniel with a shiver. How much did Romulus know about him, and how had he learned it? Daniel had not spoken openly about his past, his politics, or his feelings. If Romulus knew anything of Daniel's disenchantment with the government in particular and politics in general, he had either inferred it . . . or obtained information from Brad Hunter. Lauren wouldn't tell Romulus anything; her suspicion of him had intensified to the point where she refused to be in his presence unless absolutely necessary.

"Politics *are* like opinions—easily voiced and easily changed." Daniel smiled and settled his hands into his pockets. "And I must thank each of you for this opportunity to meet and work with you. I'll be in Europe for at least three more weeks, working with the engineers who will design the Millennium Chip. So I'll consider your offer, then give you my answer in a few days."

"We'd make it worth your while." Romulus's smile deepened. "Trust me."

Daniel stood and nodded formally to Romulus, then began the laborious process of shaking hands with each councilor at the table. As he muttered polite thanks and farewells to each member, he found himself wondering if he could convince Lauren to stay in Europe if he accepted Romulus's offer.

Probably not.

-0100111100-

Lauren thought she might have enjoyed her time in Brussels if Daniel had not been living in the same hotel. His presence was a constant thorn in her flesh, a visible reminder of her own stubbornness and intractability. Brussels was a beautiful and romantic city, but she had declared it a war zone, an edict that seemed to suit Daniel far too well.

Lauren's days were filled with public appearances—luncheons, concerts, and day trips to historical points of interest—at which she waved, made polite speeches on behalf of America's gracious first lady, and smiled through a blinding array of photographer's strobing flashes. Her picture appeared on the cover of several Belgian and English tabloids, and she soon realized that the reporters were comparing her with Diana, the late Princess of Wales. "So Tall, So Elegant, So Blonde," read one headline beneath her picture. "So Where's Her Prince Charming?"

Her Prince Charming, had she been willing to give Daniel that appellation, had closeted himself in his hotel suite, surrounded by schematics, computers, and European techno-wizards who drank coffee out of Styrofoam cups and looked at Lauren as if they expected her to break out in some sort of Marilyn Monroe-sings-happy-birthday-to-the-president routine whenever she visited. She thought it common courtesy that she drop in to see Daniel at the end of her day, but after a week, when it became clear that he had no intention of stopping his work for dinner or conversation, she quickly ended the practice.

Despite her busy schedule, she was lonely. And irritated. And very, very frustrated.

After three full weeks of soaking up the romance of Brussels alone, she ran into Brad Hunter in the hotel lobby. After her initial exclamation of surprise, she invited him to join her in the restaurant for a cup of tea. Though Brad looked a bit uneasy and seemed eager to be on his way, Lauren would not let him leave. "You wouldn't leave the president's executive assistant alone when she's desperate for a little American company, would you?" She gave him her prettiest smile, then remembered that he was a newlywed and decided that flirting was a bad idea. "Please, Brad," she begged, "it's Saturday, and I'm bored. Just sit for a few minutes and let me complain about Daniel. Then I'll let you go on your way."

Brad grinned at that, and before he knew it, they had taken a small table in the hotel cafe. She told Brad about Daniel's workaholic habits, his success in convincing the Europeans to adopt the Millennium Code and his Millennium Chip system, and his developing relationship with Adrian Romulus. "Romulus seems like a perfectly charming man," she confessed, stirring milk and sugar into her tea, "but he gives me the creeps. Or maybe I'm just jealous of the attention Daniel gives him."

"Are things getting serious between you and Danny boy?" Brad grinned. "I can't wait for him to fill me in."

"There's nothing to fill in. We're friends—and that's it. I made him promise that we'd behave as two professionals on this trip, and—" she felt her smile droop—"that's exactly what he's been. One hundred and ten percent professional. He works night and day, day and night. When he's not with that blasted EU committee, he's with a bunch of computer gurus in his suite. I had hoped we'd have at least *some* time to spend together, but I can't get him out of that stuffy hotel room."

"Let me have a talk with him." Brad pushed his coffee cup away and checked his watch. "I don't have to be anywhere for another half hour, so let me run up to the fortress and see if I can knock some sense into him."

"Good luck." Lauren shook her head. "I hope you have more success than I've had." A sudden thought struck her, and she caught his arm as he stood. "By the way, Brad, you haven't said much about what you're doing here."

It was a reasonable question, but his head jerked back as if she had stabbed him with it. "I'm staying in this hotel. I was just passing through."

"I meant what you're doing in Brussels."

"Security. You know that."

She regarded him with a speculative gaze. "Whose security? I've only seen you a couple of times, and Daniel hasn't seen much of you, either. Something tells me that you're not very worried about either of us being threatened, so what *are* you doing here?"

A lethal calmness filled his eyes. "I'm concerned with the security of the United States, Lauren. That's why I'm here." He gave her a quick, almost apologetic smile, then walked away.

Lauren fought down the frustrated scream that rose in her throat. Several times in her work she had run into roadblocks with the NSA and CIA, and each time she'd been frightened to realize that certain government agencies seemed to think they could operate independently of the White House.

She pulled her notepad from her purse and made a note to ask the president about Brad Hunter the next time she called the White House. General Archer had already returned to Washington, so maybe the president should ask him what he and Brad Hunter had going in Brussels.

-01001111100-

The hotel hallway shimmered in the first tangerine tints of the rising sun, and Daniel paused in the rectangle of light from the window before knocking on Lauren's door. Brad's visit yesterday had been brief and his message to the point: "Danny, old boy, if you're still serious about winning that woman, you'd better come out of hibernation."

Like an Old Testament prophet, Brad had breathed his warnings and dire predictions of romantic gloom and doom, and Daniel had listened. Last night he had swept the papers and laptop from his bed by midnight, and after a good night's sleep he felt rested and refreshed. From Brad, he had learned that Lauren's schedule was clear today, and so Daniel had decided that they would spend this Sunday together. A surprise date.

He glanced at his watch and noted the time: precisely 7:30. She ought to be awake, and if she wasn't, she wouldn't mind waking.

He rapped on the door, then waited patiently until he heard a muffled voice from the other side. "Yes?"

"Lauren." Daniel stooped and smiled into the peephole. "Get dressed, Miss Mitchell. I'm taking you out for a day on the town."

He heard a soft groan, then assorted clicks and jangles as she turned locks and undid chains. Finally, the door opened a crack, and he stared into one wide blue eye.

"Daniel, are you crazy?" He caught sight of her mouth—and it wasn't smiling.

"No, I'm not." He launched into his prepared speech. "I've come to my senses, Lauren, and I realize that we can be professional and still enjoy ourselves and this beautiful city. So get dressed, put on something comfortable, and let me take you to breakfast. I thought we could do some shopping in Porte de Namur, then perhaps take in some of the attractions at Bruparck."

Her forehead came to rest against the doorframe. "Brad visited you yesterday, didn't he?"

Daniel considered lying but thought better of it. "Yes. And, happily married man that he is, he pointed out the error of my ways. He convinced me that I have been neglecting the better half of the human race. And you, Lauren, are by far the best of the better half, so if you'll come—"

The door closed; the latch clicked with a definite, final sound. Daniel stood there, blank, amazed, and shaken, then he pressed both hands to the door and lowered his forehead until it rested just above the peephole.

"I'm sorry, Lauren." His voice was shakier than he would have liked. "I've been unfair. I know you wanted us to come to Brussels as business partners, but I took things too far. Even if I cared for you only as a friend, I was wrong to ignore you—and I'm terribly sorry. Please come out with me. It's Valentine's Day."

He waited, letting the silence stretch, then heard another muffled reply. "Give me half an hour."

"All right." He exhaled a long sigh of contentment, then made his way back to his room.

-0100111100-

Lauren arrived promptly thirty minutes later, then Daniel led her from the hotel. Obeying their whims and the spirit of adventure, they caught the subway at Schuman station, then exited at De Brouckere. Wandering through the picturesque streets of Old Brussels, they stared up at the dazzling white stone of Theatre Royal de la Monnaie, the opera house and ballet theater, then stopped for brunch in a delightful restaurant on the Rue de la Fourche.

Looking like a dream in a cream-colored cashmere jumpsuit, Lauren laughed and chattered and seemed more at ease than Daniel had ever seen her. After brunch, they walked to the Grand'Place and gazed in wonder at the buildings' ornamental gables, medieval banners, and gilded facades. "It's like Cinderella's village," Lauren breathed, her voice tinged with a little girl's wonder. "My goodness, Daniel, I had no idea such places still existed!"

Daniel didn't answer but took her hand and guided her to a charming statue of a flower-bedecked boy. While Lauren snapped photos, Daniel fished a coin from his pocket and bought a bag of bread crusts from a street vendor. First Lauren laughed at his impulsiveness, then she joined him in tossing the crumbs to a flock of pigeons.

Being Sunday, many of the shops were closed, but Lauren talked Daniel into stopping at a corner bakery where a tempting assortment of croissants filled the display window. Lauren shamelessly asked for two large chocolate-chip croissants and refused to blush when the baker pointedly asked, "So much food for such a skinny lady?"

Daniel stood in the shadow of the baker's doorway, enjoying the sight of Lauren clutching her treasures, then turned and lazily swept his gaze across the wide plaza. His heart skipped a beat when he recognized a familiar shadowy form—the Jew. The man stood among the crowd at the little statue, but he wasn't facing the adorable boy. He was staring directly at Daniel.

"Lauren," Daniel called over his shoulder, not daring to take his eyes off the man. "Wait here. I'll be right back."

Without waiting for her acknowledgment, Daniel sprinted across the cobbled plaza. He expected the man to duck and scurry away as he had before, but to his surprise the fellow just stood there, an expectant look on his face.

Daniel was breathless when he reached the man. "You," he gasped, raking hair from his forehead. "You were following me the other day."

He expected denial, but the old man nodded, his brown eyes piercing the distance between them.

He wore the same long, black coat and dark trousers he had worn the other day. The same wide-brimmed hat sheltered his head from the bright sun, and a tangled beard flowed from his chin and over his collar. Winding, curled earlocks, the mark of truly orthodox Jews, hung from his temples. A prayer shawl peeped from beneath the coat, its fringes evident at the man's waist. His dark, deeply wrinkled eyes and thick brows rose above a line of black beard while an aura of melancholy radiated from his seamed, tired features.

"You must come with me." His voice was low and controlled, with an undertone of desolation.

"I'm sorry, but I'm with a friend." Daniel gestured toward the bakery but kept his eyes fastened on the stranger before him.

"You must come. Please, Mr. Prentice." His voice wasn't much above a whisper, but the effect was as great as if he'd shouted in Daniel's ear.

Daniel's mind spun with bewilderment. "How do you know who I am? And why have you been following me?"

The old Jew crossed his hands, then looked down the street, his expression fixed in the desperate lines of a hunted animal. "I have read about you in the papers. And you must come with me. Please."

"I can't." Daniel strengthened his voice. "Not today. Later, perhaps, you could come to my hotel." Despite the primitive warnings ringing in his brain, the old man intrigued him. "I'm staying at the Eurovillage Brussels. Why don't you stop by?"

"No." The man shook his head, as patient as an instructor with a slow pupil. "You must come to my house, Mr. Prentice. This is the address."

From a pocket in his massive coat he produced a card scrawled with wide, black lettering. *Rabbi Yacov Witzun,* the card read, *93745 Rue Blaes, Apartment 5D, Brussels.*

"Daniel?" He turned at the sound of Lauren's voice, then lifted his hand and gestured to her. She hesitated to allow a woman and her children to pass, then gracefully made her way through the pedestrian traffic.

Daniel turned back to the old man, but he had vanished. The space he had occupied seemed to vibrate softly, as if a remnant of his image was dissipating into the air.

"What are you doing over here?" Lauren asked.

Daniel stared at the empty space and asked himself the same question. Lauren obviously hadn't seen the man. If he told her that a Jewish rabbi with earlocks and a prayer shawl was following him, she'd undoubtedly think he'd been working too hard. But he had proof—he held the rabbi's card in his hand.

"Nothing." He slipped the card into his pocket, then jerked his chin toward the bag in her hand. "Get enough croissants?"

"Yeah." She bit her lip in a teasing smile. "Enough to last all week."

"Good." He slipped his arm around her shoulder and led her away, but not before glancing over his shoulder one final time.

-0100111100-

Despite the easy familiarity with which Daniel held her, Lauren knew his thoughts were miles away. Something had happened on the plaza, something he didn't want to share with her.

They had turned onto a narrow side street, one designed more for tourists than traffic, and they wandered quietly through newsstands, flower vendors, and souvenir stands for fifteen minutes. As they neared another busy intersection, Daniel suddenly lifted his head and stared off into the distance.

"Lauren," he slipped his arm from her shoulder, "will you wait here? I'll be back in a moment. I promise."

And just like that he was off, jogging through pedestrians and dodging cars as if he had been born to the helter-skelter patterns of European traffic.

Well, he did live in New York.

Bemused but not completely surprised by his erratic behavior, Lauren turned to a flower seller on the street. Her cart brimmed with forced spring bulbs of fragrant hyacinths, colorful tulips, and bright golden daffodils. Obeying an impulse, Lauren pulled her wallet from her purse and counted out a handful of Belgian franc notes.

"How much for a hyacinth bouquet?" she asked the woman behind the cart.

The woman smiled. "For you, mademoiselle, three hundred francs."

About ten dollars. Not bad. Lauren counted out the bills, then chafed her cold hands while the woman assembled the bouquet and wrapped the stems in waxed paper.

"You have a beautiful necklace," the woman remarked, eyeing the cross that hung from a gold chain at Lauren's neck.

"This?" Lauren's fingers flew to the cross. "Thank you. It was a gift."

From Mrs. Stedman, but she didn't want to mention that. Though it usually hung under her blouses, she always wore the gold cross, for it meant more to her than any other piece of jewelry. Victoria had given it to her right after Jessica died, and to Lauren it symbolized Victoria's affection as well as her strong faith.

The flower lady's sparkling blue eyes sank into nets of wrinkles as she smiled. "Are you a Christian?"

Lauren blinked. Of course she was a Christian. She was, after all, a God-fearing American. "Yes."

The woman lifted her chin and nodded toward a storefront behind the row of cart vendors. "Come. You will like this."

Puzzled, Lauren took a step forward, then turned to glance down the street for a glimpse of Daniel. He had vanished, following some random thought that had sprung into his brain, and Lauren knew it might be half an hour before he returned.

She sighed. Developing a relationship with a genius was no piece of cake.

The flower vendor was holding out her hand, a lovely, wide, warming smile on her face. Lauren clutched her bouquet and took the woman's hand, then followed her toward the storefront. A sign above the wide glass windows proclaimed, in English and French, that the building was home to a bookbinder.

What are you doing? You could be wandering into a den of thieves or a gang of kidnappers—

The woman opened the door, and the rhythmic sound of a man's voice reached Lauren's ear. A moment later she had passed through the doorway and gazed in surprise at the scene before her. At least a dozen people were seated in the tiny open space at the front of the shop, some in chairs, some on the floor. Before them all, using the bookbinder's counter as a pulpit, an auburn-haired man in shirtsleeves held an open Bible and read from the Scriptures.

"'I write these things to you who believe in the name of the Son of God,'" he said, his voice a velvet murmur in the small space, "'so that you may know that you have eternal life. This is the assurance we have in approaching God: that if we ask anything according to his will, he hears us.'"

The preacher reverently closed his Bible, then bowed his head. "Heavenly Father," he prayed, his deep voice simmering with barely checked emotion, "hear us now. We know that the whole world is under the control of the evil one. But we also know that the Son of God has come and given us understanding so we will know him who is true. Jesus Christ is the true God and eternal life. Keep us close to him as the days grow short. In his holy name we pray. Amen."

A woman stood and turned to face the small congregation. As the preacher came out from behind the counter, she—his wife or sister, certainly—nestled under his arm and began to sing. The others joined in, and something in the lyrics tugged at Lauren's heart. She had sung this song, too, years ago when she visited church with her mother . . . before poverty forced them out of their home and into government housing projects. Her mother had no use for God after their reversal of fortune.

The flower vendor leaned toward Lauren's ear and whispered in a husky voice. "I am sorry the service is nearly finished. I believe you would have enjoyed it."

"Why do you meet here?" Lauren whispered back. "Aren't there churches in Brussels?"

"Not so many English churches." The woman shrugged. "The merchants in this alley speak English, and they enjoy worshipping together." The gold in her brown eyes flickered as she smiled. "The Lord drew me to this place, just as he drew you."

"Oh, I don't know. . . ." Lauren's voice trailed off as she listened to the singing. The music acted as a balm; she felt as though something inside her was easing, almost as though she had suffered from a chronic pain that was now being assuaged.

The song leader's clear soprano voice rang out above the others and spoke directly to Lauren's heart. "Redeemed and so happy in Jesus, no language my rapture can tell. . . ."

So happy in Jesus. How many truly happy people did Lauren know? Only one—Victoria Stedman. Even in the face of sorrow and grief, even under constant and critical scrutiny, Victoria Stedman displayed a persistent joy while Lauren had yet to find real happiness or contentment. She loved working for the president and Mrs. Stedman, but had she ever found peace?

She felt herself drowning in a wave of confused thoughts and feelings, and one frantic thought rose to the surface—*escape.*

She took the flower vendor's hand and offered her most diplomatic smile. "Thank you for inviting me. I really have to get back. I have to meet a friend."

"You will come again?"

"Perhaps." Lauren turned and put her hand on the doorknob, then leaned back. "You meet here often?"

"Every day, at lunch. We would be happy to have you join us."

"Thank you."

The haunting melody followed her out onto the street as Lauren slipped through the doorway and threaded her way through the vendors' carts.

-0100111100-

"Lauren!" Daniel lifted his hand to his mouth and yelled. She was hurrying down the side street, a bouquet of flowers in her hand, but she turned at the sound of his voice, a smile of relief breaking across her face.

Daniel hurried toward her. "Hey, what's your rush? You looked like somebody just propositioned you."

"Nothing like that." She gazed at him with a bland half-smile. "Where'd you go?"

Daniel scratched his cheek, then pointed down the road. "I thought I saw a Jewish man—a young guy, and I hoped he'd know this orthodox rabbi I met, but it was a false alarm. I mean, I never found either one of them." He looked back at her, and noticed that her face was pale and drawn. "What's wrong? You look a little upset."

Lauren pressed her lips together, then nodded as if she'd just decided something. "I just attended church."

"Church?" Daniel thrust his hands into his pockets and looked around. "I didn't think there were any churches around here."

"It wasn't a real church—an *official* church, I mean. The people met in one of those storefront shops—a bookbindery, in fact. One of the flower ladies saw my cross and invited me in."

For the first time Daniel noticed the gold cross dangling against the creamy cashmere. "So—you wanted to go?"

"I went, but just for a bit. I was curious, that's all." She paused for a moment and looked away, then shivered as a cold gust of wind blew down the street and rattled the street signs.

"It was strange, actually." She watched a stray sheet of paper blow across the street, and her eyes seemed to water in the wind. "They sang a song I haven't heard since I was a girl, but my mother used to sing it— 'Redeemed. His child and forever I am.'" She frowned. "At least, that's how I think it goes. It's been a long time."

"You used to go to church?" Daniel took her hand and they began to walk.

Lauren nodded. "When I was a kid—before the hard times set in. Mom had no use for a God who would desert us, so she stopped going to church entirely when we had to move to the projects. When she died, I told the funeral director to perform a short civil ceremony. I knew Mom wouldn't want anything religious."

Daniel said nothing for a moment but guided her around an elderly couple out for a leisurely afternoon walk. "You never told me how you met the Stedmans, you know. I thought you might have been friends through your mother."

"Heavens, no." Laughter floated up from her throat. "I met Jessica Stedman first—I was working for a caterer in Raleigh, and we catered this big shindig at the senator's house. I didn't know who Jessica was—I just noticed that one girl at the party wasn't enjoying herself at all. She hid out in the kitchen most of the time, and we started talking while everyone else was having fun around the pool."

Daniel noticed that the color had risen in Lauren's cheeks; either the wind was chilling her or she was self-conscious about discussing her past.

"Jessica and I made a real connection that day, and the next thing I knew she was inviting me over for girlfriend-type things. We went to movies together; we laughed and talked. When she told me she was going to Sweet Briar College in Virginia, I told her I'd dreamed of going to college but that my mother couldn't afford it. Then out of the blue Sweet Briar offers me a full scholarship, based on my grades and Senator Stedman's recommendation. Jessica and I were roommates, sorority sisters, as close as two girls could be . . . right up until the day she died."

A group of rosy-cheeked children ran by, leaving a trail of laughter along the sidewalk. Daniel waited until they had passed, then dared to ask the question uppermost in his mind: "Were you there . . . at the accident?"

"No." She looked at him, her eyes soft with pain. "I had to study, and Jessica . . . well, she was hanging around with some people who were really into the party scene. She went out to Smith Mountain Lake with a group of guys from Lynchburg College. The next thing I knew, someone from her father's office was calling to tell me that Jessica was dead. They said I should put all her things in a suitcase and not let any reporters into the room." Her faint smile held a touch of sadness. "Then Mrs. Stedman came to the dorm, and I helped her get Jessica's things together. And Victoria hugged me, and we both cried, and—"

Her voice broke. Daniel put his arm around Lauren's shoulder and squeezed it in quiet sympathy. "And you've been close to the Stedmans ever since," he finished for her. "I understand."

She nodded her head slightly, then looked up to the blue sky as if seeking comfort from heaven itself. Silvery tracks of tears marked her perfectly oval face.

"It's okay, honey." He pulled her closer and whispered into her hair. "Let me take you home now. And thank you for a wonderful Valentine's Day."

Nineteen

9:16 A.M., Monday, February 15, 1999

DANIEL STEPPED OUT OF THE HOTEL LOBBY AND BLINKED IN THE BRIGHT WINTER sunlight. He had canceled three appointments to free a block of time for his interview with the old Jewish rabbi because he could not stop himself from thinking about the man. Some rational, detached part of his brain kept repeating that the old man might be one of those dangerously odd people attracted to celebrities, but intelligence and determination had gleamed in the rabbi's eyes. Furthermore, in the entire winding length of Daniel's memory he could not recall a single kidnapping or assassination by an orthodox rabbi. Murder and its attendant publicity were very unorthodox.

The old man was a mystery, and Daniel had to see him.

He dredged that admission from a place beyond logic and reason; but once having admitted it, Daniel found it easy to clear his calendar, set his work aside, and dress for a winter walk through Brussels.

The day was cold, but bright; the sun jabbed brilliant fingers of light through cracks in the aging hotel awning. Daniel had requested a taxi from the concierge, and after a few moments, a black and white cab pulled up at the curb. Daniel slid into the back seat, read the rabbi's address from the card, and settled back to watch the city slide by.

His mysterious contact lived in what appeared to be a middle-class section of the city. Tall apartment buildings rose behind skeletal trees that lined the street. At one intersection a jackhammer crew busily shredded a sidewalk.

The taxi jerked to a halt outside a peach-colored apartment complex. "This is 93745 Rue Blaes, monsieur," the driver said, tossing Daniel a glance over his shoulder. "The fare is four hundred francs."

Daniel counted out the proper fare, added a generous tip, and stepped out of the cab. A reeking fog of diesel and gasoline fumes hung over the boulevard, and Daniel saw that the apartment complex was composed largely of concrete and glass. Rigid and unimaginative in design, the building testified that Brussels' modern builders cared more about housing its nearly one million inhabitants than creating beauty.

Daniel followed a curving stone pathway into a courtyard, then looked for an elevator and found none. He groaned. As he had suspected, Yacov Witzun's apartment was located on the fifth floor.

A series of concrete steps divided the center of the U-shaped building. Daniel took a deep breath and began to climb, hoping that the morning would prove profitable. He didn't want to climb five flights just to pacify a religious lunatic.

A couple of minutes later, Daniel caught his breath, then knocked on the rabbi's door. A moment passed, the door opened, and Daniel found himself staring into eyes that gleamed like glossy volcanic rock.

"Rabbi Witzun?"

"God is good." The old man reached for Daniel's hand, then fairly pulled him into the apartment. As he took Daniel's coat, he said, "I prayed you would come. I knew you would come."

Daniel found himself standing in a crowded parlor, filled from floor to ceiling with books. The rabbi, or someone close to him, had constructed what Daniel always thought of as "student shelves"—long pine planks supported by stacks of bricks. But if the rabbi had skimped on shelving, he had obviously spared no expense on his library. Gilded, leather-bound books, most of them with the worn look of rare editions, lined the shelves and overflowed onto a husky oak table in the center of the room.

The rabbi did not wear his coat now but moved through the apartment in a long-sleeved white shirt with his prayer shawl around his neck. A heavy set of keys jangled from a chain at his belt and clicked against his legs as he bade Daniel come in and have a seat at the table. Seen indoors, without his wide-brimmed hat, he appeared younger than he had on the street. His hair was still thick and heavy; his long beard was only lightly sprinkled with gray.

"Can I offer you some refreshment? Coffee? Tea?"

"No, thank you." Daniel took a seat in one of the high-backed wooden chairs at the table.

"Are you certain?"

Daniel hesitated. Lauren hadn't specifically mentioned whether refusing a Belgian rabbi's offer would constitute bad manners, but Daniel had a suspicion that his refusal might offend this particular Belgian rabbi.

"All right. Some tea, please."

The rabbi's lids slipped over his eyes. "Very good. I shall have tea, too."

He walked slowly toward the kitchen, leaving Daniel alone in the front room. The place smelled of leather and old books, a cozy, warm scent that reminded Daniel of his father.

A memory played in his head like a film shining on the backs of his retinas. The sounds of running water in the rabbi's kitchen faded, for Daniel was on the floor in his father's study, surrounded by books and plastic models of navy fighter jets.

He rose to his knees and reached for one of the jets, but his father gently moved his hand away from the fragile model. "When you're older, Danny boy," his father said, his voice calm and low, "then they'll be yours. Just like all my books will be yours."

Daniel sank back to his heels, his eyes widening at the prospect of owning such treasures. The books were nice, he was certain, for his father held a different one every night. His eyes would skim the pages in a regular pattern, halting occasionally as he reached for a pencil to scribble something at the edge of a page. But it was the thought of owning his dad's jets that made Daniel's heart turn over—

Abruptly Daniel pulled the plug on his memories. After his father's death, the jets and the books had gone into boxes that Daniel never reopened. The models, in fact, had been donated to Goodwill, and he had given all but one of the book boxes to a local library, where blue-haired ladies sold them ten for a dollar to raise money for a new addition.

The rabbi came back into the room, a steaming mug in each hand. "Do you care for milk or honey?"

"No, thank you." Determined not to be a bother, Daniel accepted the mug and took a perfunctory sip. The rabbi settled himself in a wide wooden chair at the end of the long table, then lowered his eyes to his mug.

Silence sifted down like a snowfall.

"I read about you in the newspapers." The rabbi's voice, though quiet, had an ominous quality. "I read about many things. And I see how the pieces are coming together, like bits of glass in a mosaic."

"What pieces?" Daniel placed his mug on a coaster, then rested his elbow on the table. "I'm sorry, but I don't understand."

"Let me show you." The rabbi pulled a thick, leather-bound volume from a stack of books in the center of the table. He opened the back cover, then flipped through the pages from right to left.

"I am reading from the Mishneh Torah." He looked up, and his eyes caught Daniel's. "You are familiar with Talmud and Torah?"

"Only slightly," Daniel admitted, feeling suddenly ignorant.

The rabbi smiled. "The Talmud is a collection of ancient rabbinical writings, the Mishnah and the Gemara, the basis of our religious authority. The Torah, strictly speaking, is the Pentateuch, the first five books of the Hebrew Scriptures and your Christian Bible."

While the rabbi ran his finger from right to left over the page, Daniel lifted his mug and took another sip of the fragrant tea.

"Here." The rabbi tapped the page. "In the fourteenth volume of the Mishnah Torah the great rabbi Moses Maimonides declared, 'In the future the King Messiah will arise and renew the Davidic dynasty, restoring it to its initial sovereignty. He will rebuild the Temple and gather the dispersed remnant of Israel.'"

Daniel lowered his mug, then rubbed his temple in thought. "The *Messiah* will build the temple? For years I have heard that some religious Jews are planning to rebuild it. I recall a CNN report several months ago on the subject, and the reporter said that many of the gold and silver objects used in temple sacrifice have been newly constructed and are waiting in Israel."

The rabbi shot him a twisted smile. "You listen, then, to news about Israel?"

"Of course." Daniel laughed softly. "Who can ignore it? Sometimes I think the world revolves around Jerusalem."

The rabbi snorted with the half-choked mirth of a man who rarely laughs. "Ah. Yes. Well." He intertwined his fingers and rested his hands atop the open book. "A number of other ancient sources, including the Zohar and the Rosh Hashanah, declare that the temple will be built by the Jewish people just before the coming of the Messiah."

"Perhaps both statements are true." Daniel lifted one shoulder in a shrug. "Often the truth is found in combining two truths, rabbi. Perhaps the Messiah and the Jewish people will build the temple together."

"That," the rabbi held up a slender finger, "is precisely what drove me to talk to you, Mr. Prentice." He reached under another stack of books and withdrew a plain manila folder, then opened it. From where he sat Daniel could see that the folder contained several newspaper clippings and photocopied reports.

"Are you aware—" the rabbi lifted one report and slid it over the polished table—"that your associate Mr. Romulus has begun secret negotiations with leaders of the PLO to allow the Jews to rebuild the temple on the Temple Mount? It will have to be built, of course, next to the existing Muslim Dome of the Rock."

"No, I didn't know." Daniel examined the article before him. A headline ran across the top of the page—"Temple Mount: Classified Report." A black-and-white photo of a smiling Adrian Romulus and a man identified as Abd al Bari, servant of Allah, dominated the page. The first paragraph reported that Adrian Romulus, a European negotiator, had spent several days in conference with al Bari, an Islamic leader, at the Romulus estate in Paris. In the interest of peace, the PLO and the Muslims were willing to consider allowing Israel to rebuild the temple on the Temple Mount and to allow Jerusalem to be recognized as Israel's capital. The price for this startling concession would be Israel's surrender of the territory of the West Bank and Gaza, as well as the return of the Golan Heights to Syria.

"I should think you would be delighted by this news." Daniel pushed the photocopied report back to the rabbi.

"The few rabbis who are aware of this development strongly support Romulus." The rabbi took the article and stared at it with deadly concentration. "But I cannot forget something written twenty-five centuries ago in the Book of Zerubbabel. The writer refers to a false messiah by the name *Armillus*. He is also known by the name *Romulus*.

A wave of anxiety passed through Daniel. "You can't believe that Adrian Romulus is a false messiah." He grimaced in good humor. "These books are filled with ancient prophecies; they have nothing to do with those of us who live in the twentieth century."

"What good are prophecies if they don't tell us about our future?" Witzun looked at Daniel with a vague hint of disapproval in his eyes. "These things will come to pass, Mr. Prentice, and prophecies found in the Bible we share indicate that they will come to pass very soon."

Daniel gritted his teeth. Now that his Millennium Project was close to uniting the world, the *last* thing he needed was resistance from a religious faction. "But other than a similarity in the names, what makes you think Adrian Romulus is connected in any way to these ancient writings?" If Adrian fell under suspicion solely because he had inherited an unfortunate surname. . . .

"There are more definite connections." Rabbi Witzun folded his hands in a pose of tranquillity. "First, there is his work on behalf of the Jews in regard to the Temple."

"That would seem to indicate that he was your messiah, not a *false* messiah."

Something that looked like a smile twitched among the tangles of Witzun's beard. "A false messiah must have the appearance of a true messiah, or he would never develop a following." The rabbi spoke patiently, as if he were explaining things to a small, stubborn child. "Second, the calendar itself seems to suggest that Adrian Romulus is this false messiah."

"The calendar?" Daniel moved his hand to his chin. "Excuse my ignorance, rabbi, but you'll have to explain."

"The ninth of Av, to be precise." Witzun's eyes shone moist, and his voice grew suddenly husky. "Several ancient rabbis speak of the 'spirit of Hadrian' rising in the last days to attack Israel until the Messiah—*true* Messiah—defeats him. The Roman emperor Hadrian, as I'm sure you'll recall from your history lessons, destroyed over one and a half million Jews on the ninth day of Av, A.D. 135."

Daniel searched his memories and found a recollection of Hadrian's Wall in Scotland, but nothing more. The fact that the man was an anti-Semite had not been mentioned in Daniel's school.

"I fail to see the connection."

A tremor touched the rabbi's firm mouth. "For some reason known only to the Master of the universe, the ninth of Av has often elicited the wrath of men imbued with an evil spirit. On that date in 587 B.C., by the Gregorian calendar, the Babylonians burned King Solomon's temple; on that day in A.D. 70, the Romans burned the second temple. In 1290, the Jews were driven from England on the ninth of Av; on the same date in 1492, Spain expelled her Jewish population."

The rabbi's overwhelming anguish was palpable; Daniel could almost feel the laboring, grieving presence of millions of murdered Jews.

"On the ninth day of Av in 1914, the Russians killed a hundred thousand of my people as they mobilized for World War I."

The atmosphere thickened with the heaviness of despair. Daniel pressed his hand over his mouth, unwilling to break the respectful silence, but still he could not see any link between Adrian Romulus and the tragic history of the Jews.

"Your associate, the powerful and charming Monsieur Romulus," the rabbi went on, his lips pale within his beard, "has chosen a date upon which everyone will receive a computer chip, a key to enter his false system. Gentiles and Jews alike will be implanted with these, these *things*—"

"Personal identification devices," Daniel offered.

"It does not matter what you call them." His dark eyes impaled Daniel. "Note this, Mr. Prentice—this year, the day he has chosen, the twenty-second of July, is the ninth of Av."

A thunderbolt jagged through Daniel. July 22 was a tragic Jewish anniversary? Surely the date was only a bizarre coincidence. Romulus had nothing against the Jews, and there was absolutely no anti-Semitic element to any aspect of the Millennium Project. Everyone was to be implanted with a Millennium Chip; no particular sect was to be particularly sought out or ignored. At present there were no plans to even record a person's religious preference in the PID code.

Daniel leaned forward and stretched his hand toward his host. "Rabbi Witzun," he said, the grim line of his mouth relaxing, "I can assure you that the Millennium Project and the PIDs are as safe for the Jews as for any other people. I have nothing against the Jewish people, and neither does Adrian Romulus. If I thought he was an anti-Semite, I would not work for him."

"He is the next Hitler."

Their eyes locked tight, and neither man moved for a long minute.

"He is not," Daniel said finally. He stood, nodded formally at his host, and plucked his coat from the back of a chair.

Before leaving, he threw a quick message over his shoulder. "Thank you, Rabbi, for the tea."

TWENTY

11:58 A.M., Monday, February 15, 1999

RETURNING TO THE HOTEL, DANIEL PAUSED AT A NEWSSTAND ON THE SIDEWALK and picked up a copy of the *International Herald Tribune*, wondering all the while if he should tell Lauren about the rabbi's troubling suspicions. Daniel had known few Jewish people in his life, and had never knowingly held a conversation with a rabbi. But Lauren encountered all types of people in her work; perhaps she could give some rational explanation for the rabbi's dire warning. Though Daniel knew she wasn't overly fond of Romulus, she was politically savvy and could certainly offer an insightful opinion on the matter.

Daniel thanked the vendor, pocketed his change, and paused to skim the morning headlines. He had just begun to move toward the hotel when the lobby's revolving door disgorged a slurry of guests. Daniel blinked in surprise when he saw Lauren's blonde head bobbing amidst the crowd. She hadn't mentioned a lunch appointment, but why would she? In the three weeks they'd been in Brussels, Daniel hadn't inquired more than once or twice about her plans. No wonder she had told Brad she was lonely.

His thoughts clouded with uneasiness as he watched her move away. Should she go out without an escort or guard of any kind? Her picture had been in the papers enough that anyone might recognize her, and she was an official representative of the president of the United States.

More than a little perturbed, Daniel tucked the folded newspaper under his arm, then waited on the sidewalk to see if Lauren would ask a bellhop to call a taxi. If she did, she undoubtedly had a luncheon appointment, but if she did not, perhaps he ought to join her and make up for his inattention of the last few days.

A group of women walked by, chattering like bright parrots, and by the time they had passed Daniel could no longer see Lauren. For one black instant he panicked, then he caught sight of her farther down the street. She had wasted no time but walked at a brisk pace, her slender legs moving beneath the hem of her coat in a quick, even rhythm.

Drawn by curiosity and the challenge of the chase, Daniel threaded his way through the hotel crowd and followed her. A thousand thoughts zipped through his mind as he hurried forward—where was she going, and why had she chosen to go alone? Brad was supposed to be in charge of security, so where in the world was he?

Lauren moved down the Boulevard Charlemagne and turned onto the Rue de la Loi, passing between the Berlaymont Palace, home of the European Commission, and the EU Council of Ministers building without slowing her pace. Daniel's alarm grew as she skipped lightly down the subway stairs at the Schuman Station. He followed, his heart in his throat, and slipped into a subway car just before the door closed and the train pulled away from the station.

Closing his ears to the babble of languages around him, Daniel swayed to the train's gentle rhythm and kept his eyes upon Lauren. She rode the train with a distant, distracted look on her face, as if she were deep in thought.

That look did nothing to ease Daniel's fears.

She stepped off the train at the De Brouckere station, and Daniel followed, glad that at least they were on familiar territory. This was the way they had traveled on Sunday; maybe she merely wanted to revisit a shop or pick up a fresh bag of croissants.

But even once they hit the row of shops, Lauren showed no signs of slowing. On and on she walked, past the bakery, past the little shop where they sold all sorts of goods emblazoned with the European symbol—a circle of gold stars on a bright blue background. Finally, just as Daniel was beginning to wonder if this was some sort of lunchtime aerobic program, Lauren paused by a side street. She slowed her pace and looked hesitantly around, then lifted her chin and moved past a row of vendors' flower carts.

Daniel stopped, suddenly remembering. Lauren had found a little church in one of these storefront buildings, and the discovery had left her in a thoughtful mood for the rest of the day. What could have driven her back to this place?

He stood in the center of the bustling sidewalk and debated his options. If he turned around and went back to the hotel, Lauren would never know he had followed her. His indifference might have suited her three weeks ago, but since that time Daniel had sensed a remarkable thawing of her resolve to keep him at a professional distance.

On the other hand, he could follow her inside the building. She would be surprised, perhaps annoyed, but at least she would know he cared enough to worry about her safety. And, since he had come this far, she'd want him to stay with her a while. But then the church, or whatever it was, would reach out for *him*, wrap its tenuous and persistent arms around *his* thoughts and feelings— and the one thing he didn't need right now was a muddled head.

He took a deep breath and felt a dozen different emotions collide. He wanted the woman, not the religion. He wanted Lauren's strength, intelligence, and stability, not an emotional panacea.

He exhaled in a long, slow stream. He was strong, and so was Lauren. She'd come back to this place because she was feeling nostalgic and probably missed Victoria Stedman.

Daniel shoved his hands into his pockets and forced a grim smile to his face as he wended his way through the flower carts. The faintly muffled sounds of music reached his ear, and as he opened the door he braced himself against the sentimental pull of a familiar melody.

They were singing "The Old Rugged Cross."

-01001111100-

Lauren felt a shock run through her as her eyes met Daniel's. He hesitated just inside the door, then seemed to make some sort of decision. As the dozen or so men and women around her continued to sing, Daniel hunched forward and slipped into the empty chair beside Lauren.

"I saw you leave the hotel," he said, by way of explanation, "and I thought you shouldn't be out alone."

Lauren gave him a wintry smile. "I can take care of myself, Daniel. And this is personal, not business."

He crossed his legs and nodded politely at a man who'd shifted in his seat to give Daniel a curious glance. "Celebrities do not have personal time." He leaned slightly and whispered the words. "You must be more careful."

Ready to argue the point of her so-called celebrity, Lauren took a quick breath, then released it in an audible sigh. She couldn't argue in the middle of a church service, even if it was being held on Monday afternoon in a bookbinder's shop.

The song ended, several of the worshippers shouted in enthusiastic agreement, and the preacher-bookbinder stepped out from behind his tall work counter.

"The Lord has urged me," the man began, a glow rising in his ruddy face, "to speak to you from the fourth and fifth chapters of Paul's first letter to the Thessalonians. Listen, friends, to what our Lord would have us hear about the coming resurrection."

Daniel shifted in his chair, and Lauren braced herself for a cutting comment of some sort. But he said nothing. The leg he had crossed, though, began to swing back and forth like a hyperactive pendulum.

"'Brothers, we do not want you to be ignorant about those who fall asleep, or to grieve like the rest of men, who have no hope.'" The preacher spoke in a tone filled with awe and respect. "'We believe that Jesus died and rose again and so we believe that God will bring with Jesus those who have fallen asleep in him. According to the Lord's own word, we tell you that we who are still alive, who are left till the coming of the Lord, will certainly not precede those who have fallen asleep. For the Lord himself will come down from heaven, with a loud command, with the voice of the archangel and with the trumpet call of God, and the dead in Christ will rise first. After that, we who are still alive and are left will be caught up with them in the clouds to meet the Lord in the air. And so we will be with the Lord forever. Therefore encourage each other with these words.'"

"Maranatha!" The woman next to Lauren whispered the word in reverent wonder.

Lauren thought the preacher had finished; in her church the minister rarely read from the Bible at all. But the bookbinder brought the leather-bound book closer and kept reading.

"'Now, brothers, about times and dates we do not need to write to you, for you know very well that the day of the Lord will come like a thief in the night. While people are saying, "Peace and safety," destruction will come on them suddenly, as labor pains on a pregnant woman, and they will not escape.

"'But you, brothers, are not in darkness so that this day should surprise you like a thief. You are all sons of the light and sons of the day. We do not belong to the night or to the darkness. So then, let us not be like others, who are asleep, but let us be alert and self-controlled. . . . For God did not appoint us to suffer wrath but to receive salvation through our Lord Jesus Christ.'"

Lauren threw a sidelong glance at Daniel. His swinging leg had slowed its pace; his eyes had narrowed. He was either listening with great concentration or mentally writing computer code. She turned back to the preacher, relieved that Daniel was not fretfully bored, then winced when his voice cut through the gathering like a knife.

"Would you mind explaining that, please?"

Shock flickered over the preacher's face like summer lightning. "I beg your pardon?"

"Please excuse the interruption, but I really want to know." Daniel uncrossed his legs and leaned forward in his chair, resting his elbows on his knees. "*What* will come like a thief in the night? Nuclear war? And if so, which country is going to drop the first bomb?"

Despite her embarrassment, Lauren looked to the preacher for an answer.

The marks of astonishment faded as the preacher's mouth curved into an unconscious smile. "Why, the day of the Lord, or Tribulation, will come as a thief in the night," he said, his eyes sparkling as he rose to the challenge. "The day of the Lord will begin when the leader of the revived Roman Empire will consolidate his ten-nation confederacy and sign a seven-year peace treaty with Israel and its enemies. According to the prophet Daniel, the signing of that treaty by the Antichrist will mark the beginning of God's judgment upon sinners, a terrible time of war, famine, attacks by wild beasts, and plague, as well as the commencement of a seven-year countdown to the Battle of Armageddon. At the conclusion of Armageddon, Jesus Christ will descend to earth with his armies of saints from heaven. On that day, the Lord will defeat the Antichrist and establish his righteous millennial kingdom on earth."

Lauren's mind reeled with confusion. What in the world was he talking about? She recognized a few of the words—*Armageddon* and *Antichrist*—from popular movies and books, but surely none of that stuff was real.

Daniel brought his hands to his chin in a reflective pose, but Lauren wanted more answers. "What armies of saints in heaven?" she asked, thinking of her mother and Jessica Stedman. "Are you talking about people who have died?"

"*Believers* who have died." Every eye in the room shifted toward Lauren and Daniel as the minister took a step forward. "And of course, the living believers will be absent at the day of the Lord—they will have been previously taken away at the Rapture, literally snatched up from the earth."

Daniel looked at the minister with amused wonder. "Like the Heaven's Gate cult who waited for the aliens trailing the Hale-Bopp comet?"

Lauren expected Daniel's cynical response to bring a frown to the minister's face, but he responded in a pleasant and calm voice. "There will be no mass suicide at the rapture of the living saints. There will be no bodies left behind. The Lord will appear in the heavens, and all who believe in him will vanish from the face of the earth. Those who have died before will be resurrected and taken to heaven as well, forever to be with the Lord."

The minister's kindly blue eyes searched Daniel's face, as if reaching into his thoughts. "Do you, young man, know any believers in Christ?"

Daniel lifted his head from his hands. "Yes. My mother."

The preacher nodded. "If she remains alive until the trumpet call, she will vanish at the Rapture, or Resurrection. And all who remain on earth will be left to face the Antichrist alone."

"Wait a minute." Daniel held up his hands and leaned back in his chair. "I've heard about this Antichrist, and I'm not buying it. The Antichrist is probably a system opposed to organized religion, not an individual. I saw *The Omen*. You can't convince me that there's some little kid out there marked with a 666 tattoo and destined to destroy the world."

"*The Omen* was a filmmaker's distortion of the truth." A light bitterness filled the preacher's voice. "Satan would like us to think his coming puppet is a mere fantasy or a symbol, but I can assure you that he is real. He may be alive even now. He may be in a position of power, preparing himself to do his evil work. But his true nature will not be revealed until after the believers are taken to be with the Lord."

Daniel made a quiet sound of disbelief and looked away, but Lauren could not let the subject pass. "You said the believers would be taken." Her throat tightened as she thought of Mrs. Stedman. That gracious lady was a *believer* in every sense of the word. And while Lauren called herself a Christian and believed that Jesus Christ lived and died and taught many good things, she knew she lacked the qualities Mrs. Stedman exhibited. She wasn't as good, or as committed, or something. . . .

"What do you mean by *believer?*" she blurted out, looking around the small gathering. "What makes a person good enough to be taken up with the Lord?"

The woman sitting in the next chair reached out and caught Lauren's hand. "None of us is good enough," she said simply, her voice low and smooth. "We are accepted by God because of Christ's perfection, not our own."

"A believer is one who has placed his life in God's hands." The minister studied Lauren for a moment. "Excuse me, but you are an American, right?"

"Yes."

He smiled. "What do you do in America?"

Lauren felt herself blushing. "I, um, work in the political system."

"Very good." The preacher lifted his bushy brows. "Then let's consider a simple analogy. The American president now is Samuel Stedman, yes?"

Lauren nodded.

"And you believe with your head, your intellect, that this Samuel Stedman exists? You have seen his picture, heard his voice?"

Lauren nodded again, smiling. If only this preacher knew *how well* she knew Sam Stedman!

"Very good." The minister was counting on his fingers; he moved from the first finger to the second. "Did you believe in Samuel Stedman enough to vote for him in the election? Do you believe in him with your heart because you agree with his principles and policies?"

"I do."

The minister smiled and pointed to his third finger. "So you believe in him with your head and heart. This is good. But do you believe in Samuel Stedman enough to be assured that he would save your life? If you were kidnapped on the streets of Brussels by a group of terrorists, do you believe the American president Samuel Stedman would come personally with his armed forces to rescue you? Could you trust him with your life?"

Lauren lowered her gaze as the question hammered at her. Would

Samuel Stedman—her president, her employer, and her *friend*—risk his life to rescue her?

She looked up at the minister. Obviously, he expected her to answer no, but he had no way of knowing that Lauren and Samuel Stedman were nearly as close as father and daughter. Despite the affection and love that existed between them, however, Samuel Stedman was president of the United States. He *couldn't* risk his life for one insignificant woman, no matter how dear she might be.

Shattered by the realization, her voice trembled as she answered, "No."

The preacher looked directly at her, his eyes dark with wonder. "The Lord Jesus, Son of God, cared enough to leave heaven for you. Though he could have summoned the armies of heaven to prevent his pain, he suffered and died for you." He placed his Bible on the work counter, then lifted his hand and slowly curled it into a fist. "He will hold you tight, young woman, if you trust him with your *life*. That is what true believers do, and those are the people who will leave the earth at the Rapture."

Lauren lowered her gaze as she took the words in. A shrill electronic beep rang through the bookbinder's shop, signaling the time, and the preacher took a backward step, effectively dismissing the meeting. The others stood and moved toward the door, sharing smiles and handshakes as they filed out, but Lauren scarcely noticed, so intent was she upon her thoughts.

She felt a hand at her elbow and looked up to see Daniel standing by her side. "Don't you have afternoon appointments? Shouldn't we get back to the hotel?"

"Yes."

They stood and turned to follow the others, but another touch stopped Lauren.

The minister stood behind her, a printed leaflet in his hand. "Please come back." His dark blue eyes were soft with kindness. "But if you cannot return, you can read this material. If you cannot read this material, you can still trust Jesus Christ with your life. It is a simple thing, an act of the will and an attitude of the heart."

"Thank you." Lauren reached out and took the leaflet, then slipped it into her pocket. "I am glad I came."

She followed Daniel onto the sidewalk, then walked by his side for two blocks, neither of them speaking. She was about to ask for his thoughts about the meeting when he stopped and abruptly turned toward her.

"I wanted to ask you about something," he began, his eyes narrowing in concentration.

Lauren stopped, too, and put her hands into her pockets, warmed by the thought that he cared about her opinions. "Yes?"

"Adrian Romulus has offered me a permanent position with the European Commission. I think I'd be doing pretty much what I'm doing for the American government, but it'd be a bigger opportunity, of course, because the European Union will be a larger entity than the United States. And there's always the possibility that I'll be able to extend the Millennium Project throughout the world. It's almost a given necessity, for once a nation uses the Millennium Code to fix their Y2K problems, it's only natural that they would want to sign on with our other Millennium advances."

Lauren stared wordlessly at him, her heart pounding. Was he actually considering Romulus's offer?

His eyes burned with the clear light that shines in the heart of a flame. "Of course, I'd still be spending quite a bit of time in Washington and Mount Vernon," he went on, reaching out to take her hand. "And I'd make a point of seeing you whenever I could." He lowered his gaze into hers, and seemed to probe her very soul. "I don't want to lose you, Lauren. I want to spend as much time as possible with you, whether we're here in Europe or back in the United States. You could take some time off and travel with me; you'd be right by my side every step of the way."

Lauren drew a deep breath and flexed the fingers of her free hand until the urge to strangle him had passed. Had he no loyalty at all? He obviously considered his responsibilities to President Stedman a trivial obligation, easy to shrug off whenever a better prospect appeared on the horizon.

And he hadn't even considered *her* loyalty to the president. He seemed to think she'd be thrilled to quit her job and fly around the world, that she'd be content to stand by his side and bask in the light of his egotistical, arrogant genius.

"You'd better make your decision quickly." Her voice was hoarse with frustration. "Because we're going home. The president sent a cable just this morning—he wants us back in Washington by Friday. We're supposed to meet with General Archer for a debriefing."

Daniel's face went blank with shock. "Why is he calling us back?"

"Because he can."

Before Daniel could offer another word to confuse her, Lauren whirled away and left him on the sidewalk.

Twenty-one

10:18 A.M., Thursday, February 18, 1999

"Will there be anything else, Mr. Prentice?"

The uniformed bellhop stood in the foyer of Daniel's suite in a deliberately nonchalant pose, waiting for his tip.

Daniel pulled four hundred-franc notes from his pocket and placed them in the bellhop's hand. "No, just take good care of the bags, will you? Especially the briefcase."

"Of course, sir." The bellhop turned, then pointed toward the black leather satchel on the dining room table. "Are you forgetting something, sir?"

Daniel followed the man's glance, then smiled when he saw that the bellhop was referring to his laptop case. "No, I'll carry that myself."

The bellhop nodded and slipped out of the room. Daniel took a last look in the bedroom, double-checked the garbage cans for any sensitive paperwork that ought not to be left behind, then peered into the bathroom to be certain he hadn't left his toothbrush by the sink. It was an old habit his mother had drilled into his psyche—the toothbrush was the first thing unpacked, last thing packed. With all the rich food he'd been eating in Europe, Daniel might die from a heart attack, but at least he'd depart this world with healthy teeth.

He pulled several additional hundred-franc notes from his wallet and dropped them on the bureau for the chambermaid. The abrupt departure order had surprised everyone—even Daniel, who hadn't realized that President Stedman knew many details about Daniel's activities in Europe. The American Millennium Project was progressing on schedule; Daniel received encrypted e-mail updates from Taylor Briner and Dr. Kriegel nearly every day. The European Millennium Project, which should have been of vital interest to the Americans, was proceeding apace as well. All the major European Union banks, government offices, hospitals, and international trading agencies had already begun to run the Millennium Code to correct their Y2K mainframe problems, and Daniel had engaged four major computer corporations to produce PIDs based upon the American design.

A rap on the door interrupted his thoughts. Daniel hurried to answer it, hoping that Lauren had decided to share a taxi to the airport. She had scarcely spoken to him in the three days since he had mentioned Romulus's offer of a position with the European Council, and he wanted to clear the air. If she'd only broaden her horizons, she'd see that the world consisted of more than Samuel and Victoria Stedman.

He opened the door and groaned inwardly when he saw the bellhop again.

"Excuse me, Mr. Prentice, but this was waiting for you at the front desk. Since it was marked urgent, I thought I should bring it right up."

Daniel reached for his wallet as his eyes scanned the manila envelope in the man's hand. His name had been written in block letters across the front; the nondescript handwriting could have belonged to anyone.

"Thank you." He took the envelope and handed the man another tip, then closed the door.

A simple typewritten slip of paper lay inside the envelope: "Danny boy, I must speak with you before you leave for the airport. Room 411. Come now."

Daniel frowned as he read the note. The tone and lingo were Brad's, and the fact that he'd written seemed to indicate that Daniel's phone wasn't secure. And a clandestine meeting in a hotel room could only mean that Daniel was under surveillance as well.

With only a quick backward glance, Daniel reached for his computer case, then slipped out of the suite and took the stairs down to the fourth floor. When he arrived outside room 411, he listened for a moment, fearing he'd fallen for some sort of trap. Hesitantly, he knocked on the door.

Brad opened it a moment later. His eyes were serious, but one corner of his mouth turned up in an irrepressible grin. "Danny boy! It's about time. Get in here."

Daniel followed Brad, then frowned when he realized the heavy curtains were drawn. The television poured a loud and melodramatic French soap opera into the room, and a single lamp burned over the corner table. Brad's briefcase lay open on the bed, but there was no sign of any other luggage.

A thrill of frightened anticipation touched Daniel's spine. "What's going on, Brad?"

Brad motioned Daniel to a chair, then sat on the edge of the bed. He lowered his gaze and let out an anxious cough, then looked up and gave Daniel a troubled smile. When he spoke, he was careful to pitch his voice below the frenzied voices from the TV. "Long time, no see, friend."

"I know." Daniel tapped his fingers on the table next to his chair. "Now are you going to explain all this cloak-and-dagger stuff, or am I going to have to bribe it out of you?"

"Daniel." Brad's brows drew together in an agonized expression. "I could get in a lot of trouble for what I'm about to tell you. I got this hotel room because I know there's a tail waiting for you downstairs. I think we're okay here, but in this business you can never be sure."

"Who would put a tail on me?" Daniel hesitated, blinking with bafflement. "Brad, everything we've done here is totally above board."

"Nothing is ever what it seems, Daniel." Brad nodded decisively. "You've got to remember that."

"Okay." Daniel leaned back in the chair and raked his hand through his hair. "So who are we hiding from? My people or yours?"

"I thought we were working for the same people." Brad's eyes darkened and shone with an ominous light. "We don't have a lot of time, Daniel; if you're late to the airport they'll wonder where you were. So let me just lay the cards on the table."

"I wish you would." Daniel sighed in exasperation. "Is this about Adrian Romulus?"

"It's about *you*, Daniel." Brad's mouth thinned with irritation. "We know Romulus offered you a job. We know he wants you to fill some position working for the Council of Ministers. We know a lot more about him, too, but I can't tell you everything. I'm overstepping my authority to tell you this—the man is dangerous, and he wants you. That worries us."

Daniel snorted in derision. "Do you have nothing better to do than sit around and dream up these fantasies? If you know so much, you've obviously been following me and tapping my phones—a practice that, quite frankly, offends me." An unsettling thought suddenly came to him. "Did you follow me to the old rabbi's apartment?"

"One of our agents did."

Daniel gave him a black look. "Did you eavesdrop even there?"

Brad shook his head. "No, we weren't that interested in the old man. We just had a tail on you for security reasons. We've had a tail on Lauren, too, but she's not nearly as interesting to Romulus as you are."

Daniel laughed. "Oh—that's flattering." His laughter stopped suddenly. "How do you know Romulus isn't interested in her?"

A feral light gleamed in the depths of Brad's dark eyes. "You see a lot when you're watching someone, Danny boy. And we saw that we weren't the only ones shadowing you around town."

Daniel felt his stomach drop. "You saw someone else?"

"Romulus had people on you, too. Everywhere. That was quite a parade through the Grand'Place last Sunday. Between you and Lauren darting to and fro, you had us all going a little crazy trying to keep up. But Romulus's people didn't follow her—only you."

The empty place in Daniel's gut filled with a frightening hollowness. "So, what am I supposed to do?"

"It's easy." Brad leaned forward. "Just watch yourself . . . and call me if Romulus does anything suspect."

"You've just said the man himself is suspect."

"He is, but I want you to call me if he says anything that might undermine American interests in any way, shape, or form. You've got to promise me, Daniel."

Brad and Daniel stared at each other across a sudden ringing silence.

Daniel laughed to cover his rising uneasiness. "You never did tell me how you got a copy of the Millennium Code. Now's a good time, don't you think?"

Brad drew an exasperated breath. "I'll tell you—if you promise to call me about Romulus."

"All right." Daniel threw up his hands. "I'll call if Romulus says anything suspicious, but don't hold your breath. I don't think he gives two figs about American interests. He has spoken of uniting the world in some kind of interconnected community, but he's never implied that he intended to be at the center of power." His eyes locked on Brad's. "Now spill it—tell me how you tapped into our system and got the Millennium Code program."

Brad leaned back and wrapped his hands around his knees. "We knew your Dr. Kriegel was working on the Y2K fix. On the afternoon you went to Canada—our computers logged your flight number, destination, and arrival time—a nondescript van parked on the street outside your head-quarters in Mount Vernon. While people shopped and walked around it, the agents inside used a Talegent electronic surveillance device to isolate the electromagnetic radiation from Kriegel's computer, revealing everything that danced across your professor's computer screen—that's how they got a copy of his e-mail to you. Anyway, they knew he'd been successful."

"No way," Daniel said, irked by Brad's cool, matter-of-fact manner. "We encrypt all our e-mail with PGP. It's a nearly unbreakable code."

"You didn't have your laptop." One corner of Brad's mouth pulled into a slight smile. "You were fishing, remember? You had the little Nokia phone with you. The professor knew you were trying to relax, and he got lazy and sent the message without encrypting it."

Daniel combed his hand through his hair, feeling restless and irritable. Brad was right. He hadn't taken the laptop to the cabin; he had told the professor he wanted to leave the office behind. He groaned as his stomach churned with anxiety and frustration. If they had a device good enough to pick e-mails out of thin air. . . .

"Go on," he said, knowing what Brad was going to say next. "You knew the professor had the bugs out. So how'd you get the program?"

Brad cocked his head and gave Daniel a jaunty smile. "It's a beautiful thing, really. As I said, the Talegent had isolated the professor's computer. We just commanded it to run the program on your network, and after that, copying the program was simple. As the program played on the monitor in your company vestibule—only a few yards from the van's parking space—they were able to record every digit, every keystroke."

"You probably broke about ten thousand laws," Daniel drawled, his voice ringing with distinct mockery. "The CIA and NSA are not allowed to spy on Americans in the United States."

"So sue me." Brad grinned. "And don't take it personally, Danny boy. I had the same kind of surveillance on at least twenty other techno-wizards. You came through for me."

Daniel shook his head. "Unbelievable."

"No," Brad's face went suddenly grim, "*Adrian Romulus* is unbelievable. Listen to me, Daniel. The man is a charmer, he's brilliant, and everyone loves him. But we've heard reports that he is currently exerting tremendous pressure on three of the nations in the European Union. His agents are inciting unrest in one country, undermining the economy in another, and there's talk that he has developed some sort of Svengali relationship with the prime minister of yet another—and that's not good." Brad's mouth dipped into an even deeper frown. "No one knows, of course, but last year that prime minister attempted suicide. We fear he might actually succeed in a suicide attempt if Romulus yanks his string hard enough."

Daniel looked away, trying to comprehend all he was hearing. If this was true—and Brad's intelligence reports, it seemed, were rarely wrong— which of the council members was Romulus undercutting?

"You're sure about this?"

"As certain as we can be. And so I wanted to tell you, Daniel—you've got to be careful. Romulus is the ultimate wolf in sheep's clothing. Not only is he on the brink of betraying three of the EU councilors, but in the past two months he's dined with the president of Iraq, the leaders of the PLO, and the emperor of Japan. He's already the hero of unified Korea, and he's scheduled to visit the United States later this year."

Daniel frowned, searching for the significance of Brad's words. "So?"

Brad spread his hands wide and made an imaginary globe. "The four corners of the earth—the Pacific Rim nations, the Middle East, Europe, and the Americas. If Romulus establishes alliances with all four, he could conceivably become the most powerful man in the world."

Daniel couldn't restrain his burst of laughter. "Brad, that's crazy! The world is a very big and complicated place; even Adrian Romulus couldn't hold it together. People are too independent; countries like the United States will cling to their sovereignty until they pry the last shotgun from the last redneck's hands."

"Just look at this, will you, Daniel?" Brad pulled a shiny brochure from his open briefcase and handed it to Daniel. "Don't worry, it's not classified. No one will arrest you for having it. Just look it over and then tell me what you think. See if I'm not right about Adrian Romulus's intentions."

Daniel glanced at the brochure. It was titled "A New Europe, A New Community" and featured a full-color illustration of Europe's new symbol, a picture of Europa riding Zeus, the bull. Daniel could find nothing incriminating in the picture; the same image was represented on the euro currency and the official stamp of the European parliament.

"Europa," he said, musing aloud. "Let's see, if I remember my Greek mythology, Europa was a princess who was abducted by Zeus. He took her to an island—Crete or Cyprus or something."

"Close, Danny boy. You remembered more about it than I did. Europa was a Phoenician princess abducted by Zeus, who assumed the form of a white bull and carried her across the sea to Crete. There they had three children: Minos, Rhadamanthus, and Sarpedon."

"Oh, yes, that's certainly incriminating. It's terribly politically incorrect, what with Zeus oppressing the helpless woman and forcing her to bear his children. He'd never get by with *that* in America."

"Cut the sarcasm and consider the implications, will you? Three children, and there are three sectors of the world waiting to join Romulus."

"You didn't mention Africa," Daniel remarked, turning to the inside of the brochure.

"Africa will go with the Middle East," Brad growled, resting his fist on his hip. "Read it later, and you'll see what I mean. Now you've got to get going. Your plane leaves in less than ninety minutes, and you'll have to clear customs."

Daniel gave the brochure a last glance, then tucked it into his coat pocket. What more could he tell his best friend? Romulus *had* spoken of uniting the world in a global community, but he'd made no direct statements about wanting to lead this new amalgamation. He'd led Daniel to believe that he wanted to *influence* the world, which wasn't so terrible an ambition—Daniel wanted the same thing.

But Brad wouldn't understand. He and his cronies at the NSA were hyper-paranoid, eager to find dictators and tyrants where none existed. And they were ethnocentrically American, refusing to believe that perhaps the Europeans' idea of unity was a good idea.

Or maybe they were peeved because Europe was stealing a distinctly American concept. Several independent states into one union? Who'd have ever *dreamed* it could work?

Daniel stood and looked at Brad for a long minute, then shook his head. "Sorry, Brad, but your suspicions are pretty hard to swallow. I honestly think your people got their wires crossed on this one. Romulus is energetic, true, and I can see where his intelligence and ambition might be intimidating to some people in power. But his favorite refrain is about community and the renaissance of Europe—I've never heard him say anything about wanting to rule the world."

Brad stood, too, and put his hands in his pockets. "Just be careful, will you? Open your eyes and consider what I've said." A smile tugged at his mouth. "As much as I'd like to get out of paying for your honeymoon, I don't think Lauren would ever forgive me if you got hurt. And this is a dangerous business."

Daniel snorted as he picked up his laptop and moved toward the door. "Your spies are slipping, Brad, or you'd know that Miss Mitchell and I are currently on the outs. I told her about Romulus's job offer, and she pretty much threw up her hands in disgust." He grinned. "She's like you—she doesn't like Romulus, either."

"I don't get paid to like or dislike people." Brad's voice was calm, his gaze steady. "I get paid to *understand* them."

"Better you than me." Daniel reached out, shook his friend's hand, then opened the hotel room door. "See you soon. Let me know when you get back to the good ol' USA."

"I will."

With an impertinent grin, Daniel moved through the doorway and left Brad alone with his suspicions.

−0100111100−

In the cab, Daniel leaned back against the seat, closed his eyes, and tried to reset his mental relays. So much had happened in the last week; so many strange and unexpected ideas had been tossed at him. Lauren's awakening interest in religion had come from nowhere, and Brad and his conspiracy theories had caught Daniel by surprise.

When it all boiled down to basics, Daniel reminded himself, he had a simple job to complete. It was already February 18, and in only 316 days the world's mainframes would either go berserk or pass quietly into the year 2000. Before the worst happened, Daniel had to oversee the production of more than 600 million Millennium Chips for the United States and Europe—and pray that the rest of the world would buy into the Millennium Code Y2K fix.

His mouth curved in a faint smile. Adrian Romulus may have never dreamed of changing the world, but Daniel had. In order to be truly effective, his Millennium Code *had* to be the world's standard.

And if, by some miracle, he could convince Lauren that her life would be infinitely more fulfilling if it were linked with his, well, Daniel would know he'd been a true success.

"Which airline, monsieur?" The cabbie looked into the rearview mirror for Daniel's answer.

Distracted, Daniel muttered the name of the airline and looked out the window for a sign of Lauren's blonde curls. The clerk at the hotel desk had told him that Lauren had already checked out, so Daniel knew she was still miffed.

Lauren was nowhere to be seen outside the terminal, so Daniel paid the taxi driver, paid an attendant to check his luggage, then raced through the security checkpoints and customs areas. He neared the gate just as a tall, Nordic-looking stewardess announced the final boarding call. Daniel lengthened his stride and was breathless by the time he reached the jet and found his seat in first class.

Lauren sat in the seat next to his, but she barely even glanced up as he shrugged out of his overcoat.

"Glad you made it," she said, with a marked lack of conviction. "I'd have hated to tell Sam that you chose to remain behind."

Daniel tossed his coat into the overhead bin, then sank into the seat next to her. "I don't want to remain behind." He lowered his voice. "It's just a job, Lauren, and Romulus would be just another client. It's not like I'm surrendering my citizenship or anything."

"Oh." She turned a page of her magazine without looking up.

Sighing, Daniel stretched his legs beneath the seat in front of him, then crossed his arms. Apparently this would be a chilly flight home. But perhaps he could find something to occupy his time. . . .

"Excuse me?" He waved to catch the nearest flight attendant's attention. "Would you happen to have a Bible aboard?"

"Shhh, sir!" Turning in the aisle, the steward frowned and placed a finger across his lips. "Not so loud! Do you want to panic the other passengers?"

"I only want to read—"

"We do not carry that sort of material aboard the aircraft." The fussy steward pulled a stack of magazines from a narrow shelf. "I have *Esquire*, *Newsweek*, *Europe Today*, and *Investor Weekly*. Which of those would you like?"

Daniel glanced at Lauren, half-hoping she'd be warmed by the thought that he'd asked for the Holy Scriptures, but her eyes were still glued to the glossy pages of her magazine.

"Give me *Europe Today,* please." He took the magazine from the steward, then settled back to read. He could wage war in this battle of the sexes, too. He would read the entire magazine without even glancing her way, just to prove that he was immune to her charms and that delightful scent that always lingered in her hair. He would recline in this chair and apply his mind to this magazine, absorbing every detail of the lead story, even if it had to do with Belgian tulips.

He opened the magazine, flipped past the opening ads and the masthead, then found himself staring at a full-page, glossy picture of Adrian Romulus.

Lauren's voice rattled against his eardrums. "You can't escape him even for a minute, can you, Daniel?"

–0100111100–

An hour later, Lauren stepped over Daniel's long legs, then moved into the aisle. Pressing her hands to the small of her back, she stretched and glanced down at the sleeping man beside her.

Daniel Prentice was amazing. Stubborn, bright, and generous; sharp, thoughtful, and bull-headed.

Why had her treacherous heart fallen for him?

She moved toward the lavatory, then smiled politely as another woman exited. Once Lauren had locked herself into the tiny cubicle, she dampened a paper towel, then pressed it to her right temple. A persistent thumping inside her skull signaled the advent of a killer migraine, and Lauren wanted to blame the weather, the altitude, or the stress of the journey.

But responsibility for this headache belonged solely to Daniel Prentice.

He had wanted to remain in Brussels. He came to life when he talked about his work with Adrian Romulus; he glowed as he described the changes his brilliant Millennium Project would bring to the world. Better accounting, less crime, more responsible citizens and government. More fairness, more equity, more truth. She had the sneaking suspicion he wanted to make a major mark on the world, with the Millennium Project as his pen. Bill Gates brought simple personal computers into 55 percent of American homes, but Daniel Prentice wanted to bring his Millennium Code to the entire world.

It was, she thought, like the Tower of Babel story in reverse. God had confounded the nations by making them speak in different languages; Daniel would bring them back together by teaching their computers to speak the same code. Already he had found a way to link every single American to the national network. And now, every European.

Her head pounded at the thought. Lauren groaned and closed her eyes, holding the damp towel over the pulsing vein in her temple. Daniel had come willingly enough once she told him that the president wanted them home, but she suspected that he'd only remain stateside long enough to check in with the president and his associates in New York. Then he'd be off again, back to Brussels or even France, where Adrian Romulus owned a palatial estate. Perhaps Daniel would buy the mansion next door, maybe even Versailles! After this European deal, he'd certainly be able to afford it.

She opened her eyes and peered woefully at her bleary reflection. "Get used to it, kid. See that footprint in the middle of your back? That's Daniel Prentice's mark. He's used you as a stepping stone, just like all the others."

She should have known not to trust him. She had trusted that widowed freshman senator from Minnesota who came calling with roses and perfume, but then she'd discovered that he had a living wife and six kids tucked away in a remote hamlet. The press nearly had a field day with *that* one; only Mrs. Stedman's promise of an in-depth interview with the leading news organizations had managed to bury the story. In the end, the national networks decided that the first lady was of far more interest than a broken-hearted executive assistant, so Lauren watched in silent agony as Victoria faced harsh questions about her faith, her husband's fidelity, even her deceased daughter. In gratitude to Victoria, and with the bitterness of experience, Lauren had vowed to forever bar any and all politicians from her personal life.

Daniel wasn't a politician, but she should have seen the signs. Just like most statesmen, he was ambitious, charming, and quick with a sound bite. He was rich enough to buy luxury and attention, and shameless enough to enjoy them.

That thought had barely crossed her mind before another followed— Victoria Stedman *liked* Daniel, and Victoria had a gift for discerning the truth about people. So Daniel couldn't be all bad—*of course he wasn't*—but he still had broken Lauren's heart.

She sank to the closed seat. "Merciful heavens, I can't trust anybody."

She had learned that lesson in her first year of politics, but sometimes she needed to be reminded. Public servants, even unelected ones like Lauren, couldn't confide in just anyone. Your best friends could sell out your secrets and broadcast your most personal feelings to the tabloids. No one was completely trustworthy, no one so selfless that they didn't have their own personal agenda. Even Victoria, who was as saintly a person as Lauren could imagine, had to support and protect her husband's position and reputation before anyone else's.

Loneliness welled up in Lauren, black and cold. The old feelings of loss and grief surfaced into her consciousness like a powerful undertow that pulled her under against her will.

Whom did she have? Lauren mentally listed the people who cared for her. The Stedmans loved her, but even their affection had its limits. Her mother was dead; her father gone only God-knew-where. Daniel probably cared about her, but he cared more for ambition and power. There remained a couple of casual girlfriends, a handful of ex-boyfriends who wouldn't hesitate to sell stories to the *National Inquirer* if there had been any juicy tales to tell, and a dozen White House staffers who would glee-fully stab her in the back if she dropped her guard for one instant.

Her dog adored her, but even Tasha could be wooed away with a hand-ful of kibble.

The memory of the bookbinder-preacher brought a wry, twisted smile to her face. *If you were kidnapped on the streets of Brussels by a group of ter-rorists, do you believe the American president Samuel Stedman would come personally with his armed forces to rescue you? Could you trust him with your life?*

No. No one in the world was crazy enough to value her above all else, devoted enough to rescue her from a band of terrorists . . . or unending loneliness.

Like peeling an onion, Lauren stripped the layers from her life and found—emptiness. She had no center, no reason for being. So why was she alive?

She gulped hard, then looked into the mirror and saw tears sliding down her cheeks. "Oh, God," she prayed, lifting her eyes to the molded ceiling above, "I have nothing. Nothing to believe in, no one to trust."

She stood silently, tasting her tears, then a memory ruffled through her mind like wind on water. *His child and forever I am.*

The old song. They had sung it in the little bookbinder's church, the song about being redeemed.

Redeemed and so happy in Jesus, no language my rapture can tell.

"God will hold you tight, young woman, if you trust him with your *life.*" She heard the preacher's voice again, saw the earnestness in his eyes. Belief, she remembered, meant more than knowledge or intellectual agreement—it meant complete and unconditional surrender to Christ.

Caught by surprise at the memory, Lauren gave the mirror a wry smile. Why would Jesus want her? She was nobody's daughter, a child of the projects, an adaptable woman who'd had the good fortune to be loved by a powerful man's family. She was pretty, but no knockout; bright, but not brainy; kind, but no saint. If Jesus had given his life to redeem hers, he had definitely gotten the weak end of the bargain.

His child and forever I am.

The lyrics moved in her heart, stirring passions and desires buried beneath years of denial. His child. How she had longed to be a father's child! She had never even known her own father, never heard a single favorable word about him from her mother's lips. Yet Lauren used to lie in bed and dream of a loving, gentle man who would invite her to curl up in his lap and fling her arms about his neck. The dream of a caring, sheltering father had sustained her throughout the tumultuous years of adolescence, and then she'd discovered the Stedmans. Though Samuel Stedman had maintained a stately, dignified distance, he had provided for her, encouraged her, and trusted her with responsibility. Lauren had delighted in his regard, even while she suspected that he cared for her mainly because he wanted to care for Jessica—and Jessica was forever out of his reach.

His child and forever I am.

Could she find in Jesus a God to call Father? A Father she could trust with her secrets, her failings, her faults, and her fears?

Victoria Stedman had never found fault with him. And she suspected that none of the believers in the bookbinder's little church had, either.

"All right, Jesus, I surrender," she whispered, tears blurring her vision. "Unconditionally. Take my life and use it for something. I've wasted thirty years chasing foolish dreams; forgive me for that. Take what's left of my life and do whatever you want with it."

She waited, half-expecting to see a bright light or hear an angelic choir, but she heard only the roar of the engines and the soft murmur of voices outside the lavatory. Had anything happened in that instant of surrender? She had skimmed the pamphlet the preacher had given her; it spoke of becoming a new creature, of old things passing away and a new life beginning when an individual believed in Christ. Lauren looked into the mirror and saw her familiar reflection, the tears still streaking her cheeks, and yet she felt as though a warm kernel of joy now occupied the center of her being, sending little sprouts of hope through the surface of her broken heart.

She dampened a fresh paper towel, then wiped her tears away. The towel took most of her makeup, too, and when Lauren looked in the mirror again, she had to smile at the sight of her plain, scrubbed appearance.

"Might as well make a fresh start of it," she murmured, dropping the paper towels into the trash receptacle.

And as she made her way back to her seat, Lauren realized that her headache had disappeared.

-0100111100-

In the back of the first class section, Kord Herrick lifted his head and watched as Lauren Mitchell stepped over Daniel Prentice and fell, rather ungracefully, back into her seat.

Kord lifted his newspaper again, concealing his face. Neither Prentice nor the woman had recognized him in the false beard and hat, and Kord had kept to himself as he waited to board the plane. He had been fortunate to get aboard the flight; if a certain Mr. William Geiger had not been quietly attacked in the airport parking lot, Kord would not have a seat at all.

"Mr. Geiger?"

The flight attendant's voice startled Kord, and he glanced up. "Yes?"

"You pre-ordered a kosher meal. I just wanted to be certain you were in the proper seat. We'll be serving dinner soon."

"Thank you." Kord nodded and returned to his newspaper. When the stewardess had moved back down the aisle, he lowered the edge of the paper again, just enough to see the top of Prentice's dark head.

Romulus had insisted that Kord follow Prentice back to Washington. He was not completely certain of his pet genius's loyalty, and it was absolutely imperative that Prentice and the woman convince President Stedman to link his Millennium Network with that of the European Union.

Kord noticed that Prentice had shifted and turned his face toward the aisle. He was awake, then, and deliberately avoiding conversation with Miss Mitchell.

Kord smiled. This romantic spat was an interesting development, to be sure, and one that might work in his favor. The young woman was a staunch Republican, and that political party was founded upon a platform of American conservatism. Such traditional thinking could only hinder the new community, so the less time Prentice spent with her, the better.

Satisfied that Romulus had nothing to worry about, Kord lifted his newspaper and chortled at the cartoon antics of Blondie and Dagwood.

TWENTY-TWO

11:28 A.M., Friday, February 19, 1999

"NEVER, NEVER, NEVER!" THE PRESIDENT'S FIST POUNDED THE DESK WITH EVERY word, and Daniel flinched with each separate thump. "*Never* will I surrender our national sovereignty. You can just go back to Brussels or Paris or wherever that fellow is and tell him that America may stand apart from the others, but she will always stand on her own two feet."

President Stedman glared at General Herrick, who had joined the briefing with Daniel, Lauren, and General Archer. General Herrick had graciously opened the meeting, relaying the continuing good wishes of the European Union's Council of Ministers, and then had stunned Daniel by announcing that the Commission president, Adrian Romulus, wished to invite the United States to join the European Community.

Herrick had lifted a sheet of paper and read from it as he concluded his greeting. "For years, Mr. President, our nations have been aligned in economic and military treaties through NATO and the UN. We have formed a beneficial partnership, and we have benefited from each other. Since we will be operating on identical Millennium computer systems, both designed and implemented by Prentice Technologies, doesn't it seem that the time is ripe for our two confederacies to move toward unification?"

The president, Daniel deduced, was most definitely *not* interested in Romulus's offer.

"Mr. President—" General Archer threw a nervous glance at Daniel, then slid to the edge of the sofa. "Sir, the European Union does not want us to surrender anything. They are asking that we link our Millennium Network to theirs, that we participate in a mutual sharing of resources. Surely you agree that we ought to become part of the global community of nations?"

Silence reigned in the Oval Office for a moment, then the president leaned back in his chair and pressed a finger across his lips. "No. I don't like it. I don't think the American people will like it. Oh, they may be dazzled by the idea of traveling to Europe without a passport, but let's get real. This arrangement takes far more from our people than it gives."

"I fail to see how that could be true." Herrick, who sat beside General Archer, lifted an elegant silver brow. "Consolidation always simplifies things. For instance, European Union countries now enjoy one citizenship and passport, one high court, one central bank and currency, one foreign policy and army. We have replaced the barriers and confusion of the past with one body to govern political, economic, and military control."

"That's just it." The president pounded the desk again. "You expect us to give up our Supreme Court, our Congress, and our system of administration? Ha! You folks in Europe don't know what you're asking if you want a piece of this American pie."

General Herrick looked at Daniel, obviously waiting for him to say something, but Daniel wasn't certain what Stedman wanted to hear. He couldn't forget that Lauren was in the room, too, her face pale and drawn.

Daniel plunged in. "Think of the advantages." He glanced at Herrick, then gave the president what he hoped was an encouraging smile. "One citizenship and passport—we're practically at that stage now in our relationship with Canada. Why not include Europe? And one central bank—the world markets are already linked by instantaneous computer transactions, so why not adopt one global currency? A dollar no longer represents its worth in gold; its value is subjective. So why not tie our currency to the one being developed in Europe? Together Europe and North America control over 70 percent of the global economy. If we unite, the Pacific Rim nations are sure to join us."

Warming to his subject, Daniel leaned forward and looked into the president's eyes. At least the man wasn't pounding the desk. "Within the Millennium Network, sir," he began, spreading his hands, "are all the tools we need. In less than ten months our system will be operational, and *at your urging* I designed a virtually identical Millennium system for Europe. Why not link them? The idea is cost-effective, simple, and incredibly logical."

The president did not answer but swiveled his chair toward Lauren.

She sat at the side of the president's desk with a polite, frozen look on her face.

"What do you think, Lauren?" The president's eyes fastened on her. "You were over there, you have a sense of these things. Will our people take to the idea, or will they think we're selling out?"

Lauren lowered her gaze as if gathering her thoughts, then tilted her head. "There is a marked difference between our people and the Europeans. The concept of unity might be more popular in a few years, after our citizens have had a chance to warm to the idea. But right now I believe the average American is more concerned about crime on his own street than political movements coming out of Belgium."

Daniel caught Lauren's eye and grinned, silently congratulating her on her diplomacy. He had not had an opportunity to speak to her alone since he arrived at the White House this morning, but he fully intended to take her to lunch and bury the hatchet—if she'd let him.

The president's chair creaked as he leaned forward and folded his arms on the desk. "Well, gentlemen, thank you for your time. But I'll be honest with you." His gaze shifted from General Archer to General Herrick. "General Herrick, we've heard some disturbing intelligence reports on Mr. Romulus's activities. For one, we still believe Saddam Hussein is hiding chemical and biological weapons, and I can't understand why Romulus would want to have dinner with that fellow. Second, some of his personal relationships seem a little bizarre, and I don't want to align my country's interests with somebody who ought to be reclining on a psychiatrist's couch three or four times a week."

"I'm certain I don't know what you mean." Huffing in indignation, Herrick drew himself upright. "I cannot sit here and allow you to insult Mr. Romulus."

"Well, sir, I can't help telling the truth. It comes from being a country boy, I guess. But I can tell you one truth, and you can take this back to Europe and repeat it to anyone who's interested." He pointed his index finger directly at Herrick, then lowered it to tap the desk emphatically. "The United States will join the European Union in a new world order over my dead body. That's the end of it, I promise you. You can sweet-talk some senators and congressfolk while you're here, but I really don't think you're going to win many points for your boss. Americans love their country, and they're pretty darn independent."

President Stedman glanced at his watch, then stood and buttoned his jacket. "Thank you, gentlemen, but I believe I have another appointment."

Daniel rubbed his hand over his chin, hiding a smile as he stood with Lauren and the two generals. Sam Stedman was not always the most diplomatic man, but he was definitely a man of conviction. If Adrian Romulus wanted to visit the United States without a passport, he'd have to wait at least until after the year 2000 election.

Daniel followed the others out of the office, then lingered in the hall until Lauren came out and closed the door. "Lunch?" he asked, giving her his most charming smile.

"I'm sorry," she said, smiling back, "but I have another appointment. I probably won't have time for lunch today."

"Oh." Daniel swallowed his disappointment and found it more bitter tasting than he'd expected. He shrugged. "Perhaps later. But I'm not sure how long I'm going to be in Washington."

"I don't imagine you'll be here long at all." She took a deep breath and softened her smile. "I'm sorry, Daniel, that sounded catty. What I meant to say was that I know you have a lot of work to do back in New York. And the president was quite firm—I really don't think this subject is open for further discussion. So unless you have some other great idea to unite the world—"

"Sorry. Fresh out." Daniel slipped his hands into his pockets and struggled with the sense of confusion her presence always elicited. "Look me up, then, if you come to New York."

"Sure." She nodded, and he thought he might have seen a faint shimmer of moisture in her blue eyes. Maybe it was the light.

"See you later, Lauren."

Without any further delay, Daniel turned and left the woman of his dreams standing in the hallway outside the Oval Office.

–0100111100–

Kord Herrick picked up the safe phone, then pressed the button that automatically encrypted all calls. The feature was annoying, for the transmission was delayed a few seconds, but in this case, encryption was absolutely necessary.

Charles, Romulus's butler, took the call, and Kord leaned back against the leather seats in the limo, imagining the dignity with which the old man carried the phone into the room where Romulus waited.

"Yes?"

Kord cleared his throat. "It's just as you feared. He won't listen. His exact words were, 'over my dead body.'"

The phone line hissed for a moment as the limo passed under a high-voltage wire, then Kord heard Romulus's low, throaty laugh. "Make it so, then," he said. "If not dead, then at least nearly so. All obstacles must be removed."

Kord waited until he was certain Romulus had finished speaking. "I'll handle it."

He disconnected the call, then dropped the phone back into its leather case. He leaned back against the leather upholstery, then pressed the electronic window switch and let the balmy breezes of Washington blow over his face. Ah, America, the land of the free. Perhaps, one day, Romulus would let Kord live here.

TWENTY-THREE

FIVE MONTHS PASSED. THE BREEZY DAYS OF MARCH AND APRIL YIELDED TO THE calm warmth of May, June, and July, but Daniel spent little time in anything but the filtered, climate-controlled air of Prentice Technologies. To take his mind off Lauren, he dove into his work for both the American and European Millennium Projects, purposely replicating the parameters in both systems. Even if President Stedman did not want to directly affiliate the American network with the European Union's, the Millennium Chip would still provide a common code through which all transactions could be easily monitored and recorded. Despite the president's reluctance, Daniel still fostered the hope that the nations of the world would soon join the Millennium Project. No matter how nervous Adrian Romulus made the NSA, the man had the right idea. The world had shrunk to an amazing degree in the last few decades, and mankind needed a common language and means of trade. The Millennium Chip would provide just that.

By July first, Prentice Technologies had supervised the production of over 600 million Millennium Chips. Manufacturers in California, Singapore, Munich, and Hong Kong had scrambled to meet Daniel's demanding specifications, and boxes of the tiny chips were now being stored in local post offices across the United States and Europe. Newly trained data entry specialists encoded the basic data to be keyed into each individual Millennium Chip; bank account numbers, organ donor, medic-alert, and health insurance information would be added at implementation time.

Every American over the age of ten had received a notice to report to his local post office sometime between July 4 and December 31, 1999. And the inaugural implementation day had been a rousing success. On July 4, post offices across the country remained opened with extended hours so citizens could come in and receive their Millennium Chips. Hot dog stands, puppet shows, and balloon vendors lined the sidewalks, offering goodies for the children and fun for all. Several enterprising bankers set up cash receipt booths where newly-chipped clients could turn in their cash and have an equivalent amount scanned onto their Millennium stored-value cards. Local merchants offered special discounts to those who purchased over fifty dollars of merchandise with a Millennium Card. Since the beginning of July, a host of televised public service announcements featured shots of happy shoppers grinning at the camera and assuring television audiences that the convenience of a Millennium Chip was the best thing since sliced bread.

Even President and Mrs. Stedman had gone to a great deal of trouble to put the public's fear to rest. The morning news shows all featured video footage of the White House staff receiving their Millennium Chips. "This tiny white bandage," the president told a television camera as he pointed to the back of his right hand, "is a badge of honor. Everyone who participates in National Identification Day is joining us as we take a bold step into the future."

On Sunday morning, July 18, Daniel and Dr. Kriegel sipped coffee in Prentice Technology's company cafeteria. They'd just put in an all-nighter double-checking their subcontractors' delivery dates for the latest European Millennium Chip shipments. Daniel wanted to be certain Adrian Romulus and his fellow European commissioners would have the required number of chips on July 22, the day they were now calling "the birthday of one Europe." Though the sheer number of Millennium Chips required that they be distributed over a six-month period, early reports indicated that Europeans would follow the Americans' example and rush to receive their implants. Polls indicated that the only individuals resisting the idea of a convenient identification chip were those who called themselves "born-again Christians."

Daniel felt a wry smile creep over his face as he thought of his mother. She would definitely be among the resistant group, but she had been wary of her debit card and the Internet, too . . . until Daniel had demonstrated and explained their convenience. In the same way, time and education would convince all but the most radical Christian holdouts. After all, there was nothing in the law that *required* an individual to be microchipped. But if a man or woman wanted to work, go to a hospital, receive any sort of government benefits, or shop, he or she would have to be implanted with a Millennium Chip.

Satisfied that the Millennium Project was safely on course, the professor's conversation turned to the Millennium Code program. The Y2K fix for First Manhattan had been finished since March, and the bank's final installment payment had just been sent to Prentice Technology's accounting department. Dr. Kriegel assured Daniel that the bank considered their $400 million well spent. "Their mainframes are now up to speed for the Millennium Network," he explained as Daniel sipped his coffee. "First Manhattan is miles ahead of their competition."

Daniel put down his coffee cup and nodded, only half-listening. A CNN report whispered from the wall-mounted television in the corner of the room, and Daniel couldn't help but notice that the camera was trained on the front of the White House. The president and first lady walked under the portico and waved to the cameras, then Mrs. Stedman gracefully took a seat in the back of the black limo and tucked her legs out of sight. The president paused to wave at a crowd well beyond the barriers outside the White House grounds, then Daniel's heart lurched when he saw Lauren step forward and tug at the president's sleeve.

Daniel felt his mouth go dry. He hadn't seen her in five months, but every day he had debated whether or not he should pick up the phone, call her, and confess whatever had offended her—he'd admit anything as long as she said she wanted to see him again. He didn't know exactly what had driven the wedge between them, but it had all begun the day they visited that small church and he told her about Adrian Romulus's offer.

The CNN White House reporter was speaking to the camera now, and Daniel interrupted the professor's rambling by putting his hand on the doctor's arm. "Hold that thought, will you, Professor? I'd like to listen to this."

Daniel reached for the remote and jacked the volume up, then leaned back in his chair and folded his arms.

"The first family is on its way to church today," the reporter was saying, her hair blowing in a light breeze. "Since neither the president nor the first lady were able to travel to Brussels for the coming celebration of One Europe, we had expected the president to make a short statement in honor of the occasion. But, as you can see, an urgent phone call has diverted him for a moment. . . ."

The reporter droned on about the scheduled festivities in London, Paris, Bonn, and Brussels, but Daniel scanned the background for another glimpse of Lauren. She had been wearing a summery white dress, not her typical business attire, and he didn't think her usual routine called for her to be in the office on Sunday morning. But perhaps she planned to join the Stedmans at church.

Desperate to fill air time, the reporter, Kathleen somebody-or-other, turned to ask another broadcaster for his opinion about the upcoming European celebration. As they babbled about trivialities, Daniel saw Mrs. Stedman's hand float out of the limo's backseat. She gracefully gestured toward the portico where a host of dark-suited Secret Service agents waited, then her hand reached out to close the door. The stately automobile rolled forward, probably to collect the president, and an agent stepped up as if to reopen the door. Daniel leaned toward the television, hoping for another glimpse of Lauren, but a sudden blast nearly jarred him out of his chair.

Fear shot through Daniel as smoke and flames abruptly filled the screen. The jabbering reporter flew forward, the camera tilted crazily, and Daniel caught a glimpse of blue sky and gauzy clouds before the screen went black and the roar of absolute silence filled his ears.

"No!" A cold sweat prickled on Daniel's jaw as his mind slowly took in the obvious, inconceivable truth. His heart pounding like a trip hammer, he stood, then turned toward the professor and pointed to the television, unable to speak.

"I saw." A tremor passed over the professor's pale face, and a sudden spasm of grief knit his brows. "What is the world coming to? Who would do such a thing?"

Daniel pressed his hand to the back of his neck and paced in a tight little square, his eyes fixed to the television screen. In less than ten seconds the director cut to the CNN newsroom, but the reporters in Atlanta wore blank looks and spoke with heavy, stumbling tongues—as numb with disbelief and shock as Daniel.

He heard the soft sound of sobbing in the newsroom. They watched the television, waiting, watching for someone who could give a word of explanation . . . or hope.

After a moment woven of eternity, one clear thought surfaced in Daniel's mind. "I've got to call Lauren."

"You'll never get through." The professor sank slowly back to his chair and pushed his hand through his thinning hair. "Wait. The television will tell us . . . as soon as they know."

Daniel tried to sit, but in less than a moment he was pacing again, his stomach twisting in knots of anguish. Lauren had been standing under that portico when the bomb went off—if it was a bomb that caused that blinding flash. Was she hurt? In the hospital? Was anyone looking after her, or was everyone concentrating on saving the president and the first lady?

Just when Daniel thought he would explode from frustration, the news camera returned to Pennsylvania Avenue. A different reporter stood behind the tall black bars surrounding the White House, his face contorted in a spasm of grief.

"This is a scene we thought we'd never see," he yelled into the microphone as sirens wailed in the background. "Apparently—from what we can gather—the president's limousine exploded a few moments ago. The driver, a Secret Service agent, and the first lady were inside the car, and two agents were standing within ten feet of the vehicle. Kathleen Winstead, the CNN White House correspondent on the scene, was knocked off her feet and is being tended by the paramedics. The president was *not* inside the car. I repeat—the president was not harmed in the blast."

"Where's Lauren?" Daniel ground the words out between his teeth.

The reporter paused to wipe his cheek with the side of his hand. "I have heard an unconfirmed report that everyone inside the car, as well as the two agents standing nearby, were killed instantly. As you can imagine, debris from the explosion struck others in the vicinity, and several ambulances are lined up at the security check points. Officials will not allow ambulances into the area, but several wounded are being carried out on gurneys, and others are being airlifted to Walter Reed."

Daniel drew a deep breath and forbade himself to tremble. "I'm going to Washington."

He turned and looked at the professor, who nodded. "Go." He waved Daniel toward the door. "Take care of her."

Daniel did not have to be told twice.

-0100111100-

For security reasons, Ronald Reagan Airport was shut down, but Daniel told his pilot to fly into Dulles instead. He didn't care how long it took to get there, but he would reach Lauren if he had to dig under those barricaded walls and crawl through the infamous escape tunnels under the White House grounds. As a kid, he had prowled around the external tunnels at the Canadian NORAD SAGE complex, and none of the guards had ever caught on. Daniel had made a game out of it—lying low when the video cameras scanned the passageways, moving so slowly that the motion detectors didn't pick up his movements, even coming in dripping wet from the lake to hide from the infrared sensors. He had never actually made it *into* the SAGE base, but he had undoubtedly annoyed more than a few security guards.

At the thought of guards, he opened his briefcase and double-checked his security passes. He had rummaged through his desk and files in a mad rush, tossing anything that might prove useful into his briefcase. In the clutter Daniel found three different security passes, two name badges, and a half-dozen letters from Lauren and President Stedman. He'd also tossed in an envelope filled with hundred dollar bills, in case a bribe should prove necessary. He didn't think the White House staff would be particularly susceptible to bribery, but there were probably a million reporters and traffic cops around the place by now. A well-placed c-note could save lots of time.

Daniel settled back in his seat as the jet began its descent. An urge rose up within him—born of desperation, probably—but Daniel obeyed it and whispered an urgent prayer: "God, be with Lauren. Please. And help me find her."

He repeated the prayer over and over again as the plane touched down. He didn't think that God needed to be reminded in a continuous verbal loop, but something about the act of asking for help soothed Daniel's spirit.

He was still silently reciting the prayer like a mantra when he hailed a cab and told the driver to take him as close to the White House as possible.

-0100111100-

Three hours and a thousand dollars later, Daniel began to make progress in his search for Lauren. The sight of cold, hard cash prompted a cameraman outside Lafayette Park to divulge the fact that Lauren had been airlifted from the White House with an injured Secret Serviceman. The president, the cameraman remarked, apparently thinking that Stedman was Daniel's main interest, remained inside the White House under a doctor's care. He had not been injured in the blast, but the assassination attempt and the loss of his wife had severely shaken him.

Daniel thrust a couple of wadded hundred dollar bills into the man's hand and turned away, grateful to be away from the media circus that had besieged the president's home. The country was mortified that a terrorist could strike within the walls of America's power center, but Daniel could not share in the shock. He felt sorry for Samuel Stedman, for Victoria had been a gracious lady and a loving wife. But few nations had managed to escape terrorism as well as the United States. Statistically, Washington was long overdue for a terrorist strike.

No one was invincible or completely safe. Each time the security experts came up with new technology to foil terrorists, the merchants of mayhem went a step further and foiled the security experts. It was all a deadly game, a race to stay one step ahead of the competition. And whoever had planted *this* bomb ran at the front of the pack. Daniel knew comparatively little about who was capable of what in the dark world of international terrorism. He suspected, though, that Brad would confirm that there were probably only two or three groups with access to the kind of technology that could have planted and exploded a device in the White House's driveway.

The cab driver wove in and out of the snarled traffic, barking curses at other drivers and leaning on his horn. Daniel sat silently in the backseat with his arms crossed, his mind swimming in a tide of frustration, until the cab turned onto the avenue that led to Walter Reed Army Medical Center.

"Let me out here," Daniel said, tossing the man one of the bills from his briefcase. "I'll get there faster on foot."

He didn't wait for a response but slammed his briefcase shut and threw open the car door. In this area traffic had come to a virtual standstill as the media, the curious, and the naysayers gathered to make pronouncements and offer opinions.

Daniel prayed that security wouldn't be too tight around the hospital. After all, the president was still back at the White House; only the support staff had been taken to Walter Reed.

He shouldered his way through the crowd, flashed one of his badges at a few cops and hospital security officers, then found himself in the long corridor that served as the main artery of the emergency wing. His pulse quickened as he hurried past open cubicles and peered behind curtains. Finally he stopped in an open doorway, his heart hammering. Inside the room, Lauren sat upon a gurney, a white bandage covering half her forehead, her hair mussed. Her eyes were wide, and unmistakable bloodstains marked the jacket and skirt of her white dress.

But she was sitting up . . . and alive.

Daniel whispered her name on a tide of relief. "Lauren."

She lifted her head at the sound of his voice, and her blue eyes filled instantly with tears. A nurse turned and lifted her hand as if to ward Daniel off, but he ignored her and hurried to gather Lauren into his arms. She buried her face in his shoulder and clung to him like a frightened child.

"It's okay," he told the nurse, who glared at him with her hands on her hips. "I have a right to be here."

It seemed an inane thing to say, but the nurse shrugged and threw up her hands, then left the room. Daniel ran his hand through Lauren's hair and held her close, whispering comforting sounds while she choked on the words that rose to her lips.

"I tried—I tried to reach her, Daniel." Lauren's voice broke in a horrible, rattling gurgle. "But I couldn't see anything. And the fire was so hot, and I couldn't get near her—"

"It's okay, honey. You tried. But no one could have saved her."

She yielded then to the compulsive sobs that shook her, and Daniel held her tight, grateful that she had accepted his comfort.

Twenty-four

9:45 A.M., Tuesday, July 20, 1999

Two days later Daniel sat very still in Lauren's small office, his eyes wide and contemplative as he watched her work. She had insisted upon reporting to the White House the day after the accident, and even in the midst of chaos, grief, and confusion her sheer organizational muscle had kept everyone else from falling apart. But she had sobbed in his arms on Sunday, so he knew a layer of vulnerability lay beneath that granite strength.

Would she ever reach out to him again?

Now she was studying her computer monitor, taking a video condolence call from the governor of Arkansas. Lauren thanked the governor for his concern, assured him that she would see that the president received word of his sympathy, then disconnected the call.

Her posture slumped in the instant the governor's image vanished from the screen. "Another one," she said, noting the time and message in her computer log. After fretting at the keyboard for a moment, she lifted her hands and wearily tucked her hair behind her ears, then gave Daniel a tired smile. "Why don't you go see if Francine can order in some lunch? It's after two; you must be hungry."

"What about you?" Daniel's eyes narrowed in concern. In the last forty-eight hours Lauren had responded to nearly a hundred phone calls from high-ranking government officials, sent thank-you telegrams to foreign leaders, and arranged for the computer system to apply the president's signature to each and every condolence letter that arrived at the White House.

She had removed the bandage from her forehead, revealing a cut with six stark black stitches, but she wore her bangs curled over the wound in an attempt to avoid expressions of sympathy. She had eaten only two meals—at Daniel's insistence—and though he had ordered her to go home, change, and get a few hours rest, he suspected that she had done nothing but toss and turn throughout the past two nights.

Daniel had again taken up residence in the Lincoln Bedroom, much to the chagrin of the federal agents prowling the grounds. They didn't like civilian personnel on the premises, and at the moment anyone but President Stedman, regular White House staff, and professional security people fell under suspicion. But Lauren had asked the president to approve Daniel's presence, and the dazed president had complied, so the Secret Service could do nothing to evict him.

Daniel's thoughts filtered back to the moment he'd first seen the president after the explosion. Samuel Stedman had not been injured in what was now officially labeled as a terrorist attack, but Daniel could not shake the impression of Stedman as an injured man. When Daniel saw him on Monday morning, the president's head bobbed uncertainly at every sound, presenting his advisors with a haggard, starved-looking gray face in which scared blue eyes occupied most of the available space.

Daniel glanced up at Lauren. "How's the president doing today?"

The question caught Lauren off guard, and she looked up from her keyboard, surprise in her eyes. "As well as can be expected, I suppose. He's still in shock." She lowered her gaze to the computer monitor. "I think we all are. But he's scheduled a meeting in half an hour with General Archer." She gave Daniel a brief, distracted glance, and tried to smile. "I have to go, so why don't you come with me?"

"Me?" Daniel laughed. "I came to Washington for you, not for General Archer. I've had enough of his politics."

"But the president trusts you . . . and so do I."

Daniel felt his resolve melting under her soft blue gaze. What harm could it do? This was closet politics, not the public arena, and no one would know or even care that he was lingering in places where he had no business being.

"Okay." He eased into a smile. "For you."

At 2:30 he followed Lauren into the Oval Office and was surprised to find both Generals Archer and Herrick sitting on one of the striped sofas. Archer's brows shot up as Daniel entered the room, and Herrick's thin mouth twisted in a wry smile.

"Daniel Prentice," Herrick said, his tone cool. "Imagine finding you here."

"I might say the same to you, General." Daniel took a seat next to Lauren on the opposite sofa. The president had not yet appeared, and an atmosphere of waiting filled the room.

Daniel tapped his knees and cast about for a topic of conversation. He suspected that he was not very popular with Herrick or Adrian Romulus at the moment. Though he had successfully met his goals for a very workable Millennium system, he had failed to convince President Stedman to join the European Union's computer network. He had also failed to convince himself that working for Romulus was the right career move.

"I was speaking to Mr. Romulus just this morning," Herrick said, a silken thread of rebuke in his voice. "He remarked that he has not heard from you. Apparently he made you a rather generous offer before you left Brussels—"

"Please tell Mr. Romulus that I cannot accept his offer at present." Daniel cast a quick glance at Lauren, hoping she would understand the significance of his statement. "I have been distracted by certain situations in this country that demand my full attention."

Herrick's features hardened in a stare of disapproval. "Mr. Romulus will be most disappointed to hear the news." He lifted a brow. "Perhaps I can tell him you might be available in a few months?"

Torn between his ambition and his conscience, Daniel looked away. Lauren would not want him to work with Romulus, but Lauren thought in terms of America first. Her thoughts were tinged with grief at the moment, though; she might not even care what Daniel did in Europe.

Daniel gave Herrick a bland, noncommittal smile. "Have Mr. Romulus keep the position open. I'll be in touch with him later."

The curved door abruptly swung open, and each person in the room automatically stood as Samuel Stedman entered the room. Shock flew through Daniel as the president nodded and took a seat in the velvet wing chair by the fireplace. Anxiety and grief had etched that handsome face; dark loss still shadowed his eyes. His cheekbones looked like tent poles under stretched canvas; his lips had shrunk to thin gray lines.

Daniel caught Lauren's eye as they sat down. *Is he all right?*

She gave a quick nod, acknowledging his anxiety, then smiled and turned to the president. "I thought it might be good to have Daniel Prentice join us, since he has worked with both of these gentlemen," she said smoothly, pulling a printed agenda from her leather notebook. "And I'm sure you'll remember that this meeting was scheduled last week to discuss a possible merging of our military bases in Europe with those of the European Community. And there's the matter of the official Day of Peace—"

"If you don't mind," General Herrick interrupted and leaned toward the president, "my superior, Mr. Romulus, has expressed his desire to participate in this meeting via telephone. I told him I thought a video call at 2:45 might be in keeping with our schedule."

A flicker of surprise widened Lauren's eyes, but the president merely rubbed the slight stubble on his chin. "Fine," he answered, his eyes as flat and unreadable as stone.

Lauren glanced down at her notes, then rose. "I'll have your secretary set up the camera link," she said, moving toward the door that opened to the reception area.

Daniel leaned back against the sofa, watching his companions in the resulting silence. On any other occasion they might have told jokes or shared political gossip, but an uncomfortable stillness hung over the room, an almost palpable residue of grief.

The heavy atmosphere dissipated to a remarkable degree when Lauren returned. "Francine will be right in," she said, sinking to the sofa next to Daniel. "She says Mr. Romulus is already on hold."

Francine Johnson, the president's secretary, entered a moment later, then moved to a tall wooden cabinet and opened the polished doors. A twenty-two inch monitor sat on a shelf inside, and Francine pressed the power on, then stood back and watched as Adrian Romulus's image filled the screen.

"Mr. Romulus," she said, gazing up at the tiny camera which sat atop the monitor, "can you see everyone in the room?"

"Yes." Romulus's chiseled, handsome face was furrowed with sadness. He turned slightly, seeming to seek out the president's eyes. Daniel had to remind himself that Romulus was staring into a camera, just as they were.

"Mr. President." Unspoken pain was alive and glowing in Romulus's eyes. "Please, sir, allow me to extend my sincere condolences on the loss of your beloved wife. I did not have an opportunity to meet her, and I shall always regret that unkind twist of fate. But, if it is any comfort, know that her memory shall always remain in my heart. The joy and graciousness that characterized her daily walk and the beauty that she exhibited shall continue as long as I am alive to recall her."

The president made a small, strangled sound deep in his throat. From where he sat, Daniel couldn't tell if anger or grief moved the president.

"General Herrick—" Again, Romulus's eyes seemed to move and find the man he sought—"let's postpone the discussion you were scheduled to hold today. Why should we talk about military bases when our hearts are heavy with sorrow? Let us allow President Stedman to keep council with his own thoughts."

If Herrick was surprised, he gave no sign of it. "Of course, sir."

"President Stedman." Slowly, almost imperceptibly, Romulus's image grew larger and seemed to fill the screen. Intrigued, Daniel leaned forward. A professional had to be running the camera in Europe, zooming in for effect at just the right moment.

"This is an uncertain world," Romulus went on, his dark eyes artless and serene. "And it is all the more important that you join us on January 1, 2000, as we proclaim an International Day of Peace. We have already garnered the support of more than three dozen world leaders who have agreed that their governments and citizens will lay down their weapons for a single day—January 1—and issue a proclamation of peace."

"You want me to issue a general stand down to all American troops on a given day?" The president's voice, so flat a moment ago, vibrated now with restrained fury. "You want us to leave our national defenses open to whatever enemy might want to approach us—an enemy that might have had months to prepare for an attack? What kind of fool do you think I am, sir?" The lines of heartache lifted from his face as he glared into the video camera. "I am the American commander-in-chief. I took a vow to provide for the continuous defense of the United States, and I intend to keep it."

Romulus stared blankly into the camera, with only a wary twitch of his eye to indicate he knew he had wandered onto shaky ground. "Please, President Stedman—" his dark eyes widened—"I can understand if your tragic circumstances have led you to become unreasonably suspicious, but the Day of Peace has been under discussion for at least ten years. The concept, in fact, originated with an American in New Jersey. I can assure you, sir, if we all lay down our arms, there will be no one to launch any sort of offensive."

"The Soviets tried that same line on Ronald Reagan," the president muttered, swiping at his chin. He looked at Lauren as if for assurance. "It didn't work on him, and it certainly isn't going to work on me. The United States will remain strong, we will keep up our defenses, and we will not lay down our arms for even one hour."

Romulus stared into the camera, his eyes piercing. "You are certainly entitled to your opinion, Mr. President," he said, his voice oddly formal. "But as I reflected upon your tragedy, one rather ironic thought did occur to me—if you had come to Europe to join us in a celebration of international unity and peace, your wife would be at your side even now. In unity, we find safety. But those who stand aloof from others will always be in danger."

For no reason Daniel could name, Romulus's words lifted the hairs on the back of his neck.

Romulus smiled, and the camera pulled back slightly. "Gentlemen, it is a pleasure to see you. General Archer, give my best to your family. General Herrick, thank you for your flexibility. Miss Mitchell, I am glad you were not severely injured. And Mr. Prentice, I am grateful for your willingness to serve the human community in a time of crisis." Romulus's eyes, remote as the ocean depths, seemed to rest directly upon Daniel. "I know you will appreciate the fact that things are not always what they seem."

The camera pulled back again, and Romulus lifted his hand in farewell. "I wish you all a good day."

The screen went black. Daniel brought his hand to his chin, thinking. *Things are not always what they seem?* What things? Was Romulus referring to the Millennium Project or something altogether different? And what had he meant by reminding the president that Mrs. Stedman had been in the wrong place at the wrong time? Romulus's words could almost be seen as a threat, even a confession.

President Stedman lifted a trembling hand and pointed toward the darkened monitor. "That man," he said, his voice quavering in a most unpresidential fashion, "is the devil himself. I have suspected it for some time, and now I know—he killed my wife. He wanted to kill me, but he took Victoria instead."

Daniel listened in bewilderment, then looked to General Herrick, expecting a storm of denials. But Herrick only stared at the president, his face locked in an expression of remarkable sorrow.

"Surely it isn't true." Lauren's whisper reached Daniel's ear. "Tell the president it isn't true, General Herrick."

The general stood, bowed sharply to the president, then looked at Lauren with a smile gleaming in his dark eyes. "Of course this irrational accusation is not true," he answered, lifting one shoulder in a shrug. "He is beside himself with grief. But my presence here is causing him stress, so I will return when your president is in a more agreeable mood."

He turned and walked away, followed by General Archer, leaving Daniel with a thousand unanswered questions. One broke lose from the pack and sprang to his lips.

"Lauren," he whispered, turning toward her as the president rose from his chair and moved toward his private study, "who called him?"

Lauren looked at him and blinked hard. "What?"

"Last Sunday morning. The president was about to get into the car, but you stopped him. The reporter said that he had gone inside to take an urgent phone call. Who called?"

She slowly brought her fingertips to her lips. "It was only Charlie Marvin."

"And he is—?"

Lauren lowered her gaze in confusion. "He's nobody—at least, nobody political. He's a young minister and a friend of the family who calls them from time to time. The Stedmans financially supported him while he went through seminary, and I knew they wouldn't want to miss one of his calls."

Daniel glanced down at his hands, marveling at the irony. President quietly supports preacher; preacher quietly saves president.

"Have you considered that this Reverend Charlie Marvin saved the president's life?" Daniel turned to Lauren again. "If he hadn't called, Samuel Stedman would have been inside that car when it exploded. My mother would say that God orchestrated the entire thing."

She managed a tremulous smile. "Then why," her voice broke, "couldn't God have managed to save Mrs. Stedman, too?"

Daniel dropped his hands and looked her straight in the eye. "I'm no theologian, Lauren. I guess that's a question you'll have to ask Reverend Marvin."

Twenty-five

9:00 A.M., Thursday, July 22, 1999

CNN's newscasters dutifully turned their cameras toward Brussels and the inner sanctum of the European Union's Council of Ministers. With his fellow councilors gathered around him, Adrian Romulus gazed into the camera and announced that a new world community was about to be born.

Daniel watched the announcement from a television set up in the Oval Office. He and Lauren sat on one of the sofas before the wide television screen, both of them benumbed by tragedy and a sense of loss. The White House hummed with quiet activity; a host of dignitaries had gathered in the East Room to attend Victoria Stedman's afternoon funeral service. But Daniel's thoughts about the recent tragedy fluttered and died as Adrian Romulus declared that a new global order had been conceived with a spark of inspiration from the glorious Millennium Code.

"As the millennium turns, so do the dates on our computers and the methods by which we conduct our lives and our business," Romulus said. A flush of pleasure brightened his face, as if the idea had caused younger blood to fill his veins. "I want to assure the world community that our European Union government, in cooperation with the private sector, has taken steps to prevent any interruption in services that rely on the proper functioning of computer systems. We cannot have the European people looking to a new century and a new millennium while obsolete computers endanger our lives. Due to the extraordinary Millennium Code, that will not happen. And the Millennium Chip has guaranteed that we will move confidently into a new millennium, a nation of many nations. Our diversity, alive in our unity, is the source of our creativity, our inventiveness, and our ability to communicate in the global community. That is why I have called upon world leaders to observe the International Day of Peace on January 1, 2000."

Lauren hissed softly at the mention of that project. She'd told Daniel that the president had been upset for hours after Romulus's call. If President Stedman didn't agree to celebrate peace, the media would paint him as a warmonger; but the idea of completely dropping America's defenses ran contrary to his principles.

"We have come to the end of a thrilling decade that has seen the fall of Communism and the rise of democracy throughout the world," Romulus continued. "Our world's scientists have succeeded in mapping the mysteries of the human body and the terrain of Mars. We have created new ideas in art and literature. Now we have begun the most important exploration of all—discovering and affirming our common identity as human beings in a new and different time, coming together as one world community."

"Notice that he gives credit to the world," Daniel whispered, elbowing Lauren. "When it was *American* scientists who mapped Mars."

Romulus shifted his position and played to a different camera. "For centuries, people have wondered what the new millennium would bring. Would it signal an apocalypse or herald a brave new world of unparalleled opportunity? Would it mark a time of decline or a time of renewal? Whatever our hopes and fears, the new millennium is no longer a distant dream. It has arrived. We are present today at the birth of the future, a moment we must define for ourselves and our children."

"All around the world, citizens of this new community are planning ways to celebrate the new millennium. The United Kingdom will build bridges, museums, new parks, and a new university. Germany will hold Expo 2000, the first World's Fair to mark a millennium. Australia will host the 2000 Summer Olympics. Iceland will celebrate the thousandth anniversary of Leif Ericson's voyage to the New World. And we of the European Union will begin our celebration today, as we move forward to accept the implementation of our Millennium Chips."

Romulus's expression stilled and grew serious as he stared into the camera lens. "We must now decide how to think about our commitment to the future. Thomas Paine, a great American, once said, 'We have it in our power to begin the world over again.' He was right. We must now take it upon ourselves to commit ourselves over again for our children, our children's children, for the people who will follow us in a new century. It is the future of a united humanity we celebrate today."

A burst of applause—probably canned, Daniel thought with a wry smile—greeted the conclusion of Romulus's speech. Lauren clicked the remote and shut the TV off. For a moment they sat in silence, then Daniel reached for Lauren's hand.

"Nice speech," he said, squeezing her fingers. "Very positive, very encouraging. If I lived in Europe, I'd be inspired enough to go out and get my Millennium Chip today."

"Really?" Her tone was flat. "He had the opposite effect on me. If I could rip that blasted chip out of my hand right now, I would."

She gave him a look of regret and despair, then pulled her hand away and stood. "Sorry, Daniel, I've got to see to some of the funeral arrangements. I need to go now."

She ran out of the room, her eyes brimming with tears, leaving Daniel alone on the couch, wondering if he had done something wrong . . . again.

-0100111100-

While rockets and fireworks commemorated Europe's unity, Lauren stood between Daniel and the president and smoothed the wrinkles from her black linen skirt. The day was bright and clear; the sky above Arlington National Cemetery a faultless wide blue expanse. The national army band played softly as a long parade of mourners moved from the long line of black limousines, and Lauren's gaze fell to the golden casket beside the open grave. An elaborate spray of red roses covered the coffin, their sweet perfume wafting on the warm breeze that caressed her cheek like the soft touch of Victoria's hand.

Lauren glanced up at the suffering president and silently wished she could take his hand as a daughter might. An air of isolation clung to his tall figure, and he looked vacant, spent, as though all his emotions had been smoothed away.

The politician's curse, Lauren thought. More than two decades of public life had taught him how to hide his pain and cover his anger. She had thought herself fairly skilled at hiding her private face from the public eye, but her eyes filled with tears every time she looked at the president.

So she looked at the coffin instead, and felt her anguish fade away. For Victoria, at least, sorrow had ceased to exist. Death had taken her instantly, the doctors said, without time for pain. And so she had not suffered but was now resting in the arms of the one to whom she had trusted her life.

The band began to play another tune, and Lauren felt her spirits lift at the sound of it. Victoria had often sung the melody around the office, her voice cracking on the high notes. One particular phrase came back to Lauren's mind: *I know whom I have believed, and am persuaded that he is able to keep that which I've committed unto him against that day.*

Lauren knew Victoria would have approved of this ceremony. The president had given Lauren complete control over the arrangements, asking only for final approval, which he had given without hesitation. There had been no black-draped procession, no somber funeral music, no black wreaths upon the White House doors. The flag had flown at half-mast for three days, but Lauren had insisted that it be restored to its proper height for the funeral. A children's choir had sung gospel songs at the memorial service, and the Reverend Charlie Marvin stood at the graveside, his open Bible in his hands. The humble young pastor had been surprised by the call from the White House, but Lauren had convinced him to put his reluctance aside in order to honor a woman he had long admired and cherished.

"We are gathered here today to celebrate a home going," Charlie was saying now, his eyes sweeping over the crowd on the green hillside. "Victoria Stedman was not afraid of death. Though she did not expect to meet it last Sunday morning, I know she greeted her Lord with a cry of joy."

The minister's brown eyes gentled as they came to rest upon the president. "If some of us are sorrowing today, it is because we will miss her soft touch, her words of encouragement, and her courageous example. But Victoria never wanted to be idolized—she much preferred to reflect glory upon Jesus Christ, her Savior and Lord."

While the minister paused and glanced at his notes, Lauren looked again at the president. He stood with his head bowed, his hands clasped in front of him. Cameras clicked from a discreet distance, and Lauren knew the papers would print this picture above a caption that said, "President grieves for murdered wife." But they didn't know the truth—Sam Stedman wasn't sorrowing . . . he was praying.

The air vibrated to the long trill of a robin's song, and the minister waited until the sweet sound faded before he concluded his remarks. "Unlike many of you, I knew Victoria's daughter, Jessica Stedman, before her untimely death several years ago. Jessica had entrusted her life to Jesus Christ, too, so I know that today they are together with the Lord. We may never know the reason why Jessica preceded her mother to heaven, but I have to wonder if our merciful Lord wasn't sparing Jessica from the heartbreak of this tragic situation."

"It is on your behalf, Mr. President—" the minister paused until President Stedman lifted his gaze—"that our prayers will ascend to the throne of heaven. I know the Lord has a purpose for sparing your life, and I know he will preserve you until his purposes are complete."

Sam Stedman's chin quivered, and for an instant Lauren feared he would lose his composure. But he drew a deep breath and gave the minister a brittle smile, then lowered his head again as the children's choir began to sing the last verse of "Amazing Grace."

When we've been there ten thousand years,
Bright shining as the sun,
We've no less days to sing God's praise
Than when we first begun.

As her own heart filled to overflowing, Lauren took Daniel's strong arm and followed the president from the graveside.

TWENTY-SIX

5:43 P.M., Thursday, July 22, 1999

THE PRESIDENT LEFT FOR CAMP DAVID IMMEDIATELY AFTER THE FUNERAL. Lauren made no comment about the full calendar he left behind but calmly rearranged his schedule. The man needed time to mourn; he also needed time to consider his response to Adrian Romulus's implicit threats. Not a shred of evidence linked Romulus to the car bomb, but the president wholeheartedly believed that Romulus had ordered his assassination.

But how? Kord Herrick, Romulus's aide, had been visiting Los Angeles the morning of the attack. That almost certainly meant that some trusted individual within the White House had placed the bomb or conveniently looked the other way while covert agents hid the explosive device.

From whispered conversations with Secret Service agents, Lauren knew that a blanket of suspicion had fallen over anyone who seemed to support the movement to affiliate with Europe. That number included half a dozen top advisors, several cabinet members, and a few leaders of the military. Even the vice president, who had told the *Washington Post* that Adrian Romulus was the greatest orator since Winston Churchill, found himself under investigation, and, most personally unnerving to Lauren, the president had even looked at Daniel Prentice with doubt in his eyes.

Once the president had departed the White House, Lauren and Daniel slipped through a security checkpoint and went for a walk around the Mall's Reflecting Pool. The sun was coming down in the sky but hadn't yet reached the tops of the trees that edged the Mall's long expanse.

They walked in silence for a long time, their hands intertwined, and Lauren wondered what the future held for them. Daniel had been her Rock of Gibraltar in the last few days; he'd shown up when she needed him and remained until the worst was over. But life had to go on, and she had no idea where the path of her life was leading.

"I thought you did a nice job with the funeral service," Daniel offered, breaking into her thoughts. "I didn't know the first lady very well, but I think she would have been pleased. The other families—the driver's, and the Secret Service agents'—they seemed grateful for all you did."

Lauren looked away toward the shimmering surface of the water. "I didn't do much—no more than I should have. They gave their lives in the service of their country." She tilted her head and looked up at Daniel. "Just like you nearly did, back in Desert Storm."

Daniel laughed softly. "Please, Lauren. I was no hero. It was a job, and I was glad to do it, but I outgrew my patriotism not long after that."

Lauren let the comment pass. Daniel had made no secret of his bitterness toward the military machinations that had taken his father, but he couldn't paint the entire armed forces with a single broad brush, no more than she could color all millionaires uncaring and egotistical. She had discovered, much to her surprise, that there were exceptions to every stereotype.

"I'll miss Victoria." She whispered the words. "But I'll not mourn her. I could never mourn her life. It was too precious. And I can find joy in knowing she's with the Lord."

Daniel stopped walking and turned, eyeing her with a calculating expression. "You did it, didn't you?" His eyes sparkled as though he were playing a game. "Was it Victoria—or the preacher in Brussels? Who convinced you to become a capital-C Christian?"

Lauren felt her jaw drop. "You can tell?"

"Of course I can." One corner of his mouth twisted upward. "You forget, my mother is a Bible-reading, born-again, baptized believer. She claims a long list of other adjectives, too, but I stopped trying to keep up with them all."

Lauren wondered if she should feel guilty for the wave of relief that washed over her. She had been wondering how to tell Daniel that her life had been fundamentally changed, but now she wouldn't have to say anything. He just knew.

"Does it bother you?"

Daniel snorted, then pulled her fingers from his and cradled her hand against his chest. "Would it matter if it did? I'm not sure I understand what drives people to that kind of faith, but I know it's pretty much a done deal." He bent slightly to look down into her eyes. "Am I right?"

She nodded numbly. "Afraid so. I just got to the place where I didn't know whom to trust—and I remembered what that bookbinder said in Brussels. God is the only one to whom I could really entrust my life."

Daniel turned to face her then. He lowered his head and stared at her hand as if it were some rare treasure, then slowly began to stroke her palm. "I was beginning to hope that you could trust me."

Lauren lowered her head as unexpected tears stung her eyes. She wanted to trust him, but years of political service had taught her not to completely rely on anyone. And she couldn't lose her heart right now, not until she knew what Sam intended to do about his presidency. Eighteen months remained in his first term, and in less than a year Sam Stedman would have to decide whether or not he would run again. Before last weekend the president had been eager to continue his work through a second term, but now Lauren feared he had lost the heart for politics.

Yet her job was to remain by his side until he released her. That commitment might involve every ounce of her time and energy for the next eighteen months . . . or the next five years.

"Daniel—" Her voice, like her nerves, was in tatters. "I care for you very much. But I've told you, I cannot commit to a serious relationship right now. The president needs me—and now he needs me more than ever."

He did not look up, but his fingers were cool and smooth as they caressed hers. "Believe it or not, I understand." His voice sounded as if it came from far away. "I'm a little overcommitted myself with the international Millennium Projects. I'm sure I'll be very busy in the days ahead."

The grooves beside his mouth deepened into a full smile as he looked into her eyes. "You're a beautiful and intelligent woman, Lauren. I know what I'd like to develop with you, but I also know who you are. I won't ask for the sort of relationship that would leave you feeling torn between two responsibilities."

I'm a little overcommitted myself. . . . The words rang like a death knell in Lauren's brain. Daniel was a nice guy, but even now he was probably yearning to get back to his work. Some antiquated sense of chivalry had brought him galloping to her rescue, but Daniel Prentice did not intend to stick around for the old-fashioned business of winning and wooing.

"I appreciate your thoughtfulness." The sudden and sharp words hurt her throat. Calmly, deliberately, she pulled her hand from Daniel's grasp. "And I am grateful for your coming. In the hospital, I was feeling so alone and bewildered—well, it meant a lot to look up and see you standing there."

He looked directly at her then, a spark of some indefinable emotion lighting his eyes. Lauren felt her heart flow toward him, but she steeled herself against the tide of emotion and thrust her hands behind her back. "We'd better get going." Lifting her chin, she turned and began to retrace her steps back to the White House.

Daniel quickly caught up to her. "So this is good-bye?" he asked, lifting one brow. The look in his eyes seemed to say that it wouldn't have to end if she would just say the word, but Lauren didn't know what he expected her to say. If he wanted her to quit her job, the answer would have to be no.

"I'm afraid it is." She stopped on the sidewalk and faced him, then lightly pressed her fingertips to the front of his shirt. "Daniel, let's not make this difficult for each other. We'll go back to the office, and you can get your things and head back to New York. If something comes up with the Millennium Project, feel free to call me, but don't feel obligated. I'm not a child, and I don't like playing games."

"Fine." His voice was clipped, and for an instant Lauren feared she had offended him. But he gave her a polite smile, then extended his arm in an expansive gesture. "Shall we go? I think you're going to be just fine."

Lauren nodded, and as they walked back toward the White House she told herself that all was how it should be. They were parting amicably, as friends and professionals. She had not weakened in her commitment to the president, and Daniel had behaved like a perfect gentleman.

Why, then, did her heart feel as if it were crumbling into pieces?

-0100111100-

In the quiet of his Washington hotel room, Kord Herrick plugged in his laptop, activated the PGP encryption program, then placed his call. A moment later he heard Romulus's baritone growl rumble from the speakers of his notebook PC. "General Herrick?"

"Yes, sir." Kord couldn't keep a smile from his voice. "Did you watch the event?"

"Yes." Romulus sighed heavily. "And I was most moved, General, by the sight of you wiping away a few tears. You seemed quite the sympathetic humanitarian."

Kord moved quickly past the compliment. "I'm certain Stedman will cooperate now. The man is shell-shocked. Mitchell and the rest of his staff are trying to cover for him, of course, but it is not business as usual. You saw him in the video conference—he's clinging to reality. You could drop a bomb on London, and Stedman wouldn't bat an eye."

A deep and easy chuckle rolled over the secure phone line. "Ah, the sectors are coming together now, General! The Middle East, the West, the Pacific Rim. All are gathering around Caesar's old dominion. I wonder what that old Roman would think if he could see how the Empire has expanded."

Kord laughed softly, then felt his eyes mist in a nostalgic memory. A strange sense of déjà vu swept over him—as a young man, he had worked with another young dreamer, another brilliantly insightful would-be emperor. But Hitler had weaknesses, including a despicable desire to be dominated by women. Romulus had no such weakness.

"Tell me, General, about Daniel Prentice. He seemed a little unsettled when I glimpsed him on the video. Is he still with us?"

"He's torn by his attachment to Miss Mitchell, who stands firmly with the president." Kord rested his head on his hands but took pains to be certain his face remained turned toward the tiny microphone in the laptop. "When I spoke to him, however, he seemed unwilling to dismiss your offer entirely. I believe he is neutral at this point. But an hour ago, one of our agents learned that he has booked a flight back to New York. He's going home."

"We must win him to our side." The command contained a strong suggestion of reproach. "Have you not learned, General, that those who are not for us are against us? Daniel Prentice may be impartial at the moment, but he will not remain so. And his is a great intellect. I want it."

"Of course, sir." Kord straightened his posture. "I'll call the young man. Have I your permission to increase the offer?"

"You can promise him the kingdoms of the world if you'd like."

Sarcasm laced Romulus's dry voice. "Just get his allegiance. I want him on our side."

The telephone line clicked, and Kord sighed as he shut down the computer. He checked his watch, then looked around the room. If he was lucky, he'd have just enough time for a quick catnap, then he'd have to catch a flight to New York.

TWENTY-SEVEN

10:45 P.M., Thursday, July 22, 1999

BACK ON PARK AVENUE, DANIEL STOOD MOTIONLESS IN THE MIDDLE OF THE foyer outside his apartment and studied the carved front doors. This cold, marble place was less homelike than his cluttered office, but after the emotion of the funeral and his departure from Lauren, Daniel didn't want to face his employees and pretend that all was well.

He felt restless, disjointed, almost uncomfortable in his own skin, and the discomfort was exacerbated by the fact that Daniel couldn't figure out *why* he felt so out of sorts. His time in Washington had been stressful, of course, but he had been there to comfort Lauren, not to be comforted. His nerves throbbed with weariness, but that was as much a result of the flight and the late hour as any emotional drain. Now he wanted nothing more than to return to work, his personal consolation, but he knew he was operating at less than full power. He needed rest.

Shaking his head, Daniel turned the key in the lock, then moved through the gleaming entry and into the kitchen. He tossed his briefcase upon the counter, then opened the refrigerator, and grimaced when the odors of rotting fruit reached his nose. Slamming the door, he moved to the pantry. He wanted snack food, potato chips and pretzels and chocolate chip cookies—crunchy, salty, and sweet foods that were bad for the waistline and even worse for the heart.

The foyer phone rang, shattering the marble stillness with its shrill chirping. Daniel paused, wondering if Lauren had this unlisted number, then decided to ignore the caller ID. She wouldn't call. She'd been quite firm in her refusal of his affections, quite adamant in her instructions that they should just go their separate ways.

How had he ever imagined that they might share a future? She was married to her career in general and Samuel Stedman's presidency in particular. Her four-year stint would certainly expand to eight if Stedman proceeded with his reelection plans. With his wife murdered in the service of her country, Stedman was a virtual shoo-in for the next election. Sympathy alone would bring him at least 60 percent of the vote.

The answering machine in the library clicked on as Daniel grabbed a bag of chips and searched for the expiration date. *Guaranteed fresh until December 31, 1998.*

"Great," he muttered, crunching the bag beneath his arm. "Only seven months too old." He reached for a glass, tossed in a handful of ice from the freezer, then grabbed a can of cola. Armed for the night, he moved into the library to listen to the voice rumbling over the answering machine.

" . . . desperately need to talk to you," the caller was saying. Daniel frowned, then lifted his brows when he recognized the voice and accent— the speaker was General Herrick. Daniel was mildly amazed that the general had bothered to search for Daniel's unlisted home phone, but not at all surprised that he had managed to find it.

He sank onto the tufted leather sofa and let his head fall to the padded armrest.

"I have spoken to Mr. Romulus," General Herrick droned on, "and he is most concerned about the future global implementation of the Millennium Code. In light of recent events in the United States, we are thinking that perhaps you would be wise to move Prentice Technologies to Brussels, or even Paris. Mr. Romulus would personally cover any moving expenses, as well as provide suitable office space for you and your associates."

"How would you like that, Dr. Kriegel?" Daniel lifted a toast as if the professor sat in the wing chair opposite the couch. "Would you like to move to the French Riviera? Or perhaps London would be more your cup of tea?"

"In any case, Mr. Prentice, we want you on our team. Please call me as soon as you are available. I am in New York, and anxiously awaiting your call." Herrick left two phone numbers, then clicked off the line.

Daniel stared dumbly at the wall and ripped open the bag, then popped a chip into his mouth. It had the consistency of a manila envelope, and about the same taste.

Daniel took a big swallow from his glass, washed the chip down, then dropped the bag to the carpeted floor.

What had he done with his life? He had amassed a multimillion-dollar corporate empire, charmed world leaders, and paved a technological road into the next millennium. His picture had graced a dozen magazine covers. He had dated beautiful, successful, even powerful women. And Adrian Romulus, who would soon stand at the head of the most powerful political force the world had ever known, was practically begging him to join his ambitious enterprise.

So why was he lying here in the dark . . . alone?

A sense of anticlimax washed over him. His mother would say that he needed a wife, but the one woman he could imagine living with forever had other plans. To make matters worse, she had become a Christian, and the more she got into Jesus, the more unholy Daniel would seem by comparison. He could never measure up to what Lauren expected of a man, and the more she prayed for Mr. Perfect, the less likely Daniel would be to qualify.

He shifted onto his side and rested his head on his hand. His father hadn't been perfect, but he'd been a Christian, too—or had he?

Daniel frowned and slowly submerged himself into memory. He remembered the airplane models, his father's books, the smell of leather and dust in the little bedroom his father used as a den. He thought he could remember the man praying at his bedside, but he couldn't be sure— perhaps it was an illusion wrought by an overactive imagination and a boy's yearning for the father who would never return.

Memory closed around him, filling him with a longing to know more, to separate myth from truth. He rolled off the couch and stumbled toward the library closet, where several taped boxes lay beneath his never-used Rollerblades and his spare tackle box.

A box at the bottom of the heap was marked with a brilliant blue marker: *Dad's books.* The handwriting was his mother's.

Kneeling inside the closet, Daniel shoved the junk aside and pulled the box out from the rubble. It was not large, but it was heavy; it took both hands and a concerted effort to bring it out of the closet and into the light. Daniel pulled it toward the library table, then reached up, switched on the lamp, and began to rip away the tape.

A few moments later Daniel had lifted out more than twenty books. For some reason he had imagined that his father collected books about theology or history or warfare, but nearly all the books stacked around him dealt with biblical prophecy. He pulled another book out of the box and studied it a moment: *The Last Days and the Antichrist—A Warning for the Final Generation.*

Good grief, he didn't realize his father was a gloom-and-doomer. He flipped through the pages, recognizing his name in several places—references to the biblical book of Daniel, of course—then paused on a page illustrated by a crude sketch. The sketch showed a woman clad in a Roman toga, riding upon a bull advancing from waves onto a beach. Beneath the sketch was a quote:

The prophet John described the coming kingdom of the Antichrist in his vision of a "beast with two horns." In another passage, he described "a beast arising out of the sea." In Revelation 17, John also described his vision showing the unholy alliance between the false world church of the last days and the rising kingdom of the Antichrist. This prophecy shows the false church in the symbol of a harlot riding upon a "scarlet beast" representing the ten-nation confederacy of the revived Roman Empire. The Antichrist will persecute Israel and defile her holy temple, which will be rebuilt in the last days—after the Jews return from exile to become a nation again.

A dose of adrenaline shot into Daniel's bloodstream, and his heart responded immediately, contracting like a squeezed fist. Europa and the bull. During his weeks in Europe, he had seen nearly the exact same sketch on the stamp of the European Parliament and the new euro currency.

A confusing rush of anticipation and dread whirled inside him as he flipped the pages to check the book's publication date—1946. Long before anyone had ever begun to plan for the unification of Europe, prior even to the establishment of the State of Israel.

How could the author possibly know? When this book was written, there was no Israel, no Temple, and no European Confederacy. And yet there was the picture that now adorned postcards in every European tourist shop, and Israel had begun plans to rebuild her holy temple.

Daniel leaned back against the wall and unfolded his long legs over the carpet, then opened the book to the first chapter and began to read. He knew it might take all night to digest this information, but he had nowhere else to go, and sleep was out of the question.

By the time the first pale hints of sunrise touched the library windows, he had decided to invite his mother and Lauren to New York for a weekend visit. Of all the people he knew, they were the only two he dared to trust with his suspicions.

-01001111OO-

Wrapped in a heavy blanket of grief and exhaustion, Lauren slept like the dead, then awoke to the sound of the morning newspaper slapping the doorstep. Dawn seemed to come reluctantly, glowing sullen through her open bedroom window, but the gray light was enough to pull Lauren fully awake. She sat up in her bed, hugged her knees, and raked her sleep-tousled hair away from her face. Then she remembered—Tasha was home, for her handler had gone on the road to show a champion mastiff in several major competitions. Lauren wasn't alone.

"Tasha?"

The dog lifted her head immediately, her dark eyes seeking Lauren's face like a homing beacon. But she did not spring off the bed as she usually did; even the animal seemed to sense the sadness that felt like cold hands on Lauren's heart, slowly twisting the life from it.

Though she had found the spiritual peace Victoria Stedman cherished, Lauren had never felt more alone. Victoria was gone, and Daniel, too. Even the president had pulled away from Lauren, preferring to vent his grief in the private woods surrounding Camp David. Lauren had no one to turn to in this hour of need, no one but her dog . . . and the Lord she was learning to trust.

She hadn't expected to fall into a life of ease and perfection when she became a Christian, but she hadn't expected this kind of grief and loneliness, either.

"Lord Jesus?" Lauren's voice broke as she lifted her face toward the ceiling. "I'm not much good at asking for help. I've always wanted to be the one in charge of things; I'm always the fixer. But this is something I just can't fix, and I need you to show me what to do. We all miss Victoria, Lord, and I really miss Daniel. I know I shouldn't want something I can't have, but I can't help but think of him."

She listened for some still, small voice but heard only the dripping water from the bathroom faucet, a slow, rhythmic patting. Was this how God spoke to people? Through water droplets in Morse code? Her short laugh lacked any trace of genuine humor.

"Dear God—" she pressed her hand over her face—"show me what I should do. I'll go into the office, though there's not much to be done as long as the president stays away. I'll try to keep up a brave front, but please, Lord, help me see what I should do. And if I'm not to spend any more time with Daniel Prentice, keep him far away from me. Help me to forget him, to put him far from my mind so I can concentrate on helping the president recover from his awful loss."

She sat silently for a moment, marveling that she'd been able to be so honest. Six months ago she would have flatly stated that her busy schedule allowed no time for romance, but at least she'd been able to admit that she couldn't stop thinking about Daniel. But he was now God's problem. If their relationship wasn't meant to be—and Lauren didn't see how it *could* be part of some eternal scheme—then the Almighty would just have to obliterate it.

She jumped as the chirping of her bedroom phone shattered the stillness, then glanced at the clock—7:13 A.M. Either the president had risen early this morning, or God wasted no time in dispatching answers to prayers.

Like someone about to plunge into freezing water, with a quick intake of breath Lauren picked up the phone.

-010011100-

Immediately after calling Lauren and his mother, Daniel fell into bed and slept hard for eight hours. The alarm burbled at 4:00 P.M., and he shook off the lingering wisps of sleep, showered, then telephoned Brad Hunter at home.

"Daniel?" Brad's greeting was heavy with sarcasm. "Gee, do I know a Daniel Prentice? I thought I did, but then I hear that he came to Washington for a week and didn't even call me. So maybe I don't know the guy at all."

"Hey—it was an emergency, okay? Besides, I didn't hear that you were trying to get a hold of me." Daniel lowered his voice. "I imagine it was a hard week for you, too."

Brad's voice sobered instantly. "Yeah, you could say that. Heads are rolling; a lot of people are being questioned. No one knows how that bomb got into the car or how a car with that kind of explosive device inside it could get through the new MX3 Tetracycle scanners in the gates. But there's some pretty sophisticated stuff on the black market, and we're trying to track it all down."

"Was there anything useable in the rubble—any remains of the device?"

"Now, Daniel, you know that's classified. But as soon as the information goes public, you'll be the first to know."

Daniel snorted. "Twenty years from now I won't care—but then again, maybe I will." He shifted the phone from one ear to the other, ready to change the subject. "How's Christine?"

"Great." Brad's voice vibrated with happiness. "I tell you, Danny boy, you've got to stop messing around and get married. No matter how rough things get in the real world, I can always come home and push all that other junk aside. I don't know how I would have gotten through this week without Christine."

"I'm happy for you," Daniel said, and he meant it.

"So when are you going to take the plunge?"

Daniel sighed and stared at the empty walls of his bedroom. "I don't know. I'm working on it, but it takes two, you know?"

"I hear you." There was a silence, then Brad cleared his throat. "So, what's up? I know you didn't call just to inquire about my health and marriage."

Daniel cast about for a diplomatic way to broach the subject, but he couldn't find one. "I was up late last night, reading an old book that had belonged to my father. It was about a dictator-type, a government leader."

"Fiction or nonfiction?"

Daniel made a face. "Um—fiction, I think. Probably." He ran his hands through his hair. "At least I hope so. Some pretty ugly things happened under this guy's regime."

"So what's your question?"

"Hypothetically, if a tyrant wanted to take power right now, what sort of approach would he use?"

Over the phone line, Daniel heard the tinkle of ice cubes. Brad was drinking something, swishing the ice in his glass as he considered the question.

"Well, look at the past," he finally said. "Julius Caesar rose to power through military might. Hitler added race to the equation. He convinced his followers that the Jews were subhuman and thus fit for eradication. I would think that a dictator for today's times would have to use the military—that's a given, because clear-thinking people instinctively react against dictators—as well as religion."

"Religion?" Daniel looked at the stack of prophecy books he'd brought up and placed on his night stand. The muscles of his throat moved in a convulsive swallow. "Why religion?"

He could almost see Brad shrugging. "Look around. The world's on a spiritual kick right now. You've got the coming millennium, you've got everybody talking about peace and love and toleration. Everybody wants to love everybody else, but there are going to be a lot of people who don't want to get aboard your hypothetical dictator's love train. So they'll be outcasts. Not tolerated. And since race and gender and sexual preference are no longer politically acceptable reasons for ostracism, I'm thinking that religion will be the criterion that divides the sheep from the goats. The religions that are *intolerant*—the ones that don't practice a 'come one, come all' philosophy—those will be the ones that bear the stigma."

Daniel thought for a moment. "You're talking about Christianity."

Brad laughed. "Aw, come on. Last time I went to church, everybody was welcome."

"Welcome to *visit*, yes. But didn't you ever hear that verse about the narrow gate? Christians believe—born-again Christians, anyway—that only a few truly find salvation. I've heard it all my life." Daniel closed his eyes, remembering his mother's voice. *But small is the gate and narrow the road that leads to life, and only a few find it.* He opened his eyes. "Okay, Mr. Expert, one more question—if a dictator needed to assume power quickly—in the shortest amount of time—how would he do it?"

Brad laughed. "That's easy. Assuming he is already a leader, he'd do two things—eliminate his opposition, then declare a national emergency."

"I'm talking about a *world* dictator."

"Then he'd declare a worldwide emergency—something that would give him the legal authority to take over all communications, transportation, banking, even food distribution. Of course, he'd probably have to invent a war with aliens to threaten the entire world." Brad let out a short, embarrassed laugh. "Ambitious, aren't we? Are you planning to slip some extra little command into your Millennium Code? If you're planning to take over the world, I should probably tell my bosses to put you under surveillance."

"I'm already under surveillance, remember?" Daniel's voice rasped with irritation.

"Not anymore. You were cleared as soon as you returned from Europe."

"Good. I'll tell my people they can stop encrypting their grocery lists." Daniel paused. "Why was I cleared? Aren't your people still concerned about Adrian Romulus?"

"He's been shoved to the back burner. We decided that you were right—Adrian Romulus is focussed on European problems, and right now Europe seems to be the extent of his ambitions. So, for now at least, he's off the hot list. We're still watching him, but whoever arranged this assassination attempt is priority number one."

Daniel thought about telling Brad about Samuel Stedman's conviction that Romulus had something to do with the bomb, then decided to stay quiet. The president had been lashing out that afternoon, wanting to blame someone. General Herrick and Adrian Romulus had been unfortunate enough to push him at the worst possible moment.

"Is that it, Danny boy?" Brad laughed again. "'Cause though I'd love to sit here and speculate about dictators all night, I've a much more enjoyable prospect waiting for me to take her to dinner."

"Yeah, I've got to go, too. Lauren's coming in on the 6:30 flight from D.C."

"Well, then, remember what I said about marriage. It's worth trying."

Daniel promised to keep that in mind.

-0100111100-

Lauren smiled as she came down the ramp, and met Daniel's embrace with a kiss on the cheek. She wasn't certain why she had come, but in light of his call, coming so soon after her prayer, accepting his invitation seemed like the right thing to do. If God wasn't keeping Daniel Prentice at arm's length, maybe there was some reason she was supposed to see him.

They made polite small talk as they left the Delta gate, and Lauren lifted a brow when Daniel pointed toward another concourse.

"Aren't we going to get my luggage?"

"In a minute." Daniel smiled and pressed his hand to the center of her back. "First we've got to pick up my mother."

Lauren tilted her head and gave him an uncertain look, but she didn't protest as they walked to the other gate. After they waited for about twenty minutes, the flight from St. Petersburg arrived. Daniel stood and waved as a silver-haired woman came down the ramp.

"What's this about, Daniel?" Lauren waved at the woman, then looked up at him. "I know what it *usually* means when a man brings a girl home to meet his mom—"

"It means," Daniel said, taking her elbow and leading her forward, "that I need counseling, and you two are the most qualified counselors I know."

Lauren laughed, taking his comment as a joke, and Daniel didn't correct her impression as the woman came toward them with a welcoming smile. Mrs. Prentice, Lauren noted, was a full-figured woman of medium height. She had bright blue eyes, clear skin, and hair that framed her face in a halo of white curls.

Daniel stepped forward to hug his mother, then kept one arm around her shoulders as he introduced Lauren.

"Mom, this is Lauren Mitchell."

His mother drew in a quick breath, and her eyes brightened as she smiled. "Does this mean—?" She glanced from Lauren to Daniel, then back to Lauren. "Is something going on between you two?"

"We're good friends, Mom." Daniel took the small bag from her hand, then leaned closer as he turned her toward the long hallway that led to the baggage claim area. "And if you promise not to embarrass me, I'll tell you everything on the ride home."

Beaming with pleasure, Mrs. Prentice winked at Lauren, then let Daniel lead her through the crowd.

TWENTY-EIGHT

9:00 P.M., Friday, July 23, 1999

DANIEL CHOSE TO TAKE HIS LADIES TO ELAINE'S FOR DINNER, AND LAUREN KNEW he'd selected the restaurant precisely because it was high on every tourist's must-see list. Mrs. Prentice enjoyed everything from the table linens to the little origami treats the waiter left at their table. In between her exclamations of pleasure, she fussed at Daniel for eating too little, worrying too much, and working too hard.

Lauren smothered a smile in her teacup. Mothers. She'd almost forgotten how charming they could be . . . as long as they were needling someone else.

The conversation at dinner was pleasant and trivial, but several times Lauren caught a glimpse of some dark thought lingering behind Daniel's eyes. His mother must have seen it, too, for whenever Daniel grew thoughtful, Mrs. Prentice began a new story about her townhouse neighbor, Mrs. Davis, and Mrs. Davis's overly pushy daughter. "Of course, when she realized that my son was *the* Daniel Prentice, she was dying to meet you," Mrs. Prentice babbled as she sipped her after-dinner coffee. "Saw your picture in *People* magazine, I gather, and thought you were—how'd she put it? 'Totally gorgeous.' Of course she didn't want to meet you when she just thought you were into computers. I'd told her that you were a genius, but she wasn't at all interested until she heard you were well-off, too."

Mrs. Prentice leaned forward and lowered her voice. "She's not your type at all, Daniel, so when you come down to visit, don't feel obligated to go over there."

Lauren spooned sugar into her tea and wondered how many times Daniel had visited his mother in the last year. Given his schedule, he

probably hadn't gone more than once or twice, and Mrs. Prentice obviously felt a bit neglected. Still, it was nice of him to bring her to New York,
even if it was in the hottest part of the summer. But things had to be even
warmer in Florida.

After dessert and coffee, Daniel hailed a cab, and soon they were back
inside his cavernous apartment. From Daniel's dossier Lauren knew that
he owned an impressive bit of New York real estate, but she had no idea the
apartment would be so glamorous. The foyer, with its grand staircase and
works of art on the walls, was clean, precise, and as exalting as a museum
gallery. Daniel moved through it with a diffident air, though, as if he didn't
really feel at home in the place.

He picked up Lauren's and Mrs. Prentice's bags, then started up the
staircase. "I'll take these up to your rooms," he called. "Why don't you make
yourselves at home? There are snacks and soft drinks in the kitchen, and I
thought we could talk in the library."

Lauren lifted a brow. Talk? About what?

Mrs. Prentice waved her hand and fussed as she led Lauren into the
gleaming state-of-the-art kitchen. "That boy, ordering us about like we
work for him! Though it's not exactly obvious, Lauren, I have tried to teach
him better manners."

"I've always found his take-charge attitude rather charming." Lauren
leaned against the counter and folded her arms. "And you needn't worry,
Mrs. Prentice. He's really quite remarkable."

Mrs. Prentice paused in her search through the cabinets and threw a
glinting glance over her shoulder. "Yes, he is, isn't he?" Her eyes glowed
with tender affection. "Don't mind me, dear, I suppose all mothers fret
about their children. But truthfully, God has blessed me with Daniel. There
isn't much I would change about him." She looked back into the cupboard.
"Well, there are a few things. But those things are out of my control."

She brought three glasses out of the cupboard, filled them at the automatic ice dispenser, then pulled several cans of soda from a pantry shelf
and set them on a tray. "If you'll carry the tray, dear, I believe I can juggle
the glasses," Mrs. Prentice said, moving toward the library with three
glasses delicately balanced between her outstretched fingers.

Lauren smiled as she picked up the tray. At least she now knew how
Daniel had acquired his tendency to order people about.

Daniel was jogging down the stairs as Lauren came through the foyer. He took the tray from her and gave her a conspiratorial smile. "Is my mother driving you crazy?"

"Not at all." A thoughtful smile curved Lauren's mouth. "I think she's quite charming."

Mrs. Prentice had already arranged the glasses on a coffee table when Daniel and Lauren arrived in the library. For herself, Mrs. Prentice chose the velvet wing chair, leaving Daniel and Lauren to sit together on the couch. Lauren smiled at the tidy arrangement but said nothing as she sat down and pulled a diet soda from the tray. As she popped the top and poured soda into her glass, she glanced around. This was her favorite room thus far. The decorator had included fewer expensive objets d'art in this room, and Daniel had apparently added a few personal items—a framed photo of his mother on an end table, a crudely painted picture of a log cabin on the wall, a collection of computer books scattered around a rocking chair. The room even smelled of Daniel—a masculine scent of leather and a trace of his cologne.

"You're probably wondering why I called this meeting," Daniel joked, clapping his hands together as he sat down.

Neither woman laughed, and a slight blush warmed Daniel's cheekbones as he lowered his gaze. "Seriously, ladies, I have something important to discuss, and I knew I could trust you two. It's about Adrian Romulus . . . and the Bible's prophecy about the coming Antichrist who will rule the world."

Lauren had stiffened at Romulus's name, and she noticed a similar reaction from Mrs. Prentice at the word *Antichrist*.

"What has started you thinking about the Antichrist?" His mother's voice cracked, then one brow lifted. "Your father's books—did you finally read them?"

Daniel nodded, then his gaze shifted to Lauren. "I don't know how much you know about biblical prophecy—"

"I don't know anything about it." Lauren shifted uneasily, feeling very much out of her depth. "I only became a Christian in February, and it took me nearly three months to find a church where they actually talk about Jesus and read from the Bible on Sunday mornings. I'm still learning."

"That's okay." Daniel reached out and patted her hand. "But you know about Adrian Romulus, and you've been suspicious of him from the beginning."

"Well—yes," Lauren admitted. "A gut feeling. Mrs. Stedman didn't trust him, either."

"I'm glad you told me that." Daniel turned to his mother. "Mom, you may not know anything about Adrian Romulus—"

"Adrian who?"

"—but you know about the Antichrist. So I want to tell you both what I think—what I suspect—and I want you to tell me if I'm going crazy or if there's something there."

Lauren could see no gleam of amusement in Daniel's black-lashed eyes. This was no joke.

"I thought you admired Romulus," she said, watching his eyes. "At one point, I thought you were ready to move to Europe and accept a place in his organization."

A deep flush washed up Daniel's throat and into his face, as sudden as a brush fire. "I've had second thoughts," he said, lowering his gaze to the coffee table. "After the explosion—well, let's just say that Romulus seemed less than sincerely sympathetic. And Brad once asked me if Romulus had designs on ruling the world. At the time, I laughed and told Brad that Romulus didn't care about anything outside Europe, but now I see that I was wrong. Adrian did try, once, to tempt me with the idea of influencing what he called a worldwide community, but I didn't recognize the depth of his ambition because I was blinded by my own."

"All right," Lauren whispered after a long moment. "Let's discuss him."

Daniel tossed her a quick smile, then turned to his mother. "Tell me, Mom, everything you know about the Antichrist. Lauren and I will compare notes to see if we think Adrian Romulus fits the description."

"Son, you don't have to put yourself through this." Mrs. Prentice's hands twisted in her lap. "The Scriptures tell us that the Antichrist will seize power on the world stage after Christ takes the believers to heaven." A note of pleading filled her voice. "If you would only accept Christ, Daniel, this would be a moot point. You wouldn't be here to worry about the coming Antichrist and his evil rule."

"Mom—" a shadow of annoyance crossed Daniel's face—"just bear with me, okay? I'm not like you; I can't just accept something by blind faith. I have to be convinced by facts."

Lauren drew back at the vehemence in his words. Obviously, they'd had this conversation before, and it was a sore spot for both Daniel and his mother.

"Okay." Mrs. Prentice blinked and tried to smile, but the corners of her mouth only wobbled precariously. "The Antichrist will rise to worldwide power right after the Rapture, when the Christians are taken to be with the Lord. He will lead a ten-nation confederacy in the territory of the ancient Roman Empire and will make a seven-year peace treaty with Israel."

A tinge of sadness marked her eyes as she continued. "There will come a time of trouble unlike anything the world has ever known. Plagues, pestilence, death, and destruction. If God did not have mercy and put an end to the struggle after seven years, everyone on earth would perish."

"I need to know about the *man*." A thread of impatience lined Daniel's voice. "Not what will happen, but facts about the Antichrist himself. Who is he? What is he like?"

Mrs. Prentice ran her fingertips along the soft white curls at her temple. "He will initially be known as a man of peace," she whispered, her eyes drifting out into the empty expanse of the room. "But at his core is pure wickedness. According to the prophet Daniel, he will be a stern-faced man, a master of satanic intrigue, and very powerful. He will destroy the mighty men and the holy people—the Jews. He will cause deceit to prosper, and he will consider himself superior to all others."

"That could describe many different men," Lauren said. "Perhaps we are not meant to know who he is."

"What else, Mom?"

Mrs. Prentice pressed her fingertips together, then stared at the floor. "The prophet Daniel said he would not desire women." She looked up at Lauren. "Whether that means he is homosexual or simply uninterested, I don't know."

"Romulus is not married." Daniel prodded Lauren with his elbow. "And in all the times I've been with him, I've never seen him look at a woman—you know, in that way."

Lauren rolled her eyes. "Honestly, Daniel, perhaps the man simply has self-control."

Daniel shook his head. "I don't know, Lauren. We were together in some pretty wild places in Brussels, and saw some sights that would have turned a normal man's knees to mush. But Romulus seemed strangely unaffected."

"It doesn't fit." Lauren shook her head. "His dossier contains surveillance photos of him out with one of the female councilors." She narrowed her eyes at Daniel. "I shouldn't be telling you this, so I'll withhold the name of the councilor."

"They could have been having a simple dinner."

"The way she was dressed, I'd say *she* thought it was a date."

"This man you're discussing—" Mrs. Prentice slowly eased into the conversation—"he's the head of the European Council? Is it ten nations?"

"Not at the moment," Daniel answered. "There are fifteen nations at present, but there is an inner circle of eleven that have pledged to form one economic union with shared defense, foreign police, and one common currency." His gaze met Lauren's. "And I've heard inside information that leads me to think that Adrian Romulus may be toying with the governments of at least three of those countries. So who can say how the mix will change over the next few months?"

Mrs. Prentice lifted her hand. "It certainly will change. And you can be sure that by the time the Antichrist—whoever he is—takes the world stage, that confederacy will consist of ten nations, three of which will have been violently subdued by this false peacemaker."

Daniel twisted and stretched his arm over the back of the couch. "So you're saying, Mother, that Adrian Romulus might very well be the Antichrist."

"I'm not saying that at all." She tipped her head back and looked at him. "I'm saying that he *could* be. It's dangerous to predict the future; God forbids fortune-telling. But we have the prophetic signs, and we certainly need to be alert to them."

"But what are the odds?" Despite Lauren's reluctance to believe that a man she knew personally could actually be the evil dictator predicted in Scripture, a cold knot had formed in her stomach as Mrs. Prentice described the false Christ to come. "What are the odds, Daniel, that one man could fulfill all those prophecies at this point in time?"

Daniel looked away, his jaw tightening. "I could ask the computer to calculate it."

Mrs. Prentice shifted in her chair and crossed her legs. "Please be careful, Daniel. Sometimes things aren't what they seem. What is to prevent us from taking those same prophecies and making them fit someone else? A stern-faced man—that could be virtually anyone. A man of peace—again, that could apply to anyone from Henry Kissinger to the pope. A man who has no desire for women—the pope again, or even *you*, Daniel, since you're not married."

"That's not me." Daniel growled the words, and Lauren looked away lest he see her smile.

"So many of this Antichrist's qualities are internal and hidden," Lauren added. "He is deceitful, but so is every politician I know. No diplomat dares reveal what he's truly thinking. Diplomacy is nothing but deceit elevated to an art form."

"Now that I think about it," Mrs. Prentice said, her forehead creasing in concern, "I'm surprised that your name hasn't been bandied about as a likely candidate to be the Antichrist, Daniel. You aren't married, you have a military background, and you have connections in high and powerful places. But most important, you have been instrumental in developing this awful device—"

"The Millennium Chip?" Daniel's eyes widened in surprise. "How does that make me a candidate?"

Mrs. Prentice reached into her pocket and pulled out a small Testament, then confidently flipped to a page at the back of the book. "Listen," she said, straightening in her chair as if she'd been called upon to read in school. "'He also forced everyone, small and great, rich and poor, free and slave, to receive a mark on his right hand or on his forehead, so that no one could buy or sell unless he had the mark, which is the name of the beast or the number of his name.'" Her brows flickered as she looked at her son. "You designed a chip for the new millennium, Daniel. And without it no one can buy or sell."

Lauren saw a change come over Daniel's features, a sick shock of realization. "Mrs. Stedman quoted that verse to me once," he said, turning to Lauren. "You were there—at lunch, when we were discussing the Millennium Project. She was afraid."

"Not afraid, Daniel." Eagerness and tenderness mingled on Mrs. Prentice's face. "No Christian fears the Antichrist, for he cannot hurt us. If we worry at all, it is for those who will be left behind."

Silence loomed between them like a heavy mist. Lauren lowered her eyes, unable to look at Mrs. Prentice, whose love and concern for her son marked every line of her face, or Daniel, whose jaw was set in determined resistance.

He would never be won, Lauren knew, by emotion or pleading. He lived and breathed in a world of facts and proofs and solid concepts. It would take more than a mother's plea to bring him to the place of surrender.

"Even if Romulus is the coming Antichrist," Lauren finally dared to speak up, "what can we do about it? If a prophecy is recorded in Scripture, it will happen regardless of anything we might do. And if the Christians will be taken to heaven before he is revealed, those who know the truth will no longer be on the earth to sound the warning. So what's the sense in debating the issue?"

Daniel looked at her, his eyes dark with unspoken thoughts. He had not settled the issue in his mind, but Lauren could tell that he had wearied of his mother's concern for his soul.

She dropped her lashes to hide her own hurt. He had not yet shut her out, but he might if she pushed too hard or too quickly.

"Lauren's right, of course," he said, looking at his mother with reproach in his eyes. "What's the point? Now, ladies—" he stretched and made a poor effort of pretending to yawn—"I thank you for your insights, but I'm exhausted. The apartment is yours, of course, but I'm going upstairs."

His expression softened, and he sighed softly before giving Lauren and his mother a smile. "Sorry—I'm afraid I'm a little out of my element with all this biblical talk. I'm used to solvable equations, workable problems."

His mother opened her mouth as if she would say something else, then apparently thought the better of it and snapped her mouth shut.

"You go on up," Lauren said, smiling as he stood and squeezed her shoulder. "And since you're deserting us before midnight, I'm going to let your mother tell me every embarrassing story of your childhood."

He shook his head and walked away, mumbling something about women. Lauren watched him go, then looked at his mother and smiled.

"He's a good man," Mrs. Prentice said, her bright eyes trained on Lauren.

"I know."

-010011100-

Alone in his room, Daniel clasped his head in his hands and tried to summon sleep. Though his mind was thick with fatigue and clouded with memories, sleep danced just beyond the edge of his consciousness.

What was wrong with him? He usually fell asleep within ten minutes of stretching out, his brain as efficient at shutting down as it was at processing new information. Tonight, though, his thoughts seemed energized beyond his power to control them.

Was it Lauren? He had to admit that the thought of her resting just down the hall was not exactly sleep-inducing. She had looked so lovely and natural sitting in his library, a part of him wanted to wrap his arms around her and propose that she stay there forever. He had never really felt comfortable in any of these rooms but the library, and Lauren's presence had made it almost cozy, relaxing. Daniel had found himself wishing that he could come home to her every night.

Daniel rolled onto his side and pounded his pillow. He was not an adolescent boy prone to fantasies about beautiful women. He was a man, quite adept at controlling his thoughts, his body, and his brain.

So why couldn't he sleep?

The answer, he realized as he looked out into the darkness, had nothing to do with Lauren. Tonight, for the first time, he had encountered a realm he could not understand. The laws of science were absolute; the laws of mathematics were immutable. Two plus two always made four; the second law of thermodynamics mandated that energy would always dissipate and disintegrate. Those concepts were inherent in the fabric of the universe, its undeniable warp and woof and weave.

But tonight, as his mother had recited Scriptures from memory, Daniel had brushed up against a law he could neither accept nor understand—the law of the supernatural. His mother said that the horrible predictions about the Antichrist were not possibilities, but *prophecies*, as sure as if they had already happened. In the timeless, eternal mind of the Almighty, they already had.

A cold shiver spread over him as he remembered watching the old black-and-white version of *A Christmas Carol* on television. Ebenezer Scrooge, hunched and horrified in the dark cemetery, had peered at his own tombstone and asked the hooded figure of Christmas Yet to Come, "Are these the shadows of the things that *will* be, or are they shadows of the things that *may* be only?" The ghastly figure did not answer, but Scrooge woke up clinging to his bedpost, convinced that if he changed, the world would change, too.

Scrooge saw a vision of the future and used it to better himself and save Tiny Tim. But Dickens's story was fiction, and if Mother was to be believed, Scripture was ultimate truth. So why would God give the world a picture of years to come unless people could change things and save themselves?

Daniel turned onto his back and kicked the thin sheet away. Without being told, he knew what his mother's answer would be. She would say that for years people had been offered an opportunity to rescue their futures by changing themselves; all they had to do was accept Christ and they'd be removed from the earth before all these terrible things began to happen. Because as soon as his people were removed, God was going to send the world on an inescapable and horrendous seven-year tour of hell on earth.

His answer came, not as a dazzling burst of mental insight, but like a tiny pinhole of light. Slowly it widened, connecting with a crack of revelation there, a fissure of knowledge here. Then Daniel knew what he had to do.

He couldn't stop the Antichrist, whoever he might be, but if Adrian Romulus continued to fit the pattern of prophecy, Daniel could warn the world.

Girding himself with resolve, Daniel crossed his arms behind his head and stared at the ceiling. The relentless tides of change had already begun to erode the past and push the world into the future. The Millennium Project was being implemented; tens of millions of Millennium Chips had already been distributed in the United States and Europe. On January 1, 2000, the European Community and the United States would move their

Millennium Networks online, and the new cashless programs would begin. As long as President Stedman held to his position, those two networks would continue to be separate and distinct from each other. But what if Stedman lost the election of November 2000? January 2001 would then see the inauguration of another American president, most likely someone who held views completely contrary to Stedman's. American politics had an unsettling way of swinging from one extreme to the other.

"If Stedman loses and his successor links us to the European Union," Daniel whispered to the darkness, "Adrian Romulus will control more than half the world's economy and 75 percent of its military power. And if what Brad told me in Europe is true—if Romulus is also courting the nations of the Pacific Rim and the Arab powers of the Middle East—he may soon control the world."

The thought did nothing to calm the anxiety that spurred the uneven beat of Daniel's heart.

TWENTY-NINE

8:30 A.M., Saturday, July 24, 1999

DANIEL AWOKE TO THE SOUND OF DISHES CLATTERING DOWNSTAIRS IN HIS kitchen. For an instant the sound startled him, then he smiled. Lauren or his mother—one of them was up and probably making coffee. He threw on a pair of sweatpants and a T-shirt, then took the stairs two at a time and turned into the kitchen. Lauren stood at the stove with her back to him, her hair wet from the shower, her slender figure wrapped in a soft terry cloth robe. The Saturday edition of the *CBS Morning News* buzzed from the tiny television on the counter, and he knew she hadn't heard him approach.

The sight of her, cuddly and clean, was irresistible. He walked forward and slipped his hands around her waist, then bent and pressed his scratchy cheek to her soft one.

"Good morning."

She jumped slightly at his touch, then relaxed and leaned against him. "Good morning yourself," she answered, using a wooden spoon to stir a coagulated mixture of what looked like eggs and cheese. She turned her head and gave him an uncertain smile. "I hope these eggs are fresh. I had to cut mold off the cheese."

Laughing, he released her and leaned against the counter, then crossed his arms as he studied her. Her hair hung loose around her ears; her face was scrubbed, shining, and completely bare of makeup. This was a face he could wake up to every morning.

She looked up from the eggs. "Your manners are slipping, Mr. Prentice." Her tone was as sharp as a schoolmarm's, but her eyes sparkled at him. "Didn't your mother ever teach you that it was rude to stare?"

"You're easy to stare at." His heart thumped uncomfortably when a rush of pink stained her cheek.

"You're in my way." She lifted a brow in a prim expression, and Daniel fought the urge to reach out and kiss every last trace of diffidence from her face. His hand moved to her shoulder and he might well have pulled her into his arms, but at that moment his mother stepped into the kitchen from the dining room.

"Good morning, Daniel." She pitched her voice a tone higher than usual. "Did you sleep well?"

Daniel released Lauren's shoulder and smiled at his mother. "Not really." He crossed his arms again and glanced at Lauren. "I think I was awake half the night. I had a lot of things to think about."

"I think we all did," Lauren said, spilling the eggs onto a platter Daniel hadn't seen in ten years.

"I've got juice and coffee in the dining room," his mother said, shuffling into the kitchen in threadbare slippers. "Honestly, Daniel, you really should take better care of your kitchen. Lauren and I had a hard time finding anything in this place."

"Hey, don't blame me." Daniel lifted his hands in a "don't shoot" pose. "I don't eat here very often. I usually eat out, or the professor and I order in and eat at the office."

His mother made soft *tsking* noises as she opened cabinet doors. "You ought to at least buy some napkins. Don't you have a cleaning lady? The next time she comes, you tell her to outfit this kitchen with grocery staples—fresh coffee, fresh eggs, some orange juice, milk, and sugar—"

She went on, reciting the inventory of a small convenience store, and Daniel's gaze drifted over to the television. A news desk had replaced the morning show's cozy living room set, and the man who faced the camera now wore a serious expression.

"Excuse me, Mom." Daniel moved past her, then turned up the TV's volume. The newscaster's well-modulated voice echoed in the kitchen.

" . . . a live report with Adrian Romulus, president of the European Union's Council of Ministers. We take you now to Paris, where Mr. Romulus has called a press conference to announce the theft."

"Is that the man you were talking about last night?" Daniel's mother flinched as Romulus's handsome features flashed onto the screen. "My goodness, Daniel, look at him!"

Daniel felt warning spasms of alarm erupt within him as Adrian

Romulus nodded at a host of assembled reporters. He was standing on a broad portico of an elaborate house, probably his chateau outside Paris. His hands were thrust into his pockets in an almost casual pose, but there was no denying the dark solemnity in his eyes.

A stern-faced man . . . never had a description seemed so apt.

"Citizens of the world community, I come to you today with sobering news." His voice rang with infinite compassion. "Twenty-four hours ago I was informed by representatives from the Russian Republic of Chechnya that more than a dozen so-called 'suitcase-sized' nuclear bombs had disappeared." He paused, and his dark eyes narrowed as he stared into the camera. "*Twelve* hours ago, I learned that these devices were stolen. Forces identifying themselves as the Morning Star Trust have, in effect, taken these weapons for nuclear extortion."

Romulus held up a sheet of paper. "I will now read part of the communiqué we received last night." Romulus moistened his lips as if he were nervous, then began to read. "'We of the Morning Star Trust, in order to establish a world without tyranny and oppression, have secretly placed one dozen nuclear weapons in high-density population areas throughout the cities of the world. Unless world leaders surrender an amount equivalent to six billion American dollars to us within three weeks, we shall begin to detonate these weapons, beginning in New York City. Lest you think we are incapable of evading extreme security measures, know this: We planted the bomb that killed Mrs. Victoria Stedman, first lady of the USA. We have struck once, and we will strike again, if necessary.'"

"Daniel?" His mother's voice was hoarse with shock. "What's happening?"

Daniel held up his hand as Romulus lowered the message he'd just read. When he turned his gaze back to the camera, his compelling, magnetic eyes seemed to fill the screen. "Citizens of the world community, do not fear. We of the European Union have sent word to the Pacific nations, the nations of the Middle East, and the Americas. Together we will combine our elite security forces and we will track down those who would wrest our liberties from us. Fortunately, we have already experienced a major breakthrough in our effort to combat this threat of nuclear terrorism."

Romulus pulled out another sheet of paper and turned it toward the camera. It was an 8x10 black-and-white glossy, a photograph of a stone-faced man with thick hair and dark, slanting eyes. Though the man's dark hair was sprinkled with gray, his skin was smooth and unlined.

"This man is known is Lucius Joshua," Romulus said, his mouth twisting. "He is known to be traveling under several false names and using old American and European passports. If you see him, call the authorities immediately. Do not try to apprehend him. He is armed and dangerous, he lives outside the law, and he will not have a Millennium Chip. Do not sell to him. Do not give him shelter. And do not fear. We, the citizens of the world community, will rise up and drive this evil from us."

Romulus stepped back as a swarm of questions rose from the reporters in Paris, but the network suddenly cut to the Oval Office. Wearing a dark blue cardigan, Samuel Stedman sat at his desk with a steaming cup of coffee at his elbow. Despite an obvious attempt to appear casual and at ease, the usual expression of good humor was missing from the curve of Stedman's mouth and the depths of his eyes.

"The president?" Lauren's voice held a note halfway between disbelief and regret. "Oh no, they must have brought him back last night. He was resting at Camp David, but now this—"

"Ladies and gentlemen," President Stedman began, his brow wrinkling with concern, "let me be the first to assure you that the United States has already taken the necessary precautions to prevent terrorism on our own shores. We have heard nothing from this Morning Star Trust; and we have no evidence whatsoever that this group is behind the incident—" he turned the catch in his voice into a cough and went on—"that occurred at the White House. If this is a true threat, we will dispatch every necessary force to meet it; if it is not, we will soon put the matter to rest."

"He still doesn't trust Romulus." Lauren's hoarse whisper echoed in the kitchen. "But he looks awful. Look at him, Daniel—I don't think he's feeling well."

Daniel had to agree. Weariness and pain had carved merciless lines on the president's face; creases around his mouth and eyes muted his strength. Drops of perspiration lined the hairline above his brow.

"Do not panic," the president was saying now, his hands enfolding the coffee mug as if this were just a casual Saturday chat from the White House. "Stay tuned to your emergency stations, but go about your business as usual." A muscle quivered at his jaw as he gazed into the camera. "And may God have mercy upon us."

The program immediately returned to the CBS morning hosts. They sat on the sofa and stared at the camera with wide eyes and bland, meaningless smiles.

"Daniel, I've never heard of such a thing." His mother's mouth quirked with fear. "A nuclear weapon in a suitcase? Is it possible?"

"Yes, Mom." Daniel pinched the bridge of his nose, knowing that a monster headache would soon be hammering his brain. This felt like a bad dream, but he could feel the cool tile floor beneath his feet and smell the rich scent of coffee. This was real, he was awake, and his mother was frightened.

He softened his voice. "Yes, Mother, there are nuclear demolition packages designed for placement and detonation by special forces. Not all nukes are on the tips of missiles or torpedoes. In fact, I'd dare to say that there are scores of small tactical nuclear weapons floating around out there somewhere. Yes, it's entirely possible that terrorists have managed to get their hands on such bombs."

"From Russia?"

He shrugged. "Perhaps. The state of the Russian federation is extremely volatile."

Daniel turned to Lauren, who stood in the center of the kitchen with her hand wound in her hair. Little lightning bolts of worry flashed in her eyes. "I need to get back to Washington. I shouldn't be away now."

"All right." Daniel tried to smile. "But don't you want to eat breakfast first? After all, you cooked it."

"Maybe some coffee. But then I ought to go."

Daniel helped his mom find the coffee mugs, then stood back while Lauren rattled through canisters on a frantic search for sugar. The television newscast broke for a commercial, a mindless and irritating bit about a dancing baby amid waves of undulating toilet paper, then the baby flickered for an instant and the screen went black.

"What in the world?"

Daniel knew his mother's irritated tone only covered her fear. "It's nothing, Mom." He gave her a reassuring smile. "The station must be having trouble with its video. There must have been some confusion when they cut to the satellite feeds from Washington and Paris—"

The screen blossomed to life again, and the somber-faced newscaster was back at his onscreen desk. "This just in from Washington," he said, his voice dull and troubled. "We've received word that President Stedman has collapsed and is being transferred to Walter Reed Army Medical Center. We have no details yet, but the vice president is said to be en route to the White House." The newscaster's mouth spread into a thin-lipped grimace. "Stay tuned for further reports."

"Dear God, what is happening?"

Daniel turned at the sound of Lauren's voice. A flicker of shock had widened her eyes, and she clung to the edge of the kitchen counter as if it were the only stability to be found in an unstable and chaotic world.

Daniel stepped forward and caught her, then helped her to a chair at the bar in his kitchen. Her trembling hands had gone as cold as ice.

"I should be there with him," she whispered, staring down at the floor. "What he must be going through! I knew he was struggling with his grief, but I had no idea he was ill."

"Do you think it was a heart attack?"

She shook her head again, then pressed her hand to her face in a convulsive gesture. "No. The president is healthy; he just had his annual physical in May. Low cholesterol, low blood pressure, everything was fine. His diet was great—he and Victoria lived on salads and low-fat meats because *she* had a weak heart."

Daniel sat on the chair next to her and turned the situation over in his mind. If the vice president had been summoned to the White House, this was a serious matter. But what sort of medical condition could arise from out of thin air? A stroke, perhaps. An aneurysm. An entire host of diseases could be exacerbated by stress, and Samuel Stedman had certainly experienced a devastating level of stress in the last few days. And now, with Adrian Romulus announcing worldwide terrorism in Europe and the United States . . . no wonder the man had collapsed.

Lauren pulled her hand away from her face, then pushed herself up from the chair. "I better call the White House and see if I can get any more details. Then I have to go back to Washington."

"Do you want me to go with you?"

"No." Lauren rested her hand on Daniel's shoulder for a brief moment as a smile trembled over her lips. "Thanks, but I probably won't be decent company for a while. But excuse me while I make that call—"

Daniel sat silently and watched her stumble toward the library. After a moment, his mother sank into Lauren's chair, then her hand came to rest upon Daniel's.

"Daniel," her voice was rough with anxiety, "I don't know what's happening, but I have a feeling . . . the time is near. The Lord is returning soon."

"You've been saying that for years, Mom." His words were loaded with ridicule, and he grimaced when his mother flinched. He gentled his tone. "I'm sorry. I guess we're all upset. Why don't you go ahead and eat breakfast while I see about getting Lauren to the airport? We'll talk when I get back."

She nodded without speaking, hurt shining in her eyes, then she stood and walked toward the dining room. Exasperated, Daniel let her go, then crossed the foyer in search of Lauren.

-0100111100-

Forty-five minutes later, Lauren sat in Daniel's car, her overnight bag on her lap, her cell phone pressed to her ear. Daniel crunched the gears as the Jag tore up the expressway, trying not to listen to what was certainly supposed to be a classified conversation. After a few moments, Lauren snapped her phone shut and stared out at the road with wide, watery eyes.

"They were saying heart attack," she murmured, putting out a hand to brace herself against the dash, "but now he's slipped into a coma, so they think he mixed up his pills. The doctor had him on St. John's Wort, a harmless herbal antidepressant, but somehow he took nitroglycerin. At least that's what the preliminary blood test reveals."

"Nitroglycerin?" Frowning, Daniel leaned the car around a slow-moving Ryder truck. "I thought you said he didn't have heart problems."

"He didn't. But Mrs. Stedman did; she kept nitroglycerin with her all the time." Lauren crossed her arms. "I'm so confused, I don't know what to think. But General Archer has alerted the media, and there's going to be a herd of reporters at the airport. He wants me to handle them here, before I get on the plane. Tom Ormond held a press conference in Washington ten minutes ago, but that didn't satisfy the national curiosity."

"I would imagine that Ormond's got his hands full." Daniel smiled grimly, then leaned the Jag toward the right and the La Guardia exit ramp. A moment later they were pulling up outside the Delta gate, and, as Daniel feared, a mob of reporters stood ready, armed with cameras and microphones.

"Looks like they figured out which flight was the next one to Washington. If you want, Lauren, I can get my pilot on the phone—"

"Thanks, Daniel, but there's no time."

He stopped the car a few feet away from the horde of reporters, knowing that this might be their last private moment for a long while.

Daniel reached out and took her hand, and Lauren gave him a weak smile in return. "Are you going to make it?" he asked.

"I'll be okay." Her blue eyes brimmed with threatening tears, but none fell. "I'll collapse later, when I'm alone. Right now I've got to think about the job."

Daniel squeezed her hand. "Think about the job, but spare a thought for me, okay? I know I'll be thinking about you."

The look in her blue eyes pierced Daniel's soul. "If you think of it, ask your mother to pray for the president—and for me. You can pray, too, if you want."

Not trusting himself to answer in words, Daniel squeezed her hand. She took a moment to dash the wetness from her eyes, then gathered her bags, and opened the car door. Daniel cut the engine as she stepped out and moved toward the crowd. The reporters caught sight of her almost immediately, and Daniel watched, admiring the way Lauren plunged into the mob with her head high. She moved to a short staircase leading into the terminal, then turned at the top step and faced them like a queen granting favors.

"I have just been briefed by officials in Washington," she said, her clear voice carrying over the crowd, "and I can take a few questions before I have to board my flight." She nodded at a man in a brown tweed coat. "Tom, you first. What do you want to know?"

And so the questions came—how was the president, what was wrong, had the reins of power been officially transferred to the vice president? Daniel leaned upon the steering wheel, moved to admiration by Lauren's intelligent evasions. The woman was a wonder. Though she did not give a single specific answer, she said enough to give the press something to report, just enough to keep the viewers happy and glued to the television sets.

The president was resting comfortably, she said. The White House was firmly in control of the situation, and there was no need to panic. Vice President John Miller was at the White House, and the president's cabinet was also standing by, ready to help with any emergency situation. General Adam Archer had been at the White House all morning, so there was no reason to fear international terrorists; the military had the situation under control. "Most of all," she said, her extraordinary eyes blazing over the crowd, "there is no reason to believe the president's illness has anything to do with the Morning Star Trust and the missing nuclear warheads."

Daniel smiled in an overflow of admiration. No wonder Stedman valued Lauren. She was good at this job, probably better than the White House press secretary.

"Ms. Mitchell!" A woman from the fringe of the media mob waved her hand. "Why are you in New York?"

Lauren froze for an instant, caught off guard by the question, and Daniel feared she might look his way and set the crowd on *him*. But she only tossed her head and bent to pick up her overnight bag. "I was visiting a friend," she said simply. And then, while Daniel watched, she turned and moved through the automatic doors, leaving the airport security guards to hold the mob at bay.

Daniel turned the key and smiled as the Jag settled into a steady purring sound. He'd ask his mother to pray for Sam Stedman, but it looked like Lauren had things firmly under control.

THIRTY

10:25 A.M., Friday, August 6, 1999

UPSET BY THE UNEXPECTED TURN OF EVENTS, DANIEL'S MOTHER HAD FLOWN back to Florida immediately after news of the president's collapse. Daniel was secretly relieved to see her go—he enjoyed her company but found her constant references to the last days a bit unnerving. These were treacherous times, but life would surely go on as it had for generations. The world had been rocked before, and it would undoubtedly rock again. And as soon as Lucius Joshua was caught and the suitcase nukes were returned to safekeeping, life would return to normal.

Scarcely two days after Romulus's announcements, forces claiming to be with the Morning Star Trust exploded a nuclear weapon at the Aviano Air Base in Cavalese, Italy. Over 3,000 American navy and air force personnel were killed, along with thousands of Italian nationals in the area.

As fear of terrorism from the Morning Star Trust wreaked havoc in the world, the governments of Europe, Canada, Russia, and China declared martial law. Vice President John Miller, acting for the incapacitated president of the United States, took to the airwaves and declared a state of national emergency in accordance with terms previously signed into law by President William Clinton. To protect the American people, the United States government would immediately enact stringent antiterrorism measures. All baggage would now be routinely screened at airports, bus terminals, and train depots. Canine teams would inspect all suspicious cargo and parked vehicles on government property.

But in declaring a national emergency, the government went far beyond antiterrorism measures. Relying upon Executive Order 12919, released by President Clinton on June 6, 1994, the vice president assumed the power to control all transportation; forms of energy; farm equipment;

food resources and food resource facilities; health resources; and metals, minerals, and water resources. The writ of habeas corpus, which guarantees that the government cannot hold someone without charging them with a crime, would be suspended until the situation of national emergency ceased. Furthermore, the vice president proclaimed, as of January 1, 2000, in the interest of national security, any "untagged" individual without a Millennium Chip would be detained indefinitely and subject to questioning.

This development sent a flood of reluctant, procrastinating Americans rushing to their local post offices to receive their Millennium Chips. Each night local news reports featured footage of men, women, and children standing in long lines, eager to be tagged and counted loyal to the American government.

Meanwhile, life revolved around the television set. Daniel went back to work, his concentration interrupted by intermittent flash bulletins from Europe and Washington. The news reports stirred vague and shadowy memories of Daniel's dark time in the hospital during Desert Storm. After he and Brad had planted the hardware device that confounded the Iraqis' air defense system, they had lain in their hospital beds and watched the war on television, courtesy of CNN. "The war of the future," Brad had remarked, staring up at the screen as General Norman Schwarzkopf demonstrated how a laser-guided smart bomb found and destroyed its target. "Prime-time entertainment brought to you by the United States Department of Defense and the good folks at CNN."

Daniel realized the truth in Brad's wry statement. Just as technology had changed the face of war, it had also changed the face of daily life. Though the mastermind Lucius Joshua was rumored to be in the United States, he had managed to elude the authorities at every turn. But Daniel knew the terrorist's days were numbered if he insisted upon remaining in the land of the free past January 1. On that date every legally-registered citizen would have a Millennium Chip installed. Lucius Joshua would have to be either a genius or a ghost to evade the system for long.

Now, as in the days of Desert Storm, Americans clustered around their TVs at breakfast, lunch, and dinner to observe the progress of the world's war on the Morning Star Trust and the search for the remaining nuclear devices. Grainy footage spilled into every home and workplace: video of

French gendarmes inspecting the Eiffel Tower, British bobbies in flak jackets prowling through subway stations, United Nations forces inspecting the Millennium Chip readouts and identification cards of travelers moving across international borders.

News anchors reported that thousands of telephone calls had jammed the switchboards of every police station and military base. The man Lucius Joshua had been seen at a Wal-Mart in Wichita, on an Alaskan cruise ship, and feeding pigeons outside the Vatican. Tips poured in by the thousands, and ordinary police work took a back seat as law enforcement officers around the globe searched for the criminal mastermind.

Daniel found it extremely hard to concentrate on his work in the midst of such turmoil, but he knew the reason was more than simple distraction. Something kept niggling at his brain, some idea or fact he had processed and forgotten. As he sipped his morning coffee with the professor on the first Friday in August, he felt a momentary surge of adrenaline, a flash of alertness. The idea he sought was on the tip of his tongue—and then it disappeared.

Dr. Kriegel must have noticed his look of frustration. "Something bothering you, Daniel?" he asked, his eyes sharp and assessing. "Other than the fact that New York is first on the nuke list?"

Daniel snorted as a ripple of mirth passed through him. "Know what?" He crunched the empty Styrofoam cup in his hand. "Being nuked is the last of my problems. I'm concerned about how all this will affect the Millennium Project and that my mother thinks I may have helped usher in the beast of Revelation, and I'm worried about Lauren. I haven't heard from her in two weeks."

The professor's hand fell on Daniel's arm. "Look." He nodded toward the corner television, where a special alert screen had just replaced the regular programming. "Perhaps you're about to."

The special alert logo vanished, and Daniel felt something go slack within him as he stared up at Adrian Romulus's image. The diplomat stood before another press conference, this one from Brussels. Daniel recognized the conference room in the European Union Council of Ministers' building. Romulus was gripping the same lectern Daniel had used when he convinced the people of Europe to implement his Millennium Code.

"I have good news to report to the world community," Romulus said.

He held onto the edges of the lectern with both hands and looked out at the camera with a pleased, proud, and faintly possessive expression. "We have found, interrogated, and imprisoned one of the terrorists involved in the Morning Star Trust plot. The man was apprehended as he sought to plant one of the stolen nuclear weapons in Rome. The citizens of that city are in no danger; the weapon has been safely dismantled. The terrorist is currently in a cell in Brussels, awaiting trial at the European high court. We are certain that we have begun to contain this threat."

Romulus turned toward his left, and, as if on a prearranged signal, another camera picked him up from that angle. Daniel noted the camera work—Romulus may have wanted this to look like an impromptu news conference, but somewhere a director was calling camera shots. And Romulus had been rehearsed.

"However—" Romulus's expressive face became more somber as he gazed into the closeup shot—"we have not yet located the other missing nuclear devices. And since the danger grows with each passing hour, we are declaring a state of worldwide emergency. The man currently in our custody has confessed that these weapons of mass destruction are scattered across the globe, and we cannot take chances with human life. Martial law is therefore declared in all European countries affiliated with the European Union."

Romulus shifted again, and stared into the camera with eyes that had darkened with a sheen of purpose. "I am very pleased to report that John Miller, vice president of the United States, has joined with us in a search for these threats to humankind. This morning in Brussels, Acting President Miller and I signed the Millennium Treaty, a military and economic agreement that officially affiliates our two great nations in a new American-European Federation on January 1, 2000. With our pooled military and intelligence resources, we will find these terrorist weapons and end this threat."

Daniel felt a cold panic start somewhere between his shoulder blades and prickle down his spine. Sam Stedman, silent and comatose, would never have approved this action, and neither would Congress. Miller had acted alone, under the broad powers granted to him in a state of national emergency.

The director shifted to another camera, and Daniel saw the semicircular table of the European Council's assembly room. John Miller sat at one end of the table, his heavy cheeks falling in worried folds over his collar. Miller nodded toward the camera as if sending a silent greeting to the world, and Daniel felt his stomach sway. He was going to be sick. The world was spinning out of his control, and people he knew were caught up in the vortex.

Daniel grasped at the strings of reality and held them tightly, then gasped as the elusive thought he'd sought rose to the surface. In his conversation with Brad about a world dictator, he had asked what a dictator would do before assuming power—and Brad had laughed. "He'd do two things—eliminate his opposition and declare a worldwide emergency—something that would give him the authority to take over all communications, transportation, banking, even food distribution. Of course, he'd probably have to invent a war with aliens to threaten the entire world."

Adrian Romulus hadn't invented a war with aliens, but had he invented the Morning Star Trust? And did President Stedman's illness have anything to do with Romulus's need to rid himself of opposition?

Daniel stood, then gripped the back of his chair for support. "Excuse me, Dr. Kriegel. I have to call a friend."

Back in his office, Roberta placed the call. Daniel could have wept with relief when he heard Brad's familiar voice. "That you, Danny boy?"

"Brad," Daniel kept his voice flat, knowing that all calls to the NSA were taped. "I think it's time we got together."

There was a nearly palpable silence, then Brad's deep laughter broke the awkward moment. "Sure, buddy, come on down to Washington. Christine and I would love to see you."

Daniel closed his eyes, understanding. This had to sound like a social call, though both of them knew it wasn't.

"I can tie things up here right away. I'll see you as soon as I land in Washington, but I might check in with my girl before I stop by."

"Hey, it's Friday. No rush. Call when you get in, and I'll fire up the grill."

Daniel felt his mouth twist in a grim smile. Yeah, right. Like a leading White House security advisor was going to barbecue pork ribs while the country was being handed over to a dictator.

Daniel disconnected the call, then tapped the button that instantly connected him with the Internet. With three keystrokes he was at the site for airline reservations, and with two taps on the touchpad he had located and booked himself on the next flight to Washington. He could have called for his own pilot and jet, but preparation for the flight would have required at least two hours, and he did not want to waste a single moment.

Daniel powered off his computer, then picked up his briefcase. "I'm leaving the office, Roberta. Record, encrypt, and hold all calls until I report in, please."

"Certainly, Mr. Prentice. Have a nice trip."

"I'll try."

-01001111100-

Daniel flashed his White House security pass at the guard but had to be personally cleared before a marine escorted him into the West Wing. He knocked on the door of Lauren's office and heard her muffled voice, then he slowly opened the door.

"Daniel!" She came out from behind her desk and embraced him, then pulled back and gave him a wavering smile. "I'm so glad you came!"

A masculine voice joined Lauren's greeting. "I'm glad, too, Danny boy."

Daniel looked to the left and saw Brad sitting in a chair across from Lauren's desk. "I didn't expect to see you," Daniel began, but Brad cut him off with an uplifted hand.

"I knew you weren't coming to Washington to see me, no matter how much you like my grilled burgers." Brad's voice was light, but his eyes were dark and serious. He jerked his head toward the door. "Lauren and I were just about to go out for some fresh air. Want to come?"

"Sure." Daniel waited for Lauren to pull her purse from her desk drawer, then Brad lifted his briefcase. The three of them passed through the hallway and out of the West Wing, then blinked in the bright sunlight. The passing automobiles on Pennsylvania Avenue seemed to tremble in the shimmering heat haze.

Daniel lifted a brow—*now can we talk?*—but Brad shook his head. "Danny boy, did you rent a car at the airport?"

"Yes."

"Let's take your vehicle, then."

Daniel looked at Lauren, an unvoiced question on his lips, but she merely lowered her head and quickened her steps toward the southwest appointment gate. Within a few moments they were at Daniel's car, and as he unlocked the doors, a blast of hot air struck him in the face.

"Sorry," he said, leaning down to press the automatic locks. The mechanism clicked, and Lauren opened the passenger door and slid into the bucket seat. Not quite so eager, Brad set his briefcase on the roof of the car and opened it, pulling out a small black box with an oval head protruding from a telescopic shaft.

Curious, Daniel said nothing as Brad flipped a switch and moved the device over the dash, the seats, and the ceiling. Finally he switched the power off. "The car's clean," he said, tossing the device back into his briefcase. He climbed into the back seat and waited for Daniel to take the driver's seat. "We can talk now."

Daniel frowned as he fastened his seat belt. "Did you really expect to find a bug in this car?"

"Why not?" Brad shrugged. "Lauren's office and car are bugged, and so are mine. That little gadget has found eavesdropping transmitters in the West Wing men's room, the Oval Office dining room, and the president's private study."

Daniel gave Brad a look of disbelief. "You mean your people didn't put them there?"

"Not us." Brad rested his hands on his knees and looked pointedly at the ignition. "Are you going to start the car, or are you planning to bake us in this heat?"

Daniel turned the key and powered up the AC while Brad and Lauren began to fill in the missing pieces of the story. "It all happened right after the president went into the hospital," Lauren said, twisting in her seat to look directly at Daniel. "The vice president was in charge, of course, but I began to see people I didn't recognize in the halls—a strange janitor, a new courier. That's when I began to suspect that something was up, so I contacted Brad." She raised her eyes to meet Daniel's in an oddly keen, swift look. "I wanted to call you but was afraid the lines were being tapped. I was afraid even to use the PGP program on my computer, so I didn't e-mail you."

"The entire place has been bugged—and not by us," Brad broke in. "We haven't moved anything; we'll play the waiting game and see who's pulling the strings. I want to say it's the vice president, but frankly, I don't think he has the chutzpah to pull this off. Besides, Miller left for Belgium three days after the president went into the hospital. I don't think he knows what's going on here."

"How'd Romulus get to Miller?" Daniel asked. He glanced at Lauren. "And how'd he keep you out of his business? I can't imagine you allowing him to entertain Romulus's offer without throwing a royal fit."

Lauren groaned. "A fit wouldn't have helped. Miller and I have never seen eye to eye, and I think he's resented me from the first day of the campaign. Fortunately, Jack Peck, chief of staff, has enough respect for the president that he's kept me in the loop. First, Romulus sent Miller copies of several European papers that blasted the United States for our unwillingness to participate in the International Day of Peace. Then the vice president started getting calls from political leaders and bankers in the European Union."

"Bankers?"

"Yes. They hit him with hard facts—that the European Monetary Union has an economy larger than America's, that the world financial markets may begin trading in the euro instead of the dollar, that pressure on the dollar would force U.S. interest rates to rise and subject us to whims of the international currency markets like never before. Finally, they pointed out that if both the Europeans and Japanese stopped investing billions in American Treasury bills, our economy would collapse. Miller took one look at the possibilities and decided that if we couldn't compete, we might as well join the Europeans. He left for Belgium right after that."

As he listened, Daniel kept his eyes on the road and occasionally glanced back in the rearview mirror. A black sedan had pulled out as they left the White House, and he suspected they had picked up a tail. He moved out onto the Beltway, planning to ride the circular interstate for as long as it took to hear the truth.

"What's happening with the president?" he asked.

Lauren made a soft sound of exasperation. "The doctors say Sam accidentally took Victoria's pills, but I don't know how that could happen. I know his morning routine, and I don't think he could ever be that absentminded."

"It was early on a Saturday morning," Daniel reminded her. "And if he knew about the missing nukes, he had probably been up all night. All that, coming so soon after the explosion—"

"That's what they're saying, that he was tired and distracted by the reports about the terrorists. They say he grabbed Victoria's nitroglycerin pills from the vanity instead of his St. John's Wort, then went straight in to face the cameras. One of the agents even went into the bathroom and found a container of her pills on the counter."

Daniel glanced at her. "It sounds believable, so why don't you buy it?"

Lauren lifted her chin. "Because Victoria never kept her nitro pills in the medicine cabinet. She kept them in her purse."

Daniel drove for a moment in silence. "If he didn't take her pills that morning—"

"He didn't, Daniel. Have you ever seen one of those pills? They're tiny. The president is not a fool; no matter how distracted, he could certainly tell the difference between St. John's Wort and a small nitro pill."

"Nitroglycerin, moreover, acts almost immediately," Brad said, leaning forward. "There was a ten-minute lapse from the time the president came out of the bathroom until he sat down at the desk in his office. Give him another five minutes for the speech, and another two or three minutes before he was really sick. That's eighteen minutes. If he had overdosed on nitroglycerin in the bathroom, he'd have collapsed long before that."

"Then how did he—?"

"He was drinking coffee while the cameras got into position." Lauren answered his unfinished question. "Someone could have ground up the drug and put it in his coffee cup. He drank it after his televised speech and collapsed almost immediately." She lifted her chin in a defiant gesture. "I talked to Francine, his secretary. She said she handed him the coffee at the last minute. One of the camera crew thought it would make him look more relaxed. But he didn't touch it until after the taping was done."

"Did she pour the coffee?" Brad asked.

"No." Lauren frowned. "She said someone handed her the mug, but she didn't recall who. There were too many people in the room, and every-thing was off-kilter because it was Saturday. General Archer and his senior staff had been there since five—that's when Romulus called with news of the nukes."

"You think someone poisoned the president?" Daniel moved into the right lane, then glanced over his shoulder at Brad. "Do you have any idea how medieval that sounds?"

"I know it's crazy, but it's entirely possible." Lauren raked a hand through her hair. "We didn't think anyone could penetrate the White House, but someone planted that bomb in the limo. And someone has bugged the offices. Why couldn't we assume that someone managed to slip something into the president's coffee?"

Daniel looked up and caught Brad's eye in the rearview mirror. "I suppose you've questioned the steward, the chef, the kitchen staff—"

"Everyone." Brad stared mindlessly at the passing scenery. "You can't get within ten feet of the White House gate without the proper security clearance, so someone has to be working both sides of the fence."

"Who's on the other side?" The question hung in the air, unanswered.

"You need to pull over because I have some things to show you," Brad said, after a long minute. "But first you've got to lose the black sedan on our tail."

"Right." Daniel glanced at Lauren. "Seat belt on, honey?"

"Yeah." She sank down in her seat and braced herself against the door. "I'm ready. Let's lose 'em."

Daniel pulled to the left lane and slammed his foot to the gas pedal, handling the car—and the agents behind him—as if they needed to be taught a lesson.

-01001111100-

Once the black car disappeared, Daniel pulled off in a residential neighborhood near Georgetown. He parked on a quiet street lined with row houses, then turned as Brad pulled a sheaf of photographs from his briefcase.

"You see these?" Brad divided the photos between Daniel and Lauren. "They are surveillance photos taken by the Keyhole-9 satellite affectionately known as Big Bird. You're looking at three military bases in Chechnya where several of these suitcase nukes have been stored since the Cold War."

Daniel frowned at the grainy images. They showed the rooftops of buildings, a few scattered vehicles, and a dark and rugged landscape. Not the kind of place where you'd want to spend a vacation. "Where did you get the photos?"

"The National Photographic Interpretation Center. The folks who work there spend their days analyzing information from spy satellites. When I asked them for shots of the Russian bases that had lost their nuclear demolition packages, these were just a few of the shots they gave me."

"What does this mean?" Lauren pointed to a hand-written notation in the corner of each shot.

Brad nodded. "Whenever you see the word *constant,* it means that the computer and the navy interpreter have decided that nothing has changed—no strange vehicles on the property, no unusual building or movement, nothing out of the ordinary. The photo is pretty much identical to the one preceding it."

"These all say constant." Daniel shuffled the photos in his hand. "I can't see anything different." He glanced up at Brad. "So where are the new pictures?"

"The ones that show the theft?"

"Exactly."

Brad's mouth twisted in bitter amusement. "You've got the new pictures. You're holding pictures taken from July 15 to August 5. Yesterday. If something had changed, Big Bird would have recorded it."

Lauren tilted her brow and looked at Brad with an uncertain expression. "So you're saying—"

"Romulus is lying. There were no stolen nukes, but maybe the enemy managed to buy the one detonated in Italy. I doubt that there is a Morning Star Trust, unless Romulus himself invented it. There may not even be a criminal mastermind named Lucius Joshua."

"Hold that thought." Daniel shifted in his seat. "Brad, will you pull my laptop from my briefcase? Thanks." He glanced at Lauren as Brad brought out the computer. "I wondered if this wasn't some kind of hoax. Brad and I talked a few days ago about what it would take for a dictator to seize power on the current world stage, and Brad said he'd have to invent some kind of threat to bring the world together."

"But I suggested aliens, not nuclear warheads," Brad said, grinning as he handed the laptop to Daniel. "Personally, I'd rather fight little green men than worry about nuclear bombs. I know that nuclear warheads can destroy the earth. With aliens, there's always the thrill of the unknown."

"Actually, I think the consensus of popular hysteria now dictates that they be little gray men," Daniel muttered, booting up the machine. "About four feet tall, with big slanting eyes."

As the computer whirred and loaded its programs, Daniel's gaze moved outside the car. Beyond a row of sprawling dogwood trees, stone-faced houses of two and three stories crowded together. A pair of young boys hugged the shade beneath a dogwood not far away and sweated beneath their baseball caps. The air outside was steamy and wet, too hot to play ball.

It was also too hot to hide in a parked car.

"Brad." Lauren's voice sounded uneasy. She sat sideways in the seat, facing Daniel, but her eyes scanned the road behind them. "A car just parked on the other side of the street. There are two suits inside, and neither man is getting out."

"They're onto us." Brad leaned forward as if to hurry Daniel along. "What do you have there, Danny boy?"

"A new program I whipped up this week." Knowing that a laser within the surveillance car could pick up their words, Daniel turned on the ignition, cranked up the air, and scanned the radio dial for a soft rock station. As Whitney Houston belted out a promise to always love somebody-or-other a little too loudly for the car's small interior, Daniel spoke in a hushed voice. "You're familiar with the digital imaging technology used by police to aid with suspect identification?"

Lauren and Brad nodded.

"Watch this." Daniel snapped a key, and the screen filled with a blank oval. "I asked this program to analyze all current data on the world's registered population—statistics we've gathered to help design the Millennium Chip. I'm now going to assemble digitally a face with the world's most predominant eye shape and color, nose shape and size, mouth and chin configuration. It will also fill in other details such as the predominant skin tone, hair thickness, facial hair, etc."

Daniel tabbed through several choices, selecting the default for each field, then clicked the enter key. As the computer filled in the required features, he looked at Brad and Lauren, then resolutely pressed his finger to his lips.

The cheery sound of a bell chimed along with Whitney, and Daniel heard Lauren draw in a quick breath as she and Brad studied the computer screen. The face before them, a full-color, photo-realistic composite, was a mirror image of Lucius Joshua.

Brad groaned. Daniel silently closed the laptop and passed it to the back seat, then shifted the transmission into drive. They had other things to discuss, but this location was no longer safe. Daniel nudged the rental car onto the street, then paused and waved farewell to the agents parked at the opposite curb.

-0100111100-

They drove for ten minutes through twisting streets, effectively losing the tail, then headed back out to the busy Beltway. Once they were riding in heavy traffic, Brad dared to speak up. "So this Lucius Joshua character is a complete fake?" he asked, sinking back into his seat. "Man, I must have worked a hundred calls on him just in the District. People are seeing him everywhere."

"They only *think* they're seeing him," Daniel pointed out. "The face you saw is every man's face. The eyes of one man, the nose of someone else. But it's a truly generic profile and is virtually guaranteed to remind everyone of someone." He shook his head. "It's really a clever ruse. The age is even right—I'd guess that the man known as Lucius Joshua is between forty and fifty-two, and that's the peak of the American baby boomer years."

"So if this man doesn't exist, who's the fellow they caught in Brussels?" Lauren glanced back at Brad. "What does the NSA know about it?"

"The NSA knows nothing about the man in custody or his bomb." Brad's voice was flat and harsh. "For all we know, he's one of Romulus's own aides . . . or maybe a traitor they'd happily sacrifice to the cause. But I'd bet my pension that he never makes it to trial. He'll be killed in prison, die in his sleep, or escape in a prison transfer. But his reported existence gives credibility to Romulus's story."

Daniel drove in silence for a while, then exited the Beltway and turned into the mammoth parking lot of a country restaurant that especially appealed to wide-eyed tourists. "This public enough for you, Brad? I'm hungry."

Brad's smile widened in approval. "This is great. I can use the pay phone to call Christine. She'll wonder where I am."

After they had been seated in the noisy restaurant and Brad had called home, Daniel lowered his menu and looked across the table. "Brad," he lowered his voice, "what do you know about the Antichrist?"

Brad's dry smile flattened. "You mean the beast? Six-six-six, and all that?"

Lauren parked her chin in her hand and moved closer to the table.

Brad looked away and sighed. "I don't know, the usual stuff I guess. He's the evil guy that's supposed to lead the world into great tribulation and Armageddon."

"That's right." Lauren nodded. "He's the world dictator of the last days. He will make everyone take a mark, without which no one can buy or sell. He will head up a global government, economy, military, even a one-world religion."

Brad pointed at Daniel. "See? I told you religion would play into it."

"Brad," Daniel glanced at Lauren, "we think Romulus might be the Antichrist. And if he is, there's probably no way to stop him."

"There is no way," Lauren interrupted, her eyes meeting Daniel's. "The Bible is true, and God's word cannot be changed. The prophecy will be fulfilled."

Brad looked at Lauren. "You're sure about this?"

She shrugged. "As sure as I can be. I felt there was something about Romulus from the beginning, and the more I read about prophecy, the more convinced I am. President Stedman never trusted him, and neither did Victoria."

Brad's eyes shifted to Daniel. "Are *you* convinced?"

Daniel closed his eyes. "I'm 98 percent sure. I wasn't convinced even a few days ago, but now I don't know. Maybe my mother is right—she keeps saying this is the beginning of the end."

Brad sat silently for a moment, his hand rhythmically tapping the table. The waitress, a tall, buxom blonde, came to the table and swiped a stray hank of hair out of her eyes. "Are y'all ready to order?"

"Not yet." Brad gave her a friendly smile. "Maybe later. We're trying to save the world right now."

"Oh, you!" She slapped at his shoulder in a friendly, flirtatious way, then tucked her pad and pencil away. "I'll come back in a minute, then. Y'all want more iced tea? Sweet or unsweet?"

"Nothing right now." Daniel smiled, too. "We'll be ready in five minutes."

"Five minutes?" Lauren's voice cracked with humor as the waitress moved away. "We're supposed to save the world in five minutes?"

"What can we do?" Daniel asked, crossing his arms on the table. "If all this is supposed to happen, there's not much we can do but sit back and watch."

"We can spy on them." Brad lifted his glass of iced tea and pressed it to his forehead. "They certainly have been interested in our whereabouts. We ought to turn the tables."

"If we ever find out who they are." Daniel rested his head in his hands, feeling strangely defeated. "They might even be our own people, right? If someone high up gives an order, they won't think about the reason for it, they'll just obey. Those guys in the car this afternoon could have been FBI or CIA, just ordinary guys doing their jobs. They probably think we're the anti-American element."

"Leave it to me." Brad took a sip of tea, then lowered the glass to the table. "I have a few trusted men under my command. I'll see what I can dig up." He lifted a brow in Daniel's direction. "What about you?"

"Maybe I can sabotage." Daniel's mind went back to the incident that set off Desert Storm. He had invented a hardware virus to confuse the Iraqis; perhaps there was something he could do to thwart Romulus. "Maybe Romulus does have to rise to power, but that doesn't mean we can't warn people about him."

"You have to warn them not to take his mark." Lauren's eyes had gone soft with pain. "The Bible says that anyone who takes his mark will lose his soul forever. He will be tormented with fire and brimstone in the presence of the holy angels and the Lamb."

Daniel glanced at her in surprise. "You've been studying."

"Yes." Her voice softened. "And I was afraid at first because I thought the Millennium Chip might actually be the mark of the beast. If it is, I'm already doomed because I've got a chip, and so does the president. Even Mrs. Stedman had one."

"But now you think it's not?" Daniel was surprised at the feeling of relief stirring in his own chest.

Lauren nodded. "It's definitely not. There must be another mark of some kind, a tattoo or a brand, perhaps something that will come later to show that a person's Millennium Chip has been approved and entered into the Antichrist's religious organization. The Bible says that the people who take the mark will be publicly identifying themselves with the Antichrist, marking themselves with his name or insignia. That situation doesn't fit with the Millennium Chip."

Daniel leaned back, astonished at the sense of release he felt. His mother's concern that he might have helped usher in the end of the world had disturbed him more than he had realized.

"So what do we do?" he asked, looking at the others. "Sabotage and scrutinize? Warn everyone we can?"

"We don't say anything until we're sure," Brad said, his face going grim. "Unless you want to end up in prison—or dead. Until we know for sure, we play along, we parrot the party line."

Lauren picked up her menu as the waitress approached. "So we wait and pray. For the president, and for the world."

Daniel slipped his arm around her shoulders. "I almost forgot to ask—what is your boss's prognosis?"

"Guarded, at best." Despite her attempt to appear calm and collected, Lauren's voice was thick and unsteady. "They can remove the overdose by ipecac emesis and activated charcoal, but it will take time. And his system has been through so much, with Victoria's death and everything else—"

"Did y'all save the world yet?" The smiling waitress was back.

"Not quite, but we're coming up with a plan." Daniel squeezed Lauren's arm, then glanced over her shoulder at the menu. "What's good here, Miss?"

"Everything's good, especially if you've got your Millennium Chip." The waitress tilted her head at a jaunty angle, then batted her lashes at Brad. "We're giving a 10 percent discount to anyone who pays with a debit card and Millennium Chip instead of cash. You can even put your tip on the bill."

Brad chuckled. "What is the world coming to?"

"Honey, you wouldn't believe what they can do with a computer these days." She pulled out her pen and pad, then turned the full warmth of her baby blues on Brad. "So—what'll you have, sugar?"

"Something good," Brad said, his eyes falling to the glossy menu. "Something nice and old-fashioned."

THIRTY-ONE

8:45 P.M., Tuesday, August 10, 1999

"WELL?" ROMULUS'S EYES, BRIGHT WITH THE STIMULATION OF ALCOHOL AND adventure, seemed to bore into Kord's skull. "What are they saying about our beloved friend Mr. Stedman?"

Kord thrust his hands behind his back and lifted his eyes to the edge of the walled garden as he searched for words. They were walking amid the lush greenery outside Adrian's French chateau, but the weather was far more suited for an indoor conversation. The black clouds overhead hung so low they seemed to compress the earth itself.

"They say," Kord measured his words with care, "that he will survive. John Miller seems committed to following your leadership. The American Congress will have to ratify the Millennium Treaty, of course, but the people seem to support the emergency measures he has installed." Kord lifted one shoulder in a most unmilitary shrug. "The Americans are saying that Miller is the man of the moment, and Adrian Romulus the man of the hour." He turned and found it impossible not to return Adrian's disarming smile. "Congratulations, sir."

"This is wonderful!" Adrian stopped to clap Kord on both shoulders, then folded his arms and resumed his walk. "But what of General Archer? They do not suspect him?"

"He is in charge of the investigation into both the automobile explosion and the president's mysterious illness. He is so busy rounding up suspects that no one has dared look in his direction." He paused, hesitating to mention the niggling fear that stirred in his brain. "I am speaking, of course, of the usual investigators. There are others, I fear, who suspect Archer if only because of his close association with me on my visits. But no one would dare accuse him without incontrovertible proof."

"Good." Romulus's grin flashed briefly, dazzling against his olive skin. "I shall have to do something special to thank him. Perhaps a new position in our new community—even one to rival yours, General Herrick."

Kord flinched. "Mine, sir?"

"Yes." Adrian continued down the garden path, ignoring the rising wind that threw the tree branches first one way, then another. A flash of lightning stabbed at the sky as the darkness thickened and congealed in the garden. Kord walked on, knowing that a hard rain could fall at any moment, but Adrian seemed not to care.

"General, you are very efficient—some would say ruthless."

Kord gave him a look of gratitude, which Romulus acknowledged with just the smallest softening of his eyes.

"But I gave you a task to perform months ago, and I regret to say that you have failed me."

Kord stopped on the path, his mind congesting with doubts and fears. What had he not done? He cast about for some logical explanation of his master's abrupt statement, but he could find none.

Struggling for breath, he hurried to catch up with Adrian, who walked on as if nothing had happened. "I don't understand, sir," Kord said, his heart beating faster than usual. "I removed Stedman, and the bomb had the desired effect. The Americans have joined the community, which is what you wanted—"

"I want Daniel Prentice." The shifting storm shadows hid Romulus's face, but there was no mistaking the splinters of ice in his voice. "I specifically told you that I wanted the man's genius, and yet you have done nothing to bring him to me."

Reeling with disbelief, Kord shook his head, then brought his hand to the bridge of his nose. "You have his computer code; you have his Millennium Chip." He lowered his hand, struggling to contain his swirling emotions. "Prentice did everything you asked."

"I want *him*." Adrian's dark eyes glared at Kord, shooting sparks in all directions. "I want to know that a man of his genius would vow allegiance to our cause. I want the world to see that a man like Prentice appreciates our vision of the world community. I want *Daniel Prentice* to forsake his country and vow his allegiance to me!"

Kord stepped back, momentarily astounded. Adrian had demonstrated these fits of prideful ambition before, but Kord had never been on the receiving end of his anger. He was tempted to turn away, to leave the chateau, and not look back, but one did not walk out on the man who held the world's power in his hands.

"Prentice is not easily won," he said when he finally found his voice. "That woman in the White House, Lauren Mitchell, exerts a tremendous influence upon him. His best friend is a traditionalist, his mother a funda-mentalist Christian. Moreover, he seems content with what he has, so I cannot offer him much—"

The stark white bones of lightning suddenly cracked through the black sky, followed by a roar of thunder that shuddered through the trees like a bellow of rage.

"You should offer him glory," Adrian answered, his dark hair lifting in the wind. He lifted his face to the swirling clouds, completely unafraid. "When we return to the United States, you will find Daniel Prentice. Offer him a place at my side. If he does not have the good sense to accept, kill him. He who is not for us is against us. It is that simple, General Herrick."

Kord could not answer, but gripped his hat in the bawling winds and wondered if any of Romulus's professions of loyalty could be trusted.

Thirty-two

Summer's hot breath gradually cooled to the gentler breezes of autumn. The world continued its frantic search for the terrorists of the Morning Star Trust, and three other suspects were discovered and their weapons confiscated. All three suspects, like the one held in Brussels, died before the world court could try them. One suffered a heart attack, one was killed while resisting arrest, one committed suicide, and the fourth overdosed on drugs he had managed to smuggle into the prison.

But there were no other nuclear explosions. The people of the world inured themselves to fear just as they had learned to harden their hearts to tragedy.

By November first, President Samuel Stedman's doctors had prepared their patient for his return to the White House. Lauren watched with tears in her eyes as the tall, once-powerful man walked out of the hospital between two Secret Service agents, waved to the crowd, and slowly sank into the presidential limo. The political climate had shifted so dramatically during his three-month hospitalization that she wondered if he would be able to adjust. He had left his office determined to fight for American sovereignty; he had returned to find his country in the hands of a foreign diplomat, guided there by his own right-hand man. And as Americans dreamed of a more prosperous economy and the ambiance of Europe, each passing day increased the likelihood that the Congress would ratify the Millennium Treaty in January, after their return from the holiday break.

Lauren was afraid Samuel Stedman could do little to wrest his authority away from those who had snatched it while he slept.

If Stedman was disappointed in the turn of world events, he disguised his feelings well. On a balmy November Monday, he returned to the Oval

Office and received heartfelt welcomes from his staff and a horde of visitors to the White House.

That afternoon, after seeing that the president had a gentle schedule for his first week back to work, Lauren welcomed the opportunity to retreat to her office and gather her own thoughts. She pulled a sheet of White House stationery from her drawer and wrote Daniel—in a handwritten letter, the most secure way to communicate within her office—that Sam Stedman seemed content to finish out his term quietly. Victoria's death and his own brush with eternity had mellowed the man, and Lauren knew he would not publicly criticize the vice president. Though Stedman strongly disagreed with Miller's decision to move the United States into the evolving global community, Miller was the best Republican hope for the year 2000 election.

Lauren wrote:

I think it's terribly ironic that John Miller will owe his future to Samuel Stedman. A truly great man is stepping aside to make way for a lesser one, and the fact that he is willing to do so only emphasizes his magnanimity. This country will lose a great leader but will probably never feel the loss, for the position of president will never be what it was as long as we are confederated with the European Union. Adrian Romulus clearly controls that body now—his personality pervades every press release, communiqué, and teleconference. But Sam Stedman has resigned himself to the inevitable. Perhaps he remembers what Victoria said about the coming one-world government . . . or perhaps he is too weary and grief-stricken to care. I can't ask about his feelings. He has put up a wall of reticence that no one dares approach. I only know that a shell of the man I once admired occupies the Oval Office. His calendar is filling with senseless photo ops and hand-shaking meetings—trivialities, really. And all of us who love him count the days until January 2001, when we will depart the Oval Office and leave it to a more ambitious and flexible statesman.

As Lauren signed the letter and sealed the envelope, she took stock of her own feelings. As Sam Stedman's future had diminished, so had hers. She had committed herself to serving in the White House throughout his presidency, but that presidency had all but vanished in the wake of tragedy. More and more Lauren found herself thinking of Daniel Prentice . . . and hoping for a way to tell him that her situation had changed.

-010011100-

Throughout November, as the president resumed what remained of his schedule, Daniel and Brad sent a flurry of e-mails back and forth—all carefully encrypted. Daniel devoted himself to covert activities after the office had closed and most of his employees had gone home.

Over the weeks, as Daniel and Brad shared their thoughts and played devil's advocate, Daniel's suspicions about Adrian Romulus evolved into certainty. Samuel Stedman had his enemies on the home front, of course, but Brad insisted that only someone with advanced military technology— "make that *foreign* technology, Danny boy" one message read—could have slipped an explosive device through the White House gates. Yet this administration had managed to maintain cordial relationships with every foreign leader except Adrian Romulus, who, despite his smiles and condolences, had met his first major roadblock in the person of Samuel Stedman.

So who had Romulus tapped to do his dirty work? Any of the president's cabinet members could be working for him; Vice President Miller himself could have been on Romulus's payroll. Determined to find the traitorous link, Daniel convinced Brad to share some thoughts on how to invade the enemy's territory, then he spent several long nights at his computer, working until sunrise, then catching a quick nap on the sofa in his office.

His employees must have noticed his bleary-eyes and distracted expression, but no one dared say anything.

Meanwhile, public support for the Millennium Treaty grew with each passing hour. Public service announcements touted the glamour of traveling to London or Paris for lunch without hassle and without a passport. American companies were urged to invest in European industries because "what benefits one member of the community benefits us all." The symbol of Europa upon the bull, superimposed over a circle of stars to represent the star-spangled American flag, began to appear in travel ads and commercials for European countries.

Daniel suspected that *anyone* who publicly expressed loyalty to the idea of a sovereign United States would naturally fall under suspicion, so he ran his company as if nothing had changed. Many of his employees were quite vocal in their support of the Millennium Treaty and the nation's affiliation with the European Union, and Daniel couldn't blame them for thinking he felt the same way. Prentice Technologies, after all, had designed the computer code that served as the basis for unity.

But he and Brad had finally come up with a two-pronged plan that might delay Romulus's rise to power. Even if it failed to delay the Millennium Treaty, it would still give Daniel an opportunity to warn the American people and tell the truth about the so-called nuclear threat. If Adrian Romulus could not be stopped, he could at least be exposed.

To that end, Daniel worked on a hardware virus device similar to the one he had installed in Iraq prior to Desert Storm. Brad continued his covert operations, spying on newcomers, mostly European loyalists, who suddenly appeared in Washington. Most important, Brad tried to keep an eye on General Herrick, who had taken a suite at the Watergate Hotel and now attended every cabinet meeting and security briefing.

While Daniel searched for technological ways to thwart Romulus's purposes, he knew Lauren was corresponding with his mother to learn what she could about the Antichrist from a biblical perspective. Lauren sent encrypted e-mail messages to Daniel, too, but he asked that she send them only from her home—too many surveillance devices could literally capture computer keystrokes from the other side of a wall. No room in the White House, Daniel assured her, was truly secure.

During his annual televised Thanksgiving speech, a calm, placid President Stedman reported that 84 percent of the United States population had been successfully implanted with Millennium Chips. Thousands were already using the chip to handle their banking, shopping, and medical needs. As the president concluded his speech, he looked out at the camera with weary eyes and gave the public a smile containing only a shadow of its former warmth.

Daniel felt his heart sink. If he had not invented the Y2K fix, if he had not insisted that Millennium Chips were the wave of the future, would the world still be on this collision course with biblical prophecy? The question was unanswerable.

The first snow of winter fell on Friday night, December third. Daniel saw the snow from the PT cafeteria windows, thought suddenly of Lauren, and wondered if she would build a fire in that cozy den where he had sat with her on the sofa. He had resisted kissing her that night, but if she were to walk through the door, he wouldn't resist now.

Shaking off the counterproductive thoughts, he returned to his office and sank into his chair. The green circuit card for his new hardware device lay on the desk, and he stared at it and tried to focus on his task. He had just begun to tinker with the relay switches when Roberta's husky voice broke his concentration.

"An urgent e-mail message for you, Mr. Prentice."

"Sender, please?"

"Lauren Mitchell."

"Thank you, Roberta." Daniel moved to his computer, selected the e-mail program, then highlighted the icon that would decrypt Lauren's message. In an instant, the jumbled symbols separated into words.

> *Daniel:*
> *A stroke of luck! Just heard that AR himself is coming to U.S. to welcome in the new year. A White House reception is planned for 12-23, then AR plans to vacation over Christmas. But—get this—he wants to stand in Times Square on New Year's Eve! Something about seeing the ball drop and welcoming in the new millennium. So if you want him in your backyard, you'll have him then.*
> *Hope you are well. Let me know how I can help.*
>
> *L.*

Daniel swiveled his chair and reread the message, then considered his options. He didn't particularly want Adrian Romulus nearby on New Year's Eve or any other night. But if Romulus was planning to appear at Times Square, he was undoubtedly producing some sort of televised address with lots of corresponding fanfare. The man couldn't take a simple video call without playing to the camera. Even last year, when America had no idea who or what Adrian Romulus was, he had managed to snag prime face time on camera.

Surely this was a heaven-sent opportunity. Daniel could go to

Washington for the reception on the twenty-third, plant the Trojan horse device he'd been designing, then move out and away. With any luck the device wouldn't be discovered until after New Year's Eve, and by that time Daniel would have found a way to tell the world exactly what he'd discovered.

Smiling grimly, he typed a note to Brad:

> B:
>
> *Got a tuxedo? Keep the 23rd open. L's planning a party at Casa Blanca, and we're invited. Big wigs from Europe. Holiday celebration. Just what I need before my vacation.*
> *See you there.*
>
> D.

Daniel encrypted the message with PGP and smiled as the letters flashed into incomprehensible nonsense. Even if Brad's Romulus-loving coworkers pulled this note off his hard drive, it wouldn't matter. The message contained nothing incriminating, but Brad would understand. December 23 was the launch date, and New Year's Eve would bring a rendezvous with destiny.

Daniel leaned back in his chair, laced his hands behind his head, and stared for a moment at the garbled assortment of letters and symbols. If he proceeded with this plan, his life would change in the most dramatic way imaginable. He'd have to abandon his apartment, his company, even his loyal employees. Adrian Romulus's steadily growing web of influence now covered every part of Europe and the United States; after January first there'd be virtually no place in those countries for Daniel to hide. His Millennium Chip would set off sensors everywhere he went; even his entry into a convenience store could trigger an alarm.

Romulus would certainly brand him as a wanted and dangerous criminal. He'd be lucky if he survived two days in the United States.

Still, someone had to do something. And since he had been the ambitious fool who provided Romulus with the means of controlling the world's population, he might as well be the one to do it.

Resolved to follow his conscience, Daniel reached out and clicked the send icon.

Thirty-three

7:45 P.M., Thursday, December 23, 1999

LAUREN ANXIOUSLY SMOOTHED THE IVORY FABRIC OF HER DRESS, THEN PAUSED and stared at her reflection in the small mirror behind her door. She should have taken an hour to go home and really put on the glitz; the other women at the reception would undoubtedly sparkle like nominees on Oscar night. But she had been too nervous to worry about glamour and too keyed-up to care. She peered out of her office into the West Wing hallway. Daniel, Brad, and Christine stood outside, the men both handsome in their tuxedos and Christine elegant in a simple silver gown. Lauren had lifted her brows at her first glimpse of Christine Hunter—none of her elementary schoolteachers had ever looked that gorgeous.

Lauren painted on a fresh coat of lipstick, threw the compact into her evening bag, then took a deep breath and stepped out in the hall to join her friends. Daniel's eyes had been abstracted, but they cleared as she came into the hallway. "About time." His dark eyes held more than a hint of flirtation, and she wondered how he could even think about charming her at a time like this.

Eyeing him critically, she reached out and plucked a piece of lint off the shoulder of his black tuxedo. "There. Now you look really good."

A wry smile curled on Daniel's lips. "Gee, thanks."

"You've got your evening bag?" Brad asked, arching a brow.

Lauren nodded and pointedly adjusted the delicate chain on the beaded purse dangling from her shoulder. In it she carried only two things: her lipstick compact and her courier card, the magic key that granted her access into practically every government building in town. With exaggerated nonchalance, she opened her bag, pretended to check her hair in the compact's mirror, then pulled out her courier card and slipped it into

Daniel's tuxedo pocket. She felt a shiver as she slid the compact back into her purse. Were they watching even now? Probably.

Daniel smiled and held out his arm. "Shall we go? I hear the orchestra warming up."

His touch was reassuring. Lauren took his arm and lifted her chin. Now that the White House had no official hostess, President Stedman had asked her to help him receive guests. He had graciously added that Daniel could stand by her side, but Lauren had laughed and protested that Daniel Prentice wasn't the type to stand in a formal receiving line and make small talk.

"You should be grateful," she told Daniel now as they moved toward the Diplomatic Reception Room. "Sam wanted you to stand with me and perform the protocol bit, but I told him you'd rather visit with your friends."

He gave her an impenitent grin. "Thank heaven."

They came down the stairs just as the president stepped out of the private family quarters through another hallway. None of the guests had been allowed inside the oval reception room yet, but a dozen Secret Service men churned the empty space. Daniel gallantly escorted Lauren to the president's side, then retreated to an out-of-the way settee where Brad and Christine held hands and waited. Vice President Miller and his wife separated themselves from a knot of Secret Service agents and came to stand by Lauren's side on the oval rug bordered with symbols of all fifty states.

"Ready?" Lauren smiled at the president and felt her heart break when he glanced back toward the grand staircase as if he were waiting for Victoria. Part of him would always wait for her. In the past month Lauren had observed a thousand little things that revealed the depths of his grief. The marks of anguish were permanently etched in the lines beside his mouth; his eyes would forever be shadowed by the loss of his great love.

"Yes." The president pulled himself out of his reverie, wiped his hands on his tuxedo trousers, and gave Lauren a quick smile. "Let's do it."

A Secret Service agent mumbled into his mouthpiece, and the carved doors opened to the South Grounds. The long line of guests entered with a rush of chattering noise, and Lauren shook hands and murmured pleasantries and smiled until she thought her face would crack. Adrian Romulus arrived with Kord Herrick and Elijah Reis at his side—no women, she noticed—and it took every ounce of concentration for Lauren not to pull away when General Herrick bent low and caressed her hand with a lingering kiss. Romulus himself was diffident, barely glancing her way, and Elijah Reis had nothing to say to her. He merely walked in Romulus's shadow, his wide eyes drinking in the gathering as if he were mentally recording the names and descriptions of every individual present.

As Romulus and his companions moved away, Lauren turned to smile at a rotund congressman from South Carolina. The congressman's wife held Lauren's hand in a tight grasp, enthusing over her dress in honeyed tones. Lauren gritted her teeth against the pain of the woman's crushing grip. As she nodded intermittently at the woman's comments, she saw from the corner of her eye that Daniel was standing in the circle of Romulus's retainers. She'd have given anything for the freedom to break free of the receiving line and go eavesdrop, but she knew Daniel had no plans to confront Romulus tonight. They were probably engaging in nothing but polite political conversation.

The senator's wife finally moved on, and in the brief lull Lauren was actually able to hear part of the conversation. "It was a smooth transition, really, Mr. Prentice. Your Millennium Code surprised even me," Romulus was saying, his stentorian voice thundering throughout the oval room. "One would almost think you anticipated the coming merger of the world's systems."

"Well, sir," Daniel lifted his glass in a salute, "one must prepare for the inevitable. They say the world has been growing smaller for decades, and I had only to look at the new world of global companies to see the future. In the past two years, German Daimler-Benz merged with American Chrysler, Merrill Lynch acquired Britain's Mercury Asset Management Group, and the German media conglomerate Bertelsmann bought New York's Random House. I figured it was only a matter of time until we became one community."

" . . . so glad the president's in better health."

An ambassador took Lauren's hand, and she smiled as she transferred her attention to him. She had scarcely heard a word he said, but she could guess at the gist of the man's conversation. "Yes, we're grateful, too. We would hate to lose him."

She breathed a sigh of relief when the ambassador moved away.

When the last of the reception guests had officially greeted the president, Lauren left Samuel Stedman with Vice President Miller and his wife, then slipped away and moved toward Daniel. He was standing with Brad and Christine under a mural depicting the beauty of Natural Bridge, Virginia, and apparently fascinated by something in the painting.

She slipped her arm through his. "I hope you're having a pleasant evening," she said, well aware that at least a dozen security men mingled in the crowd. Some were Secret Service, of course, but there were others Lauren had never seen. Quietly, she squeezed Daniel's arm. "Now," she whispered.

As Lauren shifted to Christine's side, the two men slipped away down a hall Lauren had pointed out earlier. Lauren looked at Christine, whose blue eyes were wide with alarm.

"So—do you like working in the Wh-white House?" Christine stammered. Brad had obviously told her to act natural, but this kind of clandestine activity was apparently a little too risky for a schoolteacher's taste. Lauren caught herself—what Brad and Daniel were attempting was too risky even for Lauren's comfort.

"Have you seen the Map Room?" she asked, slipping her arm around Christine's narrow waist. "Why don't I show it to you?"

Shivering like a scared rabbit, Christine allowed Lauren to lead her out of the reception hall.

-0100111100-

Brad had plotted out their route. The U.S. Treasury Department was located right next to the White House, but a labyrinth of tunnels and corridors lay between the Diplomatic Reception Room and the Treasury Department basement housing the Financial Crimes Computer Network. Brad led Daniel through the White House, sliding Lauren's courier card through each checkpoint, and Daniel breathed a silent sigh of relief that the White House security system was not exactly cutting edge. Brad's plan would never have worked if the White House had installed a biometric system, but the security experts had concentrated their efforts on protecting the perimeter of the mansion. Once inside, as Daniel and Brad were, an intruder could move easily from room to room with a stolen courier card.

"There's a tunnel linking the two buildings; it runs under East Executive Avenue," Brad explained as they hurried through the halls. The building seemed deserted, and Daniel remembered that most of the staff had been released to begin an early Christmas vacation. Even if it hadn't been the holiday season, Lauren told him that a laissez faire attitude now existed among the White House staff—President Stedman's attitude of diffident resignation had spread throughout the entire administration. Everyone, it seemed, was merely going through their paces until the 2000 elections.

Brad pulled a small halogen flashlight from his pocket and shone the bright beam into the tunnel. Daniel crinkled his nose—the place smelled of mildew and dust, but the concrete floor was clean and appeared to be regularly swept. "You won't find any rats down here, Danny boy," Brad whispered, his eyes following the light as it arced from side to side. The side of his mouth lifted in a grin. "They don't have the proper clearance."

"What's the security layout?" Daniel asked, struggling to catch his breath as they jogged down the corridor.

"Cameras in the corners of the room, and sound detectors. We'll have to work silently. And they will see us, of course."

"Not for long."

The tunnel spilled into a cavernous room that clanged and hissed with the sound of archaic radiators. Brad led the way down another corridor, then paused before a broad door. A placard announced that they had reached the location of the Financial Crimes Computer Network.

"Subtle," Daniel drawled.

Brad pressed his finger over his lips, then held out his hand for Lauren's card. Daniel gave it to him, then watched as Brad swiped it. The red glowing light was replaced by a bright green one. Brad turned the doorknob, and they entered the room.

Soft blue fluorescent lighting flickered over a dozen ancient mainframes. Daniel felt his mouth twist at the sight of so many antiquated machines—*you'd think the government could afford better*—then his eyes found what he sought. A workhorse PC sat on a small desk in the corner of the room, daisy-chained to a printer, scanner, and zip drive. An ordinary office setup; nothing fancy.

Conscious of the unblinking eye of the surveillance cameras, he moved to one of the mainframes and proceeded to open the front panel. While Daniel worked, Brad took off his tuxedo coat and draped it over the surveillance camera in the right corner of the room.

Daniel disconnected the keyboard from the PC, then hooked the cable into the mainframe. Brad came over and tapped him on the shoulder, and Daniel obediently paused and shrugged his way out of his own coat. While Brad moved toward the second camera, Daniel began typing on the keyboard.

Brad shucked Daniel's coat over the second camera, then snapped his fingers. Instantly, Daniel left the keyboard and mainframe. From one pocket he lifted out a pair of cotton-lined suede gloves and pulled them on. Then, taking the hardware virus device from the other pocket of his trousers, he lifted the scanner's cover, pried out the glass panel, and pressed the small black box into the largely empty space inside the scanner. A dummy wire extended from the device, and with the tip of his index finger he deftly tapped it into place beside the scanner's power supply.

Satisfied, Daniel replaced the glass panel and checked his work. Anyone looking inside the scanner would see the box and naturally assume it was part of the equipment. The device's internal power system emitted a low frequency footprint; its electromagnetic waves would be disguised by the scanner's ordinary output. But at midnight on January 1, 2000, the device would transmit an electromagnetic viral signal over the network that would jumble the Millennium Code in any mainframe residing in Europe. Like Cinderella, the glitz and shine of Romulus's kingdom would vanish, returning the European mainframes to their former ragtag conditions.

Stepping back, Daniel slipped the gloves from his hands. He had purposely left a hundred fingerprints on the keyboard and mainframe cover, but not even latent fingerprints would show up through cotton-lined suede. They'd never know he went near the scanner.

He glanced up at Brad, who leaned on the doorframe, his arms folded as if he were patiently waiting for a bus. He had asked no questions about exactly what Daniel intended to do; he had asked only that Daniel guarantee that the United States' Treasury Department computers would not be affected. "I'm still working for the NSA," he'd written in his last e-mail. "And I'd like to think I'm still a loyal American."

Daniel moved back into his position in front of the mainframe, gave the machine a simple directory command, then nodded to Brad. In unison, they each walked to their respective coats, tugged them free of the surveillance cameras, then exited the way they had come.

Daniel knew his life would never be the same again.

-0100111100-

Lauren stopped dead, looking at Daniel, her heart beating hard enough to be heard a yard away. He and Brad entered the Diplomatic Reception Room through the carpeted hallway that led to the Entrance and Cross Halls; anyone who saw them entering now might assume they'd just stepped out for a moment.

But Lauren knew better.

Daniel came toward her, caught her hands, then gave her a quick kiss on the cheek. "Miss me?"

Her hand slipped upward, felt the hard and tense muscles of his forearm beneath his sleeve. "You know I did."

He stepped back, his dark eyes gleaming black and dangerous in the soft light of the room. "Can I bring you something to drink?"

Lauren bit her lip and resisted the urge to laugh aloud. What was it about men? If she had just returned from Daniel's errand, she'd be quivering with fright and relief. But the adventure had energized him; he looked like he was ready to sweep her around the room and waltz until daybreak.

"Do you have something for me?" she whispered, taking his arm as he swung around to her side.

"Of course." With the skill of a sleight-of-hand artist, he pulled her courier card from his pocket and pressed it into her palm. Lauren hid it with the back of her hand, then opened her evening bag and pulled out her lipstick compact and pretended to check her lipstick. Then she dropped the card and her compact back into the purse.

The orchestra in the Map Room was playing "Georgia on My Mind," and Daniel lazily swung her into his arms, then moved out into the hallway where a pair of marines stood like statues. "Lauren Mitchell," he said, his eyes gleaming as he placed his hand on her waist as if they were waltzing, "we might as well face it. We belong together, and after tonight, nothing will ever be the same. So you might as well marry me."

If he hadn't been holding her, she would have lost her balance and fallen. "Marry you?"

His eyes filled with fierce sparkling. "Yes. For better or worse, richer or poorer, in sickness and in health, till death or Adrian Romulus do us part."

Lauren swallowed hard and clung to him more tightly. "Shh, not so loud, he'll hear you. And don't joke about such things. It's not funny."

"He's deep in conversation with the vice president; he doesn't care about me. Do you?" Daniel released her right hand and brought his left under her chin, lifting her face until she looked him in the eye. The expression in his eyes took her breath away, and with pulse-pounding certainty she realized he wasn't kidding. "I need you, Lauren Mitchell," he said, speaking in an odd, yet gentle tone. "We're both at a crossroads, and I can't imagine taking another step without you by my side. So say you'll marry me. Please."

The sound of that little word—*please*—sent her fingers flying to his lips, urging him to silence. She had begun to hope she would hear words like these from Daniel, but she had never imagined hearing them so soon. The obstacles that had stood between them—her career and his enthusiasm for Romulus—had faded to nothingness, but still Lauren could not accept his offer without feeling a wave of wistful sadness.

Pain squeezed her heart as she thought of the decisions and events that had brought both of them to this place. She had lost Victoria Stedman and nearly lost the president; Daniel had discovered that his bright and shiny dreams of influencing the world tarnished in the harsh light of Adrian Romulus's ambition. And yet something had blossomed between them, something stronger than politics, something more enduring than Romulus's new global community. She had come to love Daniel Prentice.

But what would that love cost her? Daniel was right—even if by some miracle his and Brad's unauthorized visit to the Treasury Department went undiscovered, life would soon change for both of them. Daniel had already set his plan to thwart Romulus in motion; if she married him her hard-won political career would vanish at midnight on January 1, 2000. But did she want to be a part of Romulus's global community?

She did not.

"Yes, Mr. Prentice." She kept her voice light as her gaze met his. "I will marry you."

Daniel smiled down at her, his features suffused with joy, then twirled her over the carpet in athletic exuberance. A small smattering of applause greeted his enthusiastic display, and when Lauren caught her breath and looked up, she saw General Herrick standing in the doorway that led to the reception room.

"Mr. Prentice." Herrick cast a glance of well-mannered dislike in Lauren's direction, then tucked his hands behind his back and nodded at Daniel. "Sir—if we might have a word with you."

Lauren saw the Adam's apple bob in Daniel's throat as he swallowed. "Why, of course, General. What seems to be the problem?"

Herrick didn't answer, but stepped aside and extended his hand toward the reception room. Lauren looked toward the space where she had last seen Brad and Christine and saw that the couple had disappeared. Lauren hoped they had managed to slip away.

"I'm coming with you." Lauren grasped Daniel's arm, then looked Herrick in the eye. "Perhaps you did not know, General, but Mr. Prentice is my fiancé."

"Congratulations." The man's tone dripped with ridicule. "But still, we need a word. If you will come—"

Daniel lifted his head and followed the general, and Lauren clung to his arm, closing her eyes in a silent prayer as she followed.

-0100111100-

Kord turned his back on the couple sitting on the antique sofa and silently wished General Archer had offered a more Spartan room for this interview. With its soft yellow walls and formal portraits of six first ladies, the Vermeil Room was not exactly suited for an interrogation. But it would have to do.

He turned again and faced the couple. The woman, Lauren Mitchell, wore the determined look of a woman in love and clung to Prentice's arm as if his life depended upon her strength. Prentice's face was as blank as an empty page; he sat calmly on the sofa and watched Kord watch him.

"Mr. Prentice," Kord said, nodding deferentially to General Archer and the two other security agents in the room, "we know what you and Mr. Hunter did tonight. Our cameras picked you up as you exited the building. We saw you go through the tunnel, and we know that you used Ms. Mitchell's card to enter the computer room in the Treasury Building."

Daniel Prentice lifted a brow. "Congratulations. So why are we here?"

Kord clenched his mouth tighter. "You are here because your actions may have jeopardized the financial computer network we have labored to put together. So tell us—what did you do in that computer room?"

"You saw it." Prentice's eyes hardened in a challenge. "You tell me what I did."

Kord drew a long, quivering breath, struggling to master the passion that shook him. Such American arrogance! These braggarts thought they knew everything. They flouted their own laws and taunted their authorities.

General Archer pulled himself off the wall and leaned on the antique table before Prentice and Mitchell. "We saw you key into the mainframe; it's all on the surveillance video. But you know what happened next— Hunter covered the cameras. So why don't you make things easy on all of us and tell us what you did."

Daniel smiled and slipped his arm around the woman's shoulders. "I'd be delighted to tell you, General Archer. I typed the directory command." He sent a guileless smile winging around the room. "I wanted to check the directory contents. That's all. The program scrolled through the files, then I shut it down. No big deal."

General Archer looked at Kord as if to say, *Satisfied?* But the German shook his head. "Nein!" he roared, clenching his teeth. "You do not speak the truth!"

"I beg your pardon, I most certainly do." Daniel tugged on his bow tie as if the entire interrogation were nothing but an annoying irritation.

"You expect me to believe you did not damage the computers?" Kord spat out the words. "Do you take me for a fool?"

"Never, General Herrick." Prentice's suddenly cold eyes sniped at him. "I would never underestimate an enemy—that would be a fatal mistake."

His eyes shifted to Archer. "You see, gentlemen, I've been doing some research over the past few weeks. Do you recall the tragic explosion that killed Mrs. Stedman? General Herrick was in Los Angeles at the time, but you, General Archer, were here, at the White House, on a bright and beautiful Sunday morning." One of Prentice's brows lifted. "I checked the computer security logs. You had not appeared at the White House on a Sunday in eight weeks, but you showed up that morning, just in time to plant the device General Herrick had left for you."

Archer's face contorted in a grimace of pain, as if Prentice had slapped him across the face. "Liar! You could never prove that!"

"I don't need to." Lauren Mitchell's face had gone pale, but Prentice continued, his sharp gaze moving around the room. "General Archer knew about Mrs. Stedman's heart condition, too. He had access to the family quarters, and he planted the medicine that the president supposedly took by accident. But nitroglycerin is a fast-acting drug, and the only way the president could have ingested it is if someone put it in the coffee cup he sipped from after he addressed the nation regarding Adrian Romulus's warning about the missing nukes."

"Daniel." Lauren Mitchell's hand trembled as she reached out to touch his arm. "You've got to say something. You've got to tell the president—"

"I can't, Lauren." Prentice gave her the briefest of glances, then met Archer's eyes again. "I can't prove it. And the way I discovered these things—well, it's not exactly legal. We could never use any of the information in a formal proceeding, but I have taken pains to be certain it is recorded. If anything unfortunate should happen to the president, Brad, Lauren, or me, the information will be released to the world."

Prentice glared at Archer with the ears-back look male dogs give each other before deciding to fight. Kord glanced at Archer, then snorted in contempt. The American general's face glistened with tiny pearls of sweat. The coward.

"Mr. Prentice," Kord suppressed his anger under the cloak of indifference, "your assumptions are completely off the mark. I don't know what sort of conspiracy rubbish you have been reading, but—"

"I've been reading your e-mail communications, General Herrick, as well as General Archer's." Prentice lifted his chin and met Kord's gaze straight on. "We broke your encryption codes last month. I must say, the reports to and from Paris and Brussels have been very interesting." He tilted his head slightly. "Did you know, Herrick, that Romulus plans to elevate Archer above you in the new global community?"

Kord felt himself trembling all over, and a heat in his chest and belly he recognized for the pure rage it was. This American was mocking him! He was lying, but like most effective lies, he had hit upon Kord's deepest fear, as irrational as it was.

Kord drew a deep breath, stilling the spasmodic trembling within him. Prentice knew everything, and he had done something tonight, something dark and dangerous. Both he and Hunter were skillful and devious, but Prentice was a genius, and that intelligence was to be feared.

The door abruptly burst open, and Kord took a hasty back step when President Stedman walked into the room, followed by Adrian Romulus.

"What in blazes is the meaning of this?" Stedman roared, his eyes snapping with more energy than he had displayed in months. The president's gaze fell upon the trembling woman, and his mouth quirked. "Lauren, honey—are you okay? What's going on here?"

"Mr. President." Lauren Mitchell stood to her feet, and her voice wavered as she tried to answer. "General Herrick has accused Daniel of doing something to the Treasury Department's computers. Daniel has explained that he and Brad Hunter merely went over there to check the directory of the mainframes, but General Herrick remains unconvinced of Daniel's good intentions."

The president's eyes darkened like angry thunderclouds as he swung around to face Kord. "General Herrick, why are you interrogating my people?"

"Sir." Kord lifted his chin and snapped to attention. "Prentice is deceitful. We have a video record of Mr. Prentice and Mr. Hunter in the Financial Crimes Computer Center. At one point, Mr. Hunter blocked the lenses of both cameras, so we are unable to see what Mr. Prentice was doing. We can only assume that he was up to some mischief with the computer systems."

Taking a deep, unsteady breath, the president turned to Daniel Prentice. "Well, sir?" He spoke as if he were strangling on repressed epithets. "What have you to say about this?"

Daniel Prentice stood and lowered his head in a deep gesture of respect. "The honest truth, Mr. President, is that Mr. Hunter and I used Miss Mitchell's courier card to access the computer room. Mr. Hunter is a senior NSA officer, so of course we knew that we were under surveillance the entire time. Our purpose was simple—I wanted to check the computers one final time before our computers link with the European systems on New Year's Eve. I haven't been to Washington in some weeks, and do not anticipate returning before the new year."

The president nodded thoughtfully. "Was it really necessary to block the cameras?"

Prentice smiled and thrust his hands into his pockets. "Would you, sir, feel comfortable with someone peering over your shoulder as you worked? I have proved my loyalty to this country." Prentice's gaze shifted and met Kord's. "I don't need to be spied upon."

The president turned to General Archer. "Have you found any damage to the computers over there?"

Archer blanched. "No, sir. But we haven't had a chance to examine them completely."

"Well." The president nodded and thrust his hands behind his back. "If some problem does arise, I assume you know whom to call in order to fix it. As for me, I believe Mr. Prentice. I've known him for some time, and he has had White House security clearance for months. If Miss Mitchell vouches for his character, that's validation enough for me."

The President's gaze shifted toward Adrian Romulus. "And as for you, Mr. Romulus, I'd take it as a personal favor if you'd remind your security people that this is still the United States of America, a sovereign nation, and this is the people's house. Your security agents have been allowed on these premises in order to protect you, not to meddle in our affairs."

Stedman looked to General Archer, who stood silently in the corner. "General Archer, perhaps a pair of your men can see General Herrick to his hotel now. I believe it's time to break up this little party."

Seething with humiliation and anger, Kord stiffened beneath Stedman's gaze. No one had ever spoken to him in that tone, and no one had ever dared to order Romulus about. This pasty-faced president was nothing, only a figurehead, but he did not have the sense to realize it.

"You fool!" The words flew from Kord's lips like stones. "Have you no idea whom you are addressing?"

As a tense silence enveloped the room, Kord realized he had said too much. A man who could not control his tongue did not deserve to control others, but surely Adrian would forgive—

"Calm yourself, General Herrick." Romulus's low voice rang with reproach, then Adrian smiled at President Stedman. "You must forgive my security officer, Mr. President. The general has not been himself for several days; I'm afraid he encountered a light case of food poisoning. He spent several hours in an emergency room, and I fear he is rather fixated on hospitals at the moment."

Lies, lies, all lies, but Stedman did not see through them.

"The man is a disgrace." The president's disapproving eyes peered out at Kord from deep sockets like caves of bone.

"I believe he has spoken and acted only out of concern for our pending Millennium Treaty." Romulus now spoke in a pleasant voice, hypnotically lilting. "In the interest of peace and cooperation, why don't we put this unfortunate incident behind us?"

Apparently somewhat mollified, the president nodded. "Fine. But I want it understood that you must leave my people alone. We have agreed to enter into a cooperative association on January first, but at this moment you are still standing on the sovereign shores of the United States of America."

"Of course we are." Romulus turned his gaze from the president to Prentice, and Kord saw the tightening cheek muscles that turned Romulus's smile from a social grace to a rictus of necessity. "And if there should prove to be some problem with the computers in the Treasury Department, Mr. Prentice, can we count on you to correct the problem?"

Prentice's face split in an arrogant smile as he met Kord's gaze. "Indubitably, Mr. Romulus." He turned his eyes back to Romulus. "It would be my pleasure—provided I'm available. I'm planning to take an extended honeymoon trip. Tonight I have asked Miss Mitchell to marry me, and she has accepted."

"Really?" A smile gathered up the wrinkles by the president's mouth. "Now that is good news! Come, you two, and tell me all about it!"

And with that, the American president escorted the prisoners out of the room and down the hall. Kord, Romulus, and Archer watched them go. A trace of laughter lined Romulus's voice as he turned toward the doorway. "General, are you ready to leave for the ambassador's residence? Apparently we have overstayed our welcome here."

In the limo, Romulus spoke in a quiet and controlled voice. "Don't worry, General Herrick. If we need Prentice, we will find him. A man of his stature leaves a large footprint."

"He knows everything." Archer spoke in a suffocated whisper. "What will we do? He could go to the media, he could ruin things—"

"He will say nothing." Romulus crossed his arms, then caressed his throat with his fingertips. "Mr. Prentice cannot accuse us without implicating himself in our work. After all, he did give us the Millennium Chip."

Romulus put the matter aside with sudden good humor. He smiled cruelly, ice in his eyes. "General Herrick, consider your previous orders now amended. I had asked you to invite Mr. Prentice to join our team—I no longer want him. When you are certain he caused no harm to the Treasury computers, eliminate him, and let that be the end of it."

"It will be a pleasure, sir." Kord crossed his arms and stared out the window at the brilliantly lit Capitol building, his rage fading as he thought about the satisfaction he would take when he met Daniel Prentice again.

THIRTY-FOUR

10:17 P.M., Thursday, December 23, 1999

A CHILLY WIND BLEW THROUGH DANIEL'S COAT AS HE AND LAUREN STEPPED OUT into the night air. He looked at her thin evening wrap, then slipped out of his coat and draped it around her shoulders. Despite the cold, warmth permeated his being as he put his arm around her waist and ran with her to his rented car.

They fell into the car, laughing, and Daniel paused to rake his hand through his hair before turning to her. He'd gathered the courage to plant the device and win the woman of his dreams, and the fact that he'd experienced two unimaginable successes left him feeling more than a little giddy.

"Well?" he asked, meeting her eyes for the first time since their narrow escape from Herrick. "Shall we seize the moment?"

Her eyes widened with understanding. "You mean—now?"

"Yeah." Slowly, he reached out and took her hand, then gently chafed her cold fingers with his own. "Honey, they're not going to let go. The president saved us back there, but Herrick has agents scattered throughout the country. They know I did something, and they know the clock is ticking. They're not going to let us just walk away."

"But you said you had the information recorded. I thought we'd be safe—"

"I'm sorry, Lauren, but that was a bluff. I just wanted to buy us time to get away."

She took a deep breath, then her blue eyes blazed into his. "Okay. Let's go to my place. I'll pack a bag and pick up the dog, then we can get the license and find a preacher."

"The dog?" Daniel's brows lifted in pretended horror as he started the car. "I'm marrying a dog, too?"

"For better or worse, remember?" Lauren leaned toward him and lightly kissed his cheek. "Don't worry. She's a good guard dog, and you just might appreciate that in a few days—"

Daniel smothered her last words with his lips, returning her kiss in earnest. Her nearness sent a wave of warmth along his nerves, and it was with difficulty that he pulled away after a moment and rested his forehead against hers.

"Dog, license, preacher, honeymoon," he whispered, his heart slamming into his ribs as her warm breath fanned his face. "Do we have to stick to that order?"

"'Fraid so, love." Her fingertip came to rest upon his lower lip. "And we'd better get moving. Herrick will know where I live, and he knows you're with me."

Spurred to action, Daniel kissed her once more, then released her, put the car in reverse, and pulled out of the parking space. She was right; Herrick and his men wouldn't scratch their heads for long. "Let's get the dog and whatever you need," he said, turning out of the parking area, "then wake up a justice of the peace. He can issue a license and marry us—"

"I'd rather get the license, then wake up my pastor." She snapped her seat belt, a beatific smile lighting her perfect face. "Let's go."

-01001111100-

Two hours later, Lauren stood in her pastor's living room, her hands in Daniel's, her eyes intent upon his face. Mixed feelings surged through her. She had no doubt that she was marrying the right man, a good man, but she couldn't deny that she was moving into the unknown. Daniel had committed high treason against Adrian Romulus tonight, and Romulus and his cronies knew it. Whether they would discover exactly *what* Daniel had done remained to be seen, but the gauntlet had been thrown down. Lauren knew General Herrick would eventually rise to the challenge.

The bleary-eyed minister paused and looked at Lauren. "Is there anything you would like to say to each other?" Reverend Scarborough had the sort of round, cheerful face whose natural expression was a smile, but even he had been caught off guard by Lauren's knock at the door. They had awakened his household at one-thirty in the morning, after a quick trip to

Lauren's townhouse and a visit to a justice of the peace across the border in Virginia, where blood tests weren't required and there was no waiting period for a marriage license. At first the official had sputtered and flatly refused to issue a license, but after Daniel flashed an obscene amount of cash, the man relented.

Now Rev. James Scarborough stood before them in house slippers, a pair of plaid shorts, and a Washington Redskins jersey. His wife, wide-eyed and frowning, wore a terry cloth robe and sat in a corner wing chair with their sleeping two-year-old in her arms.

"Yes, pastor, I would like to say something." Lauren smiled up into Daniel's eyes. "Daniel Prentice, I have come to respect, appreciate, and understand you. And in the time we have known each other, God has moved in my heart; he has moved me to love you. I can't explain why or how, for both you and I know this love could be a risky business. But I've come to see that faith is not an intelligent understanding and calculated risk. It is a deliberate commitment to a person," she smiled to herself, "even if I can see no earthly chance of success."

The minister stuttered in surprise, but Daniel's eyes flashed with humor and understanding. "Lauren Mitchell," he answered, lightly squeezing her hands, "you are all I could ever hope for, and far more than I deserve. The fact that you are willing to stand beside me now means more than any earthly possession, achievement, or success. I freely give up whatever I must in order to be with you, . . . for as long as God allows us to be together."

In spite of her resolve to control her emotions, Lauren's chin wobbled and her eyes filled. She hadn't expected Daniel to accept her faith; she knew he would have to confront God in his own time. And yet he had just proven that he was willing to meet her halfway, to respect her beliefs. And with everything in her heart she believed that Daniel would surrender his life to Christ. He had seen too much to deny God's hand, and he would undoubtedly see more as time grew shorter.

"Well, as you are both willing to marry, I suppose I can pronounce you man and wife." The preacher closed his little black book and smiled at them. "My wife and I will sign the license, but you'll have to go down to the courthouse and let the clerk scan your Millennium Chip if either one of you wants to change your name."

"Whatever." Daniel did not take his eyes from Lauren's face. "Didn't you forget something, Reverend?"

"What?"

The minister's wife spoke up from her chair. "The kiss, Harold. Tell him to kiss her."

"Ah." Lauren tried to suppress a giggle as the minister cleared his throat, then announced in a booming voice, "You may now kiss your bride."

Her giggles surrendered to a wave of warmth as Daniel tenderly cupped her chin in his hand and kissed her cheek and forehead and eyes and lips. Lauren closed her eyes, relishing the feel of his arms around her, then the minister's wife broke the silence with a discreet little cough. "I'm, um, assuming you'll want to leave for your honeymoon now."

"Right." Daniel whispered. He pulled away from Lauren for a moment, handed the minister a hundred dollar bill, then took Lauren's arm and led her out to the car. As they walked, Lauren was conscious only of his nearness, his strength, and the fact that they were now Mr. and Mrs. Daniel Prentice.

Adrian Romulus might as well have been a million miles away.

-01001111100-

Lauren sat in dazed, happy silence as Daniel started the car and drove off into the night. Tasha rode in the back seat, her dark eyes following every movement with interest, and Lauren suddenly realized that the dog knew as much as she did about Daniel's plans. "Do you know where we're going?" she asked, amazed that he seemed to know the streets so well.

"Yes." He looked at her with a smile in his eyes. "Brad and I talked this all out. If there was any trouble at all—and we were pretty sure there would be—we knew neither of us could return to our homes. Brad has a car waiting for me in Fairmount Heights; he was going to take Christine home and then hide out in a hotel room for a few days. The less she knows, the better."

Lauren said nothing, but some of the shine wore off her happiness as she considered the facts. They were running even now. At her house, she'd quickly packed a bag with three changes of clothes, a handful of toiletries, her Bible, her cell phone, and a framed photograph of her with Victoria Stedman. Then she had grabbed a bag of dog food from the pantry while Daniel hooked Tasha's leash to her collar. They'd only been in the house for ten minutes, but Daniel had been nervous even during that short time.

He didn't seem nervous now. He took an interstate exit and turned onto a side street, then pulled into a deserted gas station. A row of dilapidated cars lined a back fence, and Daniel pointed to a dark clunker with a red sweater wadded up against the back windshield. "That's the one."

"That's our car?" Lauren swallowed her surprise. Somehow she had imagined that a millionaire would go on the lam in a Porsche or a Mercedes, at the very least. This was a nondescript Chevy something-or-other, about thirty years old and dinged on every side.

Lauren glanced nervously around, then stepped out of the car. She grabbed her purse and her hastily-packed bag, then slammed the door and walked toward Daniel. Holding Tasha's leash with one hand, he ran his other hand under the chassis above the right front tire. After a moment, he grinned and pulled a sliver of duct tape from the dark space. "The key," he explained, pulling the gooey tape away with greasy fingers.

Lauren shook her head. Brad Hunter worked with some of the most expensive high-tech equipment in the world, and yet tonight he'd resorted to common dirt and duct tape. Then again, she thought, moving closer to the battered automobile, maybe a low-tech approach was the best way to hide from their enemies.

"Here we go!" Daniel's voice was almost cheery as he unlocked the car. He opened the door and whistled for the dog. "Here, Tasha! Good girl! Hop in!"

Lauren tossed her purse and bag on the back seat next to Tasha, then pressed her hands to the small of her back and watched as Daniel moved to the trunk and opened it. Inside the dark space she saw a huge spool of wire, a small suitcase, and a briefcase-sized black box. Daniel opened the box, and in the orange glow of the streetlight she saw that it contained some sort of electrical equipment, a microphone, and what looked like a video camera.

"Brad's goodies." Daniel snapped the box shut. "He thinks of everything."

Lauren drew in a deep breath as Daniel closed the trunk, then followed him as he walked around to unlock the passenger door. "Are you going to fill me in on the details or keep me in suspense?" she asked, taking pains to keep her voice light. "We're married now, you know. We're supposed to share everything."

Daniel opened the door and grinned while she sat and swiveled her legs into the car. "Is that a marriage law or something?"

"You bet."

He was still grinning when he slid into the driver's seat and started the car. The engine erupted into noisy life, and Daniel revved the engine like a teenage boy with his first set of wheels.

"We're going to Canada, honey." He turned to check the seat behind him, but paused as his gaze crossed hers. "Romulus doesn't have Canada yet. We'll be safe there, at least for a while. And we'll have them off our backs long enough to make the transmission."

"The transmission?" she echoed.

Daniel nodded as he threw the car into reverse and backed out of the parking space. "We're going to tell the world about Adrian Romulus, right before the hardware virus kicks in at midnight on New Year's Eve. And while Romulus and his people are scurrying around trying to figure out what corrupted their systems, maybe people will reconsider all that has happened in the last few months."

Lauren took a long, quivering breath to quell the leaping pulse beneath her ribs. Daniel stopped the car, put it into park, and paused. "Are you okay?"

How could she explain the crazy mixture of hope and fear that whirled in her brain? She was afraid, more terrified than she had ever been in her life. She had seen what Romulus could do; she knew that his unseen agents were fast, intelligent, and nearly as adept with a computer as Daniel. More than that, she had seen the hatred in General Herrick's eyes tonight. Daniel had bested him, and she could tell that Herrick was not a man who accepted defeat easily.

He would come after them, but she would rather be with Daniel and take a chance than remain a prisoner in a country whose people didn't even realize their freedom and lifeblood were slowly draining away.

"I'm okay, Daniel." She reached out and covered his hand with her own. "And I'm with you. All the way."

Thirty-five

2:30 a.m., Friday, December 24, 1999

ALONE WITH HIS THOUGHTS, KORD HERRICK PROPPED HIS FEET ON THE velveteen ottoman and stared into the flickering fireplace. The servants had gone to bed, and Adrian had retired upstairs an hour earlier, his mood remarkably buoyant for a man who'd just been unmasked by a computer genius. Then again, Kord thought, swirling the ice cubes in his drink, nothing ruffled the master. And though Daniel Prentice seemed to know a great deal more than was advisable, he'd have to live through the night before he could wreak any real damage.

Someone had installed a Christmas tree in the corner of this ornate oak room; its tiny red lights blinked randomly through the silence, casting an eerie glow over the overstuffed chairs and needlepoint pillows. Kord sipped at his drink, feeling the burn of alcohol on his throat, and dully wondered if he had failed at his job. He did not believe that Romulus intended to elevate that fool Archer, but still, Prentice's jibe had stung. Just as Romulus's threat, spoken so many months ago in the darkness of his Paris garden, had kept Kord awake through many an eternal night.

Surely Romulus now regretted those words. In the succeeding months he had continued as always, depending upon Kord's loyalty, his insights, and his thoroughness. That snooping Israeli reporter who had attempted to locate Romulus's mother had been eliminated; the maid who had stumbled into Romulus's secret closet at the Paris chateau had disappeared without a trace.

All because Kord was good at his job. A master planner. Archer had only been the pawn, someone to file reports and plant bombs and grind pills into a coffee cup. He was a mere foot soldier in this game, and after January 1, when Romulus took control, Archer would realize that he was only a bit player in the rising world government. Kord had been the one to woo the ambitious vice president; without Kord's influence Miller would never have found the courage to commit the American military to a complete stand down on January 1.

On that day, in the name of peace, Adrian's worldwide disciples would take up the cry of unity. While the world celebrated a new millennium, several American and European military leaders would exchange places, sharing the job of maintaining peace throughout EU-affiliated nations. When the sun set on the first day of the new millennium, the formerly independent United States would bow its head and enter into the sheltering fold of Romulus's world community. Prentice's network of flawless Millennium computers would allow the American economy to be swallowed by that of the European Union, and the sheer weight of the resulting economic, political, and military amalgamation would convince the Pacific Rim nations and the Middle East to submit . . . or starve.

A shrill sound warbled through the heaviness of his wool sweater, and Kord fumbled through the rich thickness for a moment before finding his phone. "Yes?"

He grunted softly when he heard the news. Brad Hunter, the NSA agent who'd managed to slip away, had been unable to resist the temptation to call his wife. Of course, by that time she had been upset by the strangers prowling outside and, like a lovesick fool, he had rushed home to help her.

"Keep them quiet and in the house," Kord ordered, carefully setting his glass on the carpeted floor. "I am on my way." He disconnected the call, then leaned forward and stared for one last moment into the fire.

Romulus would appreciate this, too, when he learned of it in the morning.

Kord rose and stretched for a moment, then stepped into the kitchen where a pair of guards and Romulus's driver sat around a poker game. "Come," Kord said, tapping the driver's shoulder. He pulled a slip of paper from his pocket and handed it to the man. "We need to hurry."

Once in the car, Kord checked his watch and settled back with a contented sigh. 2:25 A.M. Hunter's neighbors in Arlington Heights would be nicely tucked into their colonial brick homes or vacationing at Grandmother's house.

As the driver moved with unhurried purpose toward their destination,

Kord looked out the window. America, spawn of rebels and immigrants! The people of this country oozed arrogance, and Kord had never seen more overconfident men than Daniel Prentice, Brad Hunter, and President Samuel Stedman. Like their revolutionary forefathers, those three thought themselves above the common good. They could not see that individualism contained the seeds of destruction; the roots of peace lay in community. Romulus wanted something far more than freedom for his people—he desired the common good. He would win, he would *demand* the communal enjoyment of the fruits of the earth. Individuals who got in the way would simply have to be eliminated.

The driver made a sudden right turn, and Kord resisted the urge to curse. He was lost, probably, confused by the District's twisting maze of streets. They had entered a smutty part of town, a world of neon-coated sleaze and streetwalkers, several of whom hurried toward the limo and offered tempting smiles at whoever rode in the back seat.

Kord gazed at them with passive indifference. In a year or two, once Romulus's plans had been fully implemented, this would all change. The prostitutes would be off the streets, the drug dealers resigned either to prison or life in a menial job. The cash these hookers and addicts scrabbled for would have no value; they could buy food only if they purchased it with legitimately earned currency credits.

The car stopped at a red light, and the crowd on the sidewalk edged closer. "I am sorry, sir." The limo driver caught Kord's eye in the rearview mirror. "Took a bit of a wrong turn back there."

"Just find the house." Kord lifted his gloved hand to the dark window, through which a young girl squinted in a vain attempt to peer inside the car. He bent his finger and slid it over the glass, imagining the feel of the girl's soft cheek beneath his hand.

Such typical American presumption, imagining that he might be interested in what she had to offer. But she was only a child—in time, she would come to understand that there was a better way.

The light changed, and the car moved forward. Kord folded his hands at his waist and set his jaw, ready to commence with the real work of the evening.

-0100111100-

Brad and Christine Hunter lived in a two-story Colonial, bricked in the front and edged with immature boxwoods. The limo driver stopped on the curb, opened the car door for Kord's exit, then pulled away to wait at the end of the street. Kord stood in the yellow glow of a single streetlight and sniffed the chilly air with satisfaction. Though a mad spangle of Christmas lights adorned virtually every house, only a few dim lights burned in the street's quiet windows. In the morning, none of the neighbors would be able to say they'd noticed anything unusual on this particular night.

He walked up to the front door and entered without knocking. Three of his agents stood in the living room, a sprawling space to the right of the foyer. Christine Hunter, pale and lovely in her evening gown, sat on the sofa, her hands tied behind her back and a slice of duct tape across her mouth. Brad Hunter, who concerned Kord far more than the quivering woman, lay face down on the carpet before the fireplace. Plastic rope bound his hands, feet, and knees, while duct tape covered his mouth. He lay as still as a log.

Kord frowned and glanced at the man nearest him. "He's not dead?"

"No, sir." The agent stiffened as though Kord had struck him. "You said not to kill him."

"Good." Kord walked over and knelt beside Brad Hunter's head, then smiled at the wide-eyed wife. "Agent Dengler," he called, still watching the woman, "bring me a glass of water from the kitchen. Be careful not to leave any prints."

Dengler vanished like a shadow, and returned a moment later with a glass in his gloved hands. Kord took it, swirled the liquid thoughtfully for a moment, then tossed the water into Hunter's face.

The man groaned, then his eyes fluttered open.

"Good evening, Mr. Hunter." Kord watched the American struggle, then smiled with smug delight. "I'm sorry we didn't have an opportunity to meet at the reception tonight. I have already had a meeting with your accomplices, the delightful Mr. Prentice and Miss Mitchell, but you had slipped away by the time I encountered them."

He stood, then slowly sank into a wing chair a few feet away, keeping his eyes on Hunter. "You, my friend, made a grave mistake this evening—well, perhaps more than one. But I am afraid this will prove to be a fatal error." He lifted a brow and pointed toward the woman on the sofa. "I can only assume that you called your lovely wife and were disturbed to hear that she heard noises outside. Despite your instincts, you came rushing home to comfort her."

Kord gave the woman a sympathetic smile. "He should have ignored you completely, my dear. Mr. Hunter chose to play a dangerous game tonight, but you have handicapped him. I have always believed that agents should not marry. Love makes one do . . . irrational things."

Kord began to pull his leather gloves from his hands, finger by finger. "Mr. Hunter, we are about to make a little bargain. Agent Dengler is going to remove the tape from your mouth, and you will tell us exactly what you and Mr. Prentice did tonight in the Treasury Building's computer room. For each question you do not answer, Agent Dengler is going to break one of your fingers." He bent down and leaned closer. "Did I happen to mention that Agent Dengler goes about his work very slowly? I'm afraid he does not know the meaning of a swift, clean break."

Hunter's muscles flexed as he strained on his bonds, but the ropes held tight.

Kord jerked his chin toward Dengler. The burly man stepped forward, and a loud ripping sound broke the silence as he tore the tape from Hunter's face.

"Now," Kord went on, his voice low and seductive as he watched his captive through half-closed lids, "tell me what you and Mr. Prentice did tonight."

Hunter's face was dead white, sheened with a cold sweat that had soaked his hair and white shirt, but his eyes flashed cold and blue. "We went to a party at the White House."

"Lovely." Kord clapped his hands and smiled. "You win round one. Now, tell me more, but skip the things I already know. I know you went to the Treasury Building. I know you entered the computer room with Miss Mitchell's courier card. I know you accessed the mainframe computer."

Hunter licked his lips. "Daniel typed in the directory command."

"Tell me more."

Hunter's voice was ragged with fury. "He wanted to check the mainframes to make sure they were on track for the Millennium Code."

Kord's mouth puckered with annoyance. "You wouldn't need to cover the cameras to do that, Mr. Hunter. What else did Prentice do?"

"I don't know." Hunter chuckled with a dry and cynical sound. "Daniel doesn't tell anyone exactly what he's up to. He just does things."

Kord shot him a penetrating look. "I believe you may step forward, Agent Dengler. I have won a round. Take your point, please."

Hunter glared at Kord. "Do what you like with me, but touch my wife and you die." Each word was a splinter of ice.

"You're in no position to make threats, Mr. Hunter. You are mine, and you will remain mine until I am finished with you. In the morning, or whenever anyone cares enough to come knocking on your door, your neighbors will learn that a terribly tragic home invasion occurred on these premises. Whether you and your wife will be found dead or severely beaten, however, is up to you."

A horrible keening sound rent the air; the woman began screaming beneath the tape over her mouth. As one of the agents clicked on the television and jacked the volume up, another pulled Hunter upright. Dengler grasped Hunter's wrist with his own meaty hand, then pressed Hunter's index finger flat against the top of his hand, breaking the finger with an audible snap.

Kord didn't even watch Hunter; his view of the wife was far more entertaining. The woman's blue eyes bulged, and her face went white as the sound of Hunter's scream drowned out the mindless noise of local talent singing Christmas carols.

Kord felt a small, fierce surge of satisfaction under his irritation as Brad Hunter fell and writhed on the floor like a cut snake. It might take all night, but he would learn what Daniel Prentice intended.

-01001111100-

Daniel took the ramp onto Interstate 95 and drove steadily toward Baltimore, careful to keep the car just beneath the speed limit. Lauren lay curled up on the seat beside him, and he hoped that she had fallen asleep. He wanted to put as much geographical space between them and General Herrick as possible, and driving had seemed the safest choice. Once Herrick or Archer put out a bulletin—and they'd be foolish to wait until morning—Daniel's and Lauren's Millennium Chips would alert every law enforcement authority within a hundred miles if they walked into an airport, bus station, or train depot. But the highways of America were still free.

Daniel checked his rearview mirror and exhaled in satisfaction when he saw that no one followed. His watch glowed softly in the dark, reminding him that it was three in the morning, and he wondered what story Brad had told Christine when he dropped her at their house. He suspected that Brad had put far more thought into planning Daniel's escape than he had his own, but he had always thought more of protecting his men than himself. If Brad was smart, he had taken Christine home, taken a cab to a nondescript motel in Maryland or Virginia, and paid cash for the room. Christine—who knew nothing specific about what Brad and Daniel had intended—would be safe as long as she remained ignorant. In a day or two, after Archer's men had examined the treasury computers and found nothing wrong, Brad could quietly go home.

Daniel glanced over at Lauren and felt his heart soften as her hair lifted in the heater's hot breath. He would have been honored to marry her even if he hadn't fallen hopelessly in love. He had known few women as intelligent and loyal—and courageous. Her loyalty to Sam Stedman had put her at risk, and her marriage to Daniel would certainly put her in danger. But he would protect her with his life.

Daniel grinned and shifted his hands on the steering wheel as he recalled the memory of Stedman's face as he ordered General Herrick and Adrian Romulus out of the White House. For an instant the president had been imbued with the feisty spirit with which he won the election, but that outburst would cost him—maybe not tonight, maybe not this month. But someday soon, Daniel feared that a Secret Service agent would enter the president's bedroom and find him dead. They'd say it was another accident—a heart attack or possibly a stroke—but Sam Stedman's dissenting voice would be silenced. The man was popular with the American people, and he spoke the truth—two qualities Adrian Romulus could not endure.

Truth—what had H.L. Mencken once said? "Nine times out of ten, in the arts as in life, there is actually no truth to be discovered; there is only error to be exposed."

In an effort to expose error and corruption, Daniel had just risked his and Lauren's lives to fight a man who would probably prove to be the Antichrist—without committing himself to the *real* Christ. His mother, who was certainly no logician, wouldn't hesitate to point out the illogic in that.

So what's your problem, Prentice? What's holding you back?

He glanced out the window, watching the bright beams of a semi on the other side of the divided highway. What was holding him back? For years he'd convinced himself that he didn't need his mother's religion. Christianity was for grieving widows and helpless poor people; it was a colossal waste of time and energy. In the two or three hours most people spent at church he could write two hundred lines of code; while Christians read their Bibles and prayed, he poured over textbooks and committed them to memory.

So how had his mother known so much about the Antichrist? Daniel had known about Romulus, but his mother had been able to identify the *inner* characteristics of a man she'd never met.

She'd found her answers in the Bible. Lauren had found hers in faith and surrender.

Daniel shifted his weight in the seat, then pressed his hand to the back of his neck, kneading his stiff muscles. That bookbinder-preacher had broken down belief into three neat compartments: a knowledge in the mind, a feeling in the heart, an act of the will. Daniel had no problem accepting the historical validity of the person of Jesus Christ. The idea that God could become flesh wasn't that hard to embrace, either—incarnation was the only logical way that fallible human beings could even hope to bridge the chasm between mortal man and immortal God.

The third step, the act of the will, was likewise a sensible and sound concept. Religion was worthless unless acted upon, so Daniel had no problem with the idea that an individual had to decide to invite Christ into his life, be born again, surrender, or whatever the current lingo was.

The part that eluded him, the missing ingredient, was the feeling in the heart. Daniel had never been the type to see ghosts in the attic or images in the stars; astronomy had been one of his worst subjects because he couldn't envision or identify the constellations without a celestial map. He'd lost more than one college girlfriend because he wasn't "romantic" enough, and even with Lauren he'd never felt helpless in the throes of passion. His love for her was steady and constant; it was the sure knowledge that he wanted her by his side for the rest of his life, no matter what happened. . . .

He breathed deep and felt a stab of memory, a broken shard from his past, sharp as glass. The panorama of black night deepened into the brown and gold tints of his father's library, and once again he was six, sitting by the side of his father's chair, feeling the weight of his father's hand on his head.

"Son?" His father's voice came from above, warm and crackling like the logs in the fireplace.

Daniel looked into his father's eyes and saw himself reflected there, wide-eyed and chubby-cheeked. "Yes, Daddy?"

"You know I love you."

Daniel looked up and smiled, feeling he might burst from a sudden swell of happiness. "Yes, Daddy."

He looked down, saw the Lincoln logs in his hands and scattered over the rug. Silence reigned for a moment, then his father's hand fell gently upon his head again.

"Daniel?"

"Daddy?"

"You know I love you."

Daniel lowered his head as a slow smile crept across his face. This was a game, then. His father wanted to hear something in return, something more than a simple yes.

He waited a moment, then looked up into eyes that shone with love. "Daddy?"

"Yes, Son?"

"I love you, too."

He had felt happy before, but when his father reached up and drew him into his arms, Daniel threw back his head and laughed, glorying in the simple feeling of love and being loved.

The voice and its memories passed over Daniel the adult, shivering his skin like the touch of a ghost—no, a Spirit. The Spirit of love . . . the Spirit of God. It moved through Daniel's soul like a steady, rushing wind, breaking down the barriers he had erected, breaking the lifelong strongholds of fear and anger and resentment.

Daniel drove silently as tears rolled heedlessly down his face, hot spurts of loss and love. All these years he had been deluding himself. He thought himself too intelligent for God . . . but, truthfully, he had been too angry. Too hurt. Too proud.

Those crippling emotions had prevented him from feeling much at all.

"God," he whispered, wiping his nose on his sleeve in a childish gesture, "forgive me for blaming you for my dad's death. I know you are love, and I know you didn't kill him. Take me, Father, I'm tired of hiding from you. I give you my life, my ambition, my dreams of influencing the world. From this moment on, I'm yours."

He blinked the tears from his eyes and tried to focus on the highway. The wave of riotous emotion faded like a cloud spent of its rain, leaving Daniel with a profound sense of peace.

Filled with the wonderful sense of going home, he pushed the car into the night.

-0100111100-

Lost in reverie, Daniel drove for miles, skirting Baltimore, pushing northward. The thick black sky hung over the interstate, suiting Daniel's reflective mood, but the stars seemed less brilliant than before. His eyes burned from weariness, and soon he'd have to pull over.

A car passed on the other side of the interstate with a drawn-out whooshing sound, and Daniel jerked the wheel, suddenly aware that he had nearly fallen asleep. The adrenaline that had energized him through the night had worn off; now he felt nothing but bone-deep weariness.

The sharp motion of the car must have awakened Lauren, for she lifted her head and peered at Daniel with sleepy eyes. "Do you want to stop?"

"I suppose we'd better." Daniel gave her a smile, feeling suddenly childlike and awkward. "But first, I ought to tell you something."

"Don't tell me you already have a wife and twelve children." Her hand flew to her throat in a dramatic gesture, but her eyes were shining.

"You know better than that." Daniel tried to keep his eyes on the road, but the sight of her was irresistible. "I, uh—well, I prayed. I did what you did."

Her voice went soft with surprise. "You did what?"

Daniel shrugged. "I just figured it was highly illogical to expend all this effort to expose the Antichrist without believing—*really believing*—in Christ himself. So I made it official and joined the ranks of the believers."

She twisted in the seat, her eyes shimmering with the light from the dashboard. "Daniel, you wouldn't be joking with me, would you? Because this is not a joking matter."

"No." He softened his tone as his eyes met hers. "No, it isn't. And I'm telling you the truth, Lauren. It's done."

She bit her bottom lip, then tilted her head. "So—how do you feel?"

"How do I *feel?*" Daniel searched his heart for the answer, then reached out and intertwined his fingers with hers. "I feel more than I've felt in years. Love for you, love for God, and gratitude. A deep and abiding sense of gratitude. And I'm ready to go ahead with our plan; I have this sense that it's the right thing to do."

"Peace," she whispered, nestling close to his side. "You're feeling peace."

They drove for a while without speaking, then Daniel lifted their clasped hands and pointed toward the glove compartment. "Brad said he'd put a couple of maps and some cash in the glove box. Why don't you check and see if he remembered?"

"Of course he did." Lauren turned the knob and a stack of maps spilled into her lap. A wallet had been tucked behind the maps, and as Lauren pulled it out and fanned it, Daniel saw that Brad had lined it with hundred dollar bills—at least five of which were Canadian currency.

"Cash?" Lauren laughed softly. "How far do you think we're going to get with *cash?*"

"As far as we need to. I told Brad I'd try to make it into Canada, though I didn't tell him where I'd go." Daniel lifted his shoulders to work a cramp out of his back, then pointed to the Pennsylvania map. "Take a look at that one. I think we're in Pennsylvania, but I haven't been paying much attention to the road signs. See if you can tell which major city we'll come to next."

"Which one did we pass last?" Lauren murmured, unfolding the map.

Daniel ran his hand through his hair and tried to think. Aside from his occasional visits to the lake cabin, he hadn't been on a road trip in years. "I know we passed Baltimore, because I got on I-83 there," he said. "And I think I remember seeing something about York, Pennsylvania. We can follow the interstate for a few more hours, but after tomorrow we'd better stay off the main highways. I suspect they'll put out a bulletin on us, if they haven't already. But they don't know what kind of car we're driving."

Lauren leaned forward, bringing the map closer to the light in the glove compartment. Daniel grinned, amazed that the light even worked, then remembered that Brad had arranged for the car. Brad would have checked every detail.

"The interstate will take us to Harrisburg, which is a good-sized town," Lauren said, running her finger along the map. "That's another twenty miles."

"Sounds good." Daniel checked the rearview mirror again, then smiled as Lauren moved closer so he could slip his arm around her. "I'd forgotten how nice these bench seats are," he said, grinning at her. "I'm reminded of my teenage days when I learned to drive—back before they put bucket seats in everything. My buddy and I used to double-date in a car like this."

"I don't want to hear about your old girlfriends," she whispered, her breath warm in his ear. "Just drive, Mr. Prentice. And don't forget—this is our wedding night."

Daniel didn't answer, but kissed her quickly, then urged the old Chevy to quicken her pace and wing on down the highway.

Thirty-six

10:03 A.M., Friday, December 24, 1999

After a hard, dreamless sleep, Daniel woke to the sight of sunlight leaking around the edges of the drawn curtains. Lauren lay snuggled in his arms, her sleep-tousled curls spangling her forehead and the nape of her neck. Daniel pressed a kiss to the warmth of her throat, then carefully slid away from her and pulled his watch from the night stand.

A few minutes after ten. They'd slept less than five hours, but they had to get moving.

Stumbling in the gloom, Daniel found the small suitcase Brad had placed in the back of the car and unzipped it. Knowing that Daniel could not very well travel in a tuxedo, Brad had tossed in two pairs of khaki trousers, two sweaters, socks, underwear, and a pair of loafers. Daniel held up the shoes and felt his mouth twist when he saw that the soles were scuffed and worn. A business card lay inside one shoe, and Daniel lifted it out and read the message scrawled on the blank side: "Couldn't have you getting blisters on the run, so I broke these in for you. Hope they fit! Godspeed."

Daniel showered, dressed quickly and silently, then gathered up his formalwear, and stuffed the clothes under the mattress of the extra bed. Tasha had slept there, and she looked at him now with dark, unblinking eyes.

"Shh." Daniel placed his finger across his lips, then jerked his head toward the bed where Lauren still slept. "Guard her, okay?"

The dog wagged her tail in response. Daniel slipped the room key into his pocket, then walked out to the car. The morning was chilly, quiet, and still, and he realized with sudden shock that it was December 24, Christmas Eve morning. Most people were probably relaxing at home or out scouring the malls for last-minute gifts.

He moved toward the lobby, remembering that he'd seen a pay phone there last night. He had his Nokia personal communicator with him but didn't want to use that phone unless absolutely necessary. He wasn't certain how wide Herrick's surveillance net extended, but if his agents had penetrated the inner sanctums of the CIA and NSA, he'd be able to track Daniel through credit card transactions, e-mail transmissions, or cellular phone activity. Daniel didn't want to raise any alarms, but he needed to do one more thing—for Brad.

He slipped into the lobby, nodded a silent greeting to the young clerk behind the desk, then walked up to the pay phone and punched in Brad's number. He was certain Brad would have told Christine that he'd be away for a few nights, but Daniel couldn't shake a feeling of dread. As an elementary schoolteacher, Christine knew virtually nothing about Brad's covert activities, and Daniel suspected that she didn't want to know. But she might welcome a reassuring call.

The phone rang four times, then the answering machine clicked on. "Hello, you've reached the Hunters' house." Christine's digital voice sounded upbeat and happy. "Obviously, we're not here to take your call, so leave a message and we'll get back to you. Merry Christmas!"

"Christine—" Daniel paused, uncertain how much he should say. "I, uh, just wanted to let you know that we enjoyed being with you two last night. Take care! We'll be in touch."

He hung up and scratched his chin, then checked his watch again—10:30. With no school and an absent husband, Christine could have turned off the phone and decided to sleep in, or maybe she ran out to the mall.

Ignoring the persistent voice that whispered in the back of his brain, Daniel told himself that everything was all right.

-0100111100-

A tiny chip inside the Hunter's telephone acted as a transmitter, sending Daniel's call to an unmarked white van parked a block away from the Hunters' house. Kord Herrick leaned forward as the answering machine clicked on, then he nodded in satisfaction.

"That's Prentice. I don't need a digital print to recognize that voice."

Kord jerked his chin at the man monitoring the phone line. "Where did the call originate?"

The man studied the ID box, then tapped the digital readout. "A pay phone in Harrisburg, Pennsylvania. He's probably at a hotel or rest station."

"Find out which, then alert the local authorities." Kord wrapped his heavy coat closer about him, then pulled the van door open. "And get me a helicopter. I'm going to personally bring him in."

Kord paused outside the van, his breath steaming in the chilly air as he glanced back at the Hunters' house. Built on a gentle hill, the brick house sat in peaceful repose, the little white Christmas lights still twinkling from the scrawny boxwood hedges. The newspaper boy had tossed a paper on the porch, and tomorrow he'd toss another one. He might not think there was anything odd about a pile of papers on the porch during the holidays, but eventually someone would come to investigate. Maybe by New Year's Day someone would discover the truth.

Mr. and Mrs. Hunter had not had a very merry Christmas.

-0100111100-

The bed was empty when Daniel returned to the hotel room. He stood inside the door for a moment and listened to the sound of running water. *His wife* was taking a shower. The thought sent a thrill shivering through his senses.

Lauren stepped out of the bathroom a moment later, her hair wet and dripping, her face clean and freshly scrubbed. Wrapped in a towel, she came toward him and caught his face in her hands, then gave him a lingering kiss. Daniel locked her into his embrace, then held her for a long moment before she spoke. "Where'd you run off to?"

"The pay phone." Daniel reached up to swipe a strand of wet hair from her forehead. "I was worried about Christine. I just wanted to reassure her."

"Thinking about another woman already?" She grinned as she moved away, then rummaged through her suitcase for clean clothes. "I should have brought more—by the way, what'd you do with the tux?"

He pointed toward the bed where the dog lay. "Stuffed it under the mattress. By the time they find it, no one will remember who put it there."

"Good idea. Should I do the same with my dress?"

"No." Daniel shook his head. The dress had been her wedding gown. "Keep it."

"I'll just be a minute." She gathered up a handful of clothing and walked back toward the bathroom. "Got to put on my face."

"Okay." Daniel moved to the window, looked out at the silent parking lot, then let the curtain fall. He turned on the television, then heard the dog's soft woof.

"What's wrong, Tasha? Hungry?" He found the bag of dog food and spread a handful of kibble on the bedspread, but the dog didn't seem interested. She jumped from the bed and moved toward the door, then scratched at it—just in case Daniel missed the point.

"Oh." He found her leash, then snapped it on her collar. "Sorry, girl, but you'll have to be patient with me. I haven't had a dog in years."

He checked for the room key in his pocket, then stepped outside. A long strip of grass bordered the parking lot, and Daniel led the dog to it, then idly followed her as she sniffed the ground.

The hotel lay on a hill overlooking the interstate, allowing Daniel a clear view of the road for about a mile in each direction. The trees along the highway were bare and skeletal, stretching gray arms toward the sky, and through them Daniel saw a pair of police cars ripping over the asphalt, lights flashing and sirens blaring.

He froze as the cars took the exit ramp, then swerved in a broad left turn, nearly side-swiping an innocent Altima that sat at the light.

All Daniel's inner warning systems went off at once. *They're coming for us!*

"Tasha!" Daniel whistled sharply, then jerked on the dog's collar. Responding to the urgency in his voice, the dog trotted behind Daniel as he thrust his hands into his pockets and lowered his head. He pulled out the key, opened the door, and pulled the dog inside just as the police cars roared into the parking lot.

"Lauren!"

She peered out from the bathroom, her hair still wet and uncombed, but at least she was dressed. The look on her face told him she knew.

"Let's go."

She didn't have to be told twice. In one smooth movement she swept their toiletries from the sink and into her overnight bag, then she picked up Daniel's small suitcase. Daniel waited by the door, the dog's leash wrapped around his hand.

"It'll only take a minute for them to narrow the registrations down to us," he said, his eyes meeting hers as he took the suitcase. "We've got to make a run for it."

"I'm ready."

Sobered instantly by the frightening possibility that they might already be trapped, Daniel put his hand on the door, drew a deep breath, then walked the dog toward the car—a dark blue Chevy Nova, he saw now. Lauren followed and casually tossed her bag into the backseat. Without a word, they slammed the doors in unison, and Daniel pulled out and away from the police cars.

"Daniel," Lauren whispered, her face as pale as paper, "won't they have our license plate number? When you registered last night at the motel—"

"I made one up," Daniel whispered, driving as slowly as he dared in order to avoid drawing any undue attention. He exchanged an uneasy glance with Lauren. "Will you pull out the map? Find me a road north, but not an interstate."

"There!" Lauren pointed to a thin stretch of asphalt labeled with an arrow and the word *Marysville*.

Daniel turned the car onto the two-lane highway and settled back against the seat, adjusting the rearview mirror as he eased the car up to speed. No one followed yet, but that didn't mean no one would.

-0100111100-

Daniel and Lauren celebrated a meaningful, reverent Christmas in a little cabin in the Adirondack Mountains, then drove northward for three more days, traveling more slowly than a pursuer might expect, pacing themselves according to Daniel's plan. They paid cash for hotels, food, and gas, and avoided telephones, televisions, and the Millennium Chip scanners now prominently displayed at nearly every store. Merchants accepted Daniel's cash with reluctant laughter, and many times they were unable to give the proper change.

"We turned all our paper bills in for equivalency credits a month ago," a convenience store manager in Brookfield, New York, explained. "This bill makes a nice keepsake, but you can't expect me to make change for it."

"That's all right," Daniel said, pulling another bag of dog food from the shelf. "Keep the change and the bill, too. Who knows? If we survive the move into the next millennium, your grandkids may ask about the good ol' days when we actually used paper money."

The man's expression changed into a mask of uncertainty. "Whaddaya mean—if we survive?"

Daniel shook his head, mentally tabulating the bill as the food was totaled up and bagged. "Don't mind me. My wife says I'm the eternal pessimist."

The bill came to $45.73. Daniel left one hundred dollars on the counter and gathered the two bags in his arms. As he turned, however, the sound of Adrian Romulus's voice stopped him cold.

He turned slowly and glanced up at a television the storekeeper had mounted behind the counter. Romulus was on the screen, standing outdoors on a crowded sidewalk. He wore a heavy coat, and a wicked wind blew his thick hair away from his forehead. Daniel recognized the words engraved into the building's frieze: *Neither shall they learn war any more.*

Romulus was in New York City, outside the United Nations building. Daniel was more than a hundred miles away, and yet the sound of Romulus's voice still had the power to freeze his blood as if he were in the same room. The feeling that Romulus was evil had only intensified since Daniel's surrender to Christ.

"I'd like to remind the American people of something Franklin Delano Roosevelt said in his fourth inaugural address," Romulus told the reporter.

"And what would that be?" the reporter prompted.

Romulus's eyes clouded with hazy sadness, and his voice deepened as he gazed dramatically off into the distance. "'We have learned that we cannot live alone at peace, that our own well-being is dependent on the well-being of other nations far away.'" His voice reverberated throughout the tiny convenience store. "'We have learned that we must live as men, and not as ostriches, nor as dogs in the manger. We have learned to be citizens of the world, members of the human community.'"

Romulus's eyes shifted again, and seemed to stare right into the interior of the store where Daniel stood with the proprietor. "Because we are members of one community, it brings me great pain to announce that Brad Hunter, a senior official of the NSA and special advisor to President Samuel Stedman, was found murdered in his home this morning along with his wife, Christine. Fortunately, the police have evidence that leads to a clear suspect—Daniel Prentice, who is known to be in league with the forces of the Morning Star Trust."

Daniel stopped breathing. The world grew quiet and still; he heard only the pounding of blood in his ears and the thick, muffled thrum of Romulus's voice. "If you see this man—" Romulus continued as Daniel's photograph appeared on a split screen in living color—"do not try to apprehend him. There's no denying his genius—he helped us devise the Millennium Code—but we've recently learned that his loyalties have changed. We suspect that he has participated in the theft and dispersal of the nuclear devices with which the Morning Star Trust has threatened the world's peace."

Daniel took a hasty half-step back and prayed that the store owner wouldn't recognize him. He'd begun to grow a beard since leaving Washington, but perhaps this man had sharp eyes.

"Such a shame," the owner was saying now. His hands rested on the counter; his gaze remained fixed to Romulus's mesmerizing image. "That Romulus fellow has done so much for the world. It breaks my heart to think that one of our own would turn against him."

Not waiting to hear more, Daniel gripped his bags and slipped through the swinging glass doors.

-0100111100-

After his close call in the convenience store, Daniel abandoned his plan to move slowly. Driven by rage, grief, and resolve, he and Lauren followed back roads through Boonville, Lowville, and Harrisville. When they drove past the city limits of Morristown, a small town nestled on the shores of the St. Lawrence River, Daniel told Lauren that they were close to safety.

"Daniel," Lauren spoke slowly, and he sensed that she hesitated to voice her doubts. "Honey, how are we going to get into Canada? They're saying you're a murderer, and you'll never cross the border with a Millennium Chip in your hand."

"We're not going over the border." He cast her a smile as he drove. "We're going over the water."

"Oh." She shifted in her seat and leaned against the door, an uncertain look on her face. Daniel kept driving east through Chippewa Bay. Finally, when he reached Alexandria Bay, he pulled the car to the side of the road and took the dog for a walk on a strip of winter-brown grass along the water's edge. When he returned, Lauren was sitting on the hood of the car, her hands tucked under her legs, her eyes on the northern sky.

"Where are we?" She lifted her chin toward the water.

Daniel leaned against the car, then reached up and tried to smooth away the deep line of concern on her forehead. "That's the St. Lawrence River. And just across the water, through those islands—that's Canada."

She nodded, not speaking.

"I spent a lot of time here as a boy," he went on, his eyes sweeping the vast watery horizon. "Just north of here, off Interstate 81, is Thousand Islands. The whole area is dotted with summer cottages that will be vacant now, and most of those summer homes have boathouses."

Daniel smiled as the light of understanding filled her eyes.

"Boats?"

He nodded. "Sure. I figure we can take one and row across to Canada tonight, as long as the weather holds. It'll be cold on the water, but we'll be okay. And we'll leave this beautiful Chevy Nova to replace the boat."

"Daniel, you are a genius!" Her arms fell on his shoulders, and she pulled him toward her and planted a kiss on the top of his head. "I'm beginning to think we will make it."

"We'd better." He checked his watch—12:27 P.M. on December 30. They had less than thirty-six hours to reach safety and warn the world about Adrian Romulus. If they failed, Brad and Christine had died for nothing, and the world would fall into Romulus's hands like an overripe peach.

–01001111 00–

Kord Herrick angrily stubbed the butt of his cigarette onto the convenience store countertop, then glared at the bearer of bad news. "What do you mean, he drove away?"

"That's what he did." The manager spread his hands in a helpless gesture. "Good grief, how was I to know he was a criminal?"

"He gave you cash!"

"It's not illegal yet! And he said I could keep the change."

"That didn't make you suspicious?"

"No." The store manager folded his arms and matched Kord's glare. "Folks like you make me more suspicious than that fellow did. He bought *dog food,* for heaven's sake. What kind of terrorist loads up with Kibbles-n-Bits?"

Deciding to try another approach, Kord struggled to bury his irritation. He gave the man a half-hearted smile. "You would be a great help if you could recall if he said or did anything unusual. Did he use your phone? Ask you to contact anyone? Did he ask if you had access to a computer?"

The man's small, bright blue eyes grew smaller and brighter, the black pupils training on Kord like gun barrels. "I told you everything I remember. Shoot, it was two days ago. He was a regular guy, even a nice guy. Now you can get out of my store! The government's snooping into everything these days, and I'm tired of it!"

Arrogant American!

Shaking with impotent rage and frustration, Kord whirled, pushing past two of his agents as he strode to the van outside. Daniel Prentice was proving to be a most clever quarry, but he was running out of time. In less than thirty-five hours the Millennium Networks of Europe and the United States would officially merge. If Daniel Prentice intended to work mischief for Adrian Romulus, he'd have to do something soon.

"General Herrick?" Agent Dengler climbed into the van and took the seat behind Kord. "Sir, if I may speak freely?"

"Speak," Kord barked, his impatience growing.

Dengler rubbed his meaty hands together. "Sir, what if this Prentice is just running scared? They haven't found any problems with the computers in Washington. What's more, he can't do a single thing to hurt us as long as he's running."

"That is precisely the point," Kord answered, his tongue heavy with sarcasm. "If we stop chasing him, he might grow confident and attempt something dangerous. But I am not so certain Prentice did nothing in Washington. He is bright—far more clever than you, Dengler—and I'd wager my life that he is planning something."

Kord crossed his arms and stared out the window, thinking. His men had been over the compromised Federal Crimes computer room at least a dozen times, and they could find nothing out of place. Prentice's fingerprints were all over the mainframe and keyboard, of course, but nothing seemed amiss in the programs. Just to be on the safe side, Kord had ordered that the mainframe be wiped clean and reformatted with the program copied from an uncompromised system, but that seemed too easy a solution. Prentice would have thought of that, so whatever he did had to be much more significant.

Brad Hunter had died without revealing any useful information. Dengler had run out of fingers to break, yet Hunter had said nothing useful. Even after Dengler threatened his wife, Hunter kept insisting that Daniel had done nothing to the mainframe but type in the directory command. Perhaps that was all Prentice had done, but Kord had to be sure. Hunter raged and stormed and threatened until Dengler shot his wife; after that he maintained a stony silence, dying without another word.

If Prentice had done nothing, why was he running? If his actions had been innocent, he wouldn't be hiding. . . and neither would the woman.

Kord rubbed a finger hard over his lip, quelling the urge to laugh as he thought of the frightened minister who had come forward to confess that he had married Daniel Prentice and Lauren Mitchell, apparently just before they embarked upon a murderous rampage in Arlington Heights.

Lauren Mitchell Prentice made Kord nervous, too. Something about her was unsettling—perhaps it was the fearless way she looked at him. Months ago Victoria Stedman had looked at Kord in that same way. And even though he had been disappointed that the car bomb did not kill both the president and the first lady, he had been secretly pleased that the stronger of the two died in the blast. Stedman was a stubborn elitist, but he was like iron, he would bend in the midst of fire. Victoria Stedman and Lauren Prentice were diamond-hard; fire only seemed to fortify their resolve.

A black car pulled up alongside the van, and Kord looked out to see General Archer's rectangular form emerging from the back seat. The big man looked around, then spotted Kord in the van and lifted his hand. "General Herrick!"

Kord uncrossed his arms and reminded himself to be polite. For another day and a half, at least, this was Archer's country.

"General?"

Archer wore a broad smile. "We followed up on your suggestion about cell phones. There's no activity recorded on Prentice's frequency, but we picked up something on the woman."

Kord straightened, amazed by the unbelievable stroke of luck. "The woman has her phone?"

Archer nodded. "Yes. The scanner shows them a hundred miles north of here, pressing toward the Canadian border. Just like you thought they would."

"Let's go." Kord slammed the van door and yelled out the window for his driver. Before leaning back into the van, he called to Archer. "Prentice will not let himself be caught at any border crossing, General. I'd bet my life on it."

Archer grinned, then climbed back into his own car. The black sedan backed up, then gravel flew as the automobile moved out onto the highway.

"Follow him," Kord told his driver. He snapped his seat belt, then brought his hand to his cheek, momentarily regretting that the Americans had designed the beautiful bit of technology that enabled them to track any activated cell phone.

But no matter. On New Year's Day, everything America owned would belong to the Global Community, and Adrian Romulus would hold power over it all.

Thirty-seven

6:49 P.M., Thursday, December 30, 1999

NIGHT HAD FALLEN OVER THE RIVER BY THE TIME DANIEL AND LAUREN HAD located an empty house with a boat in dry dock. They parked the car next to the dock, then unloaded their two suitcases, the wire and other supplies in the trunk, and a shopping bag with supplies for Tasha. The Samoyed wasn't exactly thrilled by the prospect of going on the water, but she stayed close to Lauren's heels and watched silently as Daniel went into the boathouse and lowered the small fishing boat into the water.

A million sparks of diamond light brightened the dark canopy of the sky as Daniel freed the boat from its harness and tied it to the side of the dock. He lowered the bags, then helped Lauren into the craft. He had to forcibly scoop Tasha from the dock and place her in Lauren's arms, but the dog seemed content to remain on her mistress's lap as Daniel climbed in, untied the ropes, and started the motor.

He didn't think there would be much gas in the tank; most people drained the fuel tanks when they put their boats up for the winter. Predictably, the engine sputtered and died when they were only halfway across the river. When Lauren gasped in dismay, Daniel grinned and picked up the oars.

"Never let it be said that I rely *completely* on technology," he said, slipping the oars through the oarlocks. "Just be glad I grew up in the wilderness. I've been rowing my way across lakes since I was ten years old."

Lauren laughed at his efforts—he was a bit out of practice, and the boat skittered rather than glided across the water at first—but as Daniel settled back and found his stroke, he realized he was grateful for the quiet. If they had come across with the noise of an engine, someone on the Canadian shore might have noticed. As it was, no one would mark their crossing.

"You know," Lauren's teeth chattered as the wind blew her hair, "I feel bad about taking this boat. Leaving that old clunker is not exactly an even trade, you know."

"It'll be okay," Daniel assured her. "The boat is registered. We'll pull it up on shore, and when the authorities find it, they'll contact the owner." His smile turned into a chuckle. "Who knows? Maybe we'll be famous outlaws by then, sort of like Bonnie and Clyde."

"I certainly hope not! The president would be mortified."

As the silence of the lake flowed over them, Daniel found himself thinking of his mother. If she had seen those malicious lies on television, she had to be wondering about him, praying for him, at that moment.

"I should have called my mother," he said suddenly, his voice thick and heavy in his own ears. "She's bound to be worried about us."

"Why don't you call her?" Lauren gave him an encouraging smile. "We're safe on the water, and you have your cell phone, so call!"

"My phone's not working now." Daniel pulled hard on the oars and glanced behind him, searching for a smooth stretch of beach sand. "I took the batteries out. Brad told me that now the Feds can track a cell phone even if it's not turned on."

A cold wind blew past him with soft moans—an eerie sound—and then he realized it wasn't the wind moaning; it was Lauren.

He turned to her, a question on his lips, and saw that she had reached into her shopping bag. With two fingers, she gingerly lifted her own cellular telephone.

Daniel drew the oars out of the water, then swallowed to bring his heart down from his throat. From the look in her eyes he inferred the truth, but thought there might yet be a chance. "Has it been activated?"

She nodded, then shook her head. "No—and yes. No, I didn't turn it on, but yes—it's been activated." Tears spilled from her lashes, glittering like jewels in the moonlight. "Daniel—are they waiting for us on the other shore? Have they been following us all this time?"

A tremor of mingled fear and anticipation shot through Daniel. Who knew? This was not a movie where the good guys waited to come galloping to the rescue. It was real life, and he and Lauren had only each other.

Daniel felt the wings of tragedy brush past him, stirring the air and raising the hair on his forearm. The struggle might be lost even now, but he could not surrender, not as long as God gave him breath.

"Help me think." His voice sounded strangled in his own ears. "We've got to get rid of it."

She held it out over the water. "Should I just drop it—"

"No!" He took a deep breath and gentled his voice. "No, honey, they'd abruptly lose the signal and know something was up. We need something that floats, something we can put it in."

Lauren gently set the phone on the floor, then rummaged beneath her seat while Daniel searched the shore for another boat dock. If he could only find a canoe, or some other craft—

"What about this?" With a triumphant flourish, Lauren pulled a child's lunchbox from under her seat. It was insulated, sealed with a zipper, and appeared to be watertight. Daniel took it from her, unzipped the opening, then dumped a couple of moldy bread crusts into the water. "It'll do. Just drop the phone in here. If anyone's listening, we'll send them upriver to Quebec."

Lauren placed the phone in the box, Daniel zipped it shut, then flung the container out onto the river. Both of them sat silently as the lunchbox rocked on the water's surface, then rode the current upstream and disappeared into the night.

"Four or five miles an hour," Daniel remarked, squinting into the darkness. "That's how fast the river flows. With any luck, that phone will be leading them on a wild goose chase by morning."

"Do you really think they've been following my phone? Daniel, I'm so sorry. I didn't know—"

Daniel cut her off with a smile as he picked up the oars. "Honey, I should have remembered about your phone. And we've made it this far, so we're not giving up. Maybe they have been behind us, but they're not here now. So let's keep going."

She sniffed and nodded, then hugged Tasha close to her chest and stared at the surface of the lake with wide, watery eyes.

-0100111100-

Twenty miles away, General Kord Herrick frowned as Archer's limo pulled off the road and into a gas station. With an impatient gesture he directed his driver to do the same, then rolled down the window as the van followed the limo into the darkness of the deserted station.

"What is it?" he barked as one of Archer's aides came running toward his van.

"The signal is weakening," the aide explained, spreading his hands in a sheepish gesture. "The telephone battery must be going dead. But we have them moving eastward on the St. Lawrence River."

Kord bit back a curse and consulted his map. The St. Lawrence River flowed from Lake Ontario toward Montreal, then emptied into the Atlantic Ocean. If Prentice had used a boat—and he surely would, as it was an ingenious way to avoid the border guards—he could come ashore anywhere he pleased, leaving his pursuers to search miles and miles of shoreline.

Kord winced as an odd twinge of disappointment struck him. Closing his map, he pinned Archer's aide in a brutal and hostile stare. "Tell the general to regroup his men," he said. "I'm going back to New York to meet with Romulus. There has to be another way to stop this man. I'm tired of playing cat and mouse."

"Yes, sir." The aide snapped a salute, then jogged back to Archer's car.

Kord turned to his driver. "Take me to the nearest airport," he said, his voice heavy with weariness. "I am finished here tonight, but tomorrow I will find Daniel Prentice."

-0100111100-

"Mrs. Davis?"

Turning his back to the frigid wind, Daniel smothered a smile as Lauren huddled against him for warmth. They stood outside a busy market in Kingston, Ontario, at lunchtime, and Daniel had patiently fed coins to the pay phone until the call to Florida went through.

Daniel caught Lauren's eye as he tried to explain the situation to his mother's next-door neighbor. "Mrs. Davis, this is Daniel Prentice. Yes—I know, I've been on television. No, it's not true. Mrs. Davis, could you please run next door and bring my mother to the phone? No, I can't call her. Yes, I'll wait."

Daniel rolled his eyes, signaling his frustration with the talkative woman. Lauren pressed her lips to his for a brief kiss, then pulled away with a simple admonition: "Be patient."

A moment later, his mother's breathless voice rolled over the phone lines. "Daniel! Is that really you?"

"Yes. Mom—I can't talk long."

"Goodness, Daniel, why didn't you call me at home?"

"Your phones are tapped, Mom."

"They are not!" Her voice rang with indignation.

"Trust me, Mom, they are." Daniel caught Lauren's hand, then smiled into the phone. "Mom—I married Lauren. We're safe, and we're together. And we've decided to do something about Adrian Romulus. Just watch television tonight, and then be prepared. The media will probably be swarming your place by tomorrow morning."

"Daniel, they've already been here! They're saying that you killed Brad and his wife—"

"It's a lie." Despite his resolve not to dwell on the horror that had befallen Brad and Christine, Daniel felt his throat tighten. "It's the work of Romulus's general, a man named Kord Herrick. But we're safe right now, and I have a plan. But I wanted you to know I'm okay and that I love you. And I wanted you—" he stumbled over the unfamiliar words—"Mom, I want you to pray for us. Will you?"

"Oh, honey." Even a thousand miles away, Daniel could hear the love in her voice. "Daniel, I've never stopped praying for you."

"Thanks, Mom. Your prayers were answered." He caught Lauren's eye. "Lauren sends her love, too. But we've got to go now."

He hung up the phone and drew Lauren close, and both of them shivered with a cold that had nothing to do with the freezing air. The SAGE base, which had once been a part of NORAD, lay two hundred and ten miles to the northwest, and Daniel had less than twelve hours to reach it.

"What do we do now?" Lauren asked, lifting her gaze to meet his.

Daniel pulled the wallet out of his pocket and counted the money inside. Five crisp Canadian hundred-dollar bills remained. "You're going to pray that the owner of this market has more sympathy than sense," he said, tucking the empty wallet into his pocket. "And I'm going to go inside and ask him to sell a poor newlywed couple that truck and a tankful of gas—" he pointed to a pickup in the parking lot—"for a measly five hundred dollars."

A soft woebegone expression filled her eyes. "Oh, dear."

"Better start praying. If we ever needed a miracle, it's now." Tossing the words over his shoulder, Daniel walked into the store with more confidence in his step than in his heart.

-01001111100-

At a temporary command center at the UN, a uniformed Community soldier strode up to Kord Herrick and handed him a sheet of paper. "Two hours ago, sir. The giant ear picked up Daniel Prentice's voiceprint."

"Good." Kord took the paper and studied it. "Who is Charlene Davis?"

"No one important, sir. But she lives next door to Amelia Prentice, our suspect's mother. The call went out at 12:13 from a pay phone at a market in Kingston, Ontario."

Rubbing the side of his nose, Kord turned and considered the map he'd hung on the wall. They had begun to lose the cellular phone signal near Montreal, but Kingston lay just across the river from the Thousand Islands. Daniel Prentice was too clever—somehow he had managed to send them miles out of the way. Still, what was in Ontario? Prentice probably thought he was safe in Canada, and he had to be feeling a little more relaxed or he wouldn't have risked calling his worried mother.

Thoughts of the Treasury Department computers had ceased to bother Romulus. At his urging, officials from the European Monetary Union had tested the computers today, and all programs had operated without a hitch. The programmers had run a few advance deposits through the newly-merged systems, and all the post-January 1, 2000 dates had registered without a single hitch.

"Prentice must have been telling the truth," Romulus told Kord earlier this morning. "All systems are operational, and nothing seems amiss. Relax, General. He can run, but he cannot hide for long."

But Kord could not rest. Prentice was a loose cannon; he was too bright and knew too much to wander free—especially tonight, when Romulus would speak to the world from a news booth at New York's Times Square.

Romulus's advisors had been working on the plan for weeks. As soon as the fabled ball dropped, the cameras would cut to Adrian, who, in a five-minute video clip, would demonstrate how the Millennium Network would eradicate crime, simplify life, encourage productivity, and unite the world in a global community. If, however, Prentice managed to break the story of Romulus's behind-the-scene manipulation of American politics anytime between now and midnight, Adrian might not make it out of Times Square alive.

Kord sank into a chair and absently drummed his fingertips on the desk as his eyes searched the oversized map. Prentice had twelve hours between his phone call and Adrian's international speech. A man could fly virtually anywhere in twelve hours, but Prentice was traveling with a woman and a dog, and both adults had been implanted with a Millennium Chip. So he would avoid planes, trains, and buses, but he could drive twelve hundred kilometers in twelve hours. . . .

Kord stood and squinted up at the map. "Can anyone tell me," he asked, directing his comments to the bustling room filled with agents, soldiers, and security personnel, "if anything significant lies within six hundred miles of Kingston, Ontario? Narrow it down to areas in Canada, focusing on computer companies, educational centers, television stations, military installations—"

"That's easy." A nearby American soldier lifted a bushy brow. "There's Ottawa's Silicon Valley in the north, Kingston's Royal Military College, Canada's Communication Security Establishment in Ottawa, Canada's Governmental Security Administration east of Ottawa. All of those would be possible targets, and all are fully operational. And then there's the old SAGE base, right outside North Bay, near Lake Nipissing. It used to be part of NORAD, but it's been inactive for over a year. Nobody up there now but a couple of guards and a maintenance crew."

Of course. Kord's eyes sought the map again. A defensive base, even an inactive installation, would have radar equipment, a satellite dish, and rows and rows of mainframe computers, most of them still monitoring the globe.

"Get the jet." He whirled to face the American aide who'd been assigned to him. "And get me a helicopter out of—" he threw up his hand—"whatever airport is closest to North Bay. And find me two snipers, the best we have. Tell them we are leaving immediately."

Daniel drove the last twelve miles in a blizzard. The snaking black road disappeared under a blanket of white, but he plunged blindly ahead, careful to keep the old truck a steady fifteen feet to the left of a long line of telephone poles. Lauren sat next to him, her arms around the dog, her teeth chattering as she prayed aloud for guidance and protection. For the first time in a long time, Daniel discovered that prayers lifted on his behalf didn't annoy him.

The sky was black velvet, through which fat snowflakes hurtled down like falling stars. Daniel leaned forward to squint through the arc made by the windshield wipers, then jabbed his finger at the glass. "There!" he called, pointing to the small roof near the lake shore. "That's the cabin."

"That's your cabin?" Lauren's luminous eyes widened in astonishment. "That *shack?*"

Daniel grinned at her. "What did you expect, a Swiss chalet?"

A betraying blush brightened her face. "Well—yes. I read in your dossier that you had a Range Rover registered in Canada, and I imagined that you kept a nice little summer place up here."

"I garage the Range Rover at the airport. The shack is sort of a squatter's place. The government owns the land, but no one seems to mind if people fish here on occasion." Daniel swung the truck toward old Henry's cabin, then parked beneath the snow-laden branches of a pine tree.

He shut down the engine, then reached out and took Lauren's hand. "Right through there, about three hundred yards away," he explained, pointing through the whirling white snow, "is the satellite dish we need. I'm going to string our wire from that dish to this cabin. At precisely midnight you are going to go on camera and tell the world that Adrian Romulus is a murderer and a fraud."

Her breath quickened. "And that he tried to poison the president?"

"And that there is no Morning Star Trust and no nuclear threat." Daniel reached up and caressed her cheek. "And after we warn them that he just might be the Antichrist described in the Bible, we're leaving this place as quickly as we can. They'll be able to track us the instant we link to the satellite."

Lauren pressed her lips together and nodded, and Daniel smiled, realizing that he had found the one woman in a million who could pull this off. Through her role in the White House people had come to know and trust Lauren Mitchell. Most important, she possessed the courage to look into the camera without flinching and tell the truth about Adrian Romulus.

"You and Tasha can wait in the cabin." Daniel moved his hand to the door and prepared to step out into the whirling snow. "I'll get everything set up, and then I'll join you." He glanced at his watch and saw that it was eleven thirty. The storm had slowed their progress considerably, but there was still time.

"Be careful." Unguarded tenderness lingered in her eyes as she looked at him. "I'll be praying for you."

"Thanks."

Daniel drew a deep breath, then stepped out into the slashing white wind.

-01001111100-

Kord Herrick cursed as he slid on the icy tarmac and nearly fell. He should have been with Adrian in New York, surrounded by beautiful women and with a hot drink in his hand, but instead he was carrying an explosive device in the middle of nowhere, surrounded by Canadian yokels who had absolutely no concept of the word *urgent*.

Death was too merciful for a man like Daniel Prentice; he ought to be tortured, lobotomized, and pulled through the streets in a cage. Someone ought to ride before him, shouting, "*This* is what happens to those who dare to resist the good of the Community, the plans for our future! *This* is what happens to those who oppose Adrian Romulus and the powers that will unite the world!"

A gust of wind whooshed under the jet and blew past Kord, lifting the hair at the back of his head, whipping his coat tight around his middle. One of the snipers shouted something and pointed toward the golden windows of the airplane hangar, but Kord shook his head, anxious to get on with the chase.

"Where's the chopper?" he bellowed, ignoring the bone-numbing cold. "I ordered a chopper to be here!"

"General!" His American aide hurried forward, both hands clamping his hat to his head. "The chopper pilot won't fly in this storm. He says we have to wait."

"*Nein!*" A flood of curses flew from Kord's mouth, and the aide stepped back, his face going pale. Kord flashed him a look of disdain, then lowered his head and strode toward the hangar.

Slamming through the door, he marched toward a knot of men huddled around an electric heater.

"Who is the chopper pilot?" Kord demanded, spitting the words.

A tall, lanky man in a pilot's jumpsuit peeled himself off a stool, then paused deliberately to sip from the steaming Styrofoam cup in his hand. "I guess that'd be me," he finally answered, his voice flat.

Kord turned to face the man directly. "You will get your chopper and fly me to the SAGE base," he said, bridled anger in his voice. "We will leave now. It is 11:35, and I have no time for argument."

The pilot's jaw clenched as he rejected Kord's order. "I'm not flying in this weather. The wind is gusting and unpredictable; it's too dangerous."

"I command you!"

The pilot flushed to the roots of his brown hair, but he did not move. "I'm not yours to command. I'm a Canadian, and I'll have nothing to do with your cursed Community."

Kord choked on his own fury, then turned to the snipers who had come with him. "You are qualified to fly; I checked your records. Which of you will handle the chopper?"

Violence bubbled beneath the surface of Kord's skin as the two looked stupidly at each other. "Fools! You!" He pointed to the smaller of the two. "You will pilot the helicopter." He looked at the other sniper. "You will ride with us. And we will reach Daniel Prentice in time."

"General—" The first man stepped forward as if he would protest, but Kord pulled the Glock 17 from his coat and brandished it before both men's startled faces.

"I will accept no debate. Now, to the chopper, both of you." He looked at his aide, whose face had gone blank with shock. "You will wait here until we return."

The aide nodded and backed away, probably afraid Kord would change his mind and take him with them. Nothing would stop Kord now.

He moved back out into the snow-chilled wind, his heart pounding in anticipation.

In less than fifteen minutes, he and Daniel Prentice would meet face-to-face on neutral territory. And this time, Kord would walk away the victor.

THIRTY-EIGHT

11:59 P.M., Friday, December 31, 1999

DANIEL POSITIONED LAUREN NEXT TO THE CABIN WALL WITH THE MICROPHONE in her hand, double-checked his battery power, and picked up the small video camera. Though his fingers were red and numb from cold, a thread of perspiration trickled between his shoulder blades. His heart pounded in a crazy and erratic rhythm, but his mind was sharp, focused to an ice pick's point.

With the wind howling over the frozen wasteland outside, it was hard to imagine a festive party in New York, so Daniel tried to establish the proper mood. "Romulus is in Times Square right now, Lauren," he whispered, squinting at her through the camera viewfinder. "He's watching that sparkling ball as it comes down the pole, and the crowd is chanting the countdown. In a moment they'll be cheering him, and that's when we'll break in to tell the truth."

A lantern burned in a corner of the room, and in its golden light Daniel saw Lauren moisten her lips with the tip of her tongue, then insinuate her free hand into Tasha's fur. Grateful for the attention, the dog looked up and seemed to smile at her mistress.

"Okay." Daniel looked at his watch. "It's midnight." They both caught their breath—they had agreed to wait thirty seconds to let the tumult of celebration die down—and when the second hand of Daniel's watch swept past the six, he lifted his arm and brought it down in a decisive stroke.

Bright artificial light flooded the cabin. Lauren's eyes narrowed for an instant, then the professional spokeswoman in her took charge. "Good evening, all who love freedom." Because she knew every word was important, Lauren had rehearsed her speech on the long drive, but Daniel felt as though he were hearing it for the first time.

"I am Lauren Mitchell Prentice, executive assistant to President Stedman, and I have an urgent message for you. The man you know as Adrian Romulus is not the charismatic world leader he pretends to be. He is a murderer, a charlatan, and a base criminal. He is responsible not only for the death of First Lady Victoria Stedman, but also for the poisoning of the president, the deaths of Brad and Christine Hunter, and the perpetuation of the Morning Star Trust hoax. There are no world terrorists, my friends, there are no nuclear devices planted in New York, Tokyo, London, or Paris. Adrian Romulus is merely trying to subjugate the world through fear so he may rise to power as a world dictator."

Lauren's eyes glittered with intensity, and Daniel doubted that anyone in the world could watch and not believe her. "If you find this hard to accept," she went on, her voice calm and eminently reasonable, "search the ancient biblical manuscripts or any Bible you might happen to have in the house. The prophets of old predicted that a world dictator would come, that he would unite the globe in one government, one currency, and one religion. But any who follow this dictator will lose their lives and their souls, so I beg you tonight, I *plead* with you, do not believe Adrian Romulus. Do not accept his mark, which will be revealed in time. Do not—"

A sharp and bitter wind rushed through the cabin as the door suddenly swung open. Daniel lifted his head from the camera and leaned forward to see what had happened, then icy fear twisted around his heart.

General Herrick's tall and lean form filled the doorway. A briefcase hung from one hand, and a dark rope dangled from the other.

Smiling, Herrick tossed the rope toward Daniel's feet. It took Daniel a full ten seconds to realize what it meant, then his eyes met Lauren's.

The cord on the floor was no rope at all. It was the wire leading from the cabin to the satellite dish . . . and it had been disconnected.

-0100111100-

Kord stared at them for thirty seconds in full, satisfying silence. Lauren Mitchell's countenance fell at the sight of the severed wire, and Prentice's eyes blazed with indignant fury. But Kord had won.

"So delighted to see you again, Mr. Prentice." He lowered his briefcase to the plank floor of the pitiful shack, then crossed his hands at his waist and lifted a brow in Prentice's direction. "Are you ready to come with me? Or shall I kill you here and spare the Community a wearisome trial?"

Prentice shut off the camcorder and the video light, and in the sudden gloom shadows rippled over him like water over a sunken rock. He showed no more expression than a rock, either, as he sank to the floor and rested his arms upon his bent knees.

"Let Lauren go," his voice was curiously flat, "and I'll do whatever you want me to do."

Kord leaned against the doorframe and glanced outside. The chopper had landed at the SAGE base, so it was out of sight, but the snipers had walked with Kord as he followed the wire. They were hidden now behind two pine trees, ready to pick off whoever came out of the cabin.

"I'd be happy to let her go." He paused, and pulled the Glock from his pocket as casually as if he'd been reaching for a business card. "But you and I, Mr. Prentice, have a personal account to settle." He glanced up and gave Prentice a conspiratorial wink. "You have insulted my master and my honor. I cannot let you leave this place alive."

Prentice shrugged, then looked to the woman—*his wife,* Kord reminded himself.

"Daniel—" she began.

"Take Tasha and go," Prentice interrupted. He looked at her with something very fragile in his eyes. "Remember what you said at our wedding . . . and have faith."

She shook her head, obviously confused, but Prentice waved her away. She stood, about to rush to her husband's side, but Kord shoved his gun into the empty space between them. "I wouldn't want to take on the two of you," he said, shrugging. "I could shoot one of you with no trouble, but I'm too old to wrestle the other to the ground." He softened his voice. "So please. Don't make me choose between you. Do as he said, Miss Mitchell. Take the dog and go."

Wrapping the dog's leash around her arm, the woman took one step toward the doorway, then paused and glanced back at Prentice with a world of longing and sorrow in her eyes. Kord sighed impatiently, then brought his arm to her back and pushed her out into the storm.

When she had gone, he pulled the door shut and stepped into the center of the room. Prentice had not moved but sat motionless, staring at the briefcase in waiting silence.

"What's that?" Prentice finally asked, though there was little sincere interest in his voice.

Kord gave Prentice the smile he used to freeze men's blood. "It's a suitcase bomb, Mr. Prentice. Rather like the one you designed for the Morning Star Trust."

"I never—"

"Of course you didn't. But when the Canadian police find your body here—*if* they find your body here—they'll also discover whatever's left of this little device. And while it's not equipped with a nuclear warhead— you're not worth that kind of firepower—the two triggering devices are exact replicas of the so-called 'suitcase nukes' that will be discovered—and safely recovered—tomorrow." Kord smiled in the calm strength of knowledge. "Beijing, Tokyo, Baghdad, Toronto, and New York—those cities will praise Adrian Romulus's name when his Community forces enter the land and roust the terrorists from their positions."

"But most of those aren't even EU countries," Prentice pointed out, a pained expression on his face. "You can't enter them."

"We will, because we will have intelligence that tells us where the bombs are located. And, in gratitude, those countries will join our global community. Romulus will usher in an era of peace and safety, while warmongers like you, Mr. Prentice, will fall prey to an untimely end."

Prentice gave him a quick, denying glance. "Not everyone will believe your lies."

"Oh? And why not?" Kord glanced around the small space, then caught sight of a bag on the floor. A book protruded from the unzipped opening, and he bent forward to pick it up. "The *Holy Bible?*" He tilted his head, then tossed the Bible onto the floor. "Christianity is the opiate of the masses, Mr. Prentice. Hasn't history taught us that lesson? It is the panacea of fools, a delusion for the weak-minded. The new millennium will call for a new religion, a belief system in which man overcomes these fanciful notions about invisible spirits and supernatural powers."

Prentice was beaten; he did not reply. Kord leaned against the wall as a smile crept to his lips. "It was a valiant effort, Mr. Prentice. A good training exercise, in fact. You tested virtually every element of our new systems."

"How'd you find us?"

"Voiceprint technology. Our surveillance satellite, the 'big ear' as it is so quaintly known, picked your voiceprint out of the worldwide net traffic when you called your mother's neighbor. We tracked the call, then looked at a map. I realized almost instantly what you were planning."

Prentice grunted softly, then looked at the floor. "Did any of our transmission get through?"

The corner of Kord's mouth twisted with exasperation. "Perhaps—it really doesn't matter. We found your little hookup within minutes after landing the chopper, then it was a simple matter of following the wire to this place." He felt himself smile. "Rather like tracking Hansel and Gretel, I think. But now it is time for the fairy tale to end."

He gripped the Glock with both hands, then gazed at Daniel Prentice over his extended arms. "I'm going to kill you, Mr. Prentice, and then destroy this little shack. So where would you like your bullet? Back of the skull or in the forehead?"

-0100111100-

Shivering in the cold, Lauren stumbled toward the truck and moved her lips in soundless prayer. *Dear God, please help him. Show him a way. Work a miracle, deliver him. If you could deliver the prophet from the lion's den, deliver my Daniel from this evil one. . . .*

Daniel's words echoed like a broken record in her brain, but she could find no sense in them. "*Remember what you said at our wedding . . . and have faith.*" What did she say at the wedding? She had been so caught up in the unexpected turn of events, so bewildered and shaken by the confrontation with Romulus at the White House, all she could think was that she loved Daniel and wanted to spend the rest of her life with him . . . no matter how short that life might be.

The wind howled around her, a biting blast that knifed her lungs and tingled the exposed skin of her hands and face. She hesitated, blinded by the blowing whiteness, but Tasha pulled her inexorably forward. Choking on fear, sorrow, and tears, Lauren followed, hoping that Tasha had the sense to move toward the truck or some other shelter. Perhaps Daniel could overpower Herrick; perhaps he would emerge the victor. Then he'd find her, and they could find some place to live together in peace. *Oh, God, please!*

A sharp and brittle report cracked through the howling wind, and Lauren froze, recognizing the sound of gunfire. Daniel! She turned toward the cabin, ready to run back, but then another gunshot tore a hole in the snowy earth at her feet.

Someone was shooting at her.

Instinctively, Lauren jerked on the dog's leash and ran in the opposite direction, then dove behind a copse of pines and evergreen shrubs.

-0100111100-

Daniel glared up at Herrick with eyes bright with fury. "Rifle fire?" His breath burned in his throat. "You said you'd let her go!"

"I can't." Herrick jerked the gun impatiently. "Now turn around. It's late, and I'm expected at a party in New York."

Daniel lifted his hands, his thoughts racing dangerously. Lauren's words came back to him again: *Faith is not an intelligent understanding and calculated risk. It is a deliberate commitment to a person, even if I can see no earthly chance of success.*

Daniel could see no earthly chance of success now. No escape, no hope, no possible way out. Unless God provided one.

He almost laughed aloud. The Belgian bookbinder had said that God would hold him tight if Daniel trusted him with his life, but Daniel hadn't expected to put God to the test so quickly.

Heavenly Father, can't we discuss this? Even as Daniel formed the thought, he realized the answer. Faith wasn't debating or reasoning or deducing. It was accepting, with the full knowledge that God knew best.

In the next moment, he would live or die. Whatever God wanted.

"I never wanted to die sitting down," Daniel said, slowly rising to his feet. His mouth curved in a mirthless smile. "Truth is, I never wanted to die. But it seems I can see no earthly chance of escape."

His smile broadened, his spirit lifted. By heaven above, this was thrilling!

The change in Daniel's countenance seemed to confuse the general; his lips pursed in suspicion and he waved the gun dramatically. "Sit or turn, now! I will shoot!"

Almost gleefully, Daniel waved his hands above his head. "Go ahead."

Herrick's finger moved in the trigger hasp. The Glock clicked, a bullet shifted in the magazine . . . and yet the gun did not fire.

The next few seconds seemed to pass in slow motion. The general glanced at his gun with a half-frightened look, and in that instant Daniel leapt forward, his hands reaching for the weapon. Herrick pulled the trigger again, and the sound of gunfire roared through the cabin, but Daniel stood beside the gun now, his hands upon the general's arm, the German's breath in his face. Together they rolled across the rough wooden floor, then Daniel felt the gun's cold metal against his hand. He gripped it and flung it away, then felt something hit him in the face, setting off a shower of lights that rained behind his eyes like a kid's Fourth of July sparkler.

Herrick might be an old man, but he could still throw a punch. Daniel shook his head to clear it, then reached out and caught hold of the struggling general's coat. "Not so fast!" he yelled. Herrick turned, then a sharp elbow slammed into Daniel's throat, cutting off his voice in a gurgle. He gulped down a tide of rising nausea, then tasted blood in his mouth.

Forcing his eyes open, he saw Herrick on his hands and knees, crawling for the gun. Reaching forward, Daniel caught the back of Herrick's coat and pulled with all his might, climbing over the man until he brought his elbow down at the base of the general's neck.

The man folded gently and crumpled into a heap. Daniel fell backward against the wall and gasped for breath. The room flickered in the sputtering lantern light, and Daniel's nerve endings snapped at each other, bringing pain to bones and muscles he had never felt before. He leaned against the wall until his vision cleared, then his brain blazed with the memory of rifle shots outside.

Herrick wasn't alone.

Carefully, he pulled himself up and reached over Herrick for the pistol, then snapped open the magazine. Loaded and ready to fire.

Daniel slammed the magazine back into the Glock, then pulled the door open and stepped out into the whirling white world.

-0100111100-

Miles away, Amelia Prentice clenched her hands tighter and leaned her elbows on the edge of her mattress. Tears slipped from beneath her eyelids as her spirit groaned within her.

"Heavenly Father," she prayed, resisting the nauseating sinking of despair. "I don't know where Daniel is or what he's doing now, but strengthen him, Father! Please, place your angels around him, shield him from the evil one!"

Biting her lip until it throbbed like her pulse, she lowered her forehead to the bed and let her tears water the rumpled sheets. The Spirit would have to pray for her now; she had no more words. She had turned on the television to watch Times Square like Daniel told her to, and right after the sparkling ball dropped, the celebrating crowd had disappeared, replaced by a grainy image of Lauren with a microphone. With the same poise and control she had always exhibited in the White House, Lauren had introduced herself and explained that Adrian Romulus was a murderer and a fraud. She had accused him of killing the first lady and the Hunters, and stressed that there were no nuclear devices planted in New York. Then suddenly the partying crowds were back, hugging, kissing, the sound of cheering evolving from an indiscriminate roar to the sound of Adrian Romulus's name.

A five-minute video clip had followed, in which Romulus promised a bright and prosperous new world, an international community free from fear, want, and repression.

And Amelia had fallen to her knees, knowing that something had gone terribly wrong for Daniel.

-0100111100-

Gusts of wind blew over the cabin's roof, dropping clumps of snow on Daniel's head and dislodging mounds of snow from the pines. He hesitated, afraid he had just stepped into a sniper's crosshairs, then the muffled sound of barking set his blood to pumping. He ducked and ran toward the sound, weaving in a drunken pattern as tree branches snapped under his feet and in the trees beside him.

That's the sound of gunfire, not breaking branches—

"Daniel?"

Lauren's grateful shriek reached his ears, and he dove toward her like a baserunner sliding into home plate before a screaming hometown crowd. They held each other for a long moment, then Daniel lifted his head and listened.

"It's quiet." Lauren voiced his thoughts.

Daniel cradled her head to his chest and nodded. Releasing her after a moment, he crawled forward on his hands and knees, then knelt at the foot of a gnarled pine. The wind had slowed to a whisper, and the snow fell silently now, in an almost-vertical path from heaven to earth.

Daniel ducked instinctively as two dark forms came out of the woods and ran in a serpentine course toward the cabin. They went inside, and Daniel knew they'd be kneeling beside Herrick, probably helping him up, assessing the rising knot at the base of his skull.

"Did you kill him?" Lauren asked, her voice fragile and shaking.

"No." Daniel turned back to meet her earnest eyes. "He was unconscious, but alive."

"Then we'd better get out of here."

Daniel took her hand, ready to run for the truck, but he froze as the roar of an explosion scattered snow and tree limbs for two hundred yards. Daniel fell upon Lauren, pinning her to the ground as he sheltered her with his body, and they trembled together until the roar subsided to the whispering, crackling noise of a fire contentedly talking to itself.

Daniel lifted his head as Lauren stirred beneath him. "What happened?" she asked.

"I'm not sure." Daniel rolled away and stood, searching the woods for any other signs of life. Nothing else moved in the snowy landscape.

He felt Lauren's shoulder against his arm. "Herrick had a bomb?" she asked, trembling as she hugged herself.

Daniel slipped his arm around her. "Yes. He said something about the triggers—two of them. I'd bet that means one manual, one electronic."

Lauren shivered. "Surely he wouldn't trigger it himself, so how—" Her chin quivered as her gaze roved over the trees. "Is someone else out there?"

"Either it was on a timer, or—" Daniel glanced up at the cloudy sky—"or someone triggered it by satellite."

Daniel drew Lauren closer as thoughts he dared not vocalize came welling up, a persistent swarm of them. If all had gone according to plan, he and Lauren would be dead now, killed by rifle fire and gunshot. Kord Herrick had planned to plant their bodies and detonate the explosives, but an invisible beam had sliced through the night sky and triggered the bomb. . . .

Had Adrian Romulus wanted to kill his own general? Hard to believe, but in light of the evidence, Daniel could see no other explanation.

"God was good to us." He pressed his lips to Lauren's windblown hair, shivering in sudden gratitude that they had escaped the night's danger. "And we still have the truck, and my phone."

"Your phone?" Locking her arms around his waist, she looked up at him, a trace of hysterical laughter in her eyes. "Daniel, what good is a phone—without batteries out here in the middle of nowhere?"

"Brad packed batteries in the suitcase, and it's not just any phone." He took Tasha's leash and led her out of the trees, toward the ramshackle pickup. "It's a Nokia 9000 personal communicator, and it can do everything from send e-mail to balance a checkbook."

She blinked in dazed exasperation. "Daniel, we don't have a checkbook."

"We don't need one. The Nokia 9000 can access a mainframe, my computers at the office, and the Internet. We can even tap into the Financial Crimes Computer Network, which by now is in need of a little help. Romulus's European computers should be so jumbled that all the king's horses and all the king's men can't put the system back together again."

"Really?"

Daniel grinned. "Well, it's nothing that Professor Kriegel and I couldn't fix. But it's going to upset Romulus's plans for a few months, since the hardware virus makes it look like all the glitches are coming from his EU computers. No country in the world is going to want to go near his systems until the problem is straightened out." He reached up and brushed a spray of snowflakes from her hair. "Don't worry. I sent an encrypted e-mail to the president a few weeks ago, warning him of what would happen."

Lauren's gaze clouded in confusion. "I don't understand. How could you send a virus through our computers and not hurt our system?"

"The hardware virus also contained a vaccination program. All the computers are connected by network, you see, so they were all exposed to the virus, but computers registered to non-EU countries picked up the vaccination, too. American and Canadian computers won't be at all affected, but things are going to be pretty rough for the European Union countries after tonight. President Stedman is supposed to give a press conference tomorrow to explain why we have to break the Millennium Treaty with the European Union. By noon tomorrow, he'll be a hero."

"Daniel Prentice, I love you." Lauren turned to face him, and something in Daniel reveled in her open admiration. "You're not going to make it easy for Romulus, are you?"

"No." Daniel squinted up at the dark sky. "Until the Lord comes and we are snatched away, we're going to make life miserable for Adrian Romulus. We have the entire Canadian wilderness to hide in until it's safe to go home; we have the Nokia, a dog, and a pickup—what more could a couple of Americans want?"

"I know what I want." The look in her eyes made his pulse pound. "And I thank God for giving you to me."

He brushed a gentle kiss across her forehead, then opened the pickup's passenger door. "Come on, Mrs. Prentice. We've a lot to do, and not much time left."

Lauren slid in, Tasha followed, and Daniel closed the door on his little family. As he walked around the truck to the driver's side, he caught a reflection of the burning shack in the still lake. Henry's monster, the old pike, probably lay in the darkness even now, as wild and untamed as ever.

"Don't think you've escaped, Monster," Daniel whispered, jingling the truck's keys in his hand as he studied the unbroken silvery surface of the lake. "Your time will come."

EPILOGUE

SIX WEEKS LATER ADRIAN ROMULUS LIFTED A GLASS OF WINE TO HIS LIPS AND moodily sipped it as he stared out the window of his chateau. A small group of sheep clustered beneath a barren tree, and the ram, a cocky old fool, kept careful watch over them lest a single ewe stray.

Romulus should have minded his own ewes more closely. By now he should have been undisputed master of the globe, but a single meddlesome computer genius had managed to impede his plans.

Romulus swirled the wine in his goblet, then sat it upon the polished mahogany table. "Charles," he called over his shoulder, "bring my laptop, please. And the evening news."

Despite Daniel Prentice's efforts to derail the Millennium Network, the world had already begun to show signs of significant change. Cash currency was a thing of the past, outlawed in all but the most primitive countries. The Iraqis remained open to Adrian's overtures, and the countries of the European Union, though shaken by the computer fiasco, were too intimidated to reject Adrian's leadership.

The United States and the Pacific Rim had been frightened away by the European Union's Y2K computer confusion, but the coming year would bring another American election—and that quintessential nation of sheep would follow any man who promised convenience and freedom from responsibility. The computer problems would be worked out in several months, then Romulus would begin again.

He was destined to lead. From the foundations of the earth, his fate and purpose had been sealed.

"Your computer, sir." Charles placed the laptop on the table and lifted the lid, instantly booting the system. Romulus acknowledged the act with just the smallest squint of his eyes and watched with disinterest as the operating system ran through its paces. Finally, the e-mail program loaded, the automatic dial device checked the Internet, and an obnoxiously cheery voice informed Romulus that he had three messages.

The first two were routine, meaningless greetings from the emperor of Japan and the prime minister of the united Korea. The third, however, piqued his interest. The note had been encrypted, so only someone with access to Romulus's password could have sent and encrypted the message.

Romulus leaned forward and tapped the keys. The unscrambled letter was simple and direct:

Good evening, Adrian.

You will lose, you know. The Book foretells your end, and the Word of God is never wrong. If I may quote: "Then I saw the beast and the kings of the earth and their armies gathered together to make war against the rider on the horse and his army. But the beast was captured, and with him the false prophet who had performed the miraculous signs on his behalf. With these signs he had deluded those who had received the mark of the beast and worshipped his image. The two of them were thrown alive into the fiery lake of burning sulfur. . . . He who testifies to these things says, 'Yes, I am coming soon.' Amen. Come, Lord Jesus."

Romulus shivered in revulsion. A spasm of hatred and disgust rose from his core, radiating through his flesh.

Only one man could find his way through the labyrinth of safeguards that shielded Romulus's private account, and only one man would dare to insult the chief of the Community.

Daniel Prentice.

A scream clawed in Romulus's throat as he smashed his fist into the keyboard.

NEW
FROM GRANT JEFFREY

The
MYSTERIOUS
BIBLE
CODES

THE
PHENOMENAL DISCOVERY
THAT PROVES THE TRUTH
OF BIBLE PROPHECIES

GRANT JEFFREY

THE BIBLE CODES PHENOMENON REVEALED

Best-selling author and noted prophetic scholar
Grant Jeffrey discloses the most dramatic discoveries of
Bible codes in both ancient and modern times.

 WORD PUBLISHING

Available at Bookstores Everywhere.